Pr
LOVE AND OTHER WICKED THINGS

"Don't read this book if you aren't ready to lose yourself for a few hundred pages in this cozy, diverse, and magical town that Harms has created. If you are ready: take a seat at the table, open your hand, and prepare to have a reading that could change your life."

—Brianna Joy Crump, author of *Of Cages and Crowns*

"*Love and Other Wicked Things* is a perfect love letter to autumn . . . Harms packs the story with raw emotion, humor, relatability, queer joy, and magic. This book is for everyone who grew up believing in magic and never stopped."

—Loridee De Villa, author of *How to Be the Best Third Wheel*

"Bursting with magic on every page, Harms reminded me there's a witch inside everyone, my friends are my coven, and I can still be surprised by my own power. I've never wanted to jump inside a book more."

—Auburn Morrow, author of *The Trial Period*

"*Love and Other Wicked Things* is a mesmerizing tale of magic, wonder, and romance. Harms weaves a spellbinding story that will leave you captivated until the very end. Do yourself a favor and immerse yourself in this magical world."

—Rebecca Sullivan, author of *Night Owls and Summer Skies*

ALSO BY PHILLINE HARMS

Never Kiss Your Roommate

Love and Other Wicked Things

PHILLINE HARMS

wattpad books W

wattpad books

An imprint of Wattpad WEBTOON Book Group

Published in Canada by Wattpad WEBTOON Book Group, a division of Wattpad WEBTOON Studios, Inc.

36 Wellington Street E., Suite 200, Toronto, ON M5E 1C7 Canada

www.wattpad.com

First Wattpad Books edition: August 2023

ISBN 978-1-99025-994-4 (Trade Paper original)

ISBN 978-1-99025-995-1 (eBook edition)

Library and Archives Canada Cataloguing in Publication information is available upon request.

Printed and bound in Canada

1 3 5 7 9 10 8 6 4 2

Cover design by Lesley Worrell
Cover illustration by Spiros Halaris
Typesetting by Delaney Anderson

To the girls who talk to plants and find comfort in the cards.
Never lose your magic.

1

THE HIEROPHANT

family — shared beliefs — established conventions

Thank the earth and stars, Rhia thought as she sank to her knees in the middle of the woods on the evening of September 22, *that I was lucky enough to be born a witch.*

It was a thought that crossed her mind often, but never more so than during the autumn equinox. It had been one of Rhia's favorite holidays ever since she could remember. She loved the first chill of fall that accompanied it, marking the last celebration of the warm summer days before the cold settled down for good. She loved the traditions: harvesting the last of her family's little herb garden, baking the first pumpkin pie of the season, going apple picking with her sister. Most of all, she loved the feast that her family held in their garden every year, where, over food and drink, the women would thank the earth for everything it had given them throughout the summer and cast spells for protection and prosperity in the upcoming winter months.

What Rhia was doing at this moment was her own little

tradition. Every autumn equinox, in the late afternoon, she would go for a walk in the woods behind her house to look for the first signs of fall. Pine cones, chestnuts, the blushing leaves that came tumbling down—she foraged them all, carefully storing them away to decorate her altar with when she got home. Presently, she was kneeling in the middle of the woods to pick up one of the acorns she had spotted. They weren't too easy to find because she had misjudged how early the sun was setting—she'd been scavenging long enough that her only source of light was the pale moonlight that filtered through the crowns of the trees—but Rhia didn't mind. The dark had never scared her, and she knew how to find her way around these woods even after nightfall. She could always trust the trees to tell her the way back, after all.

Rhia pulled a small pouch out of the satchel slung over her shoulder. *The earth doesn't owe us anything*, her mother's voice murmured in the back of her head. *We must never take too much without giving something back.* Using her hands, Rhia dug a small pit into the soil, its texture beneath her fingertips as familiar as her own heartbeat. When she offered some seeds from her pouch, she could hear its pleased hum. "Thank you for these acorns," she softly said as she pressed the seeds into the earth. "And thank you for the summer days that have passed." It was only once she'd covered the seeds and spoken the spell that would ensure their survival in the winter that she placed the acorns in her satchel, taking care not to crush the orange and red leaves she had stowed away earlier.

Closing the satchel, she rose to her feet. Branches snapped quietly beneath her boots as she began walking again, following the beaten path that would take her towards the house. However, before she could go back, there was one more errand left to run.

The Murmuring River was easy to find, since, as its name suggested, it called out to any close passersby with its low rumbling. Although the stream was narrow and shallow in this spot, Rhia neared it with caution, taking care not to slip. She wasn't afraid of water in general, but there was something about this river in particular that always made her feel uneasy.

Crouching down, she fished out the jar her cousin had given her earlier from her satchel. The river soaked the sleeve of her dress when she dunked the glass in, but she didn't dare look down. When she was little, her aunt had told her a story of how she'd once seen something staring back at her from the bottom of the river. Rhia laughed about it in the daylight, but cloaked in darkness and with the hungry roar of the current in her ears, she was relieved when she sealed up the jar and could continue on her way.

As the Murmuring River grew quieter in the distance, she had to chuckle at herself. It was silly, letting a scary story her aunt had told her as a child get to her, especially considering *she* was the subject of many a scary story herself.

"Always acting like such a bad witch, but then you get creeped out by a stupid river," she murmured to herself. "Tristan would have a field day if he saw—"

"Am I interrupting an important monologue?"

Rhia jumped, her head snapping up to see who had spoken. "Sage," she hissed when she spotted her older sister at the end of the path. She was wearing a dark-green dress and a brown jacket that blended in perfectly with the trees around them, which explained why Rhia hadn't noticed her earlier. "You scared me!"

"Sorry." Sage laughed, falling in step beside her. "I didn't mean to. They sent me to tell you that the food is ready."

Time moved strangely when Rhia was alone in the woods, her own needs fading into the background as all her senses turned outward. She only now realized how hungry she was.

"You spent quite some time out here," her sister commented. "Did you find anything good for your altar?"

"Some acorns and leaves." Rhia cracked her satchel open a fraction to allow Sage a glimpse at her harvest. "I kind of lost track of time."

"You always do." Although Sage's tone was teasing, there was fondness in the look she sent Rhia. "Someday you're going to disappear out here and never come back."

"At least you'll know what happened to me," said Rhia, unconcerned and not entirely opposed to the idea. "I doubt anyone would be surprised."

Sage shook her head, making the golden jewelry crocheted into her box braids for the festivities glitter in the moonlight. She moved just as surely through these woods as Rhia, with her head raised high instead of having to look where her steps landed. Wherever Sage walked, the trees made way for her, pulling back their branches and burying their roots so as not to snag on her dress. They weren't quite as reverential when it was just Rhia, but she didn't mind. She preferred it when they were playful, brushing against her arms and tugging at her cardigan, leaving leaves in her hair that she could put on her altar when she got home. It was part of the reason she wore her hair down, allowing the chin-length curls to bounce freely around her face, held back only slightly by an orange headband that matched the color of her dress.

"So . . ." Rhia cleared her throat. "Did you practice any divination while I was gone?"

Philline Harms

"No. I didn't really feel like it today."

Rhia directed her eyes at the swaying treetops again. Divination, the art of telling the future, was one of the basic skills that every witch in her family possessed—every witch but her.

Sage nudged her shoulder. "Why are you asking? Is there anything you need answers to?"

"Oh, no, that's okay," Rhia quickly said. She didn't want her sister to glance at her future and report back what she thought was interesting. She wanted to see it herself, every little detail. She wanted to hold her fate in both hands and know its weight, its form, how far she could stretch it before it snapped back into shape. It was a stupid longing, considering how many years had passed since she'd last been able to do it.

"What about Grandma?" she inquired. "Did she find out anything interesting?" When she had left for her walk, her grandmother had been in the middle of a tarot reading for the upcoming months—her own take on a solitary equinox ritual.

Ducking under a low-hanging branch that wasn't quick enough to pull back, Sage expelled a quiet snort. "Of course she did. She always finds *something* interesting."

"Another looming apocalypse, then?"

"Probably. I can't remember all the cards she drew. Death, the Tower, and something else. The Lovers, maybe? I'm not sure."

"Ohhh, the Tower," Rhia said, dragging out the words in a low voice. It was a similar tone to her grandmother's ominous pitch anytime she flipped over a tarot card to find that particular image: two figures leaping headfirst from the windows of a tower struck by lightning, flames lapping at a pitch-black sky. *It symbolizes chaos, destruction, bad luck. Loss. A sudden, irrevocable change.*

"Yeah, it looks quite dramatic," confirmed Sage, sounding more amused than worried. "She's also convinced that there's a new witch in town. Says she saw it in a dream last night."

Rhia stopped in her tracks. "Really? Who did she see?"

"A girl around your age. She seems to be looking for something here, but Grandma couldn't say what."

"What could someone possibly be looking for *here*?"

"I don't know. To be honest, I can't imagine any witch coming here voluntarily, especially not without a coven. It's not like Oakriver is the place to be when you have abilities. I mean, what do we have to offer, really? One festival, a tiny shop, and the Council's ban on public use of magic," Sage listed as she started walking again.

Rhia, scandalized by this slander of her hometown, quickly rushed to its defense. Scrambling to keep up with her sister's long legs, she argued, "For how small it is, Obscura is really well stocked, though. Also, *you* are literally the one organizing the Fall Festival, so you're not allowed to bash it."

"I know, I know." Sage raised her hands in self-defense. "All I'm trying to say is that it was probably just a really vivid dream."

Rhia hummed in agreement. Still, deep down, she couldn't shake the thought that there was more to it. Her grandmother's dreams were never just *dreams*.

Before she could dwell too long on the thought, a familiar warmth draped over her and chased away her unease. A bright light flashed at the corners of her vision, heralding their return to the family's garden a heartbeat before they emerged from the tree line. It was the protective circle they had cast around the property earlier, a barrier that kept unwanted spirits and negative energy out as the family celebrated. Another step, and Rhia and Sage were fully inside, the magical sensation subsiding into a simple feeling of safety. Ahead of them, their home came into view, and in front of it the bonfire they lit every year. Its glow flickered across the faces of their family, who were scurrying in and out of the kitchen door with bowls and plates in their hands as they set the heavy wooden table perched in the tall grass.

Holly was the first one to spot them. Abandoning the pumpkin pie she'd been slicing, she skipped over to meet Rhia. "Finally, there you are! Did you get everything you needed?"

With a solemn nod, Rhia retrieved the jar of river water from her satchel. "I hope you appreciate what a sacrifice this was."

Holly grimaced. "Still that creepy?"

"Even creepier," Rhia said earnestly. "But I'll accept one bowl of moon water as payment."

"Pleasure doing business with you." With the fingers that weren't cradling the jar with all the care of handling a newborn baby, Holly firmly shook Rhia's hand. "Now come on, I'm *starving.*"

Rhia didn't need to be told twice. Her mouth watered as Holly tugged her towards the table and her eyes fell on all the food they had spent the last two days preparing. There were bowls of roasted vegetables and mashed potatoes; a pot of butternut squash soup; turnip greens and butter beans; homemade biscuits; apple crumble and pumpkin pie; decanters of grape juice, wine, and apple cider. The scent of cinnamon and rosemary mixed with the smoke of the fire, a comforting smell that made Rhia feel warm all over.

She was about to sit down next to Holly, who had already claimed a seat on one of the wooden benches, when a hand settled on her shoulder. "Hands first," her mother chided. "And bring the caramel sauce with you on your way back, would you, honey?"

With an exaggerated groan—she was the youngest of the family and therefore obligated to such antics—Rhia turned and hurried inside to wash the soil off her hands, making a brief detour upstairs to her bedroom to toss her satchel onto her bed. On her way outside, she grabbed the bowl of caramel sauce from the kitchen, neatly avoiding stepping on the cat that was curled up near the oven where the scratched-up wood was the warmest. By the time she returned to the table, the rest of the family was already seated. A smile spread on Rhia's face as she studied them: her sister, her cousin, her mother, her aunt, and her grandmother all sitting together, their dark-brown skin illuminated by the candles on the table as they chattered over cups of apple cider and wine. Like always, there was a spot saved for her between Holly and Grandma Deloris, who, as the matriarch of the family, had taken her usual seat at the end of the table.

Her grandmother looked up at Rhia when she set the caramel down in front of her. "There you are," she said. "No one saw you, did they?"

"'Course not." Rhia dropped onto the bench, slightly distracted by the sight of all the food in front of her. The autumn equinox was the *best*. "There's never anyone in these woods after dusk."

"Mmm. Better hope so," the old woman grumbled.

"Not now, Mom," Tanisha, Rhia's aunt, scolded. "We're celebrating! You can catastrophize all you want tomorrow."

Holly muttered her agreement around a mouthful of bread while the rest of the family nodded.

Grandma Deloris raised her wrinkly hands in surrender. "Fine, fine. No more."

Still, a few moments later Rhia couldn't help herself. Lowering her voice so no one else would hear, she leaned in close and murmured, "Grandma . . . Sage told me about your dream. Do you really think that it's true? That there's a new witch in town?"

For a few long seconds, her grandmother didn't react. Her eyes were fixed on one of the candles, her expression unreadable in the flickering light. "Your sister and your mother, they don't believe me. But I know what I saw, and the tarot showed me the same thing."

The wind whispered in the leaves of the trees that stretched overhead. A chill ran down Rhia's spine. "What is it, Grandma? What did you see?"

"There's danger ahead, Rhiannon." Grandma Deloris looked up, her dark eyes finally meeting Rhia's. "And I can't help but feel like you'll be at the very center of it."

2

KNIGHT OF WANDS

passion — boldness — pursuing ideas

Nothing good ever comes out of this place.

Those were the last words that Valerie's father had said to her before he'd given her an awkward hug and driven off.

Well. So far, nothing had happened to prove him correct. It had been about an hour since he'd dropped Valerie off, and Oakriver seemed just like she had always imagined: a sleepy town in the middle of nowhere, a little antiquated, but charming with its cobblestone streets and quaint middle-class homes. There was nothing particularly offensive about it, nothing at all to validate the grim expression on her father's face as he'd navigated the narrow alleyways—unless, perhaps, one had a severe aversion to red bricks or Halloween decorations put up an entire month in advance.

The dorm room she had been assigned was similarly unassuming. It was small and furnished with nothing but two desks, two beds, and two closets, but standing in it, Valerie couldn't help but grin from ear to ear. The fact that she was here at all was a small victory in itself. It had required not only several arguments with her father but also a healthy dose of cosmic intervention.

She wasn't sure which astronomical constellation she had to thank for the flooding that had damaged a large part of the college's housing and subsequently forced the school to delay the start of term to late September, but it was the sole reason she was able to study here. Had the school year started on time, she would have had neither her father's permission nor enough money to afford to live on her own, but now, after weeks of constant nagging and a summer of working several jobs, she had reached what she had been dreaming of for years.

Before leaving, her father had asked her what it was about Oakriver that attracted her so much. Valerie understood his confusion—after all, a tiny town with a population of less than ten thousand wasn't exactly where most nineteen-year-olds dreamed of going after high school. She had told him it was because of the college's good reputation. While that was partially true—its art program was nationally renowned—it wasn't what intrigued her the most.

Valerie Morgan knew exactly four things about her mother. One: she was probably a witch. Two: with red hair and green eyes, Valerie looked similar enough to her to sometimes make her father flinch when she entered a room. Three: she had lived in Oakriver. Four: seventeen years ago, she had disappeared here.

Countless times, Valerie had asked her father to tell her what had happened to her, and countless times, she hadn't gotten a response. She wasn't sure if her father simply didn't want to talk about it or if he truly did not know. Either way, the mystery around Isabelle Morgan had long ago solidified a goal in Valerie's head: she wanted to go to Oakriver to find her mother, or at the very least get some answers.

And here she was, one gigantic step closer to her objective.

But first, some smaller tasks. She had already unpacked most of her stuff, making an effort not to overstep the invisible border that divided her half of the room from her roommate's, which was already fully furnished and decorated. If the sketchbooks littering the desk and the art prints covering the wall were anything to go by, her roommate was probably an art student like Valerie. The two small pride flags above their desk—nonbinary and pansexual—made her lips tick up. She carefully stored the knowledge away.

Her last thing to unpack was her deck of tarot cards. Valerie placed them gently onto her bedside table, keeping her hand on the topmost card a few seconds longer to ground herself. It showed a man on horseback with a wooden staff in his hand, his body a vibrant blur of reds and oranges as he charged forward. It was the Knight of Wands, a recurring motif for her. She'd painted this deck herself—her favorite art project to date—and so she didn't need a handbook to understand the card's meaning; just by looking at it, she could feel the energy it held. The Knight of Wands was passion, movement, progress. He was fire, raw and reckless, filled with the same potential that she felt coursing through her own veins. The unbridled power packed into his frame was enough to make her fingertips tingle.

Valerie pulled back her hand and pocketed her keys. She paused only once more to grab the flyers from her desk, studying them as she pulled her dorm room door shut. They were made of lilac paper with an illustration of a crystal ball at the top and some text in a whimsical font beneath it: *Tarot readings — astrological forecasts — palmistry. Want to know what the future holds for you? Contact this number!*

She had designed them at home before she left in hopes that they would not only help her make some money on the side but also allow her to meet new people here. She didn't expect too much to come from them, but she tacked them to every bulletin board she encountered anyway.

Self-advertisement completed, she left the building and strolled out onto the campus. Oakriver College was of the smaller variety, offering around four dozen courses with a focus on the arts. Like most of the town, it looked ancient; a handful of ivy-covered stone buildings strewn near the edge of the woods as if some clumsy hand had carelessly dropped them there, connected by narrow paths left in the tall meadow by generations of students. Valerie followed the makeshift trails at random, passing the art studios and the main building that housed the cafeteria along the way, until she was spat out at the edge of campus. From there, she wandered into the town.

There weren't many people on the streets, which Valerie blamed on the weather. It was a gloomy day with an overcast sky, the cold biting enough to make her bury her hands deep in the pockets of her denim jacket. The few people that she did cross paths with tended to stare at her and then quickly avert their gaze when Valerie stared back. Valerie didn't care. From what she'd gathered from the town's website, it was rather liberal—it had to be, since so many of its businesses relied on the college students and their families. Still, it was a given that she would stand out with her bright-red hair, the slit in one of her eyebrows, the heavy combat boots, and the piercings in her ears.

As she drifted aimlessly past the residential houses, she tried to imagine her mother behind their windows, hurrying down the stairs, sitting on the porch. Would she live in that one, with the overgrown garden? Or that one, with the neatly trimmed rosebush?

There was one house in particular that caught her eye. It looked older than most as ivy climbed its brick façade and green paint chipped from the window shutters. Mismatched flowerpots in bright colors stood in the windowsills, and a cat dozed on the porch while Stevie Nicks's voice drifted onto the street, begging her lover to *stay with me, stay.* However, what gave Valerie pause wasn't the house itself—it was the girl behind one of the windows on the second floor.

She was tending to plants on the windowsill, a contented smile on her lips as she watered them. It was hard to tell from the street, but she looked to be a good deal shorter than Valerie, and significantly curvier. She wore a yellow knit sweater that was luminous against her dark-brown skin and a headband in the same color, which allowed only a few curls to bob around her face as she worked. Even from a distance, there was something *warm* about her, a strange charm that slowed Valerie's steps without her doing.

She only realized she had stopped in her tracks when the girl turned around, disappearing out of sight. Valerie peered up at her window a few seconds longer before she started walking again.

And her father had said nothing good could ever come out of this town.

As she continued, the music fading in the distance, she found her way right into the heart of the town. The family homes soon made room for little shops and restaurants, each more picturesque than the last. There was a café called Sugar & Spice that Valerie stopped in front of long enough for a blond-haired boy to catch her gaze through the large window. He paused while wiping down the tables to offer her a toothy grin. Valerie returned it with a smile of her own and vowed to pay the café a visit over the next few days. The cakes she could see in the display case looked *delectable*—even more so when she saw the handwritten sign that proclaimed that all of them were vegan.

She truly didn't think things could get any better than that until, through sheer coincidence, she stumbled onto one of the narrower backstreets. The building that had caught her attention was at the very end, so secluded that the light barely reached it. It appeared to be even older than the house that Plant Girl lived in, and, if she wasn't mistaken, it stood at a bit of an angle, leaning onto the building next to it like a weary elder might lean on a friend. The large shop window was so dusty that she could see nothing but the reflection of her own eyes blinking curiously back at her. On the door, there was a small wooden sign that read OBSCURA ODDITIES.

Looking at it from the outside, nothing gave the impression it was open. Still, guided by a sudden instinct, Valerie walked up to the door and gave it an experimental push. The jingling of a bell drowned out her soft sound of surprise as she all but stumbled into the shop, jumping when the door fell shut behind her with a loud bang.

For a few long seconds, all Valerie could do was wait until her eyes adjusted to the half-light, a blend of different herbs tickling her nose. Finally, some of the darker shadows revealed themselves as shelves. The floorboards creaked under her boots as she neared one of them to investigate the objects on display. Candles. Not of the scented Yankee Candle variety, but ones that looked like they belonged in fancy candelabras or scattered around a pentagram. They came in all sizes, colors, and shapes—one of them, Valerie noted as she squinted, was suspiciously phallic. Interesting.

On the next shelf, there was a row of incense burners and matches, along with a few sticks of cedar, which Valerie could now recognize in the overwhelming mix of scents. There were other things she knew—cauldrons in all sizes, rune stones, different tarot decks, dried herbs, crystals—and some things she had no name for.

As she trailed her fingers along the spines of books with titles like *The Garden Witch's Guide to Botany* and *Contacting the Dead: A Practical Handbook to Necromancy*, she felt a pleasant shiver running down her spine. There was an unmistakable energy in the air, a static crackle that made the hair on the back of her neck stand up: magic, so strong it was almost tangible. Valerie had never felt anything like it. In a trance, she wandered between the shelves, so caught up in seeing and touching and *feeling* that she startled violently when a voice sounded somewhere to her left.

"Can I help you with anything?"

"Holy sh—" Pressing a hand to her chest, Valerie spun around to see who had spoken. "Where the hell did you come from?"

The person turned out to be around her age, sitting behind the register a few feet away with their chin propped in one hand, curls of dark-blue hair flopping onto their face. At Valerie's question, they cocked their head with a puzzled frown. "I've been here the entire time."

"Then why didn't you *say* anything?"

"I didn't want to disturb you while you were browsing." With a sheepish shrug, they lifted the small gaming console that was sitting on the counter in front of them. "And, uh . . . *Animal Crossing.*"

The sight of the Nintendo was so unexpectedly mundane against the backdrop of peculiar items that Valerie couldn't help the laugh that escaped her. Walking over to the counter, she stretched out a hand. "I'm Valerie. I use she/her pronouns."

"Quinn. I use they and them."

Valerie's eyes widened when she remembered the name that had been scrawled on the covers of the sketchbooks sitting in the other half of her dorm room. "Wait, Quinn Jiang?"

Quinn blinked once. "Yes?"

"No way. We're roommates for this year! You're also majoring in art, right?"

With a nod, Quinn raised their hands so that Valerie could see that the pads of their fingers were stained black with charcoal. "I am."

"Guess we'll be seeing a lot of each other then, huh?"

"Looks like it." Tugging the sleeves of their black sweater down over their knuckles, Quinn offered her a smile. "So, is there anything specific you were looking for here?"

Valerie glanced around again, shaking her head. With bundles of herbs hanging from the low ceiling and jars of magical ingredients (some of them labeled CAREFUL: POISONOUS!), the shop seemed like a dream that might disappear if she so much as blinked. "No. I wasn't really expecting . . . anything like this." She looked back at Quinn. "It's so cool that you work here."

"It is." Quinn's eyes lit up as they glanced around the room.

"I started here a few months ago, and I really love it. We have so many interesting people coming in every day."

"Do a lot of witches live here?"

"Not in Oakriver itself. This shop is the only one of its kind in the region, so most of them come from nearby towns." Even though there was no one else around, Quinn lowered their voice and leaned a little closer. "There are three large family covens in this area that practice, but I only know because they shop here sometimes. They're very careful to not let the townspeople here know about magic. You probably should be too."

"Why, are they still hunting witches around here?" Valerie joked.

"Well, not actively. But . . ." Quinn rubbed at their neck, glancing around again as if they were worried some eavesdropper might materialize from between the shelves. "From what I've gathered, there was an incident that led to the Council of the Three—the three big witch families that live here—swearing an oath not to reveal their abilities to the town. I think there's some kind of punishment if you do, but I don't know too much about that."

In one of the little bottles on the counter—a sample of a beauty potion, naturally—Valerie could see her own wide-eyed reflection. The Council of the Three sounded like something straight out of *Hocus Pocus*. She was instantly intrigued. Gesturing at their surroundings, she asked, "But then why have a shop like this one? Doesn't this make it a bit obvious?"

"No. Because not everyone can find it," said Quinn. "The owner of this shop put a spell on the building. Unless it is directly pointed out, only those who have abilities or are at least drawn to magic will notice it."

"Oh! So, you also practice magic?"

"No. I suppose I must have a small affinity for it, but nothing full-fledged. No, you know—" they paused to give a vague wave of their hands "—*actual* magic."

Valerie, being her own only point of reference, wasn't sure what *actual magic* looked like, but she figured now was too early for any probing questions. Switching gears, she asked instead, "And you still have enough customers?"

"We also have an online shop." Quinn chuckled. "A lot of my job is just packaging orders and bringing them down to the post office."

"I see. So advertising, say, tarot readings wouldn't be a smart idea? Hypothetically?"

Quinn quirked an eyebrow. "Hypothetically?"

"Uh-huh."

"Would you listen if I said it's best to be as subtle as possible about it in this town?"

Valerie scratched at her neck, her mind flashing back to her flyers hanging all over campus. "Depends. Is this ominous council going to put a hit out on me if I'm not?"

Quinn scrunched up their nose as if they honestly weren't sure. "I don't know. I'm from a town an hour away from here, and I've only been staying here since July. I . . . don't think so?"

"Huh. Then I guess I'll take my chances. Being subtle isn't really my strong suit."

Quinn looked like they didn't know whether to be amused or concerned. "Oh dear. I have a feeling you're going to stir things up around here."

"I have a feeling you might be right about that." Pointing at one of the shelves, Valerie said, "So, about those crystal balls . . ."

3

WHEEL OF FORTUNE

fated encounters — unexpected events — a turning point

Rhia was *not* having a good day.

First, she had overslept. Then, to make it to work on time, she'd needed to take her bike, only to discover that it had a flat tire. (Holly: *I told* you the Uranus transit was going to impact your short-distance travels!) When she was finally on her way, the light drizzle that had been going on all morning turned into a full-blown rain shower, leaving her drenched by the time she made it to Sugar & Spice. And as if all of that hadn't been bad enough, her first task was to shelve the books that had arrived earlier that week.

Usually, Rhia loved her job. She *did*. The café was tucked away on the first floor of an old building with creaky floorboards and old chandeliers, containing a cluttered mix of beaten-up couches and newer coffee tables. The second floor was Rhia's favorite area: it served as a bookstore, where comfy old armchairs were hidden away between the tall rows of shelves. She could remember countless afternoons spent curled up in one of them as a kid, flipping through any book that caught her fancy while her mother had coffee with a friend downstairs.

The sheer nostalgia of the place, plus the fact that she got to work with Tristan, her best friend for over a decade, was enough to make her prefer this job over any other. She dreamed of owning the café one day, with her own cakes and pastries on the menu, her favorite books on the shelves . . . and someone else to do the tedious work of shelving. Tristan and Rhia took turns with every new delivery, despite her constant complaining that it was much easier for him, as he was at least four inches taller than her and, being a lacrosse player, had *muscles*. Her nagging never got her anywhere, though—in the three years they'd worked here together, she'd only gotten out of shelving a handful of times, mostly through bribery. Once, she'd threatened to put a hex on him, but to no avail. As it turned out, it was kind of difficult to intimidate someone who had seen her with braces at thirteen and shared a bed with her during countless sleepovers.

Today it was her turn once again. Rhia grunted as she carried a box of picture books over to the children's section, almost tripping over her own feet in the process. She felt unbearably hot under her woolen sweater, which was still wet to the touch from the rain outside. Her hair—which she'd spent two hours on just *yesterday*, for crying out loud—was already starting to poof up, straining against the hair tie she'd used to pull it back. She swore quietly as she set the heavy cardboard box down in front of one of the shelves, glad there were no children around to hear her. Her grumbling became even more heartfelt when she realized that most of the books had to go on the very top shelf. Cursing the existence of every author who had the audacity to have an

A for their initial, she got on her tiptoes to sort them into their respective places, only to almost drop all of them when a snicker sounded from somewhere behind her.

"You know, I would feel sorry for you, but it's kind of hilarious that you're making this so difficult for yourself."

Rhia spun around to face Tristan. He seemed to have made it to the café before the rain had started, his unruly mop of blond hair blessedly dry, the only stains on his hoodie caused by his inability to eat anything without mild spillage. Even several years after Tristan's infamous eighth-grade growth spurt, Rhia still resented how far she had to tilt her head to scowl at him. "How am I making this difficult for myself? It *is* difficult!"

"You could always just . . ." Cheeks dimpling, Tristan waved his hands around in a dramatic gesture that clearly indicated lifting the books through telekinesis. "You know?"

"Tris," groaned Rhia. She briefly poked her head around the bookshelf to make sure no one was within earshot. "I'm not Holly. Earth magic, remember? I can't move things. And even if I *could*, I wouldn't. Someone might walk by any moment and see."

Shaking his head, Tristan moved to lean against the bookshelf. "I seriously don't get how all of you can be so disciplined about this. If I had your abilities, I'd constantly be using them to do cool stuff. Like pranking people."

"Of course you would. You know, every morning I wake up and thank the universe for not giving you any abilities. I can only imagine the chaos."

"Okay, rude. You looked so pitiful, I was going to ask if you'd like me to do the rest for you, but I guess not."

"You would do that?" Rhia gasped.

"Well, not anymore! I am *shattered* that you would think—"

"Thank you, Tristan!" Rhia cut him off, careful to avoid the tomato sauce on his hoodie as she moved to hug him. "You're the best."

"And you're *wet*," he said, but he didn't try to shove her away.

Rhia shook her head in response, sprinkling him with the last raindrops that were caught in her hair. Then she let go of him. "Seriously, thank you. I owe you one."

"Yeah, yeah." Tristan made a shooing motion before pulling a tangled pair of earphones from the pocket of his jeans and getting to work.

Rhia didn't need to be told twice. As she made her way to the first floor, the familiar noises of the café got louder. Laughter and animated chatter mixed with the whirring of the coffee machine, spoons clinked against porcelain cups, and rain thrummed against the windows, all while a calm acoustic playlist drifted from the speakers. Rhia inhaled the scent of coffee and books and felt something in her shoulders loosen, utterly at ease in the familiar chaos—

Until the energy in the café suddenly shifted.

The cause, Rhia quickly realized, was the girl who had just stepped through the door. She was tall, white, with bright-red hair and a smile that promised trouble. Over her shoulder, she carried a canvas tote bag with a drawing of a skeleton giving a thumbs-up, the speech bubble next to the skull declaring *'Til death we do art*. Rooted in place on the stairs, Rhia watched as she shrugged off her oversized denim jacket and took a few purposeful strides towards a table where a girl with blond curls was waiting for her.

Rhia's attention was only directed elsewhere when Anne, the

owner of the café, called her name. Letting go of the handrail, she hurried over to the counter. "Sorry. Do you need me in the kitchen, or should I serve?"

"Serve," Anne said, handing her a notepad and a pencil. "It's a bit busy down here today."

Tucking the pencil behind her ear, Rhia spun around and got to work. Anne was right; the rain seemed to have driven half the town through their doors, so it took her a while to get everyone's orders. In the end, whether it was conscious or not, the red-haired girl's table was the last one left.

Rhia didn't know what it was about the girl that made her heart beat just a little bit faster as she neared the table. "Hey," she said, putting on her brightest waitress-smile, her voice a few octaves higher in what Tristan called her *working voice*. "What can I get you guys today?"

"I'd like a slice of the vegan dark chocolate cake," the blond girl, whom Rhia recognized as one of the regulars, chirped, "and a small cappuccino. With almond milk, please."

"I'll have some of the carrot cake," the red-haired girl said.

Keeping her eyes trained on her notepad, Rhia gave a nod. "Awesome! Anything to drink for you?"

"Do you have any recommendations?"

Rhia finally looked up to find the girl watching her with attentive green eyes. Her stare was enough to momentarily make her forget every single beverage the café offered. "Um . . . I'm more of a tea drinker, so . . . I really like the apple cinnamon tea, especially during fall."

"Sounds good. Thank you."

Rhia nodded, glad that she could break eye contact. She froze when, for the first time, her gaze drifted down to the table.

Spread out in a deliberate arrangement lay eight tarot cards, three of them already turned face up. They were far more whimsical than the standard deck that Rhia knew, each card holding a vibrantly colored painting that showed sensual bodies and lush greenery, beautiful animals and vivid landscapes. Rhia snapped out of her state of shock when the blond girl quietly cleared her throat. "Awesome," she rushed to say. "It'll be just a moment."

As she made her way back, Rhia could faintly hear the red-haired girl say, "Right. As I was saying, the Queen of Cups usually stands for a very nurturing, loving person in your life. She could be your mother or a good friend, someone you can trust and go to for advice . . ."

When Rhia returned to the counter, she was glad to find Tristan standing by the coffee machine. "Putting those books away didn't even take that long, you dramatic—" Noticing the look on her face, he broke off. "Hey, what happened to you? Rude customer? Who do I need to fight?"

Rhia shook her head, hands moving to tighten her ponytail as she tried to calm herself. "Have you ever seen her here before? The girl with red hair?"

Tristan briefly glanced over her shoulder to see who she was talking about. "Oh, yeah. I saw her walking by the other day. I think she's new in town."

"I can't believe it," Rhia said. Her skin suddenly felt itchy under her heavy woolen sweater. "Grandma said that there was a new witch here, but I didn't think she was right—"

"Wait, she's a witch too?"

"Shhh, be quiet!" Rhia whispered. "She's reading tarot cards for that girl right now, which is just stupid for so many reasons. If the Council of the Three found out—"

"The what?"

"The witch council I told you about," Rhia quickly explained. "Us, the Lightbourns, and the Fairloves. If there's one thing that Grandma drilled into us growing up, it's to adhere to our promise to never use magic in public. She could be banished from town for this."

"Ohhh. Right." Tristan glanced over at the girl again. Instead of getting hung up on the laws of the secret witch society on whose outskirts he moved, he offered, ever practical, "I'll bring their order over if you want."

Rhia was so grateful she could have cried. "Thank you, Tris. Second favor of the day, huh?"

"I'm expecting at least a whole cake in return."

Rhia was too preoccupied to muster more than a small smile. She did her best to steer clear of the red-haired girl as she continued serving, but she couldn't stop herself from glancing her way every now and again. Her mood darkened further when, having finished the tarot reading, the girl started using a pendulum next, a look of utter concentration on her face as she dangled it from her hand and tracked its movement. Rhia hated the casualness with which she did it almost as much as the acidic taste of envy in her mouth.

It wasn't often that she got genuinely mad, but that afternoon, after the flat tire and the rain and the book delivery and now *her*, Rhia could feel her blood boiling. All things considered, it wasn't a surprise that she couldn't stop herself from marching over to her as soon as the blond girl had left.

"You can't just *do* that."

The girl looked up at her, seemingly in no hurry to leave as she idly stirred her tea. "Do what?"

"You know exactly what I'm talking about," Rhia said, trying her best to keep her voice low.

The other witch didn't seem impressed. "I don't think I do." She paused, her dark-red lips twitching in amusement. "But why don't you sit down and explain it to me?"

Rhia stared at her. This girl, whoever she was, *reeked* of danger. Rhia felt like she was breaking all her family's rules simply by standing at her table. Then again, it wasn't as if she could just walk away and let her continue whatever she was doing.

After casting a glance over her shoulder to make sure that Tristan had everything under control, she noisily pulled the chair out and sat, arms crossed in front of her chest to clearly convey her displeasure at doing so.

"I'm Valerie," said the girl. With one hand, she pushed a strand of flaming-red hair out of her eyes. "And you are?"

"Rhia."

"Unique," Valerie commented, leaning slightly forward. "Is that your full name?"

"What are you doing here?"

"I'm drinking tea," she said, as if it were obvious. "Apple cinnamon *is* nice, by the way. Thanks for the recommendation."

Rhia had to take a very deep breath to stop herself from snapping. With a pointed look at the door, she said, "Your tea has gone cold."

Valerie cupped the porcelain mug in both her hands as if to confirm the fact. There was a small furrow between her brows, a whisper drowned out by the chatter inside the café. A heartbeat later, Rhia watched speechlessly as translucent tendrils of cinnamon-scented steam rose from her cup.

"I don't know what you're talking about." Valerie's eyes

sparkled with triumph as she lifted the tea to her mouth to blow on it. "It's almost too hot to drink."

"You—you can't be serious," Rhia said. "There are other people here! You can't just waltz in here and use—" She broke off, lowering her voice. ". . . use magic. Do you have any idea how fast word spreads in this town?"

Valerie let out an unconcerned laugh. "I doubt anyone noticed anything."

"Really? You don't think anyone noticed the extremely flashy tarot deck you had spread out here for a good thirty minutes?"

"Extremely flashy?" Valerie chuckled. It was a low, raspy sound that only added to the unease in Rhia's stomach. "I hate to break it to you, pumpkin, but everyone has tarot cards these days. It's trendy."

"But it's still dangerous to do something like that in such a public place! You didn't even bother to cast a circle, let alone *cleanse* the space—"

"Why would I do that? It's just tarot."

"I can't believe I have to explain this to you," Rhia hissed. Just how untrained was this witch? "Using tarot cards is a form of divination, yes? Divination means opening yourself to the spirit world. In an old, crowded place like this one," she said, waving a hand around to indicate the entire café, "there's tons of different energies, maybe even a few spirits that are stuck here. Some of them might be dangerous. You're asking for trouble by offering yourself to them without any kind of protection. Don't you know that?"

Valerie hesitated for a second before she simply shrugged, making the checkered flannel she was wearing slip down her shoulder. There was a splatter of freckles dusted over her upper arms and collarbones. Not that Rhia noticed. "Nothing like that has ever happened to me, and I've never cast a circle before."

Rhia couldn't believe what she was hearing, but at this point she was too annoyed to press on. "You know what, I don't really care. Get possessed if you feel like it. Just . . . go somewhere else to do it."

"Fine," Valerie agreed. "But only if you let me have a look at your hand first."

"What?"

"Your hand. Let me have a look."

"Why?" Rhia asked suspiciously.

"Why not?" Valerie's eyes glittered with mischief. Under the table, her knee brushed against Rhia's. "Scared?"

Yes. By now, every hair on Rhia's body stood on end. Sitting with Valerie felt like communing with a thundercloud; there was a static hum between them, an energy that felt like it might split the earth in two if it were released. Rhia knew she should probably walk away. Unfortunately, she'd been raised by three headstrong women who had taught her early on to stand as tall as the trees she revered, and just as steadfast. (Also: she was a Taurus.)

"If I give you my hand," she said, raising her chin, "do you promise to leave?"

"Deal."

Rhia offered the other girl her hand, palm facing up.

"Thank you," said Valerie. Her polite tone did nothing to counteract the positively impish smile she flashed Rhia.

To her own contempt, Rhia couldn't quite stop a shiver from running down her spine as Valerie traced the lines on her palm with a featherlight touch. She had long, elegant fingers, beautiful despite the black polish chipping from her nails. Her middle and ring finger were each adorned with a small tattoo; a crescent moon and a Venus symbol respectively, both of which looked suspiciously like they had been done with a stick-and-poke needle.

"This line right here says that you'll likely have a very intense love life. A deep, soulful connection with someone that will make a lasting impact on you," Valerie murmured. "This one here shows that you're going to live pretty long. Probably at least eighty years."

Even though Rhia tried hard to seem disinterested, she couldn't stop herself from leaning in. She had never been able to decipher the predictions in her hand and would have felt ridiculous asking her family, to whom this was child's play. "Uh-huh."

"These three little lines here say you'll have three children." Valerie was silent for a few moments, her eyebrows furrowed in concentration. "This one's a bit hard to read, but . . ." She looked up, meeting Rhia's eyes. "Ah, yes. It says you're a buzz-kill and taking this whole magic thing way too seriously. But the good news is you're cute, so—"

Cheeks burning up, Rhia abruptly pulled her hand back, her chair scraping loudly across the floorboards as she got to her feet. "I need to get back to work."

"Bye, Rhia," Valerie called after her. "It was nice meeting you."

Rhia didn't share the sentiment, but she didn't care to stop and tell her that.

When she risked a look over her shoulder a few minutes later, Valerie was gone; all that proved she had ever been there was a generous tip and the smoky scent of fire magic still hanging over the table where she had sat.

Philline Harms

4

QUEEN OF PENTACLES

stability — earthly comforts — self-sufficiency

"May these ingredients bond and bring calm and understanding," Rhia murmured. *"May they cleanse this space and banish negative energy."*

It was the afternoon, and she was baking. The cleansing lemon cake she was making was one of her great-grandmother's recipes that had been passed down in the family, only slightly tweaked over the years to replace cow's milk with oat milk and butter with oil. As one of the most harmless rituals for beginning witches, Rhia had known it by heart by the time she turned twelve. Countless times, she'd peeked over her mother's shoulder while she made it, until one day her mother had handed Rhia the spoon and told her to try it herself.

Since then, kitchen magic had been Rhia's favorite practice. Compared to the finicky business of brewing potions, this was easy: select the ingredients that would bring about the desired effect (today, Rhia had added some poppy seeds for relaxation and improved sleep and a tiny bit of ginger for self-assurance), channel a positive intention while baking, and you had a delicious treat that, when eaten, had just as strong of an effect as any other spell. As Rhia placed the baking pan into the preheated oven, she felt more at ease than she had since the incident at the café the day before.

"Feeling calmer yet, Elphie?" she softly asked as Elphaba, one of the many cats of the household, nudged her tiny head against Rhia's leg. "Yeah, me too."

Walking over to the windowsill, she picked up the cup of cinnamon tea she had left there. It had cooled down a little by now but still made her feel warmed from the inside out as she looked out the window at the garden. The sun was just starting to set behind the trees, glinting off the windows of the greenhouse and pouring the last rays of golden evening light onto the wooden floorboards of the kitchen.

The sound of the front door opening ripped Rhia out of her thoughts, followed by Holly poking her head into the kitchen a moment later. "Hey. Are you almost done, or should we come back later?"

"You're good." Rhia set her cup down on the windowsill again. "I'm pretty much finished."

At that, Holly stepped fully inside, tugging Tristan with her by his hand. While she was dressed to the nines as always, Tristan was wearing dark sweatpants and another one of the many old hoodies he refused to let go of.

When he saw what was going on, he abruptly stopped in his tracks. "Dude. It looks like a battlefield in here."

Glancing around, Rhia scratched lightly at her neck. The kitchen was always a bit cluttered; not only did it have to contain a table large enough to fit the entire family but also several tall shelves that brimmed with neatly labeled jars containing all sorts of magical ingredients, from devil's shoestring to witch hazel. Cupboards were packed full with pans, pots, and the odd cauldron, and every free space was occupied by greenery, whether that was the basil in the pot on the windowsill or the rosemary hanging in bundles from the ceiling. The thing that Tristan's eyes had zeroed in on, however, was the kitchen table—or what was visible of it.

"I did promise to bake you a cake, didn't I?"

"*One* cake, not ten! Which one's for me?"

"That one," said Rhia, pointing at a still-warm banana bread, which she knew was Tristan's favorite. "But feel free to try the others as well."

"What's this one gonna do? Turn me into a frog?"

"Not everything I bake is magical, you know." When Tristan only stared at her, she conceded, "It's for joy and good luck. Because I care about you, dumbass."

"Aw," cooed Tristan, already heading towards one of the drawers to get a knife and three plates.

He navigated the kitchen with as much confidence as if he lived there, which wasn't that far from the truth. As Rhia's best friend since childhood and Holly's boyfriend since high school, Tristan spent so much time in their house that the women considered him an honorary family member by now.

"I thought you were at the café today," Rhia said to her cousin as she sank onto one of the chairs, accepting the generous slice of banana bread Tristan handed her.

"Oh, I was! My dad was helping me clean up the attic," Holly said. "But then I decided to pick Tristan up from practice."

"Did you make any progress?"

"We're still trying to declutter the space and figure out its dimensions." Holly stole Rhia's mug for a quick sip of tea. "There's just so much *stuff* up there. Plus, I'm pretty sure it's haunted, so I'll probably have to do a little cleanse at some point. But once it's all done, it'll be amazing!"

Rhia couldn't help but admire her cousin's unwavering optimism. It had been a few weeks since Holly had asked Anne if she could rent the attic above Sugar & Spice after Rhia had told her that it wasn't really used. Her plan was to transform the space into a workshop slash storage place for her Etsy shop. Holly had started the shop a few months earlier, not expecting much to come of it, only for it to rapidly take off—apparently, there was an unexpectedly high demand for crystal necklaces and all the other little protection charms that she crafted in her free time.

"I can help you declutter," Tristan offered.

"That would be amazing!" With a smile, Holly leaned closer and used her thumb to wipe some crumbs off his chin.

"Gross," Rhia commented.

Tristan made a face at her. "I'm sorry, was that too heterosexual for you?"

"As a matter of fact, yes," Rhia confirmed. It was a running joke. Both of them were part of the queer community: Holly was asexual, and Tristan had stated more than once that he wouldn't be opposed to starting something with a guy if he wasn't head over heels for Holly.

"So . . ." Holly shook her head, making her dangling heart-shaped earrings swing back and forth. "Are you going to tell us why you've been stress-baking all day?"

"I'm not stress-baking."

"Yeah, no, this seems totally chill." Tristan gestured at the flood of cakes in front of him. With a grin, he met Rhia's eyes again. "It's because of the new girl, isn't it?"

"I have no idea what you're talking about."

"Me neither," Holly cut in. "What new girl?"

Tristan answered before Rhia could stop him. Wiggling his eyebrows, he said, "Her name is Valerie. She wears these stompy boots and flannels and has tattoos. We're pretty sure she likes girls."

"Hey, that's awesome!" Holly exclaimed. "That just doubled your dating pool! Now it's not just you and that one girl you kissed in middle school!"

"Okay, first of all: just because no one else is out doesn't mean no one else in this town is gay. It's not like we know most of the college students," Rhia said. "Second of all: the line between art student and lesbian is a thin one, so you can't go off of appearance. And third of all: I think I would rather die than date her."

"What? Why?"

"She's the witch Grandma talked about," Rhia said, lowering her voice out of habit even though there was no one else around. "I saw her practicing divination in the café yesterday."

"No way." Holly leaned closer. "In public?"

"Yeah. When I confronted her and told her that it wasn't a good idea, she didn't take it seriously at all."

"Did you tell Grandma? Or anyone else?"

"No. I don't want them to take it to the Council and make it a huge thing," Rhia said. "I just told her not to do it at the café again. I guess we'll see if she listens."

"Wow," Holly murmured. "A new witch in town. I wonder if that will change things."

Rhia didn't like the sound of that at all. Her family had lived in Oakriver for generations without anyone, save Tristan's family, learning their well-kept secret. She didn't think she wanted to know what would happen if the townspeople found out. Historically, that kind of stuff hadn't gone over very well. "I hope not."

Holly sat cradling her chin in one hand while the other was still loosely holding on to her fork, the banana bread in front of her long forgotten. Shrugging, she finally said, "All of that still doesn't explain why you hate her so much."

"I don't hate her," Rhia said. "She just . . . I don't know, she *irks* me. She was so cocky sitting there, doing all this stuff without casting a circle, and I felt like she didn't even listen when I told her why it was dangerous. She just laughed." *And flirted*, her brain added. Her palm itched at the memory of Valerie's fingers tracing the lines on her hand, the amused glint in her eyes when she'd met Rhia's gaze and called her cute.

"Wanna know what I think?" Holly asked. Before Rhia could say no, she added, "You don't hate her. You just hate that she's something new you can't control."

Rhia's mouth dropped open. "I—What the *hell*, Holly, I didn't come here to be psychoanalyzed—"

"I like her," Tristan threw in. "She seems cool."

"Yeah, but you're like the human embodiment of a golden retriever," Rhia accused. "You like everyone."

Tristan gave a good-natured shrug that only proved Rhia's point. After devouring half a slice of banana bread in one bite, he said, "If anyone cares, this golden retriever has an invitation to a college party this Friday. The lacrosse team is organizing it, but everyone's welcome."

Philline Harms

"Oh, I'm totally in!" Holly immediately said. "Rhia, you're coming too, right?"

"I don't know. Will it be a super big thing?"

"Hard to know beforehand. Probably?" Tristan offered. When Rhia grimaced, he pursed his lips into a pout. "Come on, Rhia. It'll be fun! We haven't partied together in so long."

"Yeah, come on," Holly said. "You can't just spend every night in your room watching Studio Ghibli movies!"

"I can, actually," Rhia retorted. "Also, stop ganging up on me, that's not fair."

Holly and Tristan exchanged glances. Then, in eerie synchronicity, each of them reached for one of Rhia's hands.

"Come on," said Holly in a singsong voice. "It'll be so fun! You can put on one of those cute dresses you never get a chance to wear, and I could do your makeup!"

"I'll take care of the next two book deliveries," Tristan said. "Please?"

"Please?"

"Please?"

"Plea—"

"Okay, fine!" Rhia pulled her hands out of their grasp. "You guys are weird."

"Says the witch who spent an entire afternoon baking magical cakes," Tristan snorted.

"Maybe I *should* turn you into a frog," mused Rhia, well aware that this was entirely impossible.

"That *would* be interesting," Holly agreed, ignoring Tristan's betrayed gasp. "But wait until after the party, please."

Rhia hid her smile behind her teacup. "I'll think about it."

5

THE SUN

fruitful encounters — childlike enthusiasm — authentic self-expression

Valerie wanted to get shit-faced.

It wasn't because she couldn't enjoy herself sober or because the week had been particularly stressful—she just felt it was appropriate for her first-ever college party.

She told Quinn as much as she let herself into their room Friday evening, making her roommate momentarily glance up from the laptop in front of them. They were lying on their belly in the middle of the bed, colors dancing across their face as the sounds of a cartoon crackled through the speakers. "Uh-huh."

"You sound excited." Valerie chuckled as she shut the door behind her. "What are you watching?"

"*Gravity Falls*," Quinn replied.

"Oh, I love that show!" Valerie threw open the doors of her closet. Flicking through the hangers, she asked, "Do you already know what you're gonna be wearing to the party tonight?"

"What party?"

"Haven't you heard? The lacrosse team is organizing it. There were flyers all over campus." Valerie turned around, holding a black dress in front of her body. "Do you think I should wear this?"

Quinn paused their show and turned their head to look at her, their cheek squished against their forearm. "I think you'd definitely have to wear something underneath it. It's a bit cold tonight."

Valerie had to smile at that. After a week of knowing Quinn, she was still hopelessly endeared by them. They were probably the most easygoing roommate Valerie could have ever hoped for, especially because the two were so similar: they shared not only their passion for art but also the habit of going to sleep at ungodly times.

The result was a new nightly routine that saw them both sitting on the floor in their room at 2:00 a.m. doing homework, not really talking much but simply enjoying the company and reminding each other to stretch out their wrists every once in a while. Valerie provided the coffee; Quinn played their lo-fi playlist. All in all, an immaculate arrangement.

"Yeah, you're probably right," Valerie agreed, grimacing down at her legs. "Also hides the big-ass bruise on my shin."

"Oh shit, it did bruise?" Quinn winced in sympathy.

"Yeah. I must've really banged it against that chair."

"At least you didn't wander out into the hallway," said Quinn.

The incident in question had happened less than twenty-four hours earlier. It had been a night like any other—until Valerie had woken to find herself standing in the middle of the pitch-black room, pain blooming in her shin and a sleep-rumpled Quinn blinking at her in shock. Somehow, she'd managed to sleepwalk halfway to the door. She didn't want to think about what would have happened without the chair that had graciously stopped her before reaching it.

"Do you sleepwalk often?" Quinn questioned.

"No." Valerie turned back to her closet, biting absent-mindedly at her thumbnail. "I don't think I ever have before."

"Huh. Maybe it's because of all the stress. You know, with moving out of your parents' house and everything."

"Yeah," Valerie agreed. "Maybe." She glanced over her shoulder again. "So, are you coming with?"

Quinn made an unenthusiastic noise. "I don't even know anyone on the lacrosse team."

"I don't know anyone either," Valerie said. "But that's kind of the point. To get to know more people."

"You've already gotten to know plenty of people with your tarot stuff, though," Quinn pointed out.

"Gotten to know their relationship struggles, more like." Valerie shuddered as memories of her 3:00 p.m. appointment resurfaced. She'd spent an entire hour convincing a weepy the-atre student that the Death card didn't literally mean that he or his boyfriend were going to keel over within the next day. And that wasn't even one of the most awkward readings she'd done over the last week. When she'd put up her flyers, she'd expected deep discussions about career paths and complex self-reflections, not talking pretentious art students through breaking up with their long-distance partners. Oh well. Money was money. And if she was honest, a part of her delighted in the gossip—over the last few days, she'd truly stared into the abyss of teen-hood. For someone who had spent her formative years occupied with

Philline Harms

makeshift rituals in abandoned parking lots and figuring out how to turn off the smoke detector in her room without her father noticing, it was all oddly fascinating.

Digging farther into her closet, she finally won the game of hide-and-seek with her pair of black tights. "Please come with me?" she begged Quinn. "It's gonna be fun, I promise. And if it's not, we can leave right away."

Valerie could hear Quinn's quiet groan, followed by the creaking of their bedframe as they presumably sat up. "Okay. But I can't promise that I'll stay very long."

"Never said we had to." Triumphant, Valerie pulled the black dress off its hanger. It shimmered like a midnight sky, the golden suns and moons embroidered on it sparkling in the dim light. Everything about the garment screamed *witch*, which was something that Valerie appreciated. Certain other people probably wouldn't, but that was half the fun—one could never know who one would end up running into, after all.

The party took place at one of the lacrosse players' houses off-campus, a ten-minute walk from their dorm. By the time they got there, muffled music and loud voices were pouring out of the open front door and onto the lawn, where little groups of students were scattered on the porch and in the grass. A few of them waved when they spotted Quinn, who offered a smile in return.

"I thought you didn't know anyone here?" Valerie chuckled.

"Knowing people and knowing *of* people are two different things," Quinn said, their ears red from the attention. "Otherwise I'd be friends with the entire town."

Valerie was pretty sure that the entire town *wanted* to be friends with Quinn. They had a gravity to them that drew people in and made them feel comfortable the moment they stepped into Quinn's orbit. Valerie thought it had to do with how observant they were. There was something about the way they looked at you, like they truly *saw* you. Some part of Valerie was still in disbelief that they let *her*, out of all people, take up so much of their time.

As Valerie crossed the threshold, she was engulfed by loud music, body heat, and the overwhelming smell of alcohol. Grabbing onto Quinn's hand so as not to lose them, she wormed her way through the crowd until she found the kitchen. In there, it was quieter, only a few guys playing a drinking game at the table. At the counter with the beverages, Valerie poured them both a cup of the red wine she found. It tasted about as good as one could expect from a six-dollar bottle.

She had taken only a few sips when she was distracted by a flash of color in her peripheral vision. The cause was what had to be the most vibrant girl Valerie had ever seen. She was dressed in pink from head to toe: her tight-fitting dress, her shoes, her heart-shaped earrings, all of them were a bright fuchsia. Valerie couldn't help but admire her dedication—even her hair surrounded her head like a big, cotton candy–colored cloud. The boy she was tugging along by his hand was dressed incredibly plainly in comparison, but the smile on his face was just as dazzling as the girl's outfit. Valerie immediately recognized him as the waiter from Sugar & Spice.

And then there was Rhia.

Instead of jeans and a large sweater, she was wearing an orange dress that matched the bow in her hair, a few curls framing her face. Her hands were buried in the pockets of her dress while her eyes wandered around the room. Her expression of wary curiosity turned into a scowl when her gaze met Valerie's.

Valerie responded by wiggling the fingers of her free hand in a small wave, chuckling when Rhia rolled her eyes and pointedly looked away.

Leaning closer to Quinn's ear, she said, "I don't think she likes me very much."

Quinn followed her gaze. "Who? Rhiannon?"

"No way," gasped Valerie, instantly delighted. "That's her full name?"

"Yeah. Rhiannon Greenbrook."

Valerie craned her neck a little to catch a glimpse of the bright-pink silhouette next to her. "And the other girl?"

"That's her cousin, Holly. She's a year older, I think," Quinn said, absentmindedly circling the rim of their cup with one finger. "And the guy she's with is Tristan Moore from the lacrosse team. He's the mayor's son."

Valerie could just barely make him out through the mass of moving bodies. He was standing with a group of lacrosse players, laughing with a beer in one hand and the other arm slung around Holly's waist. "Oakriver's golden boy then, huh?"

"I guess you could say that," Quinn said. "From what I've heard, he's really nice, though."

Valerie was about to say something else when a broad-shouldered lacrosse player with long hair came sauntering over to lean against the counter next to her. "Hey. My name is Connor, he/him. And you are?"

Valerie blinked at him. "Hello. I'm Valerie. I use she/her pronouns."

"You're the girl that reads tarot cards, right?"

Valerie raised her chin a little. In her Doc Martens, she was tall enough that they were at eye level—she wasn't sure if it was that or her business endeavors that made him fidget nervously under her gaze. Over the last few days, she'd noticed more than a few people giving her a wider berth than necessary in the hallways, while others approached her with a flood of questions and dollar bills at the ready. The two camps sort of balanced each other out, really. Valerie, who wasn't in the business of paying much attention to other people's opinions about her, wouldn't have cared either way. "I practice divination, yes."

"Right. Pretty cool, all that witchy stuff."

With their shoulders pressed together, Valerie didn't miss the way Quinn physically cringed. "Uh-huh."

"Right. Um, anyways. I was wondering if you would be up for a drinking game?" Connor gestured at the beer pong game on the table. "I could use a partner."

Valerie emptied her cup of red wine in two swigs and slammed it down on the counter behind her. "You've found yourself two." When Quinn opened their mouth to protest, Valerie explained, "You play, I drink."

Reluctantly, Quinn let themself be tugged along by their sleeve. "Are you sure this is a good idea?"

"Oh, it's a terrible idea." Valerie flashed them a grin over her shoulder. "College life, baby!"

~

Three hours later, Valerie was sure she had met her goal for the night. She was warm, her hair sticking to her neck, her cheeks flushed. There was a pleasant buzz beneath her skin that made her talk a bit louder and laugh a bit easier as she swayed to the music, trying not to spill her drink all over herself.

In short, she was *smashed*.

After the drinking game, which her team had lost quite spectacularly, she had managed to get Quinn to dance with her in the living room. They were much more sober than she was but gamely went along when Valerie twirled them with her free hand, shoulders shaking in a quiet laugh. Leaning closer, Valerie shouted, "I'm sweating. Do you wanna go outside for a moment?"

Quinn held on to her hands to steady her, brown eyes crinkling with amusement. They were so warm, everything about them. Valerie was so glad they were friends. "I need to use the bathroom first. Do you want me to meet you outside?"

Valerie stifled a hiccup with the back of her hand. "Yeah, 's fine. Be quick."

Quinn let go of her, giving her a gentle nudge towards the door. The room seemed to tilt slightly beneath Valerie's feet as she navigated her way through the mass of dancing bodies, dodging elbows and covering her drink with her hand so as not to spill it.

Her goal had been to sit down on the porch, but it seemed that half of the party had relocated out there to smoke. She politely shook her head when someone offered her a cigarette and instead let her feet carry her down the steps. There was a small path that wrapped around the house that she followed, relieved when the scents of nicotine and artificial vape flavors gave way to crisp night air.

In the light of the waxing moon, she found her way into the garden. Out here, the sounds of the party were muffled and distant, leaving her own breathing and the sound of the grass beneath her boots the loudest noises around. She was sure she was alone; that was, until she caught a glimpse of an orange skirt to her left, square in the middle of the house and the edge of the woods that stretched beyond the property.

She turned and steered towards the figure, humming the first verse of Fleetwood Mac's 1975 hit "Rhiannon"—an essential track on fifteen-year-old Valerie's first witchy playlist—to announce herself.

Predictably, Rhia groaned in response. A little less predictably, she didn't immediately tell Valerie to get lost but tipped her head back to watch her approach.

Encouraged by this, Valerie redoubled her efforts, crooning the rest of the chorus loud enough for it to echo around the garden.

"Shut *up*," mumbled Rhia, unappreciative of being serenaded. "Why does it have to be you of all people?"

Valerie collapsed into the grass next to Rhia, setting her cup down next to her. "Were you expecting someone else?"

"No."

"What're you doing out here all alone?"

"I just came outside to ground myself because I don't really like parties and I—" She hiccupped. When she lowered her hands, there was regret written all over her features. "I didn't plan to get this drunk."

"Mhh. I did."

"'Course you did. You don't care about anything."

"Is that so?" Valerie laughed, leaning back on her elbows. "I wasn't aware."

Rhia lifted a hand to rub at her eyes, the movement a little clumsy. *Cute.* "Sorry, that was stupid. I don't even know what I'm saying right now."

"That's fine. I don't either."

For a few moments, both of them were quiet, the silence between them softened by the muffled music drifting from the house and the murmuring of the wind in the leaves of the trees behind them. Valerie tilted her head back to look at the sky. It was overcast, but she could still see patches of ink blue through the tears in the blanket of clouds. When she let her eyes drift back to Rhia, she found her looking up with slightly drooping eyelids, her lips parted. A chilly gust of wind prompted her to wrap her arms around herself.

"Cold?" Valerie questioned.

Rhia's teeth chattered emphatically in response.

Conjuring fire was as easy as breathing; all she had to do was curl her hand into a fist and whisper six little words. When her fingers uncurled, a small flame danced in her palm. Rhia blinked a few times as Valerie held it closer to her, its light painting her skin with a golden hue. Valerie had to grin when she saw the look on Rhia's face, torn between impressed and irritated. She wasn't surprised when the latter won.

"Valerie," Rhia groaned, closing her hand over Valerie's without a second thought. The flame went out with a faint crackle. "Not here."

With a dramatic eye roll, Valerie flopped onto her back. "Why even have abilities if you never use them?"

"I do use mine, but only where it's safe."

"So you just sit at home and do . . . What exactly is it that you do?"

Valerie was surprised when Rhia actually answered. "Kitchen magic, mostly. A lot of stuff with plants. Sometimes spell work and rituals, but usually only with my family."

Valerie wasn't entirely sure she knew what all of that meant, but she didn't want to push her luck by asking. Instead, she turned her head to look at Rhia and said, "Show me something."

"Why would I do that?"

"Because I asked so nicely?"

Rhia shook her head, a hint of a smile on her lips. "You're not nice. You're a menace."

"A menace?" Valerie gasped.

"Yes. A rascal. A scoundrel, if you will."

"Oh, pumpkin, how you wound me."

Valerie was surprised when Rhia let out something that sounded almost like a giggle. She decided that she liked the sound. She liked this carefree version of Rhia, and she liked sitting here with this magical girl, even though the sky was spinning and the wind was trying to slip its chilly fingers beneath her clothes.

"So?" she asked.

"Still no."

"You know, I'm beginning to think you're just not very good at magic."

That finally did the trick. "Okay, fine." Rhia glanced around to make sure no one else was near. "I'll show you. But only if you promise you won't tell anyone."

Valerie immediately sat up. "Promise."

Rhia reached out and picked up a leaf that the wind had blown over from the woods. Looking up at Valerie again, she said, "Hold out your hands."

Valerie, albeit bewildered, did as she was told, watching as Rhia placed the leaf into her hands. It was brown and dried up, so fragile that Valerie was afraid it would fall apart between her fingers. She truly didn't know what Rhia intended to use it for, but any teasing comment she might have had got stuck in her throat when Rhia's hands covered hers. There was a small furrow between her brows as she focused, her lips moving as she whispered something too quiet for Valerie to make out. Once the spell was finished, she dropped her hands back into her lap. Valerie, used to her own flashy magic, squinted at the leaf in confusion. It was still just a leaf, dead and dried and . . . slowly changing color. The process was so subtle she didn't notice it at first, but once she did, she watched, breath held, as color seeped into it, turning it from brown to yellow to green. By the time the leaf unfurled in Valerie's hands, it looked as vibrant as if it had just fallen from a tree.

"There," Rhia said. It was hard to make out in the dark, but Valerie thought she caught the hint of a self-satisfied grin. "That's one thing I can do."

Valerie forced herself to close her mouth. She had never seen any magic besides her own. She knew the crackling of a fire that hadn't been there a second before, the easy lighting of a candle with nothing but a whisper, the feeling of a flame licking at her skin—but not once had she witnessed anything like this.

"Holy shit," she breathed, gingerly taking the leaf between her fingers. It felt sturdy. It felt *alive*, even though it had been moments from disintegrating just a few seconds earlier. "Can you do this with anything?"

"I can do it with plants, but not with anything that has a heartbeat."

Valerie whistled quietly through her teeth, her eyes still trained on the reanimated leaf. "I can't believe you did this while *drunk*."

Laughing, Rhia brushed a dark curl behind her ear. She looked like she was about to say something, but loud voices behind them made her turn her eyes away from Valerie.

"I swear, if she's not here then I honestly don't know where else to—oh, there she is! Quinn, we found them!"

As if on cue, they both got to their feet, watching as Holly, Tristan, and Quinn peeled out of the dark. Quinn was the first to reach them, glancing between Rhia and Valerie as they handed Valerie her jacket. "You left this inside."

"Thanks." Although Valerie never got cold, she quickly shrugged it on, slipping the leaf into her pocket. "And sorry you had to search for me."

"That's all right," Quinn said. Valerie vowed to herself to treat them to their next meal in return.

"There you are!" Holly exclaimed, catching up to them. "You just disappeared."

"Sorry." Rhia buried her hands in the pockets of her dress. "I kind of lost track of time."

Tristan stepped close to her, rubbing at her bare upper arms in a show of true parental concern. "Dude, you're an ice block. Couldn't you at least have put on a jacket?"

"Guys, I'm fine, really," Rhia protested.

Holly didn't look convinced. Grabbing Rhia's hand, she said, "Come on, let's get you inside."

Rhia shot Valerie a glance. "Are you going back too?"

"I think we're leaving," Valerie said, looking at Quinn. "Right?"

"We can stay a bit longer if you want," Quinn replied, despite looking like they could fall asleep standing up.

"Yeah, we're definitely leaving."

Rhia nodded. "Okay. Well . . . good night, then."

"Good night," Valerie echoed and watched as the trio made their way back towards the house, their silhouettes slowly fading into the dark.

Quinn turned to face Valerie the moment they were out of earshot, a smile twitching around their lips. "You spent a while out here," they remarked. "Did you have a good time?"

"Yeah." Valerie started walking, her heart leaping when she tucked her fingers into her pocket and felt them brushing against the leaf. "It was pretty magical."

6

FOUR OF SWORDS

recovery — reflection — self-protection

Rhia woke up feeling like someone was crushing her head between their hands. Her stomach was queasy, and her throat felt sore, probably from being out in the cold so long with— Valerie. Squeezing her eyes shut, Rhia turned her head into the pillow to muffle a quiet groan.

She hadn't meant to get so drunk, much less get so drunk in the presence of *her*. But Tristan was good at mixing cocktails, and Holly was good at roping others into drinking games. And then there was the fact that Rhia had felt terribly flustered under Valerie's gaze all evening and had found herself sipping her drink to avoid eye contact.

A small consolation was that she could still remember everything, from the second she'd stepped foot into the party to the moment she'd face-planted on her bed with Holly pulling a blanket over her shoulders and Tristan turning off the bedside lamp. They had left the door slightly ajar so that the cats could come and go during the night.

Now that open door allowed Rhia to hear everything that was going on in the house. There was a bright clinking of tableware in the kitchen downstairs; her aunt's soft humming as she got ready in one of the other rooms; the creaking of floorboards accompanied by the faint scent of citrus as her mother walked around the corridor. It was Saturday, her mother's appointed cleansing day. Everyone else thought it was overkill, but she was set on going through all the rooms once a week to burn orange peels and cinnamon and banish all negative energies that might have been brought in throughout the week.

Knowing that her mom would come into her room any second, Rhia forced herself into a sitting position and, after that step was successful, swung her feet over the edge of the bed. Her stomach swirled a little as she stood, but it wasn't as bad as she had feared. She managed to pull her hair into two thick braids and put on her favorite denim overalls and a sweater just moments before her mother knocked lightly at the half-open door.

"Morning, honey," she said, her voice a few notches too loud for Rhia's throbbing head. "Did you sleep well?"

"Mm-hmm." Rhia rubbed at her eyes. "Time's it?"

"Just after one. It's good that you're up, I was just going to cleanse your room. In fact, while I have you . . ." She stepped closer, waving the small wooden bowl over Rhia's head and around her until her eyes were tearing up from the smoke.

"Mom." Rhia coughed, trying to bat her hand away. "Mom, that's enough. I'm cleansed, all right? No negative energy here."

Her mother put down her bowl, though not without pinching Rhia's cheek for good measure. "All right, all right. Go ahead."

"Thank you," Rhia mumbled and pushed past her into the hallway.

The whole house still smelled like sweet smoke as she made her way down the stairs, nearly stepping on Circe, the chubby cat with copper fur that was curled up on one of the steps. The closer she got to the kitchen, the more the scent of freshly baked bread and herbs took over.

"She lives!" Holly cheered when Rhia entered. Her cousin was sitting at the kitchen table, one knee pulled to her chest, a plate balanced precariously on top of it. Next to her sat Tristan, his hair sticking up wildly. His pajamas were hidden under one of Holly's fuzzy pink bathrobes.

"Why're you not dying?" Rhia slumped into a seat opposite them. "You drank just as much as I did."

"It's all Sage," said Tristan, gesturing limply at Rhia's older sister.

She was standing at the stove, stirring a pot of something that smelled like familiar herbs. She chuckled when she glanced over her shoulder to see Rhia's hopeful expression. "I take it you had fun?"

"It was all right."

"Ah. Sounds like I really missed out on something." Sage set a mug of the brew down in front of Rhia without comment. Most people probably wouldn't have been thrilled with being served a cup of dark-green, bitter-smelling liquid, but Rhia, being familiar with her sister's anti-hangover herbal tea, bravely downed half of it in one swig.

Chuckling, Sage sank down on the chair opposite her. She picked up the open notepad on the table and, after tapping the pencil against the paper a few times, began hastily scribbling.

Philline Harms

With her stomach feeling steadier already, Rhia pulled the basket filled with fresh bread closer. On the other side of the table, Tristan had his head pillowed on Holly's shoulder while Holly scrolled through her Etsy profile on her phone. From the living room drifted the sound of a Nina Simone record—"I Put a Spell on You," because her family was hilarious like that—layering over the domestic sounds of a slow Saturday morning.

Rhia was buttering her second slice of bread when her grandmother waltzed into the kitchen, stopping in the doorway with a sniff. It always astounded Rhia how such a tiny person could wield enough power to immediately draw the attention of the entire room. "Who here had a little too much to drink last night?"

Sage pointed her pencil at Rhia without looking up.

"So did they!" Rhia protested. Tristan cracked an eye open, unimpressed.

"Rhiannon." Even though her tone was chiding, there was an amused glint in her eyes. "Did I not tell you to stay out of trouble?"

"I did," Rhia lied and quickly stuffed her mouth with bread. Valerie was the definition of trouble, but she didn't need her family to know that.

Her grandmother, apparently reassured, sat down at the table's end. Directed at Sage, she said, "Darling, when you go to the shop later, would you mind picking up some candles for me? Preferably black ones."

"Sure, I can do that," said Sage without looking up. "Do you need anything else?"

"No, that's all."

"You're going to Obscura?" Rhia asked.

Sage nodded. "I need to buy some stuff for the festival, and I wanted to put up an invite there."

"Wait, the festival? When's that again?"

"Next Friday." Sage raised her eyebrows at Rhia. "Don't tell me you forgot."

Rhia had, in fact, forgotten. Which was absurd; the Fall Festival was the biggest event that there was for witches in their area. It happened once a year and took place just outside of town, in a clearing in the woods where no one would stumble upon it. Originally, it had started out as an annual meeting for the Council of the Three, but by now, dozens of witches made their way to Oakriver at the beginning of every October to celebrate, turning the once formal meeting into a raucous party.

Rhia's family was usually the most involved in the execution of the festival because of their close relationship with Sharon Moore, Tristan's mom and the mayor of the town. Seeing as Tristan had spent most of his childhood with the Greenbrooks, it was a given that she knew about the family's otherwise well-kept secret. Luckily, she was open-minded enough to not only sit down for tarot readings at their kitchen table every now and again but also endorse the festival each year.

Working full-time as an event manager, Sage usually did most of the planning. The level of her stress was usually a good indication of how close the festival was—looking back, Rhia had no idea how she'd missed the signs.

Instead of admitting that, she said, "I'll come with you to the shop."

Sage cast a brief glance at the watch on her wrist. "Awesome, I could use some help. Hurry up, though, I want to leave in a few."

Rhia quickly downed the rest of the tea and got to her feet. "Give me five minutes."

~

Oakriver was even sleepier on the weekend than it was on a weekday. Rhia and Sage barely encountered a soul as they made their way through the familiar streets, pausing at a few select houses to slip invitations for the festival into mailboxes.

Rhia was glad every time they stopped; Sage was a few inches taller than her and always walked as if she was late to an appointment, so each mailbox visit allowed her to briefly catch her breath.

"Sage," she panted as she did her best to keep up with her sister, "slow *down*." Sage reluctantly slowed her stride enough for Rhia to catch up with her. "What's wrong?" Rhia asked as she fell into step beside her again. "You seem even more stressed than usual."

"It's nothing." Sage gave a dismissive wave. "I just misjudged how busy this month would be, is all. Between all the weddings and whatnot, I feel like I started working on this way too late. Which kind of sucks, because this is the event that's the most important to me, you know?"

Rhia nodded. She'd always admired her sister for choosing to go to college and getting into event managing—a job that had nothing to do with her abilities at all, where all the earth magic in the world couldn't help if she messed up a schedule or forgot to hire a catering team. When she'd asked Sage about her decision once, she'd explained that she liked having the two things separate. To her, magic wasn't something that she wanted to make into a chore, and so she limited it to her personal life—a sacrifice to preserve the sanctity of her practice.

Most of Rhia's other relatives had gone in a different direction. Aunt Tanisha was Oakriver's most reliable meteorologist, courtesy of her air magic. Rhia's mom was a vet, using her earth magic for healing purposes. Grandma Deloris had spent decades working at a pharmacy, specializing in natural remedies over aspirin or Tylenol. One of Deloris's sisters had owned a flower shop, while another had worked as a forest ranger. When looking at their family tree, Sage was a clear outlier as far as career choices went—no potions, no spells, just a dozen day planners and an email inbox that made Rhia's anxiety spike just by looking at it.

It was a decision that every witch had to make for themselves, and one that Rhia had no idea how to approach. She knew that she wanted to use her magic to help the earth and other people, but she wasn't sure how her abilities could translate into a practical job. Hence, her gap year working at Sugar & Spice.

"I'm sure it'll be as amazing as always," she told her sister. "And if it isn't, we'll just have to buy enough hard cider to make sure no one notices."

Sage snorted a small laugh. A moment later, they reached the post office down the road. It was closed for the weekend, but they only needed the collection box in front of it. Sage slipped the invitations for all out-of-town witches into the box, each of them sporting an address in neat cursive. Grandma Deloris kept a contact list of all nearby witch families they knew of so they could write to them personally. On the off chance that a new coven found its way into Oakriver, they always left a few extra invitations at Obscura as well.

Rhia was more excited than she cared to show as they neared the ancient building. Going to the shop with her mother had been her favorite thing as a child. She could clearly recall wandering around between the tall shelves and getting on her tiptoes to see what they held while her mother told her she could pick one item to take home with her. She felt some of the same childlike excitement as she walked through the door now, the bell jingling above her like it was welcoming her back.

"No browsing," Sage reminded her, as if reading her thoughts, and tugged her along towards the register in the back. "We don't have time to waste."

Rhia was about to utter a snarky reply when she realized who was sitting behind the counter.

"Hey, Quinn," Sage said. "How are you?"

"Not bad. How about you?"

While her sister launched into pleasant chit-chat, Rhia studied Quinn. They had started working at Obscura only a few months earlier, but already it felt as if there'd never been a time without them perched behind the register. Rhia had spoken to them a few times and thus gleaned a few tidbits about their life. They studied art at Oakriver College but weren't sure what they wanted to pursue afterward. Their mom was Chinese but spoke to them exclusively in English, which was why they sometimes used the lulls in between customers to study Mandarin. They had dimples like half-moons above the corners of their mouth and a way of looking at you that made you feel like they were paying close attention to every word you said.

Of course, there was still much to learn about Quinn. So far, the biggest mystery for Rhia was their magic (or lack thereof) and what had compelled them to work at Obscura nevertheless. Now there was another: the question of what on earth could be the foundation of a friendship between caring, earnest Quinn and a girl who moved through the world like a mini inferno.

Rhia tuned back into the conversation again just as Sage asked, "Did you get the list of things I ordered?"

Quinn pointed at the cardboard boxes sitting on the counter next to them. "Incense, thirty orange candles, eight boxes of lavender sticks. Is that all, or is there anything else you need?"

"Some black candles," Sage said. Quinn made a move to leave their post behind the register, but Sage beat them to it. "Don't worry, I'll get them."

She turned on her heel and disappeared between the rows of shelves before Rhia could say anything. Clearing her throat, she turned to face Quinn again. "Good party last night, huh?"

"It was all right," Quinn said, pulling the sleeves of their dark-purple sweater over their knuckles. "We left kind of early."

"How do you and Valerie know each other?"

"We're roommates."

"That's . . . cool?"

Quinn nodded, the hint of a smile crossing their face. "Yeah. She's really chill."

Chill wasn't a word that Rhia would have used to describe Valerie. For lack of something better to say, she tilted her head to catch a glimpse of the book Quinn had been reading before they'd come in. In a whimsical font, the cover read, *Sleep Tight: Natural Remedies for a Restful Slumber.* "Having sleeping problems?" Rhia asked sympathetically.

"Not me. Valerie." Quinn grimaced. "She keeps having nightmares, and she's sleepwalked twice—last night and the night before that. I wanted to see if there's anything in here that might help her."

"Lavender, chamomile, and passionflower," Rhia said. "She can put them in a little baggie under her pillow. And juniper or thyme if you can get them. To ward off nightmares."

Quinn immediately scribbled the names of the herbs onto the back of an invoice near them.

"Also . . ." Rhia paused. "I know she'll probably laugh if I tell her this, but maybe she'll listen when it comes from you. Excessive sleepwalking could be a sign that something . . . *other* is affecting her."

Quinn looked up from the paper, brows knitted together. "You mean, like, a spirit?"

"Maybe. With her lack of proper protection, I wouldn't be surprised if something has latched on to her," Rhia carefully said. "In sleep, all her walls are down. She might want to burn some cleansing herbs in your room to make sure her subconscious isn't vulnerable to any outside influences."

"That's easy. She loves burning things," Quinn murmured, rubbing at the goose bumps on their arms. "I'll let her know. Thank y—"

Sage returned with three black candles in hand before they could finish their sentence.

"Here you go," she said, placing them on the counter, oblivious to their exchange.

While Quinn calculated their total, Sage asked, "Is it okay if I leave a few invites to the Fall Festival here?"

"Sure. I'll hand them out to anyone who hasn't gotten one."

"Awesome, thank you." Sage set the small stack of invitation cards down on the counter. "Are you going to come?"

"I don't think so," Quinn said. "I think I'd feel a bit out of place. Your total is forty-three dollars and eleven cents."

After Sage had paid, Rhia obediently accepted one of the cardboard boxes her sister handed her and followed her towards the exit. When she glanced over her shoulder once more, it was to the sight of Quinn picking up a different book called *Spirits Begone: An Introduction to Protective Magic*, Rhia's list of herbs still clutched in one hand.

Rhia was so lost in her thoughts that she almost collided with the person who had just entered the shop. "Oh," she breathed. Her heart stuttered through a few beats when she tilted her head back to find none other than Valerie standing right in front of her. "H-hey."

"Hey." Valerie grinned back at her, a brown paper bag jammed under her left arm and a Thermos bottle in her hand. There was absolutely nothing about her easy countenance that spoke of sleep problems or night terrors. If Quinn hadn't said anything, Rhia would've easily chalked up Valerie's dark under-eye circles to a long night and alcohol.

Rhia didn't know what to do with this uncharacteristic feeling of concern for someone she barely knew. In the end, she settled on a lame "I was just leaving."

Eyes still tracking her, Valerie pulled open the door, holding it as Rhia passed through. Entering the shop fully, she called out, "Hey, Quinn! I got you breakfast—you like chocolate croissants, right? If not, you can have my . . ."

The door fell shut, muffling her words. With a confused knot in her stomach, Rhia turned around and hurried to catch up with her sister.

7

PAGE OF SWORDS

intellectual debates — thirst for knowledge — new ways of thinking

The night of the party was when the trouble began.

Valerie could not for the life of her stop thinking about Rhiannon Greenbrook.

It was ridiculous, really. They'd only spoken thrice, and from those brief interactions, Valerie hadn't learned much about her aside from a few key facts. Rhia could command plants. She was friends with Tristan Moore. She liked to bake and drank hard cider and dressed like the human embodiment of fall. But Valerie had also learned that Rhia's hands were soft and moved with purpose when she performed magic. That she furrowed her brows when she was upset and got giggly when she was tipsy. And that she, for whatever reason, had made Valerie feel more at ease than she'd felt since setting foot in Oakriver.

Valerie wanted—*needed*—to know more. And so, she went back.

When she pushed through the doors of Sugar & Spice on Monday afternoon, the café was just as busy as it had been the last time she'd been here. The air was filled with the scent of cinnamon and coffee and so warm Valerie instantly felt hot under all her layers. Craning her neck, she scanned the downstairs area for Rhia, but before she could spot her, a voice right next to her made her jump.

"You're blocking the entrance."

Valerie turned around with a grin. "Nice to see you too, pumpkin."

Rhia was standing with a hand on her hip, the other balancing an empty tray. At the nickname, she narrowed her eyes and turned to leave. Valerie, having predicted this, followed her to the counter without missing a beat.

"What do you want?" Rhia sighed without looking at her as she loaded the tray with two slices of cake.

Valerie propped her hip against the counter, trying her best to appear as innocent as possible. It was a tough look to pull off for her. "Nothing. Is it so bad I want to see my favorite drinking buddy?"

"We didn't drink together," Rhia pointed out. "You just latched on to me when I was already drunk and refused to leave me alone. Like a leech or something."

"Could've at least gone with *vampire*." Valerie sniffed. "You have to admit it was fun."

Rhia gave a noncommittal hum. Today she was wearing a dark-green sweater and a matching headband. From her ears dangled earrings that looked like mushrooms; they took the edge off the scowl that appeared when Valerie trailed after her as she brought the cake over to a table.

Philline Harms

"I was wondering," Valerie began as they made their rounds between the seats, "would you like to hang out sometime?"

The look Rhia sent her was one of utter bewilderment. "Why would I want to hang out with you?"

Okay, maybe this was going to be a bit harder than Valerie had initially expected. "Because I'm an overall fun person to be around?"

Rhia didn't look impressed.

"Because I just moved here and don't have any friends yet?" Valerie tried.

"Aren't you friends with Quinn? They told me you're room-mates. Go hang out with them."

By now, they had made their rounds around the entire café and ended up at the counter again. Biting her lip, Valerie watched as Rhia flipped through the orders in her notepad, adamantly avoiding her gaze.

Finally, Valerie said, "If you hang out with me, I'll stop doing tarot readings here."

Rhia stilled. "You'd do that?"

Valerie nodded.

"Why is this so important to you? We've only talked thrice. For all you know, I might be an asshole."

"Maybe." Valerie's lips quirked into a small smile. "But at least you'd be an asshole who knows a lot about magic." From their previous encounters, she had a feeling that hanging out for the sake of hanging out wasn't enough to convince Rhia. The cover-up wasn't even a lie; she *did* want to learn more about magic. Two birds, one stone, and all that.

Rhia's eyes instinctively darted around the café, checking to see if anyone was close enough to overhear them.

"I don't know anyone else who is, you know. Like *us*," Valerie admitted. "I have no idea about half the things you talk about—casting circles and cleansing and all of that. But I want to get better at this. I want to know more."

Rhia studied Valerie, some silent fight warring behind her eyes. Valerie was already bracing for rejection when Rhia asked, "What do I get out of it?"

"What do you want?"

"For you to teach me divination," Rhia promptly returned.

"Done," Valerie easily said.

"And," Rhia continued, "for you to stop doing tarot readings, not just in *here* but also for non-witches altogether. Deal?"

Valerie winced a little, already mourning the loss of the easily earned money. But then she thought of her mother and of the things Rhia had talked about the other night—*Kitchen magic, mostly. A lot of stuff with plants. Sometimes spell work and rituals, but usually only with my family.* Her words had been like a keyhole through which Valerie could just barely make out the silhouettes of a whole world filled to the brim with magic. She would've done anything for another glimpse.

"Deal."

Rhia slowly pulled back her hand. "I'll warn you right away, though. Some of the practices that were passed down to me are not yours to learn. I won't tell you everything I know. You'll have to find your own path yourself."

"Of course," Valerie immediately said. "I don't expect you to do all the work for me. I just need a starting point."

Rhia's mushroom earrings swung back and forth as she gave a satisfied nod. "My shift ends in thirty. Is Quinn home right now?"

"No, they're doing this cooking class with their mom and shouldn't be—"

"I'll come with you to your place, then." Rhia turned around and disappeared into the kitchen before Valerie could open her mouth to respond.

Releasing a disbelieving chuckle, Valerie turned around and made her way over to an empty armchair near the staircase. She waited there, flipping through the art history book she'd brought while sipping another cup of the tea Rhia had recommended to her last time and definitely *not* heating it up again when it went cold. She paused on a page about the works of the Pre-Raphaelite Brotherhood. Most of it was taken up by John Everett Millais's painting of Ophelia in the river, her red hair floating among the flowers in the water, her gaze turned to the sky. Valerie had been fascinated with the piece ever since she'd seen it on a postcard in the gift shop of her hometown's tiny museum at the tender age of ten. She still vividly remembered what her art teacher had explained to her when she'd found Valerie making eyes at it: that, in the Victorian era, each flower that surrounded Ophelia had been assigned a meaning. Willows for love. Daisies for innocence. And violets, fashioned into a necklace around her throat, for death of the young.

Valerie was absentmindedly tracing the forget-me-nots dotting the riverside when Rhia reappeared and said, her tone that of a convict ready to step up to the gallows, "Lead the way, then."

Valerie snapped the book shut without having to be asked twice.

~

The walk to the dorms was a silent affair. As they made their way down the cobblestone streets, past weary houses and shivering trees, Valerie kept stealing glances at the other girl's face. Most of the time, she was looking either straight ahead or down at her scuffed-up boots, but once or twice their eyes met, and Valerie could've sworn there was a hint of a smile twitching around Rhia's lips.

Eventually, the dorm came into view, red bricks hiding behind an ivy cloak. It was strange, leading her across the campus. Normally, the sober backdrop of college buildings and groups of droopy-eyed students inhaling energy drinks seemed dreadfully dull to Valerie. With Rhia there, admiring the tall oak beside the main building and pointing out the wildflowers that hid amidst the tall grass, Valerie suddenly felt a surge of reverence similar to the first time she'd stumbled upon Obscura. It was a slight shift in her perception, a gentle tingling up her spine. A new awareness of the magic that surrounded her, even here, peeking through the cracks in the mundane.

"After you," Valerie said when they reached the door to her dorm, beckoning Rhia inside with an exaggerated wave of her arm.

Rhia stepped past her, eyes darting curiously around the entrance area. Valerie's room was on the ground floor, so they didn't have to take the stairs. Instead, Valerie led her down one of the many hallways, carefully studying her reactions as they passed the tiny community kitchen and the vending machines, the rec room with its wobbly billiard table, and the staircase where a group of freshmen had made camp. Valerie was so focused on Rhia, she almost jumped when one of them called out her name.

"Valerie, hey!" Mateo Cortes, one of the less pretentious students from her art history class, came jogging over to her. "I was hoping I'd run into you. I heard that you were doing tarot rea—"

"I was," Valerie quickly said. Next to her, Rhia was pinching the bridge of her nose, her eyes directed at the ceiling as if asking for heavenly support. "Not anymore, though."

Mateo visibly deflated. "Oh. So, you couldn't give me a reading? Lucy Chang was raving all week about how accurate your advice about zir date with Malik was and I—I usually don't buy into this stuff, but I—"

"I'm really sorry." Valerie felt distinctly like she was kicking a puppy. "No can do. Just do what's in your heart, man. You'll figure it out." With that, she gave his shoulder an awkward pat and tugged Rhia along, leaving the group behind. From the corner of her eye, she caught the surprised look Rhia sent her—as if, up until that moment, she hadn't truly believed Valerie was serious about this.

Joke was on her. Valerie was serious about everything.

Well, everything except the things she wasn't.

When Rhia spoke, it wasn't to comment on what had just happened but to ask, "Do you like living in the dorms?"

"Uh . . . yeah," Valerie said, distracted by the sight of the bulletin board they were quickly approaching—and her flyer tacked confidently in the very center of it. Turning so her body concealed it from Rhia's view as they passed, she blindly tore the paper down. "It's really affordable, and I got lucky having Quinn as my roommate, so I can't complain. What about you? Could you imagine studying here?"

"I'm not sure. I'm taking a gap year right now—I thought

it'd be best if I just worked at the café for a while until I figure out what I want to do."

While Rhia spoke, Valerie turned her head and whispered a spell that made the crumpled piece of paper combust into flames between her clenched fingers.

"Yeah," she said out loud. "I get that. What options are you considering?"

"I'm not sure. I was thinking geology, or maybe culinary arts—wait, do you smell that?"

"It's probably someone smoking in their room," Valerie said without missing a beat. "Super gross, happens all the time. Anyway, this is mine." She came to a halt in front of the door labeled ROOM 13 and dug her key out of the pocket of her denim jacket.

Once inside, Valerie kicked the door shut behind her and leaned against it as she tried to see her surroundings through the other girl's eyes. Since her arrival ten days ago, the space had transformed into something that looked more like an art studio than a bedroom. Several canvases leaned against the walls and sat on the windowsill, some of them still drying from the night before. Her desk was barely visible under all the paint tubes, brushes, and empty coffee cups that were scattered across it. Quinn's side wasn't much tidier; where Valerie's half of the room was cluttered with vibrant paintings, Quinn's was buried beneath a flood of charcoal sketches and magazine cutouts. Rhia's eyes lingered briefly on the little bell that Valerie had affixed to the doorknob and on the bowl on her bedside table, which contained the remains of a lavender sprig she'd burned the night before.

Valerie expected Rhia to comment on the mess, but instead, Rhia asked, "Where's your altar?"

"My what?"

"Your altar," Rhia repeated, turning to face her. "Don't you have one?"

"I . . . No? Should I have one?"

Rhia looked just as confused as Valerie felt. "I don't know? All the witches I know have one." Rubbing her temples, she sank onto Valerie's bed. "This might be more difficult than I expected."

Valerie sat down cross-legged so that they were facing each other. For some stupid reason, she felt nervous now that they were alone.

"When you said you didn't know any other witches," Rhia asked tentatively, "you really meant you've never met even one?"

"No," Valerie confirmed.

Rhia's expression was somewhere between impressed and full of pity. "So . . . everything you know you taught yourself?"

"Yeah." Valerie fiddled with one of the rings on her fingers. "For the longest time, I thought there was no one else who could do the things I could do. I would just mess around with magic to figure out how far I could go with it."

Now the look on Rhia's face was closer to horror. "How did you find out you had abilities?"

"I guess I've always felt a bit strange. Like, I would have these vivid dreams about things, and a few days later they would happen. Sometimes lights would randomly start to flicker or the temperature in a room would go from freezing cold to scorching hot within seconds." She paused. "One time, when I was sixteen, I was really frustrated with my calculus homework. I was just staring at this worksheet saying something like, 'I wish I didn't have to do this shit,' and then *boom*, the paper burst into flames. Just like that. I didn't even touch it."

"Did you tell anyone about it?"

"I tried to talk to my dad, but he got really angry for some reason. Told me to be more careful, even though I explained there wasn't a candle or anything nearby." She shrugged. "But I'm more of a learning-by-doing person anyway, so after that I tried to figure out what I could and couldn't do by myself. I spent entire afternoons staring at candles until they would light, and then I'd stare at them some more until they went out again. Once I had that down, I bought my first tarot deck and immediately fell in love with divination."

"God," Rhia mumbled. "It's a miracle you didn't turn yourself into barbecue."

Valerie huffed a quiet laugh. "So dramatic. It's not that difficult."

Rhia didn't seem amused. "Yeah, that's because you're not doing it right," she sternly said. "It's like you just . . . I don't know, took a shortcut that bypassed all of the important stuff. Sure, you know how to make your tea a little warmer, but you know nothing about actual magical rituals and rules and traditions—"

She broke off when she saw the look on Valerie's face. Valerie wasn't sure what expression she was wearing; what she did know was that her insides were squirming in discomfort. Magic was the one thing that set her apart from others; the one thing that no one could take away from her; the one thing that connected her to her mother. To hear Rhia talking to her like this, as if she were a child who needed to be lectured for sticking her hand in the cookie jar, suddenly made her feel unbearably small. Her father's face flashed in her mind—the disdainful expression he'd worn when she'd told him about what had happened with her schoolwork, and again when he had caught her sitting on her bed with a pendulum one night. Then, she had been too different to fit in with him and his pretty new family; now, she was too ordinary to fit in with Rhia and her world of magic.

"I didn't mean . . . That was a horrible thing to say," Rhia said before Valerie could put her feelings into words. "You can do more than heat up your tea."

"Yeah," Valerie agreed, trying her best to make her tone sound light. "I can also heat up coffee."

"I'm sorry, Valerie." At the sincerity in her voice, Valerie looked up to find Rhia looking back at her with genuine regret written on her face. In a softer voice than before, Rhia said, "I think it's really impressive that you managed to learn so much about magic all on your own. I don't think I could've done that if it weren't for my family. They taught me everything I know, including the most important thing there is—the rules."

Valerie realized then that the look on Rhia's face wasn't scorn or contempt like she had thought a moment earlier. It was *worry*, maybe even fear.

"Rules?" she asked.

"Yes. This isn't a game. This is stuff that might get you killed if you don't know what you're doing." She shook her head. "It's like you're playing ding-dong-ditch with the spirit world without even knowing it. So far you've managed to get away with it, but it's only a matter of time until something is going to step out of that door you knocked on. And chances are, at that point, you won't be able to run."

Valerie swallowed. Rhia's gaze was holding hers with so much intensity that her comical level of ominousness for once did not make Valerie feel like laughing. "Earlier, you were talking about having an altar. Is that the same thing they have in churches?"

"It can mean different things to different witches. Usually, it's simply a place for us to keep our most important instruments and the space where we perform a lot of our rituals." Rhia paused. "If you want, I can show you mine."

Just by the tone of her voice, Valerie could tell how difficult of an offer it was for Rhia to make. "Isn't that really personal?"

"Yes," Rhia said. There it was again: fear, a tiny flicker that vanished from her eyes as quickly as it had appeared.

Valerie felt herself nodding before she even made the conscious decision to move her head. "Okay. Tomorrow?"

"Yeah." Rhia got to her feet, brushing a stray curl behind her ear. "My shift ends at four. Meet me at Sugar & Spice, then we can walk to my house together."

Valerie stood as well, thinking it best not to tell her that she already knew where she lived. Without context, telling Rhia that she had watched her at her window that first day in Oakriver would've just sounded creepy.

Rhia took a step towards the door but stopped before she reached it, her eyes fixed on the canvas leaning against the wall next to it. "This is beautiful."

"Oh," said Valerie, not quite succeeding in keeping the surprise from her voice.

The painting in question was one she had worked on late into the night with Quinn sketching away next to her. It showed two naked women in a close embrace, one cradling the other's face while she pressed a kiss to the side of her neck. With their silhouettes painted in bold brushstrokes and the entire piece done in different shades of red—Valerie's favorite color to work with—the pair looked like they were burning up. Valerie very nearly blurted something stupid like *Wanna re-create it?* but managed to bite her tongue. Instead, she settled on the significantly more chill, "Thanks. It's part of an assignment about power."

Rhia's eyes drifted over to the other paintings leaning against the wall. Most of them showed women in various intimate positions—kissing, hugging, tangled together in bedsheets. Clearing her throat, she commented, "Interesting subject choice."

"Yeah. Personally, I don't think there's anything more powerful than owning your identity."

Rhia turned around so they were facing each other. Since three-quarters of the tiny room was taken up by art supplies, they were standing close enough that the tips of their boots were almost touching. "You like girls?" Rhia asked.

"I like pretty much everyone. But yeah, girls are . . ." Valerie looked down at her hand, tracing the Venus symbol tattooed on her ring finger. "Really good."

Rhia laughed at that, the same bright sound that had rung in the air a few nights ago. It was even lovelier in the quiet of Valerie's room. "I agree."

Valerie wasn't sure if it was the moody radiators in her room or her own magic making an appearance that suddenly made her feel warm all over. "Nice."

Rhia's eyes were still fixed on Valerie's hand. "When you looked at my palm the other day, were any of those things true?" Valerie opened her mouth, but Rhia beat her to it. "Not the part about me being cute. The other stuff."

Valerie couldn't quite hold back a grin. "No. I was messing with you." Tapping the back of Rhia's hand, she asked, "Can I?"

Tentatively, Rhia turned it over for Valerie to look at.

"If you want to read someone's palm," Valerie said, her voice dropping lower as they bent their heads together, "these are the most important lines. You've got the life line here." She traced a finger along Rhia's skin to show her. "The fate line, right here. The heart line . . ." In the quiet of the room, Valerie didn't miss the small hitch in Rhia's breath as her fingertips brushed the delicate inside of her palm. "And this one. The head line. Much more prominent for you." With a smile, she glanced up to meet Rhia's gaze again.

"I see." Rhia cleared her throat. "So, if I have a short heart line, does that mean—"

The door burst open before she got to finish. Rhia pulled her hand back as if she'd burned herself on Valerie, both of them jumping apart in an instant.

"Uh . . ." Quinn came to an abrupt halt in the doorway. "Sorry, am I interrupting some—"

"No!" Rhia and Valerie said at the same time. They exchanged short glances before looking away just as quickly.

"I was just about to leave," Rhia explained.

Valerie could only hope her cheeks didn't look as flushed as they felt. "Yep. I'll see you tomorrow."

"Tomorrow. Right," Rhia said, and fled.

In her absence, Valerie turned to Quinn. "How was your cooking class?"

"It was good," they slowly said while they nudged the door shut behind them with their foot. "My mom says hi. What was all that about?"

"That," said Valerie, flopping backward onto her bed, "was us tutoring each other."

"Ah," Quinn chuckled. "That's what we're calling it now."

Her hand resting over her still-racing heart, Valerie grinned up at the ceiling. The world of magic wasn't just a blur behind a keyhole anymore; she had gotten her foot in the door, and now, with Rhia's laugh still hanging in the air, there was no turning back.

8

TWO OF CUPS

finding common ground — mutual attraction — a deep connection

To say that Rhia was nervous would've been an understatement. Her shift at Sugar & Spice seemed to both drag on endlessly and fly by way too quickly. Twice, she found herself standing by the coffee machine, spaced out for so long that the coffee threatened to go cold, and more than once she had to ask a customer to repeat their order.

"What's up with you today?" Tristan asked her after she had narrowly avoided knocking over a cup of tea.

"Nothing," she lied. When he only shot her a pointed look, she reluctantly said, "It's Valerie. She's coming over to my house today."

"You have a *date*?"

"It's not a date," Rhia protested, speaking quietly so as not to be overheard by the patrons studying the cakes in the display. "It's part of a deal we have."

Technically, that wasn't completely accurate. Inviting Valerie over to show her Rhia's altar—something that no one besides her family and Tristan had ever seen—hadn't been a part of the promise she'd given. Tristan didn't need to know that, though. He was insufferable enough already. Case in point: the way he announced, "Here she comes" in a singsong voice even before the bell above the door chimed. Valerie was just stepping inside, cheeks flushed from the cold, red hair tousled from the wind. With her hands in the pockets of her oversized denim jacket, she leaned against the wall next to the entrance.

"What did I get myself into?" Rhia murmured.

"Some action, finally." Tristan gave her a light nudge. "Go on. Your shift ends in five, I've got everything under control here."

Despite the coil of nerves in her stomach pulling tighter, Rhia stripped off her apron and grabbed her coat from where it was stuffed behind the counter. Shrugging it on, she pressed a kiss to Tristan's cheek. "Thanks, Tris. I'll see you tomorrow."

"Text me if anything happens!" he called after her.

Rhia turned around long enough to mouth, *Nothing's gonna happen.*

Valerie was waiting for her at the door, a grin on her lips as she studied Rhia's dangly earrings. (Today, they were tiny pumpkins.) "Ready?"

"Not particularly."

With a quiet snort—the sound was distressingly endearing—Valerie opened the door. Her arm brushed against Rhia's as she held it for her, dropping into a small curtsy. "After you."

Rhia refused to be charmed.

Outside, Valerie fell easily into step next to her, her combat boots sure as they struck the slick cobblestones. It had been pouring all day, and the clouds still hung heavy above them, steely gray and promising another shower. The air smelled like rain and chimney smoke.

Rhia's house was roughly a fifteen-minute walk from the café. Like the day before, they barely spoke as they moved through the dimly lit alleyways, but strangely, Rhia didn't mind the silence. It didn't feel heavy or like it needed to be filled. The accidental knocking of their shoulders and the amused curl of Valerie's lips when their eyes met seemed to do that just fine.

Rhia's nerves only returned when the ivy-covered brick façade of her home came into view. She hoped Valerie couldn't tell that her hands were trembling slightly as she dug her keys out of the pocket of her coat. Rhia couldn't remember the last time she had brought someone home with her. Honestly, the longer she thought about it, the more she realized that she *hadn't*—all she could come up with was the first time Tristan had come over, and that had to have been at least ten years ago.

"Hello?" she called out as she pushed the front door open. "Anyone here?"

The only response was a quiet meowing from somewhere within the house. Rhia let out a relieved breath and gestured for Valerie to follow her inside. The last thing she needed was for her family to find out she had brought a girl home with her, much less the girl who also happened to be the doom-bringing witch her grandmother had predicted. She would have Rhia's head if she knew.

Though, standing by the door, Valerie looked in no way like she was the one the Tower had referred to. In fact, for a split second, she almost looked innocent. There was no smirk on her face, no teasing comment, just a wide-eyed look of wonder as she took in her surroundings.

"What is it?" Rhia asked. They were still standing in the hallway, nothing to see but scratched floorboards and a coatrack that threatened to buckle under the heap of jackets haphazardly flung over it.

"Dude," Valerie breathed, "this place is like *buzzing* with magic."

Rhia paused. Now that Valerie had pointed it out, she could feel it too: a familiar crackle that hung in the air like static, a white noise that she was so used to that she only heard it now that Valerie had pointed it out. "Yeah," she said after a few seconds. "I guess it is."

Valerie stood frozen for a few more seconds, her head tilted as she listened to the low hum of witchcraft sounding from all around. Then she directed her attention at the tote bag slung over her shoulder. "Oh, I almost forgot. I brought you something."

Rhia frowned. "You really didn't have—"

"Here." Valerie cut her off, handing her the object she had procured from her bag. It was a fern, luscious green leaves spilling over the edges of a ceramic flowerpot. "Quinn and I went by the flower shop earlier to find some plants for our room. I thought this one looked kinda cool."

Rhia could do little more than blink. "Thank you. That's . . . sweet."

Valerie nodded, awkwardly shifting on her feet.

Touching a finger to the plant in her hands, Rhia said, "My room's a bit too drafty for this one during the winter. I think it'll enjoy the greenhouse."

"You have a *greenhouse*?"

"We're a family of almost exclusively earth witches," Rhia

Love and Other Wicked Things   81 chuckled by way of explanation. She jerked her head towards the kitchen. "Come on, I'll show you."

Valerie trailed after her, out through the back door and into the garden. The tall grass was freckled with wildflowers, the bright dots swallowed by the dense woods in the distance. The greenhouse sat right in the middle between the tree line and Rhia's home, glass panes glinting in the early evening sun. It had served generations of witches, so the structure's metal bars were a little rusty, the door creaking in protest as Rhia pulled it open to welcome Valerie.

Inside, it was humid and warm enough to prompt Rhia to push the sleeves of her knitted sweater up to her elbows. The air was thick with the scent of soil and different plants—of life growing quietly, steadily. Leaves stretched towards Rhia as she passed between them, stems bending in her direction as if nodding to her. If she focused, Rhia could hear them; here a whisper thanking her for having moved it into the shade a few days ago, there a soft voice demanding to be watered.

"You got it," she said, pausing to give the plant in front of her a generous spray from a water bottle. Immediately, it straightened, lifting its head instead of slouching. Dipping her fingertips into the pot to feel its moisture, Rhia chided, "So dramatic. You still had so much water left!"

When she turned, Valerie was watching her. "You can hear them?"

With a nod, Rhia continued walking. "Garlic," she commented, pointing at the flower bed taking up most of the greenhouse. "Spinach, carrots, eggplants, potatoes." She gestured at the flowerpots in the windowsill. "Over there are the herbs: parsley, mint, and thyme, mostly."

"Sick," Valerie murmured, drifting a little closer to the windowsill.

Rhia was hyperaware of her as she moved around the greenhouse. She loved this space. Next to her cats and her family, the plants that lived here were her dearest companions; after a long workday, they were the ones who calmed her, so much less demanding than any human and always grateful for her presence. Opening the greenhouse's doors to Valerie felt like inviting her into her heart and then watching, breath held, as she explored its chambers. It shouldn't have mattered what a girl she'd only known for a week thought about it, but it did. It did.

Valerie pulled her fingertips back from where they had gingerly brushed against the leaves of a mint plant. "It's lovely."

As Rhia drew herself a little straighter, the plants in her immediate vicinity did the same, a collective exhalation seeming to sound through the greenhouse. Softly, she set Valerie's fern down in another windowsill mostly dedicated to flowers. "This seems like a good spot for you, hmm?"

From the corner of her eye, she caught Valerie's smile. For once, it didn't look teasing—just fond, and a little bit overwhelmed. "Do you talk to all your plants?"

"Only if I have something interesting to say." Rhia touched a finger to one of the leaves. It was almost completely snapped off, probably thanks to being jostled around in Valerie's bag during their walk. Closing her eyes, she said, *"Reach your roots into the earth and your leaves towards the sky. The soil, the sun, and the water will give you what you need. Grow steadily, grow healthily, grow happily."*

The familiar incantation left her mouth easily, the words well-worn from years of use. It was an old spell that could've been shortened into only a handful of syllables, but Rhia preferred it over any kind of efficiency. It was the same one that her great-grandmother, Gabrielle Greenbrook, had used while standing in this same greenhouse, the words echoing from the misted windows hundreds of times over the decades. Some witches were of the opinion that spells lost some of their power if spoken too many times. Rhia believed the opposite.

When she opened her eyes again, the leaf no longer hung limply but slowly straightened, mending where it had nearly broken off until it looked as sturdy as the others again. "Well done!" said Rhia, and after a moment added, "Yes, I also think you'll like it here."

"Man," Valerie whispered. "That's so fucking cool."

Rhia hovered her hand over the plant for a few more seconds to see if there was anything else it needed from her. When all she received was a satisfied hum, she turned around and headed back towards the door, Valerie trailing close behind.

On their way back to the house, Valerie asked, "So . . . it's true that every witch has one element they vibe with, right?"

Rhia snorted a little laugh at the way she'd phrased it. "I guess you could say that." She paused as a new thought crossed her mind. "What's it like, having fire magic?"

"What do you mean?"

"Well, you know. Witches who draw their magic from the earth and the air have it easy because we're constantly surrounded by our elements. Water witches have to search a bit more, but even they'll find their power source somewhere most of the time, even if it's just the groundwater. But for you it's different. Fire doesn't just exist in our environment. In order to draw from it, you need to create it first, either through common methods or through your magic reserves themselves. It's a cycle of sorts, isn't it? It gives you power at the same time that it takes."

"Yeah." Valerie's steps slowed as she processed. "Yeah, I guess you're right. I think that might also be part of why I realized so late that I had abilities."

Rhia nodded, quietly fascinated. She'd spoken to only a handful of witches outside her family, and none of them had had an affinity for fire. Now that she thought about it, they were the rarest kind of witch compared to the other elements. She wondered how many others like Valerie were out there, cradling the coals of fire magic inside their chests without ever knowing it.

She was so caught up in her thoughts, she almost missed it when Valerie asked, "Does your entire family draw their magic from the earth?"

"Not my entire family. My mom, sister, grandma, and I do. My cousin and my aunt can manipulate air." Stepping back into the kitchen, Rhia chuckled. "When we were tiny, Holly and I tried to teach each other our spells. I spent *hours* trying to get her stupid necklace to levitate while she whispered at plants. Eventually, we gave up."

"Does that mean your connection to the elements isn't always inherited?"

"Not necessarily," Rhia agreed, shutting the back door behind her. "Sometimes, magic can also skip a generation."

Valerie looked surprised at that. "Really?"

"Yeah. Or, well . . . it's not like it's not there *at all*. We believe that everyone has a tiny bit of magic in them. It's just that in most people, there's some kind of blockage that keeps it from surfacing—whether that's fear or a lack of knowledge that it even exists. For them, it can manifest in small things, like always knowing what song is going to be next on the radio or having an incredible green thumb." She smiled, adding, "Putting your love into a home-cooked meal for someone else can be as much of a ritual as the chanting of a spell. There's magic in everything, if you know to recognize it."

"Right. So, everyone has a baseline rate of magic, but not everyone's reaches the threshold where it manifests into abilities?"

Rhia stopped to consider. When she'd tried to explain it to Tristan once, he'd compared it to the difference between genotype and phenotype they'd learned about in biology: just because the potential for magic was there didn't mean it had to show on the outside. "Yeah. Something like that." She pointed at the staircase. "Want to go upstairs?"

Valerie, still looking a little stunned, nodded.

As they made their way upstairs, past the family pictures hanging on the wall, Rhia explained, "My sister, my cousin, and I all live on the second floor. My mom's and aunt's rooms are downstairs, and Grandma lives in the attic. It's terribly impractical with all of the stairs and her bad hip, but she insists on keeping her room up there."

"What about your dad?" Valerie asked from behind her.

Rhia's stride faltered. They were almost at the top of the stairs, right next to a picture frame that had hung there for as long as she could remember. While the other photos were constantly updated and interchanged, this particular photo remained untouched. It showed her, no older than four, sitting in her dad's lap. While she was beaming at the camera, his smile was mostly visible in his eyes as he looked down at her, one arm slung around her to keep her from toppling over. Rhia had spent so much time staring at it that every detail was engraved in her mind: the butterfly clips in her hair, the loose thread in his knitted turtleneck sweater, the way the sun made his warm brown skin look like it was glowing from the inside out.

"That's him," she said softly, running her finger over the frame.

Valerie was standing so close Rhia could hear her swallowing.

"It's okay. You couldn't have known."

"How did he . . . ?"

"Car accident," Rhia said, her voice oddly monotonous in the way it always got when she had to tell this story. "It was winter, and the roads were icy. He crashed into a tree."

Valerie was silent for a few seconds. Rhia felt like she knew what was going to come—another heartfelt *I'm sorry, that must've been so hard for your family, do you miss him a lot?*

Instead, Valerie said, "He looks so kind."

Rhia couldn't help but smile. She leaned a little closer to the photo so she could make out the dimples in his cheeks, the same spot where hers were. "He does, doesn't he?"

"Do you remember much about him?"

"Not really. I have a few memories of us playing in the garden together and the one time we went apple picking, but that's all."

"Did he also have abilities?" Valerie asked curiously.

"He had this weird knack for always being able to predict what commercial was next on TV, that was about it." Rhia laughed. "But he loved living in a family of witches. Mom always talks about how he helped prepare rituals and joined in on all the celebrations."

"What about your uncle and your grandpa?"

"Nope. That's just a statistical blip, though. In our family women seem to be favored, but people of all genders can be witches. Anyway," Rhia said with a shrug, continuing her climb up the stairs, "my grandpa used to live here with us until he passed. I was so small, I can't remember much about him, but I know that he and Grandma were absolutely besotted with each other—so much that he lived in this house with her for sixty years even though he was severely allergic to cats."

"And they say romance is dead," Valerie said wistfully.

"Jury's still out on that one. My aunt filed for divorce when my uncle kept trying to get her to stop using her magic. He takes Holly out for coffee every other weekend and is helping her build her workshop, but he hasn't showed up here in years."

"Almost seems like some men get insecure when the women around them hold more power than them, huh?"

Rhia threw a grin over her shoulder. "You said it, not me."

A moment later, they reached the second floor. Rhia's room was one of the smaller ones of the house, most of it taken up by her bed and a desk. Flowerpots stood on the windowsill and hung from the ceiling, and the walls were covered in art prints showing different plants and the phases of the moon. Right next to her bed was a calendar that Tristan had gifted her for her fifteenth birthday, a different cat for each month.

While Valerie took all of this in, Rhia steered towards the chest that was tucked away in one corner of the room. The dark wooden surface was covered in a carefully arranged selection of objects: candles, crystals, two knives, a wooden plate, a stick of lavender, a small wooden bowl filled with salt, another bowl with her share of Holly's moon water, and the acorns and autumn leaves she had collected during the autumn equinox. In the very

Philline Harms

center sat a heavy book whose cover was adorned with golden leaf detail.

"Is this . . ." Valerie asked, carefully nearing it.

"My altar," Rhia finished. "You can look at it if you want. Just don't touch anything."

Valerie nodded, already sinking to her knees in front of it. Her expression as she took in the objects in front of her was reverent.

"These are most of the things I use when I perform rituals," Rhia explained, sitting down cross-legged next to her. This close to Valerie, with her most prized possessions on display, she suddenly felt nervous again.

"What's that?" Valerie gestured at the small wooden plate holding a piece of milk chocolate.

Rhia smiled. "It's an offering. My great-grandmother loved her sweets, so I make sure to offer her some whenever I reach out to her. Talking to our ancestors is a big part of my family's practice."

"I see." Valerie seemed to have more questions, but her eyes were already darting to the next thing. "What are those knives for? You don't do animal sacrifices or anything, right?"

"No, of course not. Harming animals is against the threefold law."

"What's that?"

Rhia tried not to let any of her shock show. She'd sworn to herself that she wasn't going to slip up and make Valerie feel insignificant again, like she had the day before.

"It's the one big rule that most witches I know follow," she explained. "It basically means that whatever energy you give out will come back to you threefold. So if you do good, good things will happen to you. But if you use your magic to hurt another being . . ." She let her wince complete the sentence.

"I like that."

"Yeah. Anyways, I use this one to cut things like herbs and plants," Rhia explained, pointing at the simple kitchen knife. Then she gestured at the much duller second blade whose wooden handle was lovingly engraved with flowers. "This one is a ritual knife. I don't use it to physically cut anything—it's more symbolic. Like, if you're doing a ritual to free yourself from a toxic person in your life, you would use this knife to cut the bonds tying you to them."

"Do I need all this stuff?" Valerie asked. "I mean, am I a real witch without all of this?"

"Of course," Rhia immediately said. "Fancy instruments don't make you a witch. I've collected all of these since I was little—most of them were heirlooms or gifts from my family. But if you decide that you don't need these or that you don't want an altar, that's perfectly fine too. This way of practicing is just more traditional, I guess."

"You like your traditions, don't you?"

"I do," Rhia agreed. "But just because my family practices a certain way doesn't mean every witch should. There are no universal rules; everyone I know has cobbled their magic system together out of the things that felt truest to them or were the most accessible." She paused, cheeks warming as she realized she'd launched into yet another monologue. She finished with: "The beautiful thing about having magic is that every witch can forge their own path. You will too—it might just take a bit longer because no one has paved it before you."

Valerie nodded, chewing absentmindedly on her thumb as

she processed what Rhia had told her. Rhia liked that about her: the way one could tell just from looking at her face that she had listened, and how thoroughly she thought things over instead of simply accepting them as fact. For all her boldness, there was an unexpected earnestness to her that only seemed to reveal itself upon closer inspection.

Pointing at the book in the middle of her altar, Rhia said, "This is one thing I do recommend you do."

"What's that?"

"A spell book. It's where we write down our spells and recipes and jot down plans for upcoming rituals or record what worked well in previous ones. When a witch dies, their spell book is passed on in the family. That way, none of our knowledge is ever lost."

She looked back at Valerie to find her with a furrow between her brows, a shadow dimming her usually bright expression.

"What's wrong?"

"Nothing." Valerie shook her head. "I just wish I had something like this from my ancestors."

Rhia waited for her to say something more, but she only kept staring at the spell book, the look in her eyes equal parts longing and frustration. Quietly, Rhia asked, "Is your mom dead too?"

"No," Valerie said. "I . . . I mean I don't think so. But that's the thing. I don't know what happened to her. My dad won't tell me anything about her, and I don't know anyone else from her side of the family—the magical side. He hinted that there was some kind of conflict with her mother and aunts, but . . . all I know is that she used to live in Oakriver and that she's probably a witch."

"What's her name?"

"Isabelle." Valerie said the name softly, her lips forming each syllable like it was sacred. "Isabelle Morgan."

"I don't know anyone with that name," Rhia quietly said. "I'm sorry."

Even though she tried to hide her disappointment, Valerie visibly deflated. "It's fine. I thought maybe you might have heard something about her, but that probably would've been too easy."

Watching her, something in Rhia's chest tightened. She had grown up with a family of witches in a house where magic drenched every aspect of her life. Her childhood had been filled with memories of sitting with Sage in the trees and listening to the stories they told, planting herbs in the greenhouse with her grandmother and making them sprout with a single whisper, baking magical cakes with her mother while Holly practiced her abilities by making the ingredients float around the kitchen.

Because of her family, she'd never had to teach herself anything, always surrounded by five other women who would readily answer all her questions and a whole family line she could call on whenever their answers weren't sufficient. She couldn't imagine what it would feel like to grow up without a single soul to talk to about her abilities; no red thread to follow, not even a single bread crumb to guide her through the dark woods that witchcraft had to feel like when you were all on your own. She was still searching for the words to express this when her thoughts were interrupted by the sound of her stomach grumbling.

Valerie met her eyes again, the disheartened look exchanged for an amused one. "Hungry?"

"Starving," Rhia said sheepishly. "I haven't eaten anything since before my shift. Do you mind if I cook us something?"

"Sure, I could eat."

They made their way back downstairs and into the kitchen. While Rhia got out pots and pans and rifled through the fridge, Valerie stood in the center of the room, staring at the bundles of dried herbs hanging from the ceiling and the green shelves overflowing with mason jars, dishware, and recipe books. That was one thing Rhia had noticed: wherever Valerie went, she eagerly drank in her surroundings, as if she had been parched her whole life.

Rhia smiled when she caught her studying the basket of bread on the kitchen table with a small tag on the handle that said, DON'T EAT—SLEEP SPELL!

Meeting her eyes, Valerie quirked one eyebrow in silent question.

"That's what I meant when I was talking about kitchen magic," Rhia explained. "It's basically normal baking, but using specific ingredients and channeling a strong intention into what you're making. That bread is for Tristan's mom—she was complaining about her insomnia the other day."

Valerie looked skeptical. "Does it actually work?"

"Yeah. There's something sacred about the act of eating in general. We're taking in a part of the earth, you know? Plus, you can combine magic with pretty much anything." Rhia paused in dicing the tomatoes to glance over her shoulder at Valerie. "How have *you* been sleeping lately?"

Valerie shrugged. Still facing away from Rhia, she said, "Quinn told me about your conversation. Do you really think I'm haunted?"

"I think that there might be a possibility a spirit attached themselves to you," Rhia carefully said. "You didn't answer my question."

"I haven't sleepwalked again, if that's what you mean, so the herbs must've helped. Thanks for the tip, by the way."

"Hey, that's great!" Rhia was surprised by the intensity of her own relief. "What about dreams? Are you having any nightmares?"

"I'm not sure," Valerie haltingly said. Her fingers were tapping an uneven rhythm against the kitchen table. "I've always had vivid dreams, but these ones are different. I can never remember what they're about when I wake up, but the feeling, it . . . it *clings*."

"What's the feeling?"

"Fear." Valerie's tapping stopped as she abruptly turned to face Rhia. "Anyway. Enough about that. How can I be of help, Chef?"

A part of Rhia wanted to inquire more, but there was something about the way Valerie had changed the topic that stopped her. She wordlessly handed Valerie a knife instead.

For the next few minutes, the only sounds filling the kitchen were the sizzling of oil, the chopping of herbs, and the roaming paws of Salem—their overweight black cat—padding across the floorboards. At one point, Rhia stepped away from the stove to find the pasta water boiling when she turned back around a heartbeat later. The mischievous glint in Valerie's eyes and the faint scent of her fire magic betrayed her innocent smile. To her surprise, Rhia found herself smiling back.

There was something unexpectedly easy about being with Valerie. She wasn't as tough as her appearance suggested, and she couldn't be further from the arrogant, uncaring villain Rhia had pegged her as during their first encounter. Standing next to Rhia, with the sleeves of her jacket rolled up to her elbows and a look of utter concentration on her face as she tried not to chop off a finger, Valerie was the opposite of intimidating. She was funny and curious and so beautiful that Rhia's breathing hitched every time their hands accidentally brushed.

Rhia hadn't realized she was staring until Valerie met her eyes and said, "Thank you."

"For what?"

"For letting me in on all of this," Valerie said, her voice so quiet Rhia unconsciously leaned closer. In the setting sun streaming through the windows, her hair looked like liquid copper. "I know I must seem stupid, but I honestly never knew there were other people like me. It's nice to finally have someone to talk to about all of this."

"You don't seem stupid," Rhia murmured.

This close, she could smell the scent of smoke that clung to Valerie's hair. The air around them hummed with magic. A peculiar feeling had settled in Rhia's chest—something insistent, something familiar, something that was tethered to her very core and *tugged*.

She didn't know who leaned in first; all she knew was that Valerie's face was suddenly very close, and her head was spinning. Rhia closed her eyes, tipped her chin—and then everything happened at once. A sensation like an electric shock ran through her, strong enough to tear a gasp from her mouth; a deafening sizzling sound erupted; Salem—*chubby, slow-moving Salem*—let out an indignant hiss and darted out the door.

Rhia's eyes flew open to the sight of the pasta boiling over while the lights—which she was *sure* she had never turned on—flickered on and off. Valerie looked as shocked as she felt. They stared at each other for a split second before they sprang into action, Valerie rushing to turn off the stove and take the pot off the heat while Rhia flicked the light switch.

"What the hell just happened?"

Rhia shook her head. She felt shaky, off-kilter, the hairs on the back of her neck standing on end. "I—I don't know, I've never—"

There was a noise at the door before she could finish, followed by her mother calling out, "Hello? Anyone here?"

"*Shit,*" Rhia cursed, grabbing Valerie's arm. "You need to leave."

Valerie stumbled after her towards the back door. "Maybe we can talk tomorrow?"

"Yeah, maybe," Rhia distractedly said, already closing the door in her face.

She turned around, still in a daze, and made it back to the stove just as her mother appeared in the doorway. "Hi, honey—" Her eyes fell on the mess on the stove. "What happened here?"

"Pot boiled over. I wasn't paying attention, sorry."

Her mother shook her head and said something else before she went upstairs, but Rhia wasn't listening. Even now, the air in the kitchen was still charged, and under the burnt smell of the pasta water on the stove, there was another scent: smoke, mixed with an earthy undertone. Magic. Valerie's, but also hers.

There was one memory of her father Rhia had that she hadn't told Valerie about, frayed at the edges but still present after fourteen years. She'd been in the garden with her parents on a sunny day in spring, the sky a spotless expanse of blue. When her mother said that it was time to go inside, she had thrown herself into the grass and screwed her eyes shut, her tiny hands braced against the ground as she made herself as heavy as she

Philline Harms

could so her dad couldn't lift her. There had been a feeling like an electric shock as magic zapped from her fingertips and into the earth. When she'd opened her eyes, it was to the sight of new flowers sprouting around each of her little fingers where there hadn't been any before, an imprint of her hands visible when she lifted them. It had been the first time her grip on her abilities had slipped, and, because after that her family had begun to teach her how to use them, it had also been the last.

Rhiannon Greenbrook knew her way around magic. Rhiannon Greenbrook *didn't lose control.* Not when she was scared. Not when she was upset. And certainly not because of a girl she had only spoken to a handful of times. None of this was like her, and it made her heart pound against her rib cage even as she set about cleaning the kitchen.

The scent of burning and magic dissipated within minutes. The fear, bone-deep and visceral, stayed with her for the rest of the night.

9

FOUR OF CUPS

melancholy — frustration — feeling disconnected

Valerie had a hard time concentrating in her classes the next morning. As much as she tried to focus on the piece she was working on, her thoughts kept drifting back to the afternoon at Rhia's house—the things she had learned and the moment in the kitchen. How could they not? Sketching a stupid college assignment was so goddamn *mundane* compared to what she'd experienced just a few hours ago.

Groaning, she leaned back in the uncomfortable wooden chair. This class was held in one of the smaller rooms on the ground floor of the large art building. If she craned her neck, she could make out bits of sidewalk behind the tendrils of ivy outside the window, scattered groups of students passing by every once in a while. The sky was as gloomy as ever—by now, Valerie had come to understand that sunny days were rare in Oakriver this time of year.

She quickly lowered her gaze again when her professor, a tall woman with sharp features and wire-rimmed glasses, passed by her station. Valerie waited until she was out of earshot before she whispered, "Hey, Quinn."

Quinn responded with a questioning hum. Unlike Valerie, they were actually being productive, dark-blue locks falling into their eyes as they bent over their sketchbook.

"I messaged Rhia on Instagram last night. She read it but still hasn't replied."

Another hum.

"Is it weird to message people on Instagram?"

"I don't know," Quinn said without looking up. "Depends on your relationship with them."

Valerie made a face. What *was* her relationship with Rhia? After yesterday, she honestly wasn't too sure. "Maybe she's busy with other stuff and didn't have time to look at her phone."

"She visited my *Animal Crossing* island last night."

Valerie just barely kept her jaw from dropping. "What?"

"She saw me playing at the shop one time, and we exchanged codes. Her island is so cute, she has this really beautiful garden and a café and a replica of Obscura with potion shelves and everyth—" Quinn broke off when they saw the tortured expression on Valerie's face. "Sorry. What did you message her?"

Careful to make sure their prof was nowhere in sight, Valerie got her phone out of the pocket of her oversized jacket and read, "'Hey, Girl-Named-After-That-One-Fleetwood-Mac-Song. Earlier was pretty wild'—I was talking about the thing with the water boiling over—'I didn't even get to eat any of the pasta. Want to hang out tomorrow and make it up? After yesterday, I still owe you a divination lesson.' Eye emoji, flame emoji."

When Quinn didn't react, Valerie buried her face in her hands. "That was too straightforward, wasn't it?"

"*Straight* isn't the word I would've used."

"Not helpful," Valerie groaned.

"Sorry." Quinn's chuckle was a rare, endearing sound. "I don't think it's weird. It's direct. But that's what both of you are."

Valerie slid her phone back into her pocket and propped her chin in one hand. "It honestly *was* wild. Her house is insane. There's, like, herbs everywhere and she has an altar and there's a *greenhouse*—"

She broke off when her prof sent her a reprimanding glance.

Lowering her voice, she told Quinn, "I mean, there were *literally* sparks flying. I've never felt anything like it."

"Doesn't that worry you?" asked Quinn. "To know that you lost control of your magic around her?"

Thinking back to it, there was an unfamiliar flutter in Valerie's chest. When she closed her eyes, she could still see everything clear as day: Rhia standing at the stove in her big sweater and pumpkin earrings, unguarded and relaxed for once; the setting sun catching in her hair and her eyes, making them glow like amber; the instinctive tilt of her head as she'd leaned closer. And then, all hell breaking loose.

"No," Valerie said. "It didn't feel like losing control. It was more like—I don't know, it was like her magic was trying to *get in*, like there was an exchange. But it all happened so quickly that in the end our combined magic just hung in the air between us with nowhere to go and kind of blew up, if that makes sense."

"I've never heard of anything like that." The amusement in Quinn's voice had made room for concern.

"Me neither, but that doesn't mean it's impossible, right?"

"I guess not," Quinn allowed. Silence fell again, filled only by their professor's heels clicking against the concrete floor and the scratching of pencils against paper.

"I wanted to go to Sugar & Spice later to get coffee. Do you think it's weird if I try to talk to her?"

Quinn's fingertips furiously rubbed at the paper, blending the strokes of their charcoal pencil. "I don't think so. And even if it was, it hasn't stopped you from doing it all the other times."

Valerie nodded, a new resolve forming in her head. Glancing at the clock on the wall, she was relieved to find there were only two minutes left until the class was over.

When she looked back at her roommate, Quinn was leaning back in their seat, their hands blackened with charcoal. Valerie inched closer to see what they had spent the last hour feverishly sketching, only for a chill to run down her spine. Drawn in frantic, smudged strokes, there was a roaring river surrounded by trees pushing in on both sides, the moon spilling silver over the turbulent water. But it wasn't the scenery that made the blood in Valerie's veins run cold; it was the body of a woman in the water, facedown, arms outstretched as she was carried off by the current. She was an upside-down Ophelia; a grim parody of Millais's masterpiece lacking both color and flowers.

"What's that?" Valerie breathed.

Quinn blinked at their sketchbook as if they were seeing the piece for the first time. "I don't know." Their voice was so soft Valerie could barely make out the words. "Just . . . something I saw in a dream."

Valerie frowned. There was something stirring in the back of her mind, the faint whisper of a memory wanting to be recalled, but it stayed just out of reach. "Sorry," she murmured. "I guess I passed my weird dreams on to you."

The nasally voice of their professor dismissing the class tore Valerie's gaze away from the drawing. Shaking her head to rid it of the foggy feeling that had overcome her, she slung her tote bag over her shoulder and got to her feet. "Do you want anything from the café?"

Quinn didn't react, dark eyes still trained on the sketch in front of them.

Valerie gave their shoulder a light nudge. "Quinn?"

Quinn's entire body jerked at the touch before they, in one hasty motion, shut the sketchbook and shoved it into their bag. "I'm not hungry."

They got up and pushed past Valerie before she could say anything else. Shaking her head, Valerie walked in the opposite direction as her roommate. "This town, man." The wind took hold of her as soon as she stepped outside, whirling fallen leaves around her feet. Valerie shoved her hands into the pockets of her jacket and sped up her pace, taking the familiar route to Sugar & Spice.

When she got there, the café was bustling with the usual mix of college students getting their caffeine fix between classes, old people meeting to play cards, and moms chatting with their friends while their kids ran around in the area upstairs. The two waitresses hurrying between the tables were girls Valerie hadn't seen before, and behind the counter stood Rhia's boss. After craning her neck to see if she could spot Rhia anywhere else, Valerie moved past the lined-up patrons near the register and towards the stairs.

So far, she had only been in the café downstairs, never in

the bookshop part of the old building. When she made it to the second floor, she was surprised at how far it extended, the coffee smell giving way to the scent of paper and ink as a maze of shelves stretched in front of her. The timeworn floorboards complained under her weight as she moved between the rows.

"Rhia?" she called out, softly so as not to disturb the people browsing the shelves. There wasn't an answer, but Valerie could've sworn she heard a quiet thud followed by footsteps scurrying away from her. She started walking faster and slithered around a corner in time to catch a glimpse of an orange skirt disappearing behind another shelf. She was about to chase after it when she collided with someone who had just stepped into the aisle.

Looking up, an apology already on the tip of her tongue, she found Tristan staring at her like a deer in the headlights. "Valerie, hi! What are you doing here?"

She craned her neck, but the skirt and its wearer were long out of sight. "I thought I might be able to find Rhia up here. Have you seen her?"

"Rhia?" Scratching the back of his neck, Tristan glanced over his shoulder. The tips of his ears were bright red. "She isn't here today. Sorry."

Valerie did her best to pull together a smile. "Oh. That's odd, I thought she said something about having a shift here today."

Tristan shrugged, looking decidedly uncomfortable as he repeated: "Sorry. Uh . . . do you want me to pass on a message or something?"

Now that she was here, she honestly wasn't sure what she wanted to say. *Why didn't you respond to my message? Was it the Fleetwood Mac joke? Do you wish you'd kissed me? Did you feel it too, that strange pull in your chest?* The longer she thought about it, the more pathetic it all sounded, so in the end she swallowed the words. "No. Thanks, Tristan."

"Uh-huh." He was still looking anywhere but at her. "Did you want to get coffee or anything? I'll make one for you on the house."

Studying him, Valerie was almost certain she could've gotten him to crack and tell her where to find Rhia. But pressuring people wasn't like her, and so all she said was, "I'll have a double espresso if that's okay."

Tristan promptly took off towards the stairs. Valerie cast another glance over her shoulder before she followed him, unsuccessfully trying to stifle the disappointment that welled up in her chest. It mixed with hurt when they passed a cardboard box filled with books in the middle of an aisle, looking like it had been dropped there in haste—the thud Valerie had heard.

She was still fighting the lump in her throat when Tristan handed her a steaming paper cup. She thanked him and left the café without another word, only turning around once more when she was back on the sidewalk. There was a small window right beneath the roof of the old building that she hadn't noticed before, belonging to a third floor above the café and the bookshop. When she squinted, she thought she could make out the outline of Rhia looking down at her, but then she blinked and the shadow was gone.

Rubbing the back of her hand over her nose, Valerie turned around and headed back to the dorms, a bitter taste in her mouth that had nothing to do with the coffee.

Philline Harms

10

THE MOON

facing one's fears — uncertainty — the subconscious

Rhia rarely had sleepless nights. She made sure of it with the crystals on her bedside table, the bag of herbs under her pillowcase, and the jasmine in her incense burner. Usually, these precautions helped her drift off within seconds. Tonight, not even magic could get her mind to rest.

Whenever she closed her eyes, Valerie's Instagram message appeared on the back of her eyelids. Whenever she turned on her side, she felt like she was back in the kitchen, and her heart began to race. Whenever she thought she had managed to slip under the surface of unconsciousness, the image of Valerie's face staring up at her through the attic window of the café intruded on her thoughts, and sleep spat her out again. It wasn't often that Rhia felt guilt, but lying there with only the moon watching her, she could almost taste it, acidic and bitter. She knew that Valerie didn't deserve being treated this way—none of what had happened had been her fault, after all. The problem was that Rhia didn't know what *was* to blame for the incident in the kitchen.

By now she had come to the conclusion that it had to have been some sort of failed exchange between them. Not only had Valerie's fire magic tried to get *in*, which was terrifying in its own right, but some of Rhia's earth magic had also tried to flow over to Valerie. Rhia knew that sharing magic was a thing. She'd done it with her family before during rituals, but it had never been as sudden, as uncontrolled, as *intense*. Usually, it happened with an intention and the permission of both counterparts, one drawing from the other to achieve a mutual goal, not an erratic firework of magic that neither could rein in. None of it made any sense to her.

Groaning, Rhia blinked open her eyes and ran her hands over her face. Her phone display showed it was 2:00 a.m. by now. With one last mournful thought about her opening shift at the café the next day, Rhia admitted defeat.

She had half a mind to sit down in front of her altar and call on one of her ancestors—sometimes it helped to have someone to talk to who wasn't Tristan or her immediate family. Gabrielle Greenbrook, for example, was an *excellent* listener. Out of all her ancestors, Rhia had always felt the most connected to her. Gabrielle had lived in the same bedroom long before it was Rhia's and, according to her grandmother, had a similar way of speaking and using her hands. When it was time to come out to her family, Rhia had soft-launched the topic by pouring out her heart to Gabrielle over an offering of chocolate chip cookies she'd stress-baked (and possibly also stress-nibbled during their conference). The next morning, the flowers on her altar had bloomed encouragingly in shades of red, white, and orange.

Somehow, the topic of Valerie didn't feel like one she could

speak about out loud, though. It felt messy and sacred and altogether too tender for other people to look at. The worst thing was
that she wasn't sure she could explain *why* it was so complicated,
to Gabrielle or to herself. And so, she pulled on her cardigan and
a pair of knitted socks and slipped into the hallway.

On her tiptoes, she snuck past Holly's and Sage's rooms and
down the stairs, avoiding every creaking step until she reached
the ground floor. She had almost made it to her destination—
the kitchen sink, to get a glass of water—when she caught a light
flickering in her peripheral vision.

With her heart kicking in her chest, Rhia turned and
stepped closer to the window to see what was going on outside.
Her shoulders relaxed when she spotted who was in the garden:
it was her grandmother, her mother, and her aunt, all huddled
around the wooden table. Seeing as sleep wouldn't come anytime soon, Rhia pulled her cardigan tighter around herself and
stepped out the same back door she had pushed Valerie through
two days earlier.

"Rhiannon!" Aunt Tanisha exclaimed when she spotted her
nearing their table. "Come sit! We're having moon tea."

Moon tea was one of the many peculiar traditions the
Greenbrooks had. Every once in a while, the three women
would get together in the middle of the night to drink tea under
the night sky and read the leaves together. Rhia had never been
able to identify anything in the soggy residue and didn't see
the point in staying up until such an ungodly hour only to be
disappointed, so she never took part. This time, though, with
her aunt beaming at her and patting the spot next to her on the
bench, she reluctantly sat down. It wasn't like she had anything
better to do.

The same table that had creaked under the weight of food and drink on the evening of the autumn equinox was now littered with saucers, teacups of different sizes, and a gently steaming kettle. A myriad of candles illuminated the faces of her mother and grandmother sitting on the other side of the table, blankets draped over their laps to keep them warm, their hair hidden beneath colorful scarves and bonnets that matched the one that Rhia had put on for bed. While her grandmother was busy squinting into her cup, her mother cocked her head to the side.

"What are you doing up so late, honey?"

"Can't sleep."

"Go ahead then," said Grandma Deloris, impatiently waving at the fourth cup that stood untouched in the center of the table. "The tea has answers to all the questions that trouble you."

Rhia blinked at it, wondering if it was a coincidence that the women had taken one too many cups into the garden with them or if her grandmother, as the most clairvoyant member of the family, had known she would come down all along. Deciding that she didn't want to know the answer, she shook her head. "You know I can't do this stuff."

"Oh, come on, little bug," her aunt said in her chirping voice, giving her a good-natured nudge with her shoulder. "What do you have to lose?"

Rhia considered it for a moment, her discomfort warring with her curiosity. She'd failed at all forms of divination, but this one seemed the most harmless. She wouldn't have to lose herself in a scrying bowl or run the risk of drawing a terrifying tarot card. All she had to do was drink tea and interpret the residue.

Reluctantly, she reached across the table and took the cup. "I won't see anything anyways."

Her mother offered her a jar of loose tea leaves and a spoon. "These things take practice. It's all right if you don't find anything right away. You'll still get a nice cup of tea out of it."

"I guess," Rhia conceded as she spooned some of the tea into the bottom of her cup. As an afterthought, she lifted it to her nose to smell what kind it was.

"An herbal blend Sage made a few days ago," Aunt Tanisha told her. "It'll help you sleep later."

That, at least, was something she could appreciate. While her grandmother continued to ponder the contents of her cup, muttering unintelligibly to herself, Rhia poured the water from the kettle over the leaves.

Her mother watched with interest as she did. "What are you hoping to find answers to?"

"Nothing," Rhia lied, tugging the sleeves of her cardigan over her knuckles. "Just a general reading."

Apparently satisfied with this answer, her mother went back to her own tea, turning the cup this way and that as she studied its contents in the candlelight.

Silence fell over the table, interrupted only by the sound of the wind murmuring around the house and a quiet meowing as Circe wandered through the back door Rhia had left ajar. Rhia watched the cat slink into the shadows before she fixed her eyes on the delicate wisps of steam rising from her cup.

"I have a question," she ventured.

"What is it?" her grandmother asked.

"You know how we sometimes share our magic with each other?"

The women nodded. Rhia bit her lip, unsure how to phrase the question without sounding suspicious. "Is that something that's only possible between family members, or can it also happen with any other witch?"

Her mother and Grandma Deloris exchanged glances, one surprised, the other wary. "It's easiest with members of your own family, but it's not impossible to share magic with outsiders as well," her mother said. She was speaking in the same even tone she'd used all the other times she'd taught Rhia how to use her abilities, always patient and calm—the same way, Rhia suspected, that she spoke to her patients at the vet clinic. "The most important thing is that both parties are open to it and that there's a foundation of trust. The better you know someone, the easier it is."

Rhia frowned. Did she trust Valerie? She wasn't sure. All she knew was that she didn't trust *herself* when she was around her.

"Can . . . can it happen by accident?" she blurted.

"Yes," said her mother. "It usually happens in moments of very high emotions."

"Extremely dangerous," her grandmother grimly remarked.

In an equally serious tone, her mother asked, "Do you remember what I told you about when not to use your magic?"

Rhia nodded silently. *Do not use your abilities when you're angry, frightened, or sad. Magic is like a flame—it isn't dangerous in itself unless you put it near something flammable. Your emotions are an oil spill, Rhiannon.*

"Why do you want to know all this?" her grandmother asked. "Did you happen to share your magic with another witch?"

"No," Rhia said. "'Course not."

Her aunt saved her before she had to say anything else. "I think your tea is ready, Rhiannon," she said gently, pointing at the porcelain cup. "Drink it slowly and think about what you want to know!"

Rhia lifted the cup to her mouth, glad to have an excuse to not say anything else for the next few minutes as she carefully sipped, trying not to swallow all the leaves floating at the top. She closed her eyes as she did, partly to escape her grandmother's suspicious gaze, partly to focus. As always, the first thing that entered her mind was Valerie, but this time she didn't push the thought away. Instead, she surrendered to it, let it pull her under until all she could think about was the amused lilt in Valerie's voice when she spoke, the ease with which she conjured fire, her curious eyes, and the scent of smoke that clung to her hair. Finally, when only the leaves and about a teaspoon of liquid were left, she set it down.

Her aunt handed her a saucer and instructed, "Give it three swirls, then turn it upside down."

Rhia did as she said, carefully setting the overturned cup down on the saucer. Closing her eyes, she rested two fingers on top of it like she'd seen her family do dozens of times, channeling her question—*What's going to happen with Valerie?*—one last time. Then, she slowly turned the cup over.

The other women leaned closer as she peered inside. "Wow," she commented dryly. "Tea leaves."

"Start at the top, right below the rim," her mother advised. "It will tell you about all the surface-level issues and feelings you're facing. After that, work your way down into the deeper layers."

Rhia stared harder, but no matter how she tried, all she saw were shapeless clumps of tea. Shaking her head, she said, "I don't see anything."

Her grandmother made an impatient noise. "Focus,

Rhiannon. Don't look with your eyes—look with your heart, your intuition. What do they tell you?"

Rhia's fingers tightened around the cup. Her intuition was a rusty instrument; her heart whispered in tongues that she could rarely parse.

Still, she held the cup closer to the nearest candle and slowly turned it. One of the larger lumps near the top caught her attention. "That one looks kind of like . . . a bug?" She looked uncertainly at her family. "What does that mean?"

"Guilt," her grandmother said. Rhia absently thought that there were few people who could still appear so formidable while wearing hot-pink silk pajamas. "Something is eating away at you, like a parasite eating away at a cadaver—"

"—or a plant!" her aunt quickly threw in when she saw Rhia wincing.

Grandma Deloris carried on, unfazed. "What it indicates is up to you to figure out."

Rhia knew what it referred to. She had focused the reading on Valerie, so it wasn't the fact that she had lied to her family. The stupid insect was a reflection of her feeling bad for ghosting Valerie.

Wordlessly, Rhia trained her eyes on the cup again, continuing to twist it slowly as she made her way farther down. There was something else that caught her eye, a huge cluster of leaves right at the bottom. She looked helplessly at her aunt. "What's that?"

"Let me see . . . Oh, that's quite easy. It's fire, see?" Aunt Tanisha traced a perfectly manicured finger along the shapeless clump. "These are the individual flames."

Rhia would never in a million years have identified it on her own. "That's not good, right?"

"Depends on the situation," said her grandmother.

Rhia wasn't convinced. "I read that it means destruction."

"Not necessarily." Her mother leaned closer, brushing a finger along the rim of the cup. "Think of the Death card in tarot. It doesn't literally mean that someone is going to die—it stands for endings, yes, but not necessarily bad ones. It can also mean entering a new chapter in your life, change, progress. This is similar. What else do you think of when you see fire?"

Valerie. "Warmth," Rhia quietly said.

"Good. You see, there are many possible interpretations for fire besides destruction. Things along the lines of passion, desire, transformation."

"Infatuation," her aunt threw in with a smile.

Despite the October chill, Rhia felt her face grow hot. "So things aren't literally going to go up in flames?"

"Hopefully not, but one never knows for sure until it happens," her aunt cheerfully said.

"Do you see anything else?" her grandmother prodded.

Rhia focused on the cup again. There were a few larger clusters of leaves left, but none of them caught her attention as much as the first two had, and with the tea in her system, she felt her eyelids growing heavier the longer she searched.

Stifling a yawn behind her hand, she shook her head. "No."

"Well, go on back to bed then." Her mother chuckled. "Save all your energy for the Fall Festival tomorrow."

With everything that had happened, Rhia had almost forgotten about it *again.* Nodding, she got to her feet. "'Kay. Good night."

"Night!" her aunt called after her before she shuffled back inside.

Rhia didn't know if it was the tea or the reading that had calmed her, but this time she fell asleep as soon as her head hit the pillow, pulled under by dreams of flames cradled between slender hands and trees catching fire.

11

TEMPERANCE

moderation — perspective — blending of opposites

At the other end of town, Valerie was far from sleepy.

She was sitting on the floor in her dorm room, methodically attacking a canvas with shades of red, layering frantic strokes until they built up texture. She had no idea what she was creating, but that was fine. Tonight, the point wasn't beauty—she just needed to do something to tune out the itch beneath her skin, to turn the chaos outward, to drown out all thoughts about attic windows and unanswered texts.

"Valerie."

She moved from a deep scarlet to a screaming crimson, red bleeding into the water in her cup. The bristles of her brush scratched loudly against the canvas.

"*Valerie.* Are you okay?"

Her head snapped up. "Hm?"

From the other side of the room, Quinn raised their eyebrows at her. They were sitting on the floor by their bed, a stack of magazines in their lap and a selection of cutouts arranged on a blank paper next to them to form the beginning of a collage. "Are you okay?" they repeated.

"Sure," Valerie said.

One of Quinn's eyebrows rose a tiny bit higher. "The temperature in here just went up by at least eight degrees."

With a sigh, Valerie dropped her brush onto the newspaper she'd laid out on the floor. "Sorry." She pressed the heels of her palms against her eyes. Sweat prickled at her hairline. She'd run hot enough to take off her flannel a few hours ago, leaving her in a tank top and pajama shorts. "I don't know what it is tonight."

"Hey." There was a creaking of floorboards as Quinn padded across the room. Then a cool hand settled on Valerie's bare shoulder. "How about we stop here? You know, before you boil us alive?"

Valerie opened her eyes to survey her work again. Over the last hour, she had turned the canvas into a wildfire. Her hands were stained magenta, her wrists were sore, and her neck was stiff, and still she felt like she was going to buzz out of her skin. "Okay." She pushed to her feet. "I'll pop down to one of the studios so you can sleep."

"Wait. We could do. . . something else."

"Like what?"

"I, um." Quinn threw a glance in the direction of their bedside table. "It might be a weird idea. We don't have to do it if you don't want to."

"Is this a sex thing?"

"*No*, you rake, it's not a sex thing," Quinn sputtered. "And it concerns me that *that's* the first thing you thought of."

"You asked me if I was up for something weird and then looked suggestively at your nightstand! How does that make me—"

"Do you want to help me dye my hair?" Quinn said, raising their voice to speak over Valerie.

"Oh." Valerie's eyes darted to Quinn's hair, which, now that she really looked at it, did look a little less blue than it had the first time they'd met. "Okay."

And that was how, ten minutes later, she found herself sneaking into a bathroom on the second floor. It was labeled "Staff Bathroom," but Valerie had never seen an actual member of staff around the dorms, so she had no qualms about claiming it for their impromptu hairstyling session.

"Welcome to Valerie's Hair Palace," she announced, locking the door behind them while the light flickered on. "Please, get comfortable. Right there is perfect."

Indulgently, Quinn settled on the closed toilet. Valerie draped a fluffy towel around their shoulders and mixed the box dye Quinn apparently kept in their nightstand in a small bowl that she'd nicked from the community kitchen. "Tell me about your day?"

Quinn tilted their head, a soft breath leaving them when Valerie brushed a stray curl out of their eyes. "It was okay. I liked the lecture this morning, the one about modernism. And the ceramics class was better this week than last."

Valerie made a face. She hated the ceramics class with a passion. In her opinion, there were few sensory experiences more abhorrent than that of wet, stubborn clay. "I still don't get why we have to take that one. Neither of us wants to become a *potter*, of all things."

Quinn's shoulders shook slightly as they gave a near-silent laugh. Their eyes had slipped shut when Valerie had begun to section off some of the strands, clipping them in place. "I like that they let us experiment with a bunch of different mediums. I just wish they didn't grade us for them, you know? I mean, most of us are hard enough on ourselves as it is—we don't need someone with a PhD to tell us we will never become artists just because we fucked up a vase."

Valerie nodded in agreement.

"Anyway. After class, I had lunch with Priya and Amanda—" two girls from their dorm "—and called my mom, and that was about it."

"Nice," murmured Valerie, slightly distracted by her task. There was something unexpectedly meditative about brushing her fingers through Quinn's hair, gently working in the dye. When her fingernails scratched Quinn's scalp, they leaned into the touch in a manner that reminded Valerie of a cat requesting petting. With a smile tugging at her lips, she obliged.

"My mom always dyed my hair when I was still living at home," Quinn said.

Valerie paused, peering down at Quinn's face. With their eyes shut, their features were relaxed and open. "Are you guys close?"

"Mm-hmm," Quinn confirmed.

"What about your dad?"

"We're close as well, but it's different with him. He's an acts-of-service kind of guy—we barely ever talk, but I know that if I messaged him that something in our room was broken, he'd be here within an hour."

Valerie carefully withdrew her hands from Quinn's hair.

Philline Harms

Setting a timer on her phone, she tried to tamp down the jealousy coiling in her chest. It was an ugly feeling. She didn't truly envy Quinn—she was glad they had parents who were supportive, who they could have hour-long phone calls with and visit on the weekends, not out of duty but because both parties *wanted* to. She just wished she knew what that felt like.

A few seconds passed in silence until Quinn tilted their head back and asked, "Have you found out anything about your mom?"

"Nothing."

"I'm sure you will. I'll keep an ear out at Obscura as well. You wouldn't believe how much I've learned about everyone in this town since I've started working there."

Valerie launched herself at the distraction as if it were a life raft. "Oh? Do tell."

Quinn's cheeks dimpled. "Just today, Helen Lightbourn told me that apparently there's a whole feud going on between Mrs. Gilbert and Mrs. Clampitt over a beauty potion. Apparently, Mrs. Gilbert recommended it to Mrs. Clampitt as an antiaging thing, but when Mrs. Clampitt tried it, it turned her face green." Quinn cut themself off with a high-pitched wheeze. "Like the Wicked Witch of the West, Valerie. A real, deep, Kermit green all the way down to her neck."

At Quinn's laughter, Valerie couldn't help but chuckle as well. She was sitting criss-cross applesauce on the cold tiles at Quinn's feet by now, her chin cradled in one hand as she listened.

"So now they keep sending each other increasingly obscure potions in hopes that the other one will try it. Only, they have to try them on themselves as well to make sure they work." Quinn wiped their tears of laughter away with the back of one hand, their voice wobbly. "Eyebrows have been lost. Every day I wait for one of them to come in to buy another remedy for their self-inflicted disfigurement. It's the pettiest thing, and I *love* it. You'll have to keep an eye open for them at the Fall Festival tomorrow."

"Fall Festival?" Valerie questioned.

"Oh, I thought you'd seen the invite at the shop. It's this big get-together of all the witches in the area. I figured you'd be going."

Valerie was nodding without even having to think about it. "I will. Thanks for letting me know."

"Sure." Tilting their head, Quinn caught a glimpse of Valerie's timer. "Ready to rinse?"

Valerie pushed herself back to standing and held the towel in place around Quinn's shoulders as they shuffled to the sink. She turned on the faucet and waited for the water to come out—except all that followed was an ominous gurgling sound from somewhere deep within the pipes. "Uh." Through the mirror, she shot Quinn a look. "Is that normal?"

"They do that sometimes. Apparently, ever since the flooding, the whole water system has been a little wonky." They reached out, gingerly twisting the old faucet handle. In the next second, water sputtered into the sink with enough force to spray both of them.

While they waited for it to warm, Valerie asked, "Were you here when the flooding happened?"

"Yeah. It was my first night here, actually. A bunch of pipes burst in Dorm B. I was lucky my hometown isn't that far from Oakriver, so I could move back in with my parents for a bit and then come back when they told me a new room in this dorm was available."

"No way. So the flooding is the only reason we're roommates?"

Quinn met her eyes through the mirror. "Must've been fate."

Studying them with their dyed hair sticking to their forehead and the towel around their shoulders, their relaxed posture and the toothy grin they reserved for only a handful of people, Valerie suddenly felt unbearably fond. She really *was* grateful for the flooding.

She held a hand under the water. "I think we're good to go."

Quinn ducked their head under the stream without double-checking its temperature, hissing slightly when it hit their scalp.

"Too cold?" Valerie asked.

"Too hot! Is this how you shower?"

"Maybe," Valerie admitted, turning down the temperature. "In my defense, I think my body temperature is higher than average. Back in school I kept getting sent home because the nurse thought I was running a fever." She paused for effect. "I guess I'm just that hot."

Quinn's groan almost got lost in the running of the tap. Grinning to herself, Valerie ran her fingers through their hair, watching the blue-tinted water circle the drain until it turned clear. When they were done, Quinn moved to dry off with the towel that had been wrapped around their shoulders, but Valerie beat them to it.

"Can I?" she asked, wiggling her fingers.

Quinn tipped their head in a small nod and closed their eyes.

With a whisper, Valerie called on her fire until she could feel her palms heating up above Quinn's head. Quinn released a small, shuddery breath when they felt the warmth, a reverent smile touching their lips in the mirror as steam rose from the tips of their hair. Valerie studied their joined reflection with something like awe. Here they were, standing beneath the harsh fluorescent light in a dingy college bathroom, Valerie in a paint-splattered tank top and Quinn with hair dye staining their ears—and despite the mundanity of the moment, for just a few seconds, the scene felt close to sacred. Maybe *because* it was so mundane. The more time she spent with Quinn, the clearer it became to Valerie how hazy her idea of friendship had been before. Now, slowly, the picture grew sharper in her mind, one 2:00 a.m., overcaffeinated, half-delirious hangout at a time. Maybe this was what friendship meant: an entire string of mundane moments that, linked together, formed something quietly magical.

By the time Valerie was done, Quinn's hair was left perfectly dry, a deeper blue than it had been before.

"Neat," Quinn commented, opening their eyes.

Valerie released a disbelieving laugh. She couldn't help but be charmed by Quinn's relationship with magic. The way they treated witchcraft wasn't that different from the way they approached pottery: although they weren't keen to get directly involved with it, they observed its mechanics with interest and could appreciate the art itself.

She flicked her finger against a curl that had fallen artfully onto Quinn's forehead. "Feel free to leave me five stars on Yelp."

"Of course. How else would I rate someone so skilled *and* humble."

"Exactly," Valerie agreed, picking up the bowl and brush.

As they made their way back to their room, she felt more settled than she had all day. She had a new thing to look forward to now, a new plan of action forming. If there was one place to find answers about her mother, a witch festival had to be it.

12

THREE OF CUPS

celebration — joy — community

Night had fallen by the time Rhia set off towards the meadow outside of town. She went alone—her family had left two hours earlier to help set up the Fall Festival while she'd still been busy working her weekend shift at Sugar & Spice.

As she made her way through the woods, she could barely see where she was going; the moon was hidden behind the trees that reached into the night sky, their branches intertwined above her like fingers laced together. Luckily, Rhia didn't need the light. She could blindly follow the indented path of dozens of feet that had walked before her, until the sound of the festivities grew louder. Laughter and music mixed with the crunching of leaves under her feet before at last the trees gave way to a clearing.

Rhia's shoulders relaxed the moment she stepped out of the thicket and took in the scene in front of her. A crackling fire in the middle of the meadow illuminated the faces of dozens of witches of all ages, some standing in groups, others sitting together in the tall grass or dancing. Five women were standing on a little stage, playing violins, flutes, and tambourines while they sang at the top of their lungs, filling the night air with a song that sounded as old as time itself.

Scattered across the meadow were different stands that had been set up during the day where one could buy food and drink, protection charms and potions, astrological forecasts and tarot readings. Obscura had a stall as well, but instead of Quinn, it was overseen by a member of the Lightbourns who owned the shop.

Rhia was searching for her family when she heard her cousin calling out to her. "Rhia, over here!"

Relieved, Rhia made her way over to where Holly and Tristan were lazing near the fire. "Hey." She sank into the grass where they were sitting. "Those flower crowns are pretty."

Tristan touched a hand to the petals in his hair, a self-satisfied grin on his face. He was one of the few non-witches around, but lying with his head pillowed on Holly's lap and a bag of toasted pumpkin seeds in his hand, he seemed to be enjoying himself thoroughly. "Thanks. Holly says it matches my eyes."

"It does!" Holly brushed a stray curl off his forehead before she lifted her gaze to beam at Rhia. "We got one for you as well." Reaching behind her, she procured another flower crown. Unlike Tristan's, which was made mostly from baby-blue periwinkles, and Holly's own crown, pink to match her hair, the one she handed to Rhia was made entirely from sunflowers.

Rhia obediently inched closer and let her cousin place it gingerly onto her hair. When she was done, Rhia leaned back on her hands and let her gaze wander over the clusters of witches around them. She spotted a few familiar faces she usually saw on this occasion—Marisol and Oscar Fairlove, who had moved away from Oakriver when she was little; Eleanor Brittlebone, the kind older lady who had gifted her her first ritual knife once Rhia was old enough to be trusted with a blade; Nicolas Saltmere, the charismatic founder of the Trans Witch Association—but the rest of her family was nowhere to be found.

"Grandma and your mom are over there," Holly said, pointing at a stand that sold herbs and other magical ingredients. "My mom is over there." She gestured at a group of women chattering away near the fire. "And Sage . . . well, she's everywhere at once, as per usual."

Rhia chuckled. Especially during the beginning of the festival, Sage was always terribly nervous, running back and forth across the clearing to make sure everything was perfect. It was usually around midnight, when she had tired herself out and gotten in one or two cups of hard cider, that she calmed down enough to sit down with the rest of them.

"Want some?" asked Tristan, extending the paper bag of pumpkin seeds to Rhia.

Rhia distractedly accepted, barely looking at him as he grabbed her hand and poured some into her palm. Her wandering eyes had caught on the fortune-telling stand. It was by far the busiest, a long line waiting while the witches behind the counter read tea leaves, shuffled tarot cards, swung pendulums, and threw rune stones.

Every year before the festival, there was an application form to be filled out by any witch willing to perform divination for others in exchange for a tip. Sage often volunteered. Rhia, on the other hand, was never asked, everyone aware that she wasn't like the rest of her family but like those lining up—witches who could not see past the present and relied on others to be their eyes.

Again, her traitorous brain conjured the image of Valerie. Rhia had almost believed she'd found someone to teach her what her sister could do in her sleep, only for it all to come crashing down amidst one ill-advised almost-kiss. Of course this was what happened the one time she did something without thinking. She should've known better than to have expected anything else.

"Hey." Holly poked her cheek. "Why the long face?"

"My face is a perfectly normal length," Rhia assured her.

"Mmm, no. This won't do." Holly nudged Tristan off her lap and got to her feet. "It's the *Fall Festival*, Rhia. We can't have you brooding all night!"

Tristan quickly sat up and righted the flower crown on his head.

"Come on." Holly extended a hand to both of them. "Let's dance!"

Rhia and Tristan both knew there was no arguing with Holly when she had a goal. They stood. On their way, they passed Sage. Holly clasped her wrist and pulled her along with them before she got a chance to resist.

"What's going on? What are we doing?" Sage asked, scrambling to keep up.

"Dance break," Tristan informed her.

By the time they made it over to the band, a larger crowd of witches had gathered before the stage, winding and swaying to the music. The women had just begun to play a more upbeat song, their voices bright as they sang at the top of their lungs.

Holly let out a delighted squeak and grabbed Rhia's hand to get her to move. Rhia tolerated it for a moment, gamely letting herself be twirled around. She always felt awkward dancing in public—her moves were more appropriate for the greenhouse or for dance intermissions in the kitchen while she waited for her dough to rise. But then she glanced around at all the women moving in their own strange ways and let herself get carried away by Holly's enthusiasm.

Her laughter mixed with the night air as she twirled, her head tilted back and her hands thrown over her head. With how the sky was spinning, she couldn't distinguish between the stars and the sparks of the fire, but both seemed like they were just within reach, near enough to close her fingers around if she just got onto her tiptoes. The skirt of her dress billowed around her as she moved. There was magic in this too; a precious kind of bond forged by music and dance and the witchcraft that hummed in each of their chests, burning brighter every time their feet struck the earth, perfectly synchronous. Rhia never felt more known than during this one night of the year, when she got to drop her mask and just *be*. As the music got faster and faster, the air crackled with the combined magic of a dozen witches, and for the first time in weeks, Rhia didn't think—she just gave herself to the music, to the night, to the unbridled joy bubbling up in her chest.

That was, until she collided with someone.

"Oh," she said, stumbling back. "I'm so—" The laughter died in her throat as she lifted her gaze and saw who it was she had run into.

Valerie was standing with her hands in the pockets of her jacket, staring at her with a look that Rhia couldn't decipher. While Rhia was frozen in shock, Valerie bent down to pick up the flower crown that had fallen to the ground. Carefully, and

Philline Harms

without ever taking her eyes off Rhia's face, she placed it back on Rhia's hair. "Hey."

Rhia didn't know what to say. The world was still spinning around her, a dizzy blur of color and noise. How had she ended up on the outskirts of the crowd? She could have sworn she had been right next to her family, but when she glanced over her shoulder, she saw they were a good few feet away from her, too caught up in the dance to notice that Rhia wasn't with them anymore.

With her heart in her mouth, Rhia turned to face the other girl again. In all the excitement of the event, she hadn't for a split second considered that Valerie might be here. Ever since she'd been a little girl, she had known the Fall Festival to be the one occasion where she could let down her guard with no need to worry about running into unexpected acquaintances from her everyday life. But of course that too was different now that Valerie had set foot in Oakriver.

"What . . . what are you doing here?" she stammered.

"Quinn told me about this. They said that every witch is welcome." Valerie jutted her chin forward as she said it, like she was expecting Rhia to object.

Instead, Rhia rushed out, "Okay. Have fun."

With that, she began to walk away, but she didn't get very far before fingers closed around her wrist. "That's it?"

With Valerie's fingers resting over her pulse point, Rhia suddenly found it very hard to find words. She opted for the cowardly option: she nodded.

Valerie studied her, the light of the fire only reaching one half of her face. It didn't matter—even in broad daylight, Rhia wouldn't have been able to read the look in her eyes. In the end,

Valerie did the same thing as Rhia had: she gave a simple nod and released Rhia's wrist.

In her wake, Rhia felt like she was rooted in place. She looked down at her wrist where Valerie's fingers had lingered a moment too long, her skin cold now that their touch was gone. She looked over at Tristan, Holly, and Sage, still dancing, the soft breeze carrying their laughter over to her. And then she looked straight ahead, at Valerie's silhouette growing smaller as she walked towards the tree line.

Before she could think too hard about what a horrendously stupid decision it was, Rhia started running. "Valerie, wait!"

Valerie immediately came to a halt. Rhia threw a glance over her shoulder. From where they were standing, she could see her mother and, a little farther away, her grandmother—which meant that they could see her too.

She looked at Valerie again. "Walk with me?"

Wordlessly, Valerie followed her into the thicket. Rhia walked and walked and walked, her long skirt snagging on roots and branches as she stumbled blindly ahead, Valerie trailing close behind her. It was only when the woods had swallowed the glint of the fire and the music was so quiet it might as well have been in her imagination that she turned around.

"I'm sorry," was the first thing she said, her voice as fragile as the fallen leaves crunching under her boots, "about avoiding you."

There was a beat of hesitation from Valerie. Then: "Is this because of what happened in the kitchen?"

"Yes." Rhia wished she could see Valerie's face, but the shadows were so thick she could make out nothing but her flaming-red hair, and that only when the moonlight reaching through the treetops hit it just right.

"Then I'm sorry too." There was a quiet rustling sound as she presumably shifted her weight from one foot onto the other. "I don't know how it even happened—us almost kissing—but if I had known that you'd react like this I would've never—"

Rhia blinked. "You think this is because we almost kissed?"

"Isn't it?" Now Valerie sounded slightly unsure.

"No, I—That's not what I regret," Rhia said, hoping that the heat in her cheeks didn't also seep into her words. "It's the fact that we shared magic."

"So it *was* an exchange."

"Yes. A failed one that shouldn't have happened."

The laugh that Valerie expelled was a breathy thing. "Oh, thank God. Here I was thinking that I was so repulsive you'd rather hide in the attic than see me."

"Valerie." The tone of Rhia's voice was enough to make the laughter die in Valerie's throat. "This isn't a joke. We both lost control over our abilities. This time it was just some lights flickering and water boiling over, but who knows what will happen next time?"

Silence again. Then a whispered spell and a flame flickering over both their faces, warm and bright enough to blind Rhia. When she could open her eyes again, Valerie was studying her intently. "You're scared."

"Yes," she whispered. "Why aren't you?"

"I never said I wasn't. But I don't believe in giving things up after just one try." Valerie looked down at the fire licking at the palm of her hand. "Otherwise, I wouldn't be able to do this."

"After just one try?" Rhia echoed. "You . . . you want to try again?"

"Yes." The flames in Valerie's hand grew restless, flickering as if they were itching to find something to ignite, to consume. With Valerie's eyes burning into hers, Rhia already felt like it: ignited, consumed.

There was something hot smoldering in Rhia's chest as she thought back to the night before, to her dreams and the tea leaves. *There are many possible interpretations for fire besides destruction. Things along the lines of passion, desire, transformation . . . infatuation.*

The leaves mirror your heart's desires, her grandmother had always told her. *They know the truth even if your head doesn't yet accept it.*

"Do you trust me?" Valerie softly inquired.

Last night, Rhia hadn't been sure she did. Yet here she was, standing in the middle of the woods with no one around but this strange girl. A girl whom she hadn't even known for two weeks; a girl who seemed to crack her open and see right inside without flinching at anything she encountered; a girl who held a flame a hairsbreadth away from her face. She knew how easy it would be to get burned by Valerie, but the flutter in Rhia's stomach had nothing to do with fear. "Yes," she said.

The flame gave another flicker, a gentle shower of sparks raining from Valerie's hand. "I'll be careful with you," she murmured, her eyes bright and uncharacteristically earnest. "I promise."

Rhia closed her eyes. "I know," she said—because, for whatever reason, she did.

A branch snapped as Valerie stepped closer, the world behind Rhia's eyelids growing dark as the fire vanished.

She waited, her heart pounding faster than the drums sounding in the distance. It skipped a beat when a hand came to rest on her cheek, warm against the skin that had previously only

Philline Harms

been caressed by the autumn chill. She could hear Valerie's shaky inhalation, feel her hair tickling her face—and then, finally, her lips finding Rhia's.

The kiss was achingly tender, both of them holding their breath as they waited for something to happen. Rhia could feel her magic simmering under her skin, *alive alive alive*, but this time none of it slipped outside her reach.

Resting her forehead against Valerie's, she released a relieved breath.

"Okay?" Valerie asked.

"So okay," Rhia agreed. And then she pushed Valerie up against the tree behind her and kissed her like she meant it.

Valerie's surprised gasp got lost in her mouth before her hands slid down to rest on Rhia's waist, their heat seeping through the fabric of her dress. When Rhia had imagined what it would be like to kiss Valerie, she'd expected her to taste like smoke and spices—instead, Valerie tasted sweet, like cinnamon and sugar, and she kissed like it too, soft and yielding.

Rhia often thought about the child she'd once been, running through the woods on bare feet, unafraid of stones and splinters, laughter loud enough to startle the birds from their perches in the treetops. Never thinking farther than the next bend of the path, the next tree to climb, the next cave to clamber into. Grinning at the universe with her teeth bared, trusting implicitly that it would always catch her when she fell.

It was with a start that she realized kissing Valerie made her feel closer to that girl than she had in years: hungry, eager, reckless to her core. It should have scared her, but if there was any anxiety, it was too quiet to be heard over the riotous pounding of her heart.

By the time they separated, Valerie had chased the October cold right out of her. Rhia had already done one stupid thing, and with her head still spinning and Valerie's breath on her lips, it was easy to do another.

"Do you want to go back to the festival?"

"You mean, together?"

"Yeah." She leaned forward to bump her forehead against Valerie's. "You wanted to find magic, right? Here it is."

"Okay." Valerie grabbed Rhia's hand, her voice trembling with barely concealed giddiness.

Back they went. When they broke through the tree line, Rhia was relieved to see that Grandma Deloris, Aunt Tanisha, and her mother had vanished, probably retreating into the small tent at the far end of the clearing for their Council meeting. Still, there were eyes everywhere, and the witch community was notoriously filled with gossip, so their first order of business was to head towards the stand that sold cloaks. Secretly, Rhia had always wanted to own one of them—now she finally had an excuse to buy the dark-green cape that she'd been making eyes at all evening. Only for sneaking purposes, of course. Valerie, predictably, went for one in dark red.

With their hoods pulled around their faces, they plunged back into the festival. Rhia's chest felt warm as she studied Valerie's expression while she drank in the stalls, fascinated by things that Rhia had long been accustomed to. It was bewitching, witnessing her childlike excitement over potions and rune stones, and the way her face lit up as she watched the fire performance that the Fairlove twins put on, as if she couldn't have done the same thing with her eyes closed. Impossibly, she made the festival seem even more magical.

They only made their way back into the woods when Rhia's feet had started to hurt, the sweetness of candied apples still lingering on her tongue. She looked over at Valerie just as she pushed off her hood, red hair spilling onto her shoulders. The sight was so captivating she almost forgot what she wanted to say; even the two older women standing at the side of the path abruptly ceased their conversation, eyes widening as they caught a glimpse of Valerie's face. Rhia barely suppressed an eye roll. Sure, their community was small, but that was no reason to stare at every newcomer like they'd just seen a ghost.

Shaking off her annoyance, Rhia cleared her throat. "Hey, Valerie?"

"Hmm?"

"I was wondering . . . do you want to sleep at my place?" When Valerie didn't respond right away, Rhia rushed to add, "You know, that way you won't wake up Quinn."

Valerie blinked at her, a little dazed, the air around them still humming with magic. Finally, a grin settled on her face, brighter than the fire at the festival, brighter than any flame she could've conjured. "Sure. Anything for Quinn."

It was all the encouragement Rhia needed to grab Valerie's hand and stumble onward, away from the festivities and into the dark.

If this was the way things were going to go up in flames, Rhia dizzily thought, then maybe she didn't mind burning all that much.

13

EIGHT OF CUPS

withdrawing — disappointment — walking away

For the first time since she'd come to Oakriver, Valerie woke up feeling rested. She hadn't dreamed or sleepwalked. There was no hair sticking to her neck from sweating through nightmares, and no residual anxiety from night terrors she couldn't recall. She didn't know if it was because of the bag of herbs she'd found under the pillow last night, the crystals on the bedside table, or simply because of the girl next to her. Rhia was still asleep, curled up on her side with a hand tucked under her cheek. She looked softer when she was like this—calm and unguarded, the ever-present furrow between her brows smoothed out.

Valerie could've tried to doze off again, but this close to Rhia, she was too giddy to go back to sleep. And, either way, she preferred witnessing the room around her come to life: the hazy morning light catching in the specks of dust lazily floating about, the quiet scratching at the door from one of the cats, the smell of smoke from the fire at the festival still clinging to their hair and mixing with the earthy scent of the plants that took up the majority of the room.

Last night, after they had made it back to Rhia's house, they had gone straight up the stairs to her room, despite having the entire house to themselves since Rhia's family had still been at the festival. Once the door had fallen shut behind them, they'd both been uncertain as to what to do. In the end, they'd settled on watching a movie on Rhia's laptop. Valerie wouldn't have been able to recount a single plot point for the life of her; she had, however, learned that Rhia was ticklish on the inside of her arm and that she liked having her neck kissed, which was a win in Valerie's book.

She was ripped out of her thoughts when Rhia shifted, followed by a quiet sigh that was muffled by the pillow. A moment later, her eyelashes fluttered and then her eyes opened, squinting into the bright light.

"Morning, pumpkin," Valerie said, her voice still rough with sleep.

Rhia stilled when her eyes focused. With both of them lying on their sides, their faces only inches apart, Valerie didn't miss the slight hitch in her breath. "Hey."

"Did you sleep well?" Valerie propped herself up on one elbow.

Rhia scrubbed a hand over her eyes. "Mm-hmm. What time is it?"

"Just after eleven."

Rhia nodded, her eyes falling shut again. Valerie barely bit back a smile. There was something terribly endearing about Rhia when she was like this, the creases of her pillow indented in her cheek and her features relaxed, her walls momentarily down.

Unthinkingly, Valerie reached out and tugged the blanket higher over Rhia's shoulder.

The warmth radiating from her body loosened up Valerie's tongue enough to say, "You look pretty when you sleep."

"Were you *watching* me?"

"Maybe," Valerie said without any shame. "Is that not allowed?"

"No. In this house, we actually have a strict no-staring policy."

"Is that so?"

"Mm-hmm."

Valerie tilted her head. "Is there also a no-morning-kiss policy?"

Rhia considered it for a moment, scrunching up her nose. "Yes. It doesn't apply to weekends, though."

"How convenient." Valerie chuckled.

She inched closer, one hand moving to cup Rhia's cheek, but before their lips could brush, a loud creak sounded from outside, and Rhia's eyes snapped open.

"Shit," she swore, abruptly sitting up. "It's Saturday."

Valerie blinked up at her, disoriented. "Yeah, no morning-kiss policy, remember—"

"You need to leave." Rhia cut her off, pulling the blanket off her. "My mom is cleansing the entire house, and she's gonna come in here any second—do you think you can leave through the window?"

"What?"

Rhia didn't respond, too busy grabbing the nearest items of clothing and tossing them at Valerie. "My grandma's going to kill me if she finds out you slept here. Come on, hurry."

Outside, the footsteps moved closer. Valerie finally snapped out of her daze and scrambled out of bed, rushing to pull on the clothes. Once she'd shrugged on her denim jacket, she darted over to where Rhia had already opened the window.

With her boots dangling from one hand, she swung her legs outside. She only paused to ask, "Wait—are we, like, a thing now?"

There it was again: the furrow between Rhia's brows. "What? No, we're just casual. Right?"

Valerie felt a little bit like she'd been punched in the face. "Okay. I mean, totally, just making sure. I'll . . . see you around then."

Throwing an anxious glance over her shoulder as if she was expecting her mother to come bursting through the door any second, Rhia only said, "Yeah."

Suddenly, Valerie couldn't get out of there fast enough, and she slid out the window without a second thought. The shingles were cold and damp beneath her sock-clad feet, but she barely took notice, moving quickly to the edge of the sloping roof. As she stared down at the grass underneath her, she could hear the window shutting behind her with horrifying finality.

This was fine. She was fine. Rhia wouldn't have told her to jump if she didn't think she could make it. Taking a deep breath, Valerie squeezed her eyes shut and leapt.

The impact came sooner than she'd expected, reverberating all the way into her shins. Whispering a heartfelt "Fucking hell," Valerie knelt, getting into her boots and lacing them up as fast as she could. With her socks damp with morning dew, it was a decidedly uncomfortable affair, but there was little to be done about it now. Her heart was still racing as she rushed towards the gate that led back into the street, turning her head once more to glance at Rhia's window before she—

"Whoa."

Valerie ground to a halt seconds before she collided with Tristan.

He regarded her with a bright smile, holding up a paper bag in his hand. "Are you not staying for breakfast? I got cinnamon buns from the bakery."

Valerie was far too rattled to form an intelligent reply. Falling down a roof did that to a girl. "Uh," she said, eloquent as ever. "No, thank you. I'm not a breakfast person." She pushed past Tristan before he could reply, moving down the street as fast as her aching legs would allow. The pain only began to subside when she had almost made it to Obscura. From the outside, it looked just as abandoned as it had the first time she'd stumbled upon it, but this time she pushed the heavy door open without hesitation.

With her eyes still adjusting to the dim light inside the shop, she blindly picked her way through the shelves until she could slump onto the counter.

At her dramatic groan, Quinn glanced up from their gaming console. "Hey. What happened to you?"

"Rhiannon Greenbrook," Valerie informed them.

Quinn's eyebrows lifted, their head disappearing for a moment as they crouched behind the counter. They reappeared with a cookie jar that they wordlessly handed to Valerie. "Barely anyone comes around this early. I have time."

Valerie miserably accepted the cookies and pushed aside a stack of invoices in order to sit down on the counter, her heavy boots propped on the edge of Quinn's chair. Even now, she still felt a dull throbbing behind her shins. Her free hand absentmindedly rubbed at her leg. "I don't even know where to begin."

"Begin at the festival," said Quinn, resting their chin in the palm of their hand. "How was it?"

Valerie thought for a moment, nibbling one of the cookies. They were the chewy ones with chocolate chips that Quinn sometimes baked when they felt like procrastinating. "It was a lot. I didn't expect there to be so many witches—I mean, hell, I was already surprised when I found out about Rhia's family. If someone had told me a month ago that I'd be going to a whole secret witch party, I would've never in a million years believed them." She paused, directing her gaze at Quinn again. "Have you ever been there?"

The look on Quinn's face was hard to make out in the half-light. "No. I'm not a witch, remember? There's no point in going."

Valerie frowned. Tristan wasn't a witch either, and he'd seemed to have a grand time. Instead of pointing this out, she dug another cookie out of the jar. "Anyway. The festival wasn't the true highlight."

"Go on." Quinn chuckled.

"We kissed. This time without all hell breaking loose, thankfully." Valerie's heart skipped a little beat at the memory. Making out with Rhia with her back pressed against a tree and Rhia's hands in her hair had to rank somewhere in her top three life moments. "After that, we went back to the festival, and then to her place."

"But if everything went so well, why are you here?"

Valerie lowered her gaze, focusing on brushing the crumbs

from her jeans and . . . *Rhia's* sweater. In all the chaos, it hadn't fully set in, but she was wearing Rhia's sweater. God.

"She kicked me out because her mom was about to walk in. And she said she only wants this to be a casual thing."

"How do you feel about that?" Quinn carefully asked.

Valerie almost snorted. Quinn's mom was a therapist—apparently, she'd passed on some of her catchphrases along with a deep-rooted need to help.

"It's fine. I mean, it's better to have someone sometimes than not at all, right?"

"I don't know. Is it?"

Valerie laughed, but only because she felt like she might cry if she didn't. "Jesus Christ, Quinn. You're really getting in the way of me convincing myself that this is okay here."

"What about your mom?" Quinn inquired. "That was the main reason you went to the festival, right? Did you find out anything about her?"

"No." Valerie averted her eyes, staring at her beaten-up boots instead. "There was no one there who looked like her. And after I ran into Rhia, I was a bit distracted." How stupid, to get so caught up in a girl she'd only known a few weeks. The festival had been her biggest shot at finding answers, and she'd spent it making out in the woods and playing dress-up between stalls. An hour ago, she would've called it time well spent, but now, with Rhia's words—*just casual*—still ringing in her ears, she wasn't so sure.

Quinn gave her knee a comforting squeeze, but before they could speak, a jingle from the bell above the door made both of them sit up straighter. Together, they watched as a silhouette entered, backlit at first, then blurring into the darkness of the shop. Valerie could make out her face only when the woman had almost reached the counter.

"Good morning," she said. Her voice was low and rich, smooth like silk. "I bought a dozen altar candles at the festival yesterday but didn't want to carry them around all night. Helen said they would be available to pick up here this morning?"

"Oh, yes, she left a note about that." Quinn got to their feet. "Just one moment."

Valerie could see them scurrying into the back room from the corner of her eye—her gaze, however, was fixed on the woman in front of her. She was tall and pale and looked like she was in her thirties. Even in the gloomy shop, her copper hair shone as it spilled over her shoulders.

In Quinn's absence, the silence stretched. Valerie *knew* she was staring, but she couldn't tear her eyes away. Looking at the woman filled her with a shock similar to the impact of jumping off the roof, only times ten.

When the silence became too awkward to bear, the woman crossed her arms in front of her chest and said, "So . . . do you also work here?"

Valerie couldn't get her words to cooperate. She wanted to ask a million questions. She wanted to conjure up a flame and hold it closer to the woman's face to see if she could find herself in her emerald eyes, the slope of her nose. In the end, all she could do was shake her head, her tongue heavy in her mouth, and the moment slipped through her fingers before it had ever been truly within reach.

Reappearing at Valerie's side, Quinn handed the woman her box. "Here you go!"

She nodded, a relieved smile on her face as she accepted

it and turned. Still reeling, Valerie sat frozen while the woman crossed the store and stepped outside. It was only after a few seconds, when the door had fallen shut, that she snapped out of her daze.

"Valerie—" Quinn began, but Valerie didn't stay to listen. She simply pushed the cookie jar into their arms and ran.

Her aching legs protested as she sprinted towards the end of the alleyway, but by the time she reached the main street, the woman was nowhere to be seen. "Damnit," she whispered. There were other curses lined up behind that first one, but they were cut short by the buzzing of her phone.

The caller ID made her stomach seize up. Talk about perfect timing. Did he have some kind of sixth sense that always let him know exactly when it was a horrible moment to call? Reluctantly, she held the phone to her ear. "Hi, Dad."

"Valerie. How are you?" His voice sounded as gruff as she remembered, weighed down by the weary undertone that was ever-present whenever they spoke. Which wasn't often. The last time he'd called was almost two weeks ago, and it had only been to ask if she'd received the money he'd sent through. Really, the tuition transfers and Valerie's short thank-you messages were the only correspondence between them, which made this random phone call all the odder.

"Fine," she said, even though nothing about this morning felt very *fine* at all. "What's up?"

"Nothing. Can't a dad call his daughter just to chat? What have you been up to lately?"

Valerie exhaled. "Not much. Just studying. Getting settled. There was this witch festival yesterday that I went to with—"

"Hang on, what?" There was a noise that sounded like a

coffee cup being set down with too much force. Valerie could feel the lecture coming even before he launched into it. "Valerie, I thought we agreed that you are there to *study*, not get caught up in more of this occult nonsense."

"I don't remember agreeing to that."

"Oh, for the love of—" He cut himself off. In the background, children's voices rose over the clinking of cutlery. When he spoke again, his tone was quieter, infuriatingly level despite the frustration still simmering beneath the surface. "I want you to be very careful about the friends you make in that town, Valerie. If I see any of this affecting your grades, we'll have to talk about transferring schools."

Valerie tried to bite down on the next words with all her might, but they slipped through her teeth all the same, ugly and dripping with venom. "You know I wouldn't be here if it wasn't for you, right? If you'd tell me *anything* about her and not just pretend she never existed, then maybe I wouldn't have to go on a goddamn scavenger hunt."

"Valerie, I—"

"No." She cut him off. "You have no right to keep her to yourself. And you have no right to criticize me now that I'm going out and finding her myself."

Silence.

"What about the rest of the family?" Valerie demanded. "She has sisters, doesn't she? Aunts. Even if she isn't, one of them must still be living here. What's their address?"

"I can't tell you."

Valerie felt her lungs growing tight. For the first time, she spoke the horrible suspicion that had haunted her for weeks now. "You don't even *want* me to find them, do you? You're hoping

I'll find it all useless and come back empty-handed. You only let me come here to get it out of my system so we can go back to normal."

At the other end of the line, her father's breathing fell out of its steady rhythm. His next sentence sounded rehearsed. "I don't know what you want me to say here."

"*Anything.* Tell me where to search. Tell me about the rest of the family, where to find them. Tell me her favorite spots around Oakriver. Hell, tell me her favorite color. Just . . . anything."

The silence dragged on so long she was afraid he wouldn't answer. The domestic sounds of a family breakfast continued, radio chatter and her father's new wife chiding one of her sons for getting crumbs all over the table. Valerie wanted to scream at the injustice of it all. Finally, he said, so quietly his phone barely picked it up, "Her favorite color was maroon. Not all shades of red, but maroon, she liked."

"Thank you, Dad. That's great." Valerie's breath caught in a way that sounded painfully close to a sob. *Was.* Past tense. Why did he always talk about her in past tense? "You should join your real family for breakfast now." With that, she hung up.

Alone in the alley, her breathing echoed loud and jagged. To stop herself from crying, she pressed her fingers to her eyes hard enough to see dancing colors. The image of the Knight of Swords she'd pulled a few days ago flashed in her mind. She hated that a single call from him could turn her into this: charging forward in full armor, slicing and stabbing without pausing to consider which vulnerable parts she was striking. Her palms felt hot. She wondered if her mother was like this as well—if she too was an angry crier, or if she knew how not to reduce entire conversations to ashes in the heat of the moment.

Dropping her hands, she looked back at Obscura. Quinn was probably wondering what was taking her so long, but she couldn't go back now, not with her eyes red-rimmed and her blood still boiling. Valerie couldn't possibly explain what it felt like, chasing after the ghost of her mother while her father held all the answers hostage. She couldn't explain what it was like to constantly pick herself apart and study every piece, wondering *Is this me? Is this him? Is this you is this you is this you?*

She was so sick of all the question marks. Sick of the envy that churned in her stomach every time Quinn came back from a cooking class still faintly trailing their mother's perfume. Sick of sitting in a hacked family tree with not even the faintest understanding of her roots, nothing but her own magic and the very man who held the axe to rely on for guidance.

She was just so goddamn tired.

And so, she left the shop behind and walked back to the dorms instead. As she did, she pulled her jacket tighter around herself, tugging the sleeves of the sweater over her knuckles. The wool was softer than any item of clothing she owned, and when she closed her eyes, she could smell Rhia on it—an earthy scent with sweet undertones that made her traitorous heartbeat stumble.

Valerie was so fucked.

14

TWO OF SWORDS

tension — indecision — difficult choices

Three days passed in a daze of vague anticipation. Rhia hadn't heard from Valerie again after her rushed exit on Saturday, but that didn't stop her from perking up whenever the bell chimed above the door of the café or when a set of boots made their way up the stairs to the bookshop. She probably looked ridiculous, craning her neck every time in hopes of spotting Valerie, only to deflate when it was someone else. She sure *felt* ridiculous—she'd made Valerie climb out the *window*, for goodness' sake. It would be a bigger miracle than the existence of magic itself if Valerie went out of her way to see her again anytime soon.

All her pent-up anxiety had reached its peak. She could hardly concentrate on the cakes she was supposed to arrange in the display, much less retain any of the orders she was told. In the late afternoon, a mailman carried in a delivery of new books, and this time, instead of pretending she didn't see it or begging Tristan to take care of it, she marched right up to it. The box was so heavy that her arms began to tremble right away, but she gritted her teeth and continued. This was good. Physical strain meant that she had something to focus on that wasn't the look on Valerie's face when Rhia had told her to leave.

She almost let out a yelp when, halfway up the stairs, Tristan's voice suddenly sounded from right in front of her. "Hold on," he exclaimed. "Am I seeing things? Or is Rhia Greenbrook really taking care of a book delivery unprompted?"

"Shut up," she panted without any heat and tried to push past him.

Instead of stepping out the way, he reached for the cardboard box.

"Hey!" Rhia called out, hurrying after him as he easily took two steps at a time, carrying her only distraction away with him.

After a glance into the contents of the box, Tristan lugged the books into the very back of the shop. The shelves weren't arranged by genre but by mood—this section was labeled "Dark & Stormy" and held mostly thrillers, mysteries, and crime novels. *Fitting*, Rhia cynically thought as they came to a halt. Out loud, she said, "I could've done that myself."

"Tumble down the stairs and give yourself a concussion is what you could've done," Tristan said mildly as he set the box down in the middle of the aisle. Straightening, he gave Rhia a once-over. "You okay?"

"Yeah. Just stressed."

"You know you could just go and see her?" Tristan asked. "You don't have to wallow and wait for her to show up."

"I don't think she wants to see me," Rhia murmured, rubbing a hand over her eyes. They felt itchy and dry from hours of tossing in bed the night before.

Tristan grimaced in response. Neither of them was particularly good at problem-solving, especially when the problem had to do with feelings—that was where Holly tended to come in. Still, he tried, suggesting, "Maybe do, like, a love spell?"

"Tris, those are highly unethical. I'm not going to take away someone's free will—"

"I didn't mean that," he quickly said. "I mean the kind that Holly does. Self-love spells. So that you can be a little more confident and go get your girl."

Despite herself, Rhia felt a small smile crossing her face. "You know a lot about those spells, huh?"

"Well, yeah." He reached into his collar to show her the little charm hidden underneath. It was a tiny piece of rose quartz that dangled from what otherwise looked like a plain silver necklace. "Holly gave me this one a few weeks ago. So I have more confidence before lacrosse games and make captain next season. It's also supposed to ward off bad vibes because I'm an empath or something?"

Rhia didn't know whether to laugh or cry. "What on earth—you two are *literally* perfect for each other."

Tristan let the crystal disappear under his hoodie again. "Pretty much, yeah. So . . . can I leave you on your own here, or are you going to keep self-destructing?"

"I'm okay." Rhia sighed. "I just need to get out of my head for a bit, I think."

"All right. I'll be downstairs if you need anything." He paused to press a short kiss into her hair, the gesture so tender that all Rhia could do was blink. Then, he was off. Left alone in the aisle, Rhia turned around and got to work.

Putting away the novels was a mindless task, but that was

what she needed—taking out the books, finding the author's name, and alphabetically sorting them into their correct places made sense in a way nothing else did right now.

She was so engrossed in her work that the sound of heavy boots nearing her didn't register until they came to a halt right next to her. "Hey."

Rhia startled so violently she almost dropped the book. "Oh," she breathed. "Hey."

After thinking about her for the last three days, seeing Valerie in person was like staring into the sun. With her red hair tousled and her cheeks flushed from the cold, she looked like the personification of autumn—the crisp, cinnamon-scented kind that Rhia longed for all year. Just studying her, something inside her chest ached.

"I, um. Wanted to give you back your sweater," Valerie said without looking at her.

Rhia's gaze fell to the dark-green fabric she was clutching in her hands. Valerie was here because she was too polite to steal her clothes, not because she had been itching to see her like Rhia had.

Trying to keep her disappointment from showing on her face, she accepted the sweater and tossed it into the half-empty cardboard box at her feet. "Thanks."

Valerie buried her hands in the pockets of her jacket again. Rocking back and forth on her feet, her eyes darting aimlessly around the aisle, she asked, "It's okay that I came here, right?"

"Why wouldn't it be?"

"I don't know. We're not anything serious, so . . . I don't want to bother you at work."

"You're not bothering me," Rhia quietly said. While Valerie

studied the floor, Rhia studied her. Even in the dim light, she could tell how dark the circles under her eyes were. "Have you been sleeping?"

"I tried." Swallowing, Valerie rubbed a hand over her eyes. "I keep waking up in the middle of the night. I haven't sleepwalked again, but I'm still so *restless*. I don't know." She broke off.

"I'm sorry," Rhia said. Before she could stop herself, she added, "I've had trouble sleeping as well."

Valerie's lips attempted to quirk into a smile. "What, did you forget to cast a circle? Are you haunted now as well?"

"Only by you," Rhia said. It was supposed to be a joke, but truth added a weight to her words that made them sound like the opposite.

At last, Valerie's eyes settled on her face. Her gaze was so heavy it felt almost like a touch in itself. Her teeth were biting her lower lip and—God, Rhia remembered how Valerie's teeth had felt biting *her* lip, and she couldn't take it anymore.

Without a second thought, she grabbed Valerie's hand and tugged her along to the very end of the aisle where a door opened into a tiny storage room. Valerie went with her easily, kicking the door shut behind her while the single light bulb hanging from the ceiling flickered to life. There was a split second of hesitation, an awkward dance as they figured out how best to fit into the cramped space. Then Rhia's back hit the door and Valerie's mouth was on hers and every coherent thought left her head.

Valerie kissed her like Rhia was water and she'd been thirsty for years, both hands holding on to her face as her body pressed her against the door. Rhia was glad for it; she felt like she would have simply collapsed without anything to steady her, her hands helplessly clutching Valerie's shoulders. With her fingers curled into the sturdy denim of Valerie's jacket, Rhia's world narrowed down to nothing but the heat rolling off Valerie's body, the cold metal of her rings against Rhia's cheek—

And then, a flicker of magic that started as a prickle on the back of her neck before traveling down into her arms and then farther. Rhia could feel it rushing through her, but by then it was too late. It sparked from her fingertips to her feet and disappeared into the wooden floorboards before she could stop it.

Valerie made a small noise of surprise; Rhia's eyes snapped open just in time to see the light bulb flicker and then die with one last sizzling sound.

"Sorry," Rhia gasped. "Sorry, that was me. Did I hurt you?"

"I'm okay," came the breathless affirmation. "Really, it just felt like a tiny electric shock."

Rhia let her head fall against the door with a thud. Inhaling shakily, she breathed in the scent of soil and morning dew—the smell of her own magic, one that she had only ever known in the confines of her home.

Valerie seemed too startled to even think about conjuring any light to see by. Instead, her fingers blindly found Rhia's cheek, tilting her face. "Are *you* okay?"

"Yeah," she whispered. Her mother's voice echoed in her head again: *It usually happens in moments of very high emotions.* What was *wrong* with her?

"Sorry," Valerie quietly said.

Rhia shook her head. "It's not your fault. That was all me."

Valerie was silent for a few seconds, her palm still resting against Rhia's cheek. She immediately missed its warmth when it fell away and Valerie murmured, "I should probably go."

Rhia wanted to disagree, wanted to cling to her and tell her to stay. Instead, she nodded and stepped away from the door, pulling it open as if the act didn't feel like ripping off a limb.

Valerie stopped to press one last barely-there kiss to Rhia's temple. A heartbeat later, the door fell shut again, and her footsteps receded.

Rhia waited in the tiny space, still thick with magic she hadn't intended to unleash, until she was sure that Valerie had left. When she finally stepped out into the aisle, she was so caught up in her thoughts that she didn't notice how dark the bookshop was. Only when she was halfway down the stairs and took in the scene in front of her did the realization hit: the entire café was dark. Tristan was hastily distributing candles at every table; their flickering glow was the only thing illuminating the bewildered faces of the patrons. Without the whirring of the coffee machine, the room was eerily quiet.

With a lump in her throat, Rhia walked up to the counter where her boss was standing. "Sorry, Anne. I was upstairs."

The older woman nodded distractedly, her hip leaning against the counter. "Strange," she mused, gesturing out the window at the brightly lit storefront of the boutique across the street. "The rest of the town still seems to have power."

"Must have been a short circuit," Rhia said, her voice so quiet she wasn't certain Anne even heard her. She didn't stay to make sure—instead, she grabbed the second box of candles and turned, avoiding Tristan's glances as she clumsily moved between the tables. The lights flickered back on a few minutes later, but the jittery feeling in Rhia's chest remained.

~

Philline Harms

The rest of the day dragged. Rhia's smile fell the moment she left Sugar & Spice to walk home. The evening was dark and clammy, dead leaves rustling under the heavy fall of her boots as she wandered through the puddles of orange light the streetlights provided.

There was a heaviness in her chest—a combination of the incident in the storage closet, her own exhaustion after a long workday, and the ever-present awareness of nature that forced itself onto her. With her connection to the earth came the unfortunate side effect of having a front-row seat to its quiet suffering. There were days when she wanted to cry because she could *feel* it: the way the leaves choked on pollution, the ache that settled into scorched land where trees had stood for centuries, the sickness that had crept into the ecosystem and that spread with every passing year. Normally, it was easier to ignore; it was only in moments like this, when she was already gloomy and a little bit self-pitying, that it became quite so present.

Fumbling for her keys in her coat pocket, she heaved herself up the steps to her family home. She was lacking magic. That was probably it. As with most things in nature, there was a limit to her powers. Her magic wasn't a bottomless well—it was one that could run dry and required time to fill up again, drop by tedious drop.

In accidentally releasing magic at Sugar & Spice, Rhia had lost far more than felt comfortable. At dinner, she barely managed to finish her plate, and when her mother asked if she wanted to try out a new baking spell with her, she only shook her head. Instead, she changed out of her work clothes, huddled under several blankets, and pulled up *Practical Magic*. For comfort purposes. Also, for Sandra Bullock.

She hadn't gotten past the first twenty minutes before she got distracted. It was hard to focus on anything when her lips still remembered the softness of Valerie's, her hand the brush of her fingertips. In the low light of her bedroom, Rhia studied her palm. What was it that Valerie had said? *The head line. . . much more prominent for you.* It was true, wasn't it? That was the reason they were in this mess. Rhiannon Greenbrook couldn't let herself fall without thinking. No emotion passed through her system without being dragged under the microscope, labeled, and filed away. No intuition could be followed without reasoning.

Rhia was sure that if she were to look at Valerie's palm, she would find a heart line deeper than her life line, deeper than any human ought to have.

A knock at the door made her hand drop limply back into her lap. "Are you doing spell work, or is it okay to come in?"

With a sigh, Rhia reached out and paused the movie. "You can come in."

The door flew open and Holly strode inside, flinging herself onto Rhia's bed hard enough to bounce slightly off the mattress. Sage followed at a more leisurely pace, gently closing the door behind her before she sank down on Rhia's other side.

Reluctantly, Rhia shut her laptop and set it down on her bedside table. "What's going on?"

"An intervention," Holly declared.

"There's nothing to intervene," Rhia said, rubbing a hand over her eyes.

Holly's eyes immediately zeroed in on the motion. She reached out to tug at Rhia's sleeve. "Cute sweater," she pointedly said. "Did Valerie leave it here when you snuck her out of the house the other day?"

Rhia froze. It *was* Valerie's sweater, a dark-red turtleneck that smelled like smoke and night air and fell past her knuckles if she didn't push it up to her elbows. On one sleeve, there were specks of green paint, and the hem was frayed. Rhia shouldn't have found wearing it as comforting as she did.

Picking at one of the loose threads, she asked, "Did Tristan tell you that?"

"Maybe?"

"Of course he did," she said darkly. "Traitor."

"Hey," said Sage, her hand rubbing reassuring circles on Rhia's back, "we can see that you're not doing too well. Maybe we can help."

"Yeah." Holly peered up at Rhia from where she was lying on her belly, her chin cradled in one hand. "Come on, little bug, you know you can talk to us about anything. What's wrong?"

Sitting between them on her bed, both of them looking at her expectantly, Rhia felt unbearably small. *So much* felt wrong, she didn't know where to start, didn't know how to find words to describe the visceral fear that lingered in the pit of her stomach. In the end, all she managed was a faint: "I like Valerie. Like . . . a lot."

"Okay," Sage calmly said. "And?"

"And I don't think I should." Holly opened her mouth, but Rhia cut her off. "Not because she's a girl or whatever. But because it's dangerous. *We're* dangerous when we're together."

"What do you mean?" The frown on Sage's face was the same one she wore when she was trying to put together a schedule for an elaborate event or when she was brewing a potion that required extremely precise measurements. Her sister was good at narrowing her focus onto one thing at a time. It felt strangely reassuring to stand in the center of her attention knowing she wouldn't let up until they'd found a solution.

"Do you promise not to tell Mom or Grandma about this?" Rhia asked.

They both nodded.

"There's this thing that sometimes happens with her that has never happened to me before. Sometimes when we kiss—"

"Oh my God, you've *kissed*?"

"Holly," Sage reprimanded, pantomiming zipping her mouth closed. Holly rushed to do the same before motioning for Rhia to continue.

"Sometimes when we kiss there's this accidental release of magic," Rhia finished. "It's like a mini explosion or something. Lights flicker, pots boil over. Today I caused a short circuit in the café, and the electricity didn't come back for twenty minutes."

Holly unzipped her mouth to throw in the important addition, "Damn. Talk about sparks flying."

"It's not funny," said Rhia, hugging her knees closer to her chest. "It scares the hell out of me."

"Understandable," Sage said. "But you said it happens *sometimes*. That means there are also times you can control it, right?"

"Yeah. I think the first time was because I was so surprised she wanted to kiss me. And today it happened because I was so relieved she still wanted to see me."

"Why would she not?" Holly asked.

Rhia buried her face in her hands, the words coming out muffled from between her fingers. "After she slept here, I kind of panicked and told her I wanted things to be casual. And then when Mom was about to come in, I made her leave through the window."

"Why do you only want something casual with her?" Sage inquired, smoothly brushing past the almost-making-Valerie-break-her-neck part. "Not that there's anything wrong with that. It just always seemed like you were yearning for someone to be with, but now that love is coming your way, you turn and run in the other direction."

Rhia was quiet for a moment, her right thumb tracing the heart line in her left palm as if she could deepen it through sheer willpower. In a voice like sandpaper, she finally said, "I guess . . . if I don't let her get too close to begin with, I can never really lose her."

Sage's face softened. They both knew what loss felt like—that constant shadow, a weight they carried wherever they went. Similarly to Rhia's grief over Mother Nature, it was sometimes easy to ignore, almost like it wasn't there at all, while other days it was all she could seem to feel. Rhia hated it, but not as much as she hated the thought of her losses growing, of another stone added to her pockets to weigh her down. It was the reason her one real friend, outside her family, was Tristan, and even that was only because he had latched on to her in the first grade and simply refused to let go.

Valerie was similar in that regard, now that Rhia thought about it. Where Rhia built a wall, Valerie was like ivy, climbing undeterred and slipping through the cracks that Rhia had missed. And Rhia was so tired of pushing back. Because Sage was right: she did crave to be held and to be understood and to be wrapped up in something other than the magic she tried to fill the empty spaces in her life with. She craved it so much she sometimes felt sick with it.

Quietly, with so much understanding in her voice it felt like she had heard all of Rhia's thoughts, Sage asked, "What is she like?"

"She's a menace. I don't know anyone as reckless as her." Rhia rested her chin on her knee. "But she's also really sweet. And curious and charming and funny. And even though we're both difficult people, it's easy with her. Sometimes. When things aren't blowing up."

"What kind of witch is she?" Holly inquired.

"She's incredible at divination," Rhia said. "Even though she had to teach herself everything. And she has fire magic."

"That's hot."

"Literally." Rhia chuckled. "Being in bed with her is like sleeping next to a breathing furnace—"

Holly scrambled to sit up, jabbing an accusatory finger at the mattress. "Oh my God, did you get it on in this bed?"

"What?"

"Did you?!"

"We didn't do anything! We haven't even gone on a proper date yet—"

"You could change that," Sage pointed out. She was still leaning against the bedframe, an amused smile on her face.

"Oh, that reminds me!" said Holly. "Tristan and I want to go up to his mom's cabin next weekend. You should totally ask Valerie to come with!"

"And immediately subject her to embarrassing conversations like this? No, thank you," Rhia said. When Holly pouted, she relented. "I'll think about it. First, I have to make sure I didn't actually scare her off with my little light performance at the café."

Sage let out a snort. "I think you making her climb out the window would've already done that."

"God, I made her jump from the *roof*," Rhia whined. "I'm horrible."

"Yes, you are." Holly patted her knee. "But she still came back, didn't she?"

"Yeah. I guess she did."

"If that isn't all the confirmation you need to know that she's into you, then what is?"

Rhia gave a tentative nod. Maybe they were right. Maybe things weren't all *that* awful.

Sensing that they had reached their goal, Sage and Holly exchanged satisfied grins. A moment later, Holly levitated the laptop over from the nightstand and stretched out next to Rhia as if they'd been planning to have a movie night all along. Sage stayed seated and pulled Rhia's head into her lap, her fingers cool against her scalp as she absentmindedly braided her curls.

When Rhia's eyes started to drift shut halfway into the movie, neither of them commented. Nestled between them, Rhia could feel the hollow in her chest slowly filling with magic again, hear the rain tapping gently against the window, smell Valerie on the soft sweater that swallowed her—and for the first time that day, fear loosened its grip on her.

15

THE FOOL

new beginnings — courage — leap of faith

Valerie was spiraling.

She was sitting in her room, and all she could think about was Rhia. She couldn't focus on anything else: not her painting, not the incident at Obscura, not even the argument with her father and his subsequent generic apology text. Instead, images of Rhia fogged up every inch of her brain, rendering every other thought blurry and hard to grasp.

Valerie *hated* it.

She'd agreed to keeping things casual. What she'd forgotten at that moment was that she'd never done anything casually in her life, ever. She wasn't casual when it came to painting, staying up into the early-morning hours with her back aching and fingers cramping, running on nothing but caffeine and spite. She wasn't casual when it came to wondering about her mother; she'd moved towns, for fuck's sake, even at the risk of finding only bread crumbs. And she most definitely wasn't casual now, having a goddamn crisis over a girl she'd only known for a few weeks. It didn't help that the piece she was working on right now was another one to add to her series on power, another painting that showed two women kissing, one pushing the other up against a wall. The hands cupping her face were supposed to look tender, but somehow that had gotten lost in translation when her brush had touched the canvas. Now it looked different—not rose petals and a whisper of a touch but a fuse and a spark.

Desperate, Valerie thought as she glared at it from where she sat, cross-legged on the floor of her dorm room. The two figures looked desperate. Just like the way she'd kissed Rhia in the storage room the day before. Just like she'd been feeling ever since that moment in her kitchen.

With every brushstroke, another image of Rhia flickered in her brain, like a fire she couldn't put out. Rhia dancing at the Fall Festival, her arms raised and her face washed in moonlight. Rhia in the greenhouse, all quiet joy as she drifted between the plants, talking to them as if it was the most natural thing in the world. Rhia in her bed, her face nestled against Valerie's shoulder, her shirt riding up with every breath to expose a glimpse of a soft tummy. Groaning, Valerie dropped her brush into the paint water and slumped onto her back. She wished Quinn were there so she had someone to ramble to, but they were stuck in some graphic design class in another building.

Her one consolation, she thought as she stared up at the cracks in the ceiling, was that Rhia hadn't run away again when she'd come to find her at the café. Stolen moments in a storage room weren't much, but they were better than nothing. Valerie no longer even cared about finding out more about magic from her. She was willing to spend all her money on overpriced coffee if that was what it took to see Rhia once a day.

The sound of the door opening interrupted her in her wallowing. Craning her head back, she watched, still star-fished on the floor, as Quinn entered the room. They paused when their eyes fell on Valerie, head tilting to meet her gaze. "Hello. Comfortable?"

"No," Valerie miserably said. She didn't move to sit up. "How was class?"

"Oh, you know. About as soul-crushing as usual." Coming to stand above Valerie, Quinn nudged her shoulder with the tip of their Doc Marten. "Is this about Rhia or about art?"

"Neither," Valerie said. A beat later, she reconsidered. "Both." She limply lifted a hand to point at the half-finished painting balanced precariously against her bed. "Does that look casual to you?"

Quinn regarded the two figures with a wince. Instead of responding to Valerie's question, they sank down cross-legged next to her and opened their messenger bag. After a few seconds of rifling through it, they procured a see-through plastic container. "I made chow mein in the kitchen earlier," they offered. "Want some? I could also whip up the pasta you like? Or some more chocolate chip cookies?"

"Chow mein is good," Valerie said pitifully. Quinn was one of the few people who used the community kitchen for something other than ramen and microwave popcorn. One simply didn't pass up the chance of home-cooked food when in college, no matter one's emotional distress. As Quinn dropped some noodles and a crispy piece of tofu into her waiting mouth, Valerie felt distinctly like a baby bird being fed. She found she quite liked the idea. Baby birds didn't have to worry about missing mothers and cowardly fathers. And baby birds definitely didn't get their hearts crushed by five-foot-three witches with commitment issues.

Neither of them spoke as Quinn alternated between eating and feeding Valerie, both comfortable in the silence. It was only once the container was empty that Quinn murmured, "I wish they'd do something about the pipes in this dorm."

"What d'you mean?"

"The dripping." Quinn gestured vaguely. "I couldn't sleep last night because of it, it's so loud."

Valerie strained her ears. As hard as she tried, she couldn't make out anything but her and Quinn's breathing layered over the usual bustling of the dorms. "I don't hear it."

Quinn froze. "Oh God. Do you think there's a tinnitus that sounds like dripping water?"

"It's all those extra hours you work at Obscura," Valerie accused. "You need to chill a little."

"*You* want to tell *me* about being chill?" Quinn snorted. The words were softened by the way they'd started playing with Valerie's hair, careful not to catch the strands on their rings as they ran their fingers through them.

"I just don't know what to do." Valerie turned a little so her head was resting in Quinn's lap, her cheek squished against their thigh. "I can't figure out if she likes me or if she's just going along with it, you know?"

"Have you asked the cards?"

A small shiver ran down Valerie's arms as she glanced at the stack of tarot cards on her nightstand. "I have."

"And? What'd they say?"

"Nothing."

"You mean nothing you could understand?"

"No." With a sigh, Valerie pulled herself into a sitting position and grabbed the stack. Shuffling them with quick, practiced flicks of her wrist, she explained, "I don't think they're responding to my questions. No matter what I ask, it's always the same card."

"Really? Which one?"

Instead of answering, Valerie spread the cards out on the floor in front of her. She didn't even have to pull one—out of all seventy-eight cards, one was already sticking out, eager to be picked up. With a sinking feeling, Valerie turned it over.

The Moon.

"It's always this one?" Quinn asked, leaning closer to study the hand-painted motif. In more traditional decks, the card showed the image of a dog and a wolf howling at the moon, a river flowing past them. When Valerie had painted it two years ago, she'd reimagined it to fit what she intuitively saw when she thought of the card. It was a woman, standing waist-deep in a body of water. Her hair spilled onto her shoulders in loose waves as she stared straight at the viewer, the look in her wide eyes unreadable. Behind her rose a full moon, its pale light hollowing out her features. "What does it mean?"

"I'm not sure." Valerie tucked the card back into the stack to shuffle with the others. "It's one of the few cards I can never quite grasp. There are some that resonate with me so clearly— like Strength, or the Knight of Wands, or the Fool—but then there are others that are slippery."

She paused again, plucking out another card at random. The Moon.

While she studied it, Quinn got up and picked up the book sitting atop Valerie's desk. It was the first tarot handbook she'd bought after discovering her abilities—a thing made of yellowed pages, the smell of the antiques shop where she'd found it still clinging to the brittle paper.

"'In the dark of the night, the light of the Moon brings clarity,'" Quinn read. "'When this card appears, we are going beyond the boundaries of the known. Powerful energies call for us to tap into our subconscious. We may feel the pull of things that are unseen, recurring themes that connect our present to our past. Spend time exploring your dreams and pay attention to the cycles in your life. Channel the energy of the Moon as she goes through her phases. Face the fears that are dredged up during this time and trust in your intuition—there are hidden truths to be uncovered within ourselves that will only reveal themselves to those who look.'" Quinn made a face and set the book down. "Wow. That is unbelievably unspecific."

"I know, right?" Valerie pointed at the cards. "You try one."

Quinn sank to their knees in front of Valerie and accepted the stack she handed them. They shuffled for a few seconds, a look of intense concentration on their face. Imitating what Valerie had done, they spread out the cards and turned one over.

"Judgment," Valerie grimly observed. "Not the cards, then."

"Maybe you just need to manifest Rhia making a decision," said Quinn, who, despite having no practical experience, knew half the magical handbooks at Obscura by heart. "You know, law of attraction and all that."

"Right." Valerie squeezed her eyes shut. "Rhiannon Greenbrook will be so in love with me. She'll—"

"You need to use present tense."

Valerie cleared her throat. "Rhiannon Greenbrook *is* so in love with me. She finds me irresistible. My fire magic is attractive to her. She has a thing for girls who could commit arson. Rhiannon Greenbrook is in love with me. She finds me irresistible. My fire magic is—"

She was cut off by a knock on the door. Quinn's head snapped up. "Oh my God. What if it's her?"

"It's not. It can't be. She never—"

All thoughts about tarot cards forgotten, Quinn scrambled to their feet. "It's her. I'm *almost sure* it's her. Why wouldn't she—"

"Just open it!"

Quinn did, pulling the door open slowly, as if scared that whoever was out there would vanish into thin air if they rushed it.

The sight of Rhia standing in the hallway nearly severed Valerie's soul clean from her body. She got up so quickly she felt light-headed, ignoring Quinn's whispered, "It worked!"

"Hey." Slightly breathless, she leaned against the door frame. "What are you doing here?"

Rhia extended one of her hands, which, Valerie realized with confused delight, was clutching a paper cup from Sugar & Spice. "I figured you might need some caffeine," she said. "And . . . I felt bad that you always come to see me and never the other way around."

Valerie reflexively accepted the coffee. She was aware that Quinn was still hovering next to her, grinning from ear to ear, but the only thing she could focus on was Rhia, who, in her yellow coat, brightened up the entire hallway.

"Should we get out of here?" Rhia asked when the silence dragged on, nervously gesturing at the hallway. "I thought maybe we could take a walk?"

"Yeah. Yeah, of course," Valerie said. She glanced over her shoulder once more to see Quinn giving her an enthusiastic thumbs-up.

~

Instead of heading for the main road, Rhia led them in the opposite direction—around the dorm and down the path that led into the woods that stretched behind the campus.

Valerie sipped her coffee while they walked just so she wouldn't blurt out anything stupid. It tasted sweet but not overly so, with a hint of cinnamon that fit the autumnal scenery. By now the trees had gone from green to blazing shades of red and orange, leaves crunching under their boots as they made their way into the heart of the forest. The air was crisp and sweet with the scent of wet soil and the chimney smoke that drifted over from the town.

Even here, it seemed like the plants responded to Rhia. Sometimes they would stretch out their branches to playfully snag at her sleeve; other times they would pull back and give way to her in spots where the thicket became too dense. Surrounded by nature, Rhia looked calmer. An easy smile played on her face as she squinted into the autumn sun, tilting her head as she listened to the whispering leaves.

It was only when they had been walking for at least ten minutes and a river came into view that Rhia spoke. "Legend says that a woman drowned here."

Despite herself, a surprised laugh tumbled from Valerie's lips. "What?"

"I don't know. It's probably just some small-town rumor."

"*That's* the first thing you say to me?"

"It's not the first thing I said to you." Rhia defensively crossed her arms in front of her chest. "I also said *I thought you might need caffeine* and *let's take a walk* and—"

"And then you transitioned smoothly into tragic death." Valerie chuckled. "As one does."

Rhia rolled her eyes, but Valerie could tell by the way her lips twitched that she was trying not to laugh. "I've never been on a date before, I don't know what you're supposed to talk ab—"

"Wait. This is a date?"

"I . . . Yes?" Rhia said, but she didn't sound very certain. "That's what you do, right? You go out for coffee and talk?"

Valerie's eyes darted down to the empty paper cup in her hand. Her heart felt like it was going to pound its way through her rib cage at the implication. She wanted to ask if that meant what she thought it did. She wanted Rhia to pull her in and melt in her hands all over again. Instead, she raised a teasing eyebrow and pointed out, "You haven't even kissed me yet. For all I know we're just friends hanging out."

"You're such a—"

"A menace, a scoundrel, yeah, yeah." She grinned. "We've been over this. Come here." For all her huffing and eye-rolling, Rhia went remarkably easily, her arms looping around Valerie's neck as their lips brushed. The kiss was sweet and unrushed— steadying in a way that was uniquely *Rhia*—and for the first time that day, the fog cleared from Valerie's head. "Thank you," she said when Rhia leaned back, her voice sounding only a little bit breathless. She took a step back. Busied herself by storing the empty paper cup away in the pocket of her jacket. Definitely did *not* want to pull Rhia back in and kiss her within an inch of her life. She was *nailing* this casual thing.

Gesturing at the river, she asked, "What's the story then?"

Rhia started walking again. The river grew louder the closer they got, a low rumbling accompanied by a crashing sound every time the current met one of the larger boulders in the riverbed. "There isn't really a story. It's just a weird part of Oakriver lore. *Be careful around the Murmuring River, someone drowned in it.*" She shrugged. "I'm pretty sure it's just a scary story to keep children from going near it."

"Mmm," Valerie absentmindedly hummed. Evil river or not, she found that the water was strangely hard to look away from. It was a curious, murky color that reminded her of paint water after hours of being too lazy to exchange it. With the way the current swallowed the light, there was no way of telling how deep it truly was. Water and women. Why did everything seem to come back to that lately? "Always better to be safe than sorry, I guess."

"I don't know." There was an odd quality to Rhia's voice that made Valerie tear her eyes away from the river. "Is it?"

"What do you mean?"

Rhia's hands fidgeted nervously at her sides. Valerie frowned. Rhia never fidgeted. Brimming with restless energy was usually Valerie's thing. When she spoke, her voice was so quiet Valerie had to strain to make out her words over the rumbling of the river. "I changed my mind," she said. "I don't want this to be a casual thing."

For a second, Valerie was sure she hadn't understood her correctly. "What?"

"I'm sorry, I—I know I'm being confusing. I *thought* that was what I wanted, but it's not."

She took a step closer, the look on her face achingly open. With a start, Valerie understood what this was: it was Rhia shakily undoing her armor to show Valerie her heart beating right outside her chest, exposed and frightened and *wanting*.

"I don't want some half-here, half-there situation," she said, voice soft and sincere and somehow still unshakably firm. "I want everything."

And, fuck. It was too much—her tone, her words, her heart right within reach. "You already have everything," Valerie said—and then she finally did kiss Rhia within an inch of her life, all greedy hands and gasping breaths, and nothing about it was casual at all.

When Rhia pulled back, she did it with an incredulous laugh. "I was so scared," she said, tipping her head back to look at Valerie. "I wasn't sure you wanted me like that."

"Rhiannon Greenbrook," Valerie said slowly, clearly enunciating every syllable, "I've wanted you like that ever since the day you almost strangled me for doing a tarot reading at the café."

"I didn't *almost strangle* you, I just—"

"It's all right, pumpkin. As it turns out, I have a thing for bossy, cottage-core-looking waitresses who may or may not be able to turn me into a tree."

"And I for reckless art students who should never, ever be trusted with fire *or* magic and for some reason got both," Rhia miserably said and leaned in for another kiss.

"Why did you say you only wanted a casual thing in the first place?" Valerie asked when they separated.

Rhia's eyes turned serious again. "I don't feel in control when I'm with you."

"Is that such a bad thing?"

"I'm still trying to figure that out," Rhia murmured.

As they continued following the river, Rhia's hand slipped

into Valerie's. The weight felt as natural as the force of gravity and as steadying too. Looking down at their intertwined fingers, Valerie said, "I was worried there was something more serious."

"Like what?"

"I don't know. Some kind of internalized homophobia situation or your family not being accepting, I guess."

Rhia smiled wide enough for her eyes to crinkle at the corners. "They're accepting. I never actually came out to them. I just told them when I was fifteen that I was questioning my sexuality, and they helped me figure it out over the years—watching *Paris Is Burning* with me, asking the tarot cards, researching the different terms, the whole nine yards. My grandma knitted me a scarf in the colors of the bisexual flag, then, a few months later, one in the lesbian flag colors. It felt like a whole family project." She trailed off, looking at Valerie again. "What about your dad? Does he know you like girls?"

"I didn't have an official coming-out either." The thought of bringing it up with him made Valerie cringe, and she quickly added, "I figured out I wasn't straight when I was sixteen, but I never felt like I needed a label for it besides *queer*—anything more specific than that has always felt restricting, somehow. He found out when I went on a date with a girl for the first time."

"So, no big identity crisis there?"

"No." Valerie chuckled. "The fact that I could suddenly set things on fire with my mind was a little more concerning, you know?"

Rhia snorted a quiet laugh. They walked the next few feet in comfortable silence, until Rhia said, "You don't talk much about your dad."

Valerie kicked at an acorn on the ground, watching as it rolled into the shrubs off the path. "There's not really much to talk about. He's an okay guy. I mean, he's paying for my tuition and stuff. I don't know."

"You're not very close, are you?"

Valerie shook her head. They *had* been, but that was so long ago she'd almost forgotten what it had felt like. Before her magic had sparked, it had never occurred to Valerie just how little she knew about her mother. Once it had, something between them had shifted. Whenever she tried to get anything about Isabelle out of her father, he pushed her away; whenever he caught her playing around with magic, he yelled at her; whenever she entered a room, he averted his eyes. *Every day you look more like her*, he'd told her once. From his mouth, it had sounded like a tragedy.

Shortly after Valerie's sixteenth birthday, he'd married a woman named Laura—a colleague from work, another accountant. Before Valerie knew what was happening, Laura was already moving in, bringing her ugly furniture and two sons from her previous marriage along. *Don't scare them away*, her father had told her between moving boxes. *Keep your you-know-what to yourself. Do it behind closed doors, if you must.* Just like that, he'd cemented their new roles: Matthew Morgan, with his shiny new family, and Valerie, his strange daughter, hidden away in her room like a broom in a storage closet or an unsightly stain on the floor that had to be covered with a rug. She knew he loved her, and she supposed she loved him too. Still, Valerie couldn't help but feel like a burden to him—an unwanted souvenir from a time he desperately wanted to forget.

Even now, Valerie still wondered what her mother had seen

in him. Which sounded kind of terrible. He wasn't all bad. He hadn't batted an eye when she'd gone out with a girl two or three times, for example. He donated to charities twice a year. He'd always made sure to cook something vegetarian when Valerie was eating dinner with them and had read up on the vitamin supplements a vegan diet required. He was just so *him*. If her mother was a fairy tale, her father was a tax handbook. There was absolutely nothing in him that Valerie could relate to.

"You know . . ." Rhia's voice interrupted Valerie's thoughts. "I actually did a tea leaf reading with my family about you."

Valerie almost tripped over her own two feet at that. "You told your family about me?"

"No—I mean, Holly and Sage and Tristan know, obviously, but I didn't tell the others the question I wanted answers to. I just had them help me decipher the symbols in the cup."

Valerie tried to suppress the little pang of jealousy in her chest that came every time Rhia talked about her family. "Why? Did you not see anything by yourself?"

"I, uh . . . never really do."

Valerie ground to an abrupt stop. "You're joking."

"I really wish I were."

"I don't understand," Valerie said. "I thought all witches were clairvoyant?"

"A lot of them, yeah." One of Rhia's hands came up to scratch at her neck the way she always did when she was flustered. "Not me."

Valerie studied her. Even though Rhia's tone was light, there was an edge to it, a hint of wanting that tinged her words. Valerie knew that tone intimately. "Oh shit," she said as realization hit her. "I thought you just wanted to learn *more* about divination—you know, compare notes or whatever. I didn't realize we were starting from scratch."

Rhia shifted on her feet, her eyes darting along the forest floor. "It's okay, I . . . I don't even know why I asked. It probably won't work anyway. My family has tried to teach me, and nothing's ever—"

"Nonsense." Cutting her off, Valerie reached out and took hold of Rhia's other hand as well, tugging her closer. "We made a deal, remember? You've shown me your altar and your spell book. The least I can do is help you open your stupid third eye."

"My *stupid third eye* is very much closed," Rhia insisted. "Divination requires you to get out of your head, and I've never been good at that. How is anything you do going to change that?"

"You said it yourself." Valerie slid a hand to Rhia's neck, feeling her pulse jump under her fingertips. "I make you lose control."

At that, Rhia shivered in a way that didn't seem like it had anything to do with the autumn chill. Valerie knew she'd won from the way Rhia's breathing hitched, her face turning the tiniest bit into Valerie's palm. "Okay," she relented. "We can try."

With a triumphant grin, Valerie bridged the last inch between them and brushed her lips over Rhia's. "Thank you."

"Mm-hmm. Don't get your hopes up, though."

"Oh, they're all the way up." Valerie laughed. "One of us has to be optimistic."

Rhia gave another noncommittal hum and leaned in for another short kiss. When she pulled back, it was with a regretful look at the setting sun. "I have to go back to the café. I have the closing shift today."

Reluctantly, Valerie let go of her. There was something magical about being in the woods with Rhia; with no one but the trees to watch them, time seemed to move syrupy-slow as the entire world narrowed to just them. She wasn't ready for the spell to break, for time to snap back into its usual shape, or for the magic that saturated the air between them to be diluted by the real world again.

Still, she nodded and clasped Rhia's hand. "I'll walk you back."

Together, they turned, this time moving upstream.

Valerie didn't let go of Rhia's hand until they reached the café, and even then only to hold the door for her. Rhia stepped past her with a small curtsy. "Thank you. Do you want to come inside and warm up for a bit?"

Valerie wasn't cold—she never was—but she trailed after Rhia nevertheless, staying close behind as Rhia wended her way between the bustling tables and towards the staircase.

They'd made it halfway to the second floor when a bright voice rang out above them. "Oh, there you are, I've been looking everywhere for you!"

Valerie raised her gaze to find Holly Greenbrook standing a few steps above them, beaming at Rhia over the cardboard box she was carrying. Her grin widened when her eyes fell on Valerie.

"Hey," said Rhia. "What are you doing here?"

"I was decluttering the attic again—I'm turning it into a workspace for my online shop," she explained to Valerie. "And I found a bunch of recipe books. They're, like, really old, but I thought maybe you'd find something interesting in there. I'd feel bad throwing them all out, so have a riffle through them, and if they're all boring, I'll take them to the secondhand shop."

Rhia fumbled to accept the cardboard box her cousin shoved at her. "'Kay."

Now empty-handed, Holly skipped down a few more steps until she was right next to Valerie. "It's so nice to see you here, Valerie! Are you coming with us this weekend?"

"Uh . . . where?"

With a grimace, Rhia propped the box on her hip so as not to drop it. "Holly, Sage, Tristan, and I are all driving up to Tristan's mom's cabin in the woods this weekend. It's not a big thing, just some board games and hiking. They wanted me to ask you if you'd like to come."

"*They* wanted you to ask that, huh?" Valerie teased, reaching out to take the books from Rhia when she noticed that she was struggling.

Sounding greatly inconvenienced, Rhia clarified, "I would also really like it if you came. Happy?"

"Very," Valerie agreed. "Is it okay if I bring Quinn? I think they'd love to get away from college for a bit."

"Of course!" Holly chirped. "The more, the merrier."

Valerie smiled. "Then I'm in."

"Perfect!" Holly said. "I really have to go now. See you on Friday!"

Valerie nodded, watching as Holly's bright-pink hair disappeared down the stairs. When she was gone, she turned back to Rhia. "I love your family."

"Uh-huh." Rhia took the cardboard box from Valerie again, quietly pleased. "Let's see if you still say that after the weekend."

16

TEN OF CUPS

contentment — harmonious relationships — abundance of love

It was late in the afternoon when Rhia, Tristan, Sage, and Holly pulled up to the campus. Quinn and Valerie were already waiting on the sidewalk, one looking vaguely apprehensive, the other buzzing with excitement.

"Hey, you," Valerie said when Rhia got out of the car.

"Hey." Very aware of her family watching through the car windows and Quinn standing awkwardly next to them, Rhia got on her tiptoes and pressed a quick peck to the corner of Valerie's mouth. "Ready to go?"

Valerie nodded, casting an amused glance behind Rhia's shoulder. "Nice car."

"God, don't say anything, please. Tristan is sensitive about it." Since Oakriver was small and every place could easily be reached by bike, none of them owned a car—Tristan was, however, sometimes allowed to drive his mom's campaign bus. Perhaps *campaign bus* was a bit of an overstatement, considering it was just a large van with seven seats, but the fact that it had Sharon Moore's face printed on both sides—along with the slogan *Want Oakriver to be more? Vote Moore!*—was enough to turn Tristan's ears a bright pink every time he sat in the driver's seat.

Despite Rhia's warning, the first thing Valerie said upon clambering into the back seat was: "Hey, Tristan. Please excuse my dreadful etiquette, I always forget I'm in the presence of Oakriver royalty."

Tristan's ears turned an even deeper shade of red. "Hi, Valerie." He twisted around in his seat to watch Rhia settle down next to Sage in the middle seat. Quinn was the last one to get in, pulling the heavy door shut behind them as they squeezed in next to Valerie.

Tristan beamed at them. "Dude, it's so cool that you came! Wait—is it okay if I call you dude?"

Quinn blinked, caught off guard, before a surprised smile flickered across their face. "Yeah, *dude* is fine."

"Sweet," Tristan said. "I love your hair, by the way. I've always wanted to dye mine, but then I see how often Holly has to do touch-ups, and that honestly looks way too stressful—"

"Tristan," Sage interrupted, "do you maybe want to start driving?"

Tristan turned around in his seat again, the engine stuttering to life. "Right, yes, good call."

They rolled onto the main street, taking a left onto the road that led into the heart of the woods. It ran parallel to the Murmuring River—if Rhia craned her neck, she could sometimes catch a glimpse of it before it disappeared behind the trees again.

"Are we staying close to the river?" Valerie curiously asked.

"Yeah." Tristan wiggled his eyebrows at her through the rearview mirror. "Make sure you don't get too close to it. You don't want the lady who drowned to pull you in with her."

"Wow," Valerie snorted. "You too? Is that an actual thing that people here believe?"

"Listen," Tristan said, laughing, "that myth is one of the few intriguing things we have going for us here. If it weren't so macabre, my mom probably would've turned it into merch already."

Valerie nodded, as if to say *Fair enough.*

With several lively conversations happening at once, the ten-minute drive passed by quickly. At one point, Rhia felt a light kick to the back of her seat, followed by a hand tugging at her sleeve.

"What?" she asked, turning around in her seat to find Valerie's face inches away from her own.

"You're so far away."

"So *clingy.*" Rhia laughed. Still, when she turned around again, she reached her hand through the gap between the seats to intertwine her fingers with Valerie's.

After that, it wasn't long until the uneven road ended and the trees around them gave way to a small clearing. "Here we are," Tristan announced.

Valerie whistled quietly through her teeth.

Where *campaign bus* was an exaggeration, *cabin* was an understatement. With two stories, four bedrooms, and an enormous living room, it was bigger than most of the town houses in Oakriver, though the bright-green window shutters and fairy-tale tiles on the roof seemed like an attempt at modesty.

"One of Tristan's great-great-grandfathers built it," Rhia explained to Valerie while they got their luggage—which consisted mostly of snacks and board games—out of the back of the van. "He stayed here during his hunting trips. When Tristan's mom inherited it, the whole place was full of taxidermy deer."

Before Valerie could do more than shudder, Sage clapped her hands to demand their attention. She stood by the front door with two bags slung over her shoulders and a look that Holly and Rhia called the "event planner frown" on her face.

"All right, guys, let's talk room assignments. We're six people, and we have four bedrooms. That means the two couples can sleep together . . ." Rhia glanced over her shoulder to find Valerie already looking at her, something warm and heavy in her gaze. "And Quinn and I get our own rooms. Any complaints?"

Rhia immediately shook her head.

"Great. For tonight our agenda is: settle in, find some firewood while it's not completely dark outside, have a campfire, and then maybe some movies or board games. Got it?"

"Yes, ma'am," Rhia, Holly, and Tristan said in unison before they each grabbed their things and headed inside.

Climbing the stairs led them into a narrow corridor with walls covered in framed family photos. "Quinn, this is yours." Rhia pointed at a door to their left. "Are you sure you're okay being on your own?"

"Yeah, that's fine," Quinn said. "It'll be good not to have someone snoring next to me all night. Or, you know, standing in the middle of the room in the dead of night staring at nothing."

"And I thought we had something special." Valerie pressed a hand to her chest in feigned betrayal. In a more serious tone, she added, "But seriously, if you feel lonely you can come over."

"And walk in on you two? No, thank you," Quinn snorted and disappeared inside their room.

Rhia and Valerie exchanged glances, Rhia flustered and Valerie the opposite. Then Rhia grabbed Valerie's hand and tugged her along to the door at the very end of the corridor. It was her favorite room of the house and the one where she'd slept every other time they'd stayed here; it was the smallest, but the one with the largest bed, and from its window you could look out into the woods.

Valerie made a beeline for the bed, arms spread wide as she flopped onto the mattress. "Man. My dorm bed's got nothing on this."

With a chuckle, Rhia tossed her backpack somewhere near the door and moved to straddle Valerie's hips. Tilting her head, she asked, "Is it true that you snore? I don't think I heard that when you slept over at my place."

Valerie grinned up at her, her hands easily settling on Rhia's hips. "You mean the day you made me jump from the roof?" She pushed herself up on her elbows, eyes darting over to the window. "This house is a bit taller, so if you have any plans of making me leap to my death, please tell me now so I can call the ambulance in adva—"

Rhia leaned forward and pulled her into a kiss before she could finish her sentence. Valerie sank back into the mattress, one hand leaving Rhia's hip to cup her cheek instead. The way she immediately kissed her back, her body warm and welcoming beneath her, made something unfamiliar flutter in the pit of Rhia's stomach.

By the time she pulled back, Valerie's pupils were dilated. "Two nights together in this bed, huh?" she asked, voice a little bit rougher than it had been a few moments ago.

"Two nights," Rhia breathlessly confirmed.

She was bending down to capture Valerie's lips again when a thump at the door made both of them jump. "Hey, lovebirds!" called Sage's muffled voice. "Come out, you have firewood duty!"

With how close they were, Rhia could feel Valerie's laugh resonating in her chest.

"We should probably get up before your sister kicks down the door," Valerie suggested.

"You're joking, but she would literally do that," Rhia returned. Summoning every ounce of strength in her body, she got to her feet.

Two nights.

~

By the time they all returned to the cabin, arms full of twigs and leaves, night had spread across the sky like ink seeping through paper. Out here, the moon seemed closer than it did from Rhia's window at home; it hung pale and plump over the treetops, spilling silver over their skin. It was the night of the Hunter's Moon, the last full moon before All Hallows' Eve.

"It's also called the Falling Leaf Moon or the Dying Grass Moon," Rhia explained to Valerie and Quinn as they piled their foraged wood in the fire pit behind the cabin. "Some even call it the Blood Moon."

Holly giggled, catching herself on Tristan's arm when she almost stumbled over a branch. "You make it sound so ominous."

"I mean, it kind of is," said Sage. "The veil between our world and the spirit world is starting to lift tonight. It's one of the best nights to practice divination or contact the dead."

While Quinn shuddered, Valerie's eyes lit up. "The best time for divination, you say?"

And that was how, five minutes later, Rhia found herself kneeling in the clearing in front of the cabin with a bowl of water in front of her. "I'm not really sure this is a good idea," she said.

"Come on, you heard your sister." Valerie settled down cross-legged next to her, her knee pressing lightly against Rhia's. "I did promise to help you open your third eye. If not tonight, when?"

Touching a finger to the rim of the bowl, Rhia sighed. She could feel Quinn's gaze on her; they were sitting on the front steps of the porch, a safe distance from their makeshift ritual. "Promise not to laugh at me if I can't do it?"

In the dark, Rhia could barely make out Valerie's frown. "Why would I laugh?"

"Because I'm *supposed* to be able to do this. Every witch in my family can." Rhia rubbed at her nose. Softly, she added, "I used to be able to do this too. Just not anymore."

Next to her, Valerie stilled. "You used to be clairvoyant?"

Rhia nodded.

"What happened?"

"My dad," she said. The words came out haltingly, like they were sticking to the back of her throat and had to be coaxed out one by one. "The night he got into the accident, my grandma woke up from a nightmare. She had seen what was going to happen—she knew he was going to die minutes before he did. But it was too late. He'd already gotten into the car, and he didn't pick up his phone when we tried to call."

Rhia tilted her head back to look at the treetops. She tried to focus on the way they swayed in the breeze, not on the memories replaying in her mind—the sound of loud voices that had lured her out of bed and down the stairs to where her mother had been crying at the kitchen table, the phone clutched in her hand. Her grandmother staring out the window with unreadable eyes, completely still, save for the faintest tremor in her shoulders. She remembered the thick silence in the room, interrupted only by her mother's wet sobs and the tick-tick-ticking of the clock as its hands moved from *before* to *after*. She remembered how her aunt had pulled her against her chest when she'd noticed her standing in the hallway, explaining what had happened in a calm voice even as her tears pattered down on Rhia's head, warm like summer rain. And she remembered how, lying in bed with her mother and sister that night, all of them pretending to be asleep while the gray morning light of her first day without a father crept through the curtains, she had vowed to herself that she never wanted to know what the future held ever again.

"After that, my grandma and my sister fully committed themselves to getting as good as possible at divination, to prevent anything like it from ever happening again," Rhia scratchily continued. "Meanwhile, it took me three years until I could even stand to be in the same room as them when they did a tarot reading. By the time I agreed to try again, that tiny seed of clairvoyance I'd had to begin with was buried."

"But seeds can sprout and grow," Valerie said, offering her a small smile. "Right?"

"I guess. Under the right conditions."

Wordlessly, Valerie wrapped an arm around Rhia's shoulders. For a few moments, they simply sat there, the trees whispering above them. Then Valerie quietly asked, "Do you believe in fate?"

Rhia had thought about the question hundreds of times before—had pictured her father and icy roads and wondered whether his death really was an accident, a slip on paper crossing out what wasn't meant to be crossed out, or a carefully crafted line written by a hand that no one, witch or otherwise, could control.

"I don't know," she said honestly. "Do you?"

"Fuck, no."

The immediate response almost startled a laugh out of her. "No? Then why practice divination?"

"So that I know the future and can laugh in its stupid face when I change its course," Valerie stated as if it were self-evident.

"That's . . . oddly comforting, actually."

Grinning, Valerie tilted her chin at the bowl again. "So? Are you ready to do this?"

"Ready as I'll ever be," Rhia agreed. "But first, *I'm* going to show *you* how to cast a circle. I'm not about to open myself to the spirit world just to get possessed by some lingering souls under the Hunter's Moon, no thank you."

"Fair enough." Valerie laughed and got to her feet.

Casting a circle was one of the first things Rhia had learned as a child, along with tying her shoelaces and writing her own name. She began by dipping her fingers in the bowl and sprinkling water in a circle around them while murmuring, *"Element of water, watch over us while we work."* Then, she repeated the process, this time with a pinch of salt she had grabbed from the kitchen for this purpose: *"Element of earth, watch over us while we work."* Lastly, she had Valerie light one of the lavender sticks she'd brought and watched as she spread the smoke around them. Her movements were a little unsure, but her voice was clear and steady as she spoke.

"Elements of air and fire, watch over us while we work."

Once it was done and Rhia could feel the circle in place, she sank to her knees in front of the bowl again. "How does this work?"

"There's nothing technical to it, really," Valerie said. "That's why scrying is my favorite form of divination aside from tarot. It's the most intuitive, in my experience—all you have to do is look into the bowl and clear your mind."

"Sure," said Rhia, her fingers twitching against the rim of the bowl. "Sounds easy."

Valerie must have picked up on the anxious tremor in her voice because she suddenly inched closer until their shoulders were pressed together. "You don't have to be nervous," she said. "It's okay if you don't see anything right away. Don't force it. The visions will come to you when you're ready."

Rhia took one last deep breath. Finally, she leaned forward and peered inside the bowl.

A few seconds passed. As hard as she looked, all the bowl held was a sea of stars, twinkling in and out of existence as the water rippled gently in the breeze, and her own face, blurry and distorted. As the wind picked up, it carried over a plethora of sounds: Tristan pretending to howl at the full moon, followed by Holly's bright laughter; the insistent scratching of Quinn's pencil against the paper in their sketchbook; branches snapping in the undergrowth; the low rumble of the Murmuring River in the distance.

"Rhia," Valerie said as if sensing the dozens of directions Rhia's attention was wandering. "Focus."

Rhia stared down into the bowl again. When she squinted, there seemed to be something moving at the bottom of it, but it was just out of reach—she couldn't make out its shape or put a name to what she was seeing. It reminded her of sitting up in her

Philline Harms

bed in the middle of the night, her drawers and shelves and altar cloaked in shadows and transformed into something entirely foreign. Deep down, she knew that she would be able to make out what they were once her eyes adjusted, but until then she was suspended in an eerie feeling of vague recognition, eyes straining and heart pounding as she waited. There was something there, a *want* welling up in her chest to answer the call of the unknown swimming before her, but—

Another ripple passed over the surface, and the shapes disappeared altogether, leaving her staring at her own reflection once again. Frustration tightened her grip on the bowl. She was about to tear her gaze away from it and give up for good when a warm hand settled on the nape of her neck.

Rhia could just barely see Valerie in the reflection of the water, eyes shut as the wind played in her hair, brow furrowed.

And then she felt it: Valerie's magic seeping from her fingertips into Rhia's skin. This time, it wasn't an unstoppable wave crashing over her; it was a gentle trickle that filled up her chest one drop at a time, warmth flooding her veins. It was sunshine made liquid, a feeling so bright and golden it made her dizzy. Her eyes unwillingly fluttered shut. When she forced them open again, the water was completely still, and she didn't see her reflection—she saw right to the bottom of the bowl, where the fleeting shadows slowly solidified into an image.

"What do you see?" Valerie asked, her voice low and hopeful.

"You," said Rhia. "I see you. And a river. The Murmuring River, I think."

"What am I doing there?"

"You're . . . you're just lying in it." She swallowed. "You're facedown. And you're wearing a dress, a black one."

Valerie's hair tickled her cheek as she leaned closer. Her thumb rubbed gently up and down the nape of Rhia's neck where her hand still rested, a comforting weight. "Am I alone?"

The longer Rhia stared, the more the image frayed, dissolving in the water as it began to move again, the sudden clarity she felt slipping out of reach once more. "I can't see. It doesn't feel like it. I think there's someone watching, multiple people. But I can't see their faces, and—" She sighed, looking up. "It's gone."

Valerie slowly pulled back her hand. "Well," she said, "looks like I'm staying away from that river."

"I told you it's creepy," Rhia muttered. "This doesn't mean anything though, right? We can just take this as a warning and make sure you don't go near it?"

"Yeah, of course. Besides, maybe you just saw me going for a swim or something. I'm sure it's nothing bad." She lifted her head. "But that was amazing!"

At that, Rhia finally allowed herself to feel giddy. "I honestly didn't think I'd be able to do it. And the way your magic feels when it isn't an accident . . . I've never felt anything like it."

Valerie, looking thoroughly satisfied with herself, was about to respond when Sage's voice rang across the clearing. "Hey, you three! Dinner's ready!"

Reluctantly, they got up. While Valerie went ahead to help set the table, Rhia closed the circle and thanked the elements. She poured the scrying water into the bushes next to the cabin, ridding herself of the vision—both literally and, she hoped, symbolically.

Quinn watched silently as she did.

~

After dinner, Rhia found herself perched on one of the wooden benches that surrounded the fire pit behind the cabin. It was pitch-black by now; the only light was the erratic flickering of the matches in Tristan's hand, illuminating his face one second and being snuffed out by the wind the next. The breeze had grown much more demanding, tearing at Rhia's hair and trying to find its way under her many layers. Through the open kitchen door seeped the sounds of the others cleaning up. A smile spread on her face when she heard Valerie make a joke, followed by the rare sound of her sister's laughter.

She hadn't noticed Tristan watching her until he asked, "Happy?"

Rhia hugged one of her knees closer to her chest, resting her chin on top of it. "Very."

"She fits."

"Yeah." Rhia strained her ears to make out the words among the laughter in the kitchen. "She does."

Just then, Valerie stepped through the kitchen door carrying a tray with six glasses of hard cider wobbling precariously. Her eyebrows rose when she spotted Rhia, hunched over in hopes of saving some of her body heat, and Tristan, kneeling in a grave-yard of spent matches.

"Dude." She laughed, setting the tray down on the ground next to the fire pit before she crouched next to him. "I thought this would be lit by now. Didn't you say you were in Boy Scouts?"

"I was!" He handed her the half-empty box of matches without hesitation. "For two months."

Valerie tossed them back at him. "We won't be needing these."

Holly stepped out the door as Tristan heaved himself onto

the bench with a huff. "It's okay, baby, you still did great." She paused to ruffle his hair before she gracefully sank down next to Valerie.

Rhia leaned forward as they exchanged glances. A whisper from Holly was enough to make the wind around them still. From the way the leaves on a distant tree were dancing in the breeze, Rhia could estimate how far Holly's magic stretched, an invisible wall sheltering them.

Looking vaguely impressed, Valerie leaned forward and placed her hands directly on the firewood stacked in the pit. Now that the wind had quieted, Rhia, for the first time, could make out what she was saying.

"*Look*," Valerie murmured as her eyelids fluttered shut, "*here comes a walking fire.*" A heartbeat later, flames licked at her slender fingers, as gentle as a lover's touch.

Around her, the others cheered, but Rhia was spellbound, her eyes not fixed on the fire pit but on Valerie. With the flames flickering in her eyes and her hair cutting through the night like a torch, she looked like danger personified—and Rhia was so enchanted she couldn't breathe, couldn't do anything but laugh incredulously when Valerie met her gaze.

She jumped when Sage's hand appeared out of nowhere to lift her jaw. "Shut your mouth or you'll catch a fly."

Rhia slapped her sister's hand away. Still, she couldn't stop herself from tracking every single one of Valerie's movements as she slowly drew her hands out of the fire. The flames seemed to cling to her fingers as she did, desperate to hold on to her. Rhia couldn't blame them. She reached for Valerie the moment she was close enough, taking her hand to pull her down next to her on the bench.

"You're sweet," Valerie said, quiet enough for only her to hear, and pressed a kiss to her temple.

Rhia blamed the heat in her cheeks on the fire, grateful for the glass of hard cider Sage handed her at that moment. Tucked against Valerie's side, with the alcohol burning through her and her family chattering around her, Rhia felt like she was floating. Earlier that day, she'd been afraid that blending her two worlds was going to be awkward, but it wasn't. Valerie and Quinn had clicked right into place, like they were parts of a puzzle that had just been waiting to be assembled; Rhia felt it every time Valerie joked with Holly or when Tristan and Quinn got into an unexpectedly heated debate about whether or not banana bread was classified as cake. (Tristan: *It's got the consistency of cake, and Rhia always puts chocolate chips in it! It's obviously cake!* Quinn: *The word* bread *is literally in the name! The chocolate chips are a lie, Tristan, wake up.*) It ended with Quinn triumphantly waving an online article and Sage laughing hard enough for cider to spray from her nose.

After a few hours, when the cold had crept in despite the fire and the Hunter's Moon had wandered to the very center of the velvety night sky, Rhia tugged at Valerie's hand. "Hey," she whispered, "do you want to go inside?"

Valerie immediately downed the rest of her tea—they'd moved on from cider after one glass—and got to her feet.

A chorus of good-nights followed them as they entered through the kitchen door. Inside, it was dark, but Rhia knew the layout of the cabin by heart and blindly led Valerie back to their room.

In the soft light of the bedside lamp, she turned around to face Valerie again. She was leaning against the door, her hair disheveled from the wind, an easy smile on her face as she slowly looked Rhia up and down.

"What?" Rhia asked, her skin prickling under Valerie's intent gaze. Perching on the edge of the bed, she plucked at the embroidery on the floral-patterned throw pillow in her lap to busy herself.

"You look good out here," Valerie observed, her eyes returning to linger on Rhia's face. "More relaxed."

The throw pillow did absolutely nothing to distract her. Her voice was embarrassingly scratchy as she asked, "Come here?"

Valerie pushed away from the door. However, instead of touching Rhia, she simply let herself fall onto the mattress, hands thrown above her head in a display of oblivious innocence.

Rhia swallowed thickly as her eyes flitted along the delicate curve of her exposed neck. "That line you said earlier, where is it from?" she asked, trying her best to keep her voice level. "Is that what you always say to call on your fire?"

"Yeah." Valerie's sweater rode up to expose a tiny bit of her stomach as she stretched. Rhia's head was so fuzzy she almost didn't register Valerie adding, "It's a line from *King Lear*. We read it in school, and it's the one line that stuck. When I realized that to intentionally use magic you need to speak it into existence, it was the first sentence I could think of."

"A walking fire," Rhia absentmindedly whispered. She wanted to say something else, but words suddenly seemed very far out of reach. Valerie, on the other hand, seemed very much *within* reach, watching Rhia through half-lidded eyes as she sprawled next to her.

As if reading her mind, Valerie propped herself up on one elbow, green eyes glittering with mischief because she *knew* what she was doing. The absolute menace. "Help me out," she said, bridging the distance between them to walk her fingers up Rhia's thigh. "Where was it that we left off earlier?"

"You're impossible," Rhia breathed. In an instant, she was straddling Valerie's hips like she had earlier that day, leaning down to kiss away her satisfied expression. One of Valerie's hands slid to the nape of her neck, like she had done when they had been scrying. If Rhia hadn't known better, she would have thought she was sneakily using magic again; with Valerie's fingers gently cradling her head and the taste of cider and smoke on her tongue, everything went wonderfully hazy.

When Valerie leaned back again, her tone was more serious. "We don't have to do anything just because we're staying in the same room, you know?"

"I know." Rhia's heart did an exceptionally strange thing when Valerie's fingers brushed a stray curl out of her eyes. "We could, though."

"We could," Valerie agreed. Her smile, warm and a little bit flustered, was enough to make Rhia feel undone. Slowly, her fingertips slipped under Rhia's sweater. "Is it okay if I . . ."

Rhia stilled. Where Valerie was lithe and fine-boned, Rhia was indulgent curves and a soft belly. She was as grateful for the body that sustained her as she was for everything else the earth gave her and therefore not exactly self-conscious. The thought of someone seeing her was just . . . new.

Sensing her hesitation, Valerie tilted her head, warm hands resting against Rhia's back. "Everything all right?"

"Yeah," Rhia said and pulled her sweater over her head in one decisive motion.

It was followed by Valerie's sweater and then Rhia's jeans, an item for an item, until they were left in only their underwear. Rhia's breathing hitched when Valerie's hands gently trailed up her sides, skimming across stretch marks and sliding up her bare shoulder until she brushed Rhia's hair away from her neck.

"You're beautiful," Valerie said. Her eyes met Rhia's without a trace of the mischief they had sparkled with moments ago—instead, they were alight with something else entirely, achingly earnest in the candlelight.

It was too much for Rhia to handle. Her face felt warm, and her throat was tight, so instead of responding, she busied herself by peppering kisses from Valerie's mouth down to her neck. Valerie tilted her head back, her throat moving under Rhia's lips as she swallowed hard. When Rhia's lips grazed Valerie's collarbone her body arched, her eyes fluttering open with a soft gasp as the magical tether between them gave a sudden tug.

The three candles on the bedside table, meant for décor more than use, had crackled to life. "Sorry." A breathless chuckle tumbled from Valerie's lips. "Got a little excited there."

For a moment, all Rhia could do was stare at the candles, flickering in time with Valerie's quickened breaths. Finally, when she looked at the girl underneath her again and found her grinning sheepishly up at her, the spell she'd been under broke.

"*Valerie.*" She let out an incredulous laugh. "You're a breathing fire hazard!"

"And whose fault is that?" asked Valerie.

"Yours! Very clearly yours!"

"Now, now, pumpkin. I never lose control over my magic when you aren't around. Clearly, you're the critical factor here."

Rhia looked down at Valerie—cheeks flushed, pupils dilated, her chest still rising and falling rapidly—and, for the first time, realization set in. *She* was doing this—she affected Valerie enough for her to lose her grip on her magic. Strangely, she felt like crying. Instead, she leaned forward and kissed Valerie into the mattress, cradling her face between careful hands.

Valerie indulged her for a few moments before she flipped them around and Rhia found herself on her back, Valerie's thighs bracketing her hips.

"Hey." Valerie's hair tickled Rhia's face when she leaned down, hands braced on both sides of Rhia's head.

"Hi," Rhia nonsensically responded. She rose on her elbows to chase Valerie's lips, but Valerie pulled back, pressing Rhia down against the mattress with a hand on her sternum.

"Do you trust me?" she inquired. Her tone told Rhia that she already knew the answer to that question.

"Unfortunately," Rhia said, breath hitching when Valerie bent down to press a kiss to the side of her jaw.

Fingers splayed over Rhia's pounding heart, Valerie said, "Then let me take care of you." Another kiss, this time lingering near the corner of Rhia's mouth like a promise. "You don't need to be in control all the time." Her hands carefully tilted Rhia's head, thumb tracing the curve of her lips. "Let me take you out of your head for a bit?"

And God—what else was Rhia to do other than nod when asked so sweetly? "Okay," she whispered, turning her face into the steadiness of Valerie's palm. "I can try."

Valerie smiled again, her features hazy and open, and leaned down to kiss Rhia like she'd been aching for this entire time. Her hands—always peculiarly warm, as if they had been curled around a cup of tea seconds before touching Rhia—were so easy to melt into.

Gently, Valerie's fingers closed around Rhia's wrists, pressing them into the mattress. The reverent look that appeared on her face when she released her grasp and Rhia's hands stayed where they were was enough to make Rhia feel like she was set alight. Dimly, she thought that she'd always known Valerie was going to burn her to the ground—she just hadn't expected the flames to feel so tender, consuming her one careful touch, one kiss, one whisper at a time.

"I've got you," Valerie murmured, her lips brushing Rhia's forehead. "Just let go."

And so, for just a few moments, Rhia did.

17

NINE OF SWORDS

sleeplessness — anxiety — helplessness

When Rhia woke up, her heart was throwing itself against her rib cage. She had no idea what time it was, but judging by the thick darkness that filled the room, dawn was still a few hours away. Her head felt heavy in the way it always did when she startled out of the deepest of sleeps, and there was a pressure behind her eyes that only increased as she rubbed her hands over them. With a groan, she squeezed them shut again and turned onto her other side, reaching out to seek Valerie's warmth. Instead, her hand brushed against cold sheets. Rhia abruptly sat up. That was what had woken her: the sound of the door opening.

Squinting into the pitch-black room, she realized that the door was still ajar. With a sinking feeling, Rhia pushed off the sheets and swung her feet over the edge of the bed. Her clothes were still strewn across the floor, and she wasted no time putting them on before stepping outside.

The bathroom at the end of the hallway was dark and

vacant, but somehow she'd known Valerie wasn't there even before checking. Her heart pounded as she rushed towards the stairs, not bothering to be quiet as she raced down towards the first floor, driven by a sudden sense of urgency.

A second door was thrown open before she'd made it half-way down the staircase. "Rhia, wait!"

Rhia turned her head to find Quinn hurrying towards her, almost stumbling down a few steps as they hastily pulled a sweater over their head. "Do you know where she is?"

"The river," Quinn panted, catching up with her. "She's going down to the river."

Rhia didn't question them, didn't ask how they knew. She just turned around and ran, Quinn on her heels. When they reached the living room, they saw the front door standing wide open, the wind sending leaves tumbling across the hardwood floor.

"She went this way," said Quinn, starting towards the woods.

With a quiet curse, Rhia followed them, leaving the cabin and the clearing behind. In front of her, branches snagged at Quinn's clothes, their feet catching on roots and twigs—Rhia caught up to them and grabbed their hand, and the trees pulled back, clearing a path for them.

Was she here? Rhia asked them.

They responded like they always did, with a murmuring of leaves, an ancient chorus of brittle voices audible only to her: *Yes, yes, this way.*

"Has she made it to the river yet? Can you tell?" she breath-lessly asked Quinn.

"She's at the riverside." Quinn's fingers were cold and clammy around Rhia's, holding on to her hand so tightly it hurt. "But she hasn't gone in it yet."

Rhia gave a curt nod. The river couldn't be much farther. Ahead of her, the path was dappled in what little moonlight made it through the dense treetops. Every time she caught a glimpse of the Hunter's Moon—*the Blood Moon*—Rhia's blood froze as her sister's words echoed in her ears again: *The veil between our world and the spirit world is starting to lift tonight.* She'd heard of people going mad during the full moon—stories of witches hexing their enemies in a bout of hubris only to receive three times the bad luck, witches tumbling from roofs believing they could fly, witches forgetting to cast a circle and ending up helpless to the whims of the spirit world. She'd always chalked those legends up to be just like all the other scary stories her grandmother loved to tell: cautionary tales meant to remind them to be responsible with the heightened energy these nights brought with them. Now, with her lungs screaming for air and the Hunter's Moon watching impassively as they raced through the woods at breakneck speed, none of the stories felt far-fetched.

"We're almost there," said Quinn a heartbeat before the familiar rumbling of the Murmuring River reached Rhia's ears.

By the time they broke out of the tree line, it was deafening. There was something hungry about the sound tonight, something entirely untamable that sent a shiver down Rhia's spine. The feeling was nothing compared to the dread that took hold when her eyes spotted Valerie. She was wading through the river, the water reaching up to her thighs and soaking her dark-red nightdress. The way she moved unsettled Rhia, every motion slow and marionette-like, as if there was an invisible force playing with her strings.

"Valerie!" Rhia called out. "What are you doing?"

Valerie didn't react. Her head was bowed, her eyes fixed

on the violent current that threatened to knock her over any moment. In the unforgiving wind, her slender frame visibly trembled.

"Valerie!" Rhia tried again. Her throat felt tight as she watched her from the riverside. The images she'd seen in the scrying bowl earlier flashed in her mind again: Valerie being carried away by the river, facedown and limp.

"I don't think she can hear you," Quinn said. They had come to a halt next to Rhia, their face ghostly pale in the moonlight.

Rhia was moving even before Quinn finished their sentence, stripping off her boots with shaky fingers. Her feet went numb almost the second she set them into the water. "Val!" she called again. Already, her pants were weighing her down, heavy and clinging as they stuck to her legs. "Look at me. We need to get you out!"

Valerie waded forward, undeterred, her unseeing eyes fixed only on the water. Rhia felt a sob trying to tear free from her throat. The current was so strong she could barely move one foot in front of the other without it threatening to pull her under. Meanwhile, Valerie was getting farther and farther away from her.

"Valerie, please," Rhia tried again. It was a futile invocation. Her voice broke as she used all her strength to take another step, the water pulling and pulling and pulling her in the other direction until finally, Valerie came to a halt and leaned down to study the spot right in front of her, as if she could somehow see through the murky water to the riverbed beneath. Teeth gritted, Rhia redoubled her efforts and caught up to Valerie seconds before she could reach into the water. "Valerie." Without thinking, Rhia took her by the shoulders and pulled her up to standing.

Valerie's entire body seized up the second they made contact. She gasped, a sound so full of terror that it made something inside Rhia's chest hurt. Her eyes, when they tore away from the river and darted around to take in her surroundings, were wide and suddenly clear.

"What happened?" Her voice shook in a way Rhia had never heard before. "I—I didn't go here. Why are we here?"

"You sleepwalked," Rhia whispered. Tears were glinting in Valerie's eyes. They spilled down her cheeks as she began to shake in earnest. "It's okay," Rhia lied, wiping them away. "You're okay. Let's just get you out of the water, all right? Everything will be fine."

Valerie nodded, her jaw clenched to keep her teeth from chattering. Her legs buckled when they began to walk, but Rhia immediately wrapped an arm around her waist. Quinn was crouched at the riverside and gripped Valerie's hands the moment she was within reach. Together, they hoisted her out of the water and into the grass where Valerie slumped down. Her entire body trembled in her soaked nightdress, but she didn't seem to notice; her eyes were still fixed on the river.

"Here." Kneeling down next to her, Quinn pulled their sweater over their head and helped Valerie into it, leaving them in a pair of boxer shorts and the oversized black T-shirt they'd put on before bed.

"We need to get her back to the cabin," Rhia numbly said.

Quinn gave a jerky nod and helped Valerie get back to her feet.

Where the sprint to the river had seemed long, the trek back felt like an eternity. No one spoke; the only sounds filling the silence were the snapping of branches and Valerie's shuddering breaths, deafening to Rhia's ears.

When the cabin finally came into view, they were greeted by a distraught-looking Holly. "There you are!" she exclaimed, running towards them. Her steps slowed when she took in their drenched state. "Are you okay? What on earth happened?"

"I don't know." Tears pricked at Rhia's eyes. Her legs were threatening to give out underneath her, but she refused to give them permission, tightening her grip on Valerie instead. "When I woke up, Valerie was gone. We found her in the river."

"Jesus. Do you want to go back to sleep, or—"

"No," Quinn and Rhia said in unison, voices strained through chattering teeth.

Holly nodded. "I'll get the others."

Fifteen minutes later, Rhia found herself in the back seat of the van, holding Valerie while the woods swallowed the cabin in the rearview mirror. Wrapped in several blankets and with her head resting against Rhia's shoulder, Valerie was completely motionless, her vacant eyes staring out the window at the moon. But it wasn't Valerie's silence or empty gaze that made Rhia's stomach twist—it was the fact that, for the first time since she'd known her, Valerie's hands were ice-cold.

18

FIVE OF WANDS

testing ideas — disagreements — frustration

The rest of the weekend passed by in a haze. Valerie had caught a cold and subsequently spent Saturday and Sunday in bed. Rhia came by several times to force food and some kind of magical herbal tea down her throat, but they hadn't talked about what had happened. There wasn't much to say because, as hard as she tried, Valerie couldn't *remember*. The hours between falling asleep next to Rhia and finding herself freezing to death were a blur. She didn't remember leaving the cabin or finding her way through the woods. What she *did* recall was the river. Every time she closed her eyes, she could still hear the violent rushing of water. She was aware that she should have been terrified to go back, but all she felt was an inexplicable pull to return to the site. She had been so close to *something*, though what it was, she couldn't say. All Valerie knew for sure was that the force drawing her to the river wasn't something that would simply go away with time—not unless she went back to finish what she'd started.

~

By Monday, Valerie felt physically able to go to class, but her mind was well outside the walls of the stuffy studio. To make matters worse, Quinn wasn't there to distract her. They hadn't been spending much time in the dorm since they'd been back. Valerie had assumed it was because she was sick, but that theory wasn't holding up too well now that she was fine again. She decided to worry about it later. For now, she had more important things to do—like flee the classroom as soon as her class ended and make a beeline for the building's exit.

Outside, she found the bike she'd talked a sophomore into lending her for the afternoon. With her hands on the handlebars, Valerie stopped for a moment, considering. In the back of her mind, she could hear Rhia scolding her for being reckless, but without the sight of her reproachful stare, it was easy to push aside. Rhia wasn't here, and neither was Quinn. There was no voice of reason to stop her as she swung onto the saddle and took off towards the woods, following the same path she'd walked with Rhia only a few days earlier.

Finding her way to the spot was more difficult than she'd expected. The deeper she pushed into the woods, the more erratic the river's course became, odd twists that were hard to follow as the trees became denser.

At one point, the path seemed to disappear entirely, giving Valerie the eerie sense that she was the first person to ever enter this part of the woods—or, at least, the first in a while. Squinting through the branches, she could make out a clearing. The birdsong was quieter here, and in the center of the meadow, there was a strange array of charred, weather-worn debris. Some

Philline Harms

part of Valerie itched to get closer to see what had once stood in this place, but it was overruled by the part of her that was still listening to the roaring of the river in the distance.

When her calves began to tremble from the strain of the increasingly impenetrable woods, she hopped off the bike and walked with it until she reached the spot where she'd waded into the river a few days earlier. Even though she'd been barely conscious then, there was a vague sense of recognition as she leaned the bike against a tree and neared the water on unsteady legs.

It was a sunny day with a clear blue sky, but the river remained its strange, turbid color. Valerie stared down at it for a few seconds, shivering. She'd never liked to swim. Maybe it was because no one had ever really taught her. More likely, it was because she knew that with nothing to manipulate or draw power from, she was utterly, terrifyingly human.

She shook her head. She wasn't afraid of the water. She *wasn't*. At least not as scared as she was of never getting any answers to her questions.

With renewed determination, Valerie peeled out of her jacket and unceremoniously dropped it to the ground. Her boots, dress, tights, and sweater followed, until she was left in just her underwear. "Here goes nothing," she murmured.

The water was even colder than she'd remembered. Swearing, Valerie forced herself to take deep breaths and ignore the pins and needles shooting through her limbs. Although she found a relatively shallow spot where the water only reached up to her knees, she still felt unsteady in the strong current. *"A walking fire,"* she chanted to herself. *"A walking fire, a walking*—Oh, fuck *me."*

Inhaling shakily, she closed her eyes and tried to concentrate not on the cold but on her intuition. That night under the Hunter's Moon, she'd known there was something in the riverbed that she needed to find. Now, as she focused her energy on it, she could feel the same thing she'd felt then: something calling back to her, a pull tugging her along.

She took a few steps forward, moving slowly across the slippery riverbed. The tugging sensation grew stronger as she made her way upstream until, finally, it stopped. Valerie bent down, trying to find whatever it was that was calling out for her—

"Are you out of your mind?"

With a start, Valerie's head snapped up. Right next to the heap of Valerie's clothes stood Rhia. In her arms, she was holding a fluffy towel.

"Hey, pumpkin." The quiver in Valerie's voice and the way her entire body had begun to shake sort of undermined the nonchalance she was going for. "How'd you know I was here?"

"How did I know you were going to return to the one spot in Oakriver you were told not to go back to after having not listened to anything anyone has told you, ever?" Rhia glowered. "Lucky guess, I suppose."

"Oh. Yeah, that checks out." Valerie tried for a grin. "Want to come in? Lovely weather for a swim."

"Valerie."

"Rhiannon," Valerie parroted in the exact same tone. If they were going to bicker for much longer, she would be leaving this river with a few less toes than she'd gotten in with.

Apparently coming to the same conclusion, Rhia sighed. "What are you even hoping to find here?"

"I don't know," Valerie said honestly. "But I know there's something here I need to do. Or . . . have?" She paused. "I think something has been pulling me here ever since I came to Oakriver." She didn't say the rest: That she was sure that without Rhia's advice about cleansing herbs, she would've come here in her sleep much sooner. That something had dug its claws into her subconscious the moment she'd set foot in the town, and that she would rather face it like this: not a marionette at the whim of something unseen but lucid and on her own terms.

Judging by the look on her face, Rhia already understood. "Fine," she said, sinking into the grass next to Valerie's discarded clothes. "But don't start whining when your cold comes back tomorrow."

Valerie gave a weak thumbs-up and turned around again. She was close, she could feel it. Whatever it was lay right under her nose—all she had to do was dig it up. Bracing herself, she bent down once again, plunging her hand into the ice-cold water. The riverbed gave way surprisingly easily as she dug her fingers in and closed them around the first firm object she came into contact with. She deflated when she saw what it was. A crunched-up soda can.

Over the next few minutes, she procured several handfuls of random items: two plastic bottles, a juice box, a penny from 1986, some kid's wallet. With each of them, the sense of certainty she'd felt faded a little more . . . until her fingers brushed against cool metal and a jolt went through her entire arm, almost knocking her off balance.

"Rhia," she said, her voice shaking with barely contained excitement.

Rhia, who had spent the last few minutes watching her with something akin to pity, sat up straighter. "Did you find something?"

Valerie didn't respond as her hand broke through the surface of the river to reveal a necklace. It was a simple silver chain with a pendant in the shape of a pentagram that was about as large as a coin. Holding it in her hand, Valerie could practically feel the magic buzzing off it, its weight in her palm enough to make her dizzy. Realization hit her: for the first time in her entire life, she was holding a piece of her mother.

"What is it?" Rhia asked.

Valerie turned around, her eyes still fixed on the five-pointed star as she waded back towards the riverside. Rhia wrapped the towel around her shoulders the instant she climbed out, but Valerie barely noticed.

"Look," she said, holding it out for Rhia to see. "It's hers. It has to be."

Rhia leaned closer, her hands still rubbing Valerie's arms to warm her up. "How do you know?"

"I don't know. I can just feel it."

"So . . . what now?"

Valerie thought for a moment, her eyes still glued to the piece of jewelry. Finally, she looked up at Rhia. "I'll try a tracking spell."

Rhia's eyes widened. "Okay. But can you put on clothes first? You're going to catch your death out here."

Valerie became suddenly aware that she was still dripping and shaking all over. She kept the necklace clutched in one hand while she dried off and got dressed again, only halting in her movements when Rhia said, "I actually have something for you."

Valerie turned around to find Rhia holding something out in her hand. It was another necklace. In a delicate silver frame dangled a crystal; depending on how the light hit it, it looked somewhere between gray and lavender.

"It's smoky quartz," Rhia explained. "For protection."

At that, Valerie momentarily forgot all about the pentagram in her hand. As her fingers ran over the coarse surface of the crystal, it hummed in response, sending a warm tingle through her skin. "Thank you," she murmured, meeting Rhia's gaze again. She couldn't remember the last time someone had given her a present that wasn't money or a gift card, let alone with so much heart-aching care in their eyes. "It's beautiful."

"Want me to help you put it on?"

Moving her hair out of the way, Valerie tilted her head. There was some rustling behind her as Rhia got onto her tiptoes. Then the gentle weight of the necklace came to rest around her throat, followed by Rhia's lips pressing a soft kiss to the nape of her neck.

"There." She carefully moved Valerie's hair back into place. "All done."

"Thank you." Smiling, Valerie turned back around and leaned down for a kiss. When she backed away, she felt steadier than she had all day. "Now that I'm all safe," she said, "let's do this. I will even—" here, she paused dramatically "—cast a circle."

"How? Do you always carry salt and lavender with y—" Rhia broke off when Valerie retrieved exactly that from the basket on her bike.

Valerie grinned. "What kind of amateur do you take me for, pumpkin?"

"This is," Rhia said very earnestly, "the hottest thing you've ever done."

Trying her hardest not to make a terrible joke, Valerie set about casting the circle. Five minutes later, they sat facing each other in the grass, both leaning over the pendant in Valerie's hand.

"I've never done a tracking spell before," Rhia admitted.

"Me neither," Valerie said. "At least, not consciously. When I was a kid, I used to lose stuff all the time and find it again by *visualizing* it," she finished with air quotations. "I only realized I was performing a spell when I stumbled upon it in one of the books I'd snuck from a thrift store."

Rhia shook her head, a small smile playing around her lips. "How does it work, then?"

"It's just like divination," Valerie explained. "You clear your mind, focus your energy on the object you're seeking, and wait for answers. With people, it's more difficult—you need to have something of theirs or have some kind of emotional bond with them, otherwise it doesn't work. The rest is intuition."

Rhia nodded, though not without grimacing at the feared I-word.

Closing her fingers tighter around the cool metal, Valerie drew in a deep breath and allowed her mind to drift. While Rhia always seemed to struggle with this part, Valerie slipped into the meditative state with ease. It wasn't that different from the way she felt when she was painting, her head clear and her attention focused on only one thing at a time. It didn't take long until the black behind her eyelids began to move and take on shapes. A low brick wall with an open metal gate came into view. She imagined herself walking through it, and a narrow path appeared, leading to a small building made of coarse brick. The word *chapel* popped into Valerie's mind without her doing.

She opened her eyes. "Does Oakriver have a chapel?"

Rhia was still sitting cross-legged in front of her, her face full of wonder. "Yes."

Valerie got to her feet. "She's there."

"Valerie—"

She was already rushing towards their bikes. "Come on!"

Behind her, she heard Rhia's sigh, then a murmur as she closed the circle. A moment later, she got onto her bike next to Valerie, and they took off towards the town, the rumbling of the river fading in the distance for what Valerie hoped was the last time.

Like most noteworthy places in Oakriver, the chapel wasn't very far from the town center. When they arrived, flushed and out of breath, it looked exactly as Valerie's vision had shown: there was a low brick wall that they leaned their bikes against and a rusty metal gate that screeched in protest when pushed open. A narrow, partially overgrown path wound through the meadow and up to the door of the weathered chapel. The pebbles crunched under Valerie's boots as she strode through the gate, her chin raised and her steps determined. Rhia moved with more reluctance but stayed firmly at Valerie's side as they made their way towards the entrance of the chapel. The inside was just as Valerie had expected: several wooden pews, a small altar, a few candles silently burning away. What she hadn't expected was for no one else to be there, the heavy quiet pierced by the sound of their steps echoing from the walls.

"She's not here."

"I'm sorry," said Rhia. Nothing about the statement sounded particularly surprised.

"Don't say that yet." Valerie abruptly spun on her heel, marching back towards the door. "We haven't searched everywhere."

Rhia trailed after her, back into the autumn air. This time, they didn't stay on the path but walked through the tall grass, rounding the chapel. Behind the building stretched a cemetery with rows and rows of ancient crosses and headstones sitting in the shadows of the old trees towering above them. But they weren't what made Valerie's heartbeat stutter: it was the sight of the red-haired woman standing at one of the graves. Even though only half of her face was visible, Valerie recognized her immediately as the witch she'd seen at Obscura.

It could've very well been coincidence. Valerie, ever the optimist, decided to chalk it up to luck instead.

She didn't think or pause to plan. She just walked, her steps speeding up as she clutched the pentagram tightly enough for its edges to dig into her palm. She was close enough to be able to make out the flower pattern on the woman's dress, and she would've called out for her if a hand hadn't suddenly closed around her wrist.

Spinning around, she faced Rhia. "Rhia." She tried to yank her hand free, but Rhia held on. "What are you doing? It's *her*—"

"Valerie," Rhia said quietly.

"What?" Valerie snapped. Her voice came out harsher than she'd intended, but Rhia didn't flinch.

"Look around," Rhia said in the same soft tone. "We're in a cemetery."

"I can see that."

Rhia's eyes were warm and imploring. "Have you ever considered that maybe—"

"No." Valerie knew where that sentence was heading even before it was finished. "She's not. I *know* she's not, she's right—"

Valerie turned as far as she could with Rhia still holding on to her, but it was too late. The woman was gone, vanished as if she'd never been there in the first place.

When she turned back to Rhia, her voice was choked up. "Why did you do that? She was *right there*, I could have spoken to her—"

"No, she wasn't." There was that pitying look again. Valerie decided that, out of all of Rhia's expressions, this one was her least favorite. "That woman only moved to Oakriver two years ago. Her name is Jenny. She has two kids and a cat she brings to my mom's clinic sometimes. It's not her, Valerie."

"That still doesn't give you the right to decide if I can talk to her or not," Valerie said, trying her best to keep her voice from rising in volume. The Knight of Swords flashed in her mind again. She dug her nails into her palms to keep them from growing hot.

"You're right." Shoulders sagging, Rhia let go of her wrist.

For a few seconds, neither of them knew where to go from there. Finally, Valerie turned around and walked back in the direction they'd come from.

Rhia caught up with her when she was already climbing onto her bike. "Valerie?" she asked, sounding uncharacteristically uncertain. "Will I see you tomorrow?"

With her hands on the handlebars, Valerie studied the guilty look in her eyes, the sorry set of her shoulders. It hadn't been a real fight, but there was still an uneasy sense of confrontation squirming in the pit of her stomach, jarringly different from anything else she'd felt with Rhia so far.

"Yeah." She leaned closer for a short kiss, her hand squeezing Rhia's. "Yeah, of course."

With that she left, her head full of questions and two more necklaces than she'd started off with clinking softly beneath her collar.

19

SEVEN OF SWORDS

withheld information — acting alone — deception

Rhia had never been afraid of magic.

All her life, witchcraft had been a familiar playing field; her family's rules left little room for surprises, traditions eliminated error, and everything she had to know had been spoon-fed to her while she'd barely been able to walk. In Rhia's hands, magic was safe. At least, that was what she had thought before the night at the cabin—before her vision, before she'd watched Valerie wade into a river with unseeing eyes, before she'd followed the necklace of an unknown witch to the cemetery. None of it felt familiar, or controllable, or even safe in the slightest. It felt lawless, untamable. It felt *dark*.

Valerie didn't seem to notice, but Rhia did. She spent the two days following their frantic race to the chapel searching every inch of the cemetery for a headstone, but to no avail: Isabelle Morgan's grave was nowhere to be found. That left her with no other choice but to consult her family's spell books.

Whenever a volume was filled, it was added to the shelves in the living room, two ceiling-high beasts that threatened to buckle under the mass of felt-bound tomes and notebooks they held. Rhia had read around half of them—Gabrielle Greenbrook's notes, mostly, since she was the most powerful earth witch who had ever come from their family, and a few others by great-aunts with an affinity for earth. This time, she wasn't sure what she was looking for.

Trying to ignore the racket sounding from the adjacent kitchen—her mother was baking something cinnamon-scented while Sage and Holly bickered over their late lunch—she went to stand in front of the shelves and closed her eyes. Intuition. It always came back to the one thing she could not control.

In the end, she tried to imitate what she'd seen her sister do while picking cards during tarot readings. Stepping closer, she ran a hand along the spines on the shelf, waiting for one to feel warmer than the others or, as Sage had once described, *tingly*. All she felt was rough paper and fabric. She was a witch stripped of her sixth sense, and none of her other ones were fit to compensate for it.

With a frustrated groan, she opened her eyes, snatched the first book she honed in on, and slouched to the floor. There was no title or author on the cover, but Rhia recognized the handwriting as that of her great-aunt Cassandra, one of her grandmother's late sisters who could manipulate air. She'd always written with a flourish, her accounts rambling and filled with anecdotes. Hers were classics amongst the books that she and Holly had requested for bedtime stories when they were little, purely because of how entertaining they were. This particular tome, however, Rhia couldn't remember ever seeing on her nightstand.

Settling on her back, legs up against the bookshelf, she began to read. It was a lot of the usual: notes about rituals, some more successful than others—*I fear that I used too much witch hazel, but that's all right. Eyebrows grow back, don't they?*—stories about her life in Oakriver, observations about the witch community. It didn't take long before Rhia's eyelids started to grow heavy. It was a combination of the golden afternoon light that warmed the wooden floor and the gentle purring of Salem over on the couch. Also, possibly, a Pavlovian response instilled by years of falling asleep to Cassandra Greenbrook's words.

It was the raised voices in the kitchen that startled her back to full awareness.

"Please, Holly, it'll literally take you seconds—"

"I'm not your weather frog! Let me finish my soup!"

"It's a really important event, and the venue needs confirmation *now*. Please, Holls, I'm begging you." Indifferent silence. "I'll let you wear my black dress for Halloween. The new one with the cutouts."

There was a dramatic sigh, the scraping of a chair across the floor. Then, the creaking of the back door as Holly stepped outside. Through the open door that connected the kitchen and the living room came a gust of wind strong enough to flip a few of the pages in Rhia's spell book. She was about to cry out that Holly had made her lose her spot when she looked down at the page. It was a protocol of a Council meeting, except . . . "Council of the Four?" Rhia murmured.

Her mother glanced over at her from where she was kneading dough at the table, her cheek smeared with flour. "Did you say something, sweetheart?"

Instinctively, Rhia shook her head. Her finger traced the

faded letters. *Protocol of the Annual Meeting of the Council of the Four, October 1998.* The words settled heavy and wrong in her stomach. The rest of the page yielded no explanation. All names were shortened into initials—there was G for Greenbrook, L for Lightbourn, F for Fairlove, and then H. In her mind, she ran through all the witches she knew and their last names. She couldn't think of a single one with this initial who lived close enough to Oakriver to warrant their being in the Council.

She flipped the page, only to land on a recipe for an antigravity potion meant to make the consumer momentarily weightless. In Cassandra's books, the recipes were always collected in the very back pages. Which meant that everything in between, about ten pages if Rhia had to guess, had been torn out. With her heart pounding in her chest, she sat up. At random, she pulled out another book from around 2000. At least a quarter was missing. Another. Several pages cut clean out. Another. Incomplete.

From the kitchen, she could feel her mother watching her. Meeting her eyes, Rhia held up one of the books. "Mom? Why are there pages missing?"

"Hmm? Oh, those were private, I suppose." Her mother gestured with hands sticky with cinnamon roll filling. "Some things, you don't want your family to read."

Rhia looked back at the book she was cradling, running a finger along the jagged edges where the missing pages had once been. It made sense. She'd filled one spell book so far, and her mother had told her several times that if there was anything she didn't want included in the family archives, she absolutely had the right to remove it. It just seemed so *methodical*. Why had she never read about this Family H in any other volume before?

"It's going to rain," Holly's bright voice announced. "Better book an inside venue." Behind her, the door slammed shut.

Still jittery, Rhia slid the books back into place. It didn't matter. Whoever these ex–Council members were, they had nothing to do with Isabelle Morgan. That was the priority. She could interrogate her family about everything else another time.

With this objective, Rhia decided to change tactics. Aimlessly fishing for answers in a murky sea of information wasn't going to lead anywhere. If she wanted to get to the bottom of this, she needed to go beneath the surface. And so, she dove in.

~

"Rhia?" Quinn squinted into the dim light of the hallway. Judging by the disheveled state of their hair and the considerable time it had taken them to open the door, they'd just woken up from a nap. "Valerie is still in class."

"I know," said Rhia. "Is it okay if I come in?"

The furrow between Quinn's brows deepened, but after a moment of hesitation, they wordlessly stepped aside.

While Rhia entered and closed the door behind her, they crossed the darkened room and sat down on their bed. "Does Valerie know you're here?"

"No." Wringing her hands, Rhia wandered closer to Valerie's side of the room. Next to empty coffee mugs and the leaf Rhia had revived at the party a few weeks ago—the sight did something funny to her heart—sat the pentagram necklace. It was heavier than it looked when she picked it up, the metal unexpectedly cool to the touch. She turned around and met Quinn's gaze again. "I actually wanted to talk to you."

"Me?"

"Yes. Is it okay if I sit?"

"Sure."

Sinking down cross-legged in front of them on their unmade bed, Rhia asked, "Did Valerie tell you about the necklace?"

"She told me that it's her mom's and that it led her to a witch she knew from Obscura."

Rhia's fingers tightened around the pendant. "And what do you think about that?"

Quinn lifted one shoulder in a shrug, slender fingers plucking at the threads in their comforter. "Why does it matter what I think? I'm not like you. I don't know anything about magic except what's in textbooks."

"You don't truly believe that." Rhia laughed. Her smile faded when Quinn met her eyes again with a bewildered expression. "Wait, do you?"

"Of course I do." Quinn frowned. "I'm not a witch."

"But you work at Obscura. You can *see* the shop even though there's a decade-old concealment spell on it."

"Helen said that sometimes there are people who are clairvoyant enough to see it. People with a high degree of magical affinity, but not enough to manifest into actual powers, et cetera."

"Okay," Rhia said. "Let's say that's true. It still doesn't explain everything that happened the other night. You knew where Valerie was going. How, if not through magic?"

Quinn visibly blanched. They looked away again, but this time Rhia caught the fear flickering in their eyes before they could hide it. *That* was what had been moving in their gaze all along, Rhia realized. Quinn Jiang was terrified.

Their voice was a hoarse whisper when they said, "I didn't do anything."

"Quinn," Rhia said softly.

They were quiet for a long moment. Their hands had stilled. Their eyes were fixed somewhere on the wall as if staring into another room, another night. "There was a voice. A woman whispering. It's what woke me up in the first place."

There it was again: the sense of danger that had been clinging to Rhia like a bad perfume ever since the cabin trip. "What did she say? Did you see her?"

"I didn't see anyone, but it sounded like she was standing right next to me." There was a tremor in Quinn's voice that Rhia had never heard before. "She said, 'Valerie needs you.' And then I heard the river."

"You *heard* the river?"

"Yeah." Quinn gulped. "The water, I could hear it all the way from my room. It sounded like a bunch of voices all speaking at the same time. And then somehow I knew exactly where Valerie was."

"Water magic," Rhia breathed.

Quinn's head snapped up. "What?"

"Every witch has one element they draw their magic from. Mine is earth. Valerie's is fire. And I think yours—"

"No," Quinn said firmly, shaking their head. "That's not possible. I'm not a witch, my mom isn't—"

"She doesn't have to be. Magic can skip generations."

"But wouldn't I have noticed something earlier?" Quinn whispered, more to themself than to Rhia.

Sitting in front of them, with their hands trembling in their lap and their too-large sweater swallowing their narrow frame, Rhia felt a sudden surge of pity. Gently, she said, "Some witches realize they have abilities in their thirties, some even later. The signs are different for everyone. It's normal to be scared, but I promise that nothing has changed. You're still the same person."

Quinn was staring blankly at the wall again, their breathing shallow. "Is it also normal to hear voices?"

Rhia hesitated. "I can hear the trees if I focus. But I've never experienced anything like what you're describing. It's never a singular voice." She paused before quickly adding, "I'm sure there's an explanation for it. Another special talent."

"If this is a talent, I don't want it," Quinn said. "I don't—Fuck, I'm just trying to make it through college. Why is this only happening to me *now*?"

"I don't know." Rhia had the overwhelming urge to pull Quinn into a hug, but she didn't think they wanted that. Instead, she tried for a reassuring tone as she said, "I know this must feel terrifying. But magic isn't a curse, Quinn. Do you want to know what I believe?"

"What?"

"I believe that everyone has a tiny seed of magic in them," Rhia said, echoing the words her mother had told her over and over growing up. "For most people, it's buried all the way down, so far they may never know it's even there. Few people are aware of it and nurture it to help it grow—like my family, or the other witches in Oakriver. Yours just sprouted without you knowing." She paused, studying Quinn, before she added, "You can't bury it. Not when it's such a deeply rooted part of you. Not when it's already seen the light."

A few seconds passed without either of them speaking. Then: "It's just . . . I don't understand why no one in my family ever talked to me about it. At least one of them has to have abilities, right? So why did they never reach out to me? Why did they just leave me to figure all of this out alone?" Their voice cracked on the last word. In the low light, Rhia could see tears glittering in their eyes, though from the way Quinn angrily blinked them away, they seemed more out of frustration than sadness.

"I don't know," she murmured. "Have you ever met them?"

"A few times, but I was so small, I don't . . . Oh." In the bluish tint of the room, their face looked wearier than Rhia had ever seen, the shadows under their eyes bruising. "This is why." When Rhia only stared at them, uncomprehending, they explained. "My grandmother went back to Nanjing a few years before I was born, and since then she and my mom haven't really spoken. Mom always talked about how she felt like an outsider in the family—how she felt like there was something that connected her mother and aunts that she could never grasp. It has to be magic, right?"

Rhia swallowed. She felt terrible. This was all terrible. "Quinn—"

"It's not like I haven't had enough self-discovery arcs to last me a lifetime," they continued. "I mean, first the gender stuff, then figuring out I'm pansexual, and now magic? What's next?" A laugh clawed its way out of their throat, jagged and near hysterical. "Every time I feel like I've found my footing, another revelation comes out of nowhere. It's like I'm playing goddamn identity Jenga while the universe purposefully knocks over my tower every other second."

Rhia winced. This was the most she had ever heard Quinn talk in one sitting, and the most distraught she'd ever witnessed them. If Valerie had been there, she could have told them about how she had come to understand her magic.

All Rhia could offer was a soft: "You don't have to figure it out on your own. You have me, and Valerie, and my entire family. You don't even have to use it if you don't want to, though I think that if you did—if you learned to harness your abilities— you would be *amazing*. I mean, the way you led us straight to Valerie . . ." Rhia broke off when she saw the look on Quinn's face, their eyes darkening again like the windows of a house being shuttered. Quickly, she rushed to say, "I'm here, is all I want to say."

Quinn said nothing. Rhia felt a distinct pang of guilt as she watched the way they hugged a pillow to their chest—they'd been napping peacefully between classes until she'd come along and turned their entire world upside down in one messy conversation.

Finally, Quinn asked, "Rhia, why are you here?"

"It's nothing. We don't have to talk about it right now. I should probably just—"

"No," Quinn said. "If it's about Valerie, I want to know."

"It's about the necklace." Rhia reluctantly held it out for them. "It was in the river, and since you knew where to find her, I thought . . . maybe you'd know more about this too."

Quinn squinted at the pentagram. "What do you want to know?"

"I need to know who this belongs to and if that person is still alive."

"Why?"

"Because Valerie doesn't want to even *consider* the possibility that her mom might be dead. You know her. She'll chase a ghost to the ends of the world if she thinks there's the slightest chance she'll find her."

"Probably," Quinn agreed. "That's her decision to make, though."

Unable to sit still any longer, Rhia got to her feet. "She's already climbed into that cursed river twice," she said, pacing the length of the tiny room. "Who knows what else she'll do? She'll get herself killed if she doesn't—"

"If she doesn't what?" Quinn asked behind her.

Rhia didn't answer. Her eyes were glued to the drawing that sat on top of the mess on Quinn's desk. A woman in a black dress floating in a river, facedown. "Quinn," she said, "did you draw this?"

Quinn craned their neck to see what she was looking at. "Oh. Yeah, I did. I'm not sure wh—"

"I saw the same thing. When I was scrying with Valerie at the cabin, this is the vision that came up. It's her."

Quinn had grown very still. There wasn't a hint of sleepiness left on their face as they watched Rhia stagger back over to the bed, the drawing clutched in one hand. "You think she's going to drown?"

"I was sure I interpreted it wrong, but . . ." There was a lump in Rhia's throat that made her voice sound strangled. "You saw the same thing. It can't be a coincidence."

Quinn's jaw worked. For a few terrible seconds, neither of them spoke. Outside in the hallway, a group of college students walked by, chattering and laughing. They had no idea that just behind the door, two witches were sitting with a necklace from a cursed river and the bone-chilling knowledge that their loved one was going to die if they didn't find a way to prevent their shared premonition.

"Okay." Quinn stretched out their hand. "I'll give it a try."

Rhia placed the pentagram into Quinn's palm. Their fingers closed around the necklace slowly, each more reluctant than the one before. When they finally held it, they inhaled shakily, closed their eyes, and brought their cupped hands to their heart. Two things happened at once.

One: the door burst open, and Valerie strode inside.

Two: with the necklace clutched between their fingers and in the complete silence of the dorm room, Quinn began to drown.

20

TEN OF SWORDS

bitterness — loss — feeling betrayed

"Rhia?" Valerie sounded incredulous as she froze in the doorway. "What are you—"

A terrible gurgling sound from Quinn cut her off. Rhia's eyes snapped back to them; they were still sitting on the edge of the bed, fingers white-knuckled around the pendant.

"Quinn?" Rhia asked, her own voice ratcheting an octave higher as panic flooded her. She put a hand on Quinn's knee, but they didn't react. "Quinn, what do you see?"

They shook their head, their chest rising and falling rapidly as they gulped in choking breaths.

"What did you *do*?" Valerie whispered, dropping to her knees next to Rhia.

Rhia's own breaths turned shallow as she watched Quinn's eyes roll back into their skull. "Nothing, I just—The necklace—"

Valerie's eyes darted down to the silver glittering between

Quinn's fingers. She opened her mouth to say something, but Quinn beat her to it.

"The river. The river, the river—" They broke off into wet, gasping coughs.

While Rhia sat frozen, unable to move, Valerie reached out and curled a hand around the back of Quinn's neck, pulling their face closer as if to make them look at her. "Quinn, you can breathe, you're okay—"

"No," Quinn gasped, frantically shaking their head. "Please don't. *Please don't!*" A new scent filled the room, heavy and cloying: river water.

Valerie had to smell it too. Pressing her forehead against Quinn's, she whispered, "Tell me what you're seeing, Quinn."

"They found out." A whimper. "They're going to kill me. There's—" Rhia watched in horror as they convulsed in another coughing fit. Water sputtered from their lips, dripping down their chin and onto their sheets. "There's water everywhere," they choked out. Their voice was a horrifying rasp that sounded like two metal pieces grinding together.

"Who are *they?*" Rhia asked shakily.

Quinn cried silently, their eyes darting back and forth beneath their closed eyelids. When their lips parted again, the voice that came out didn't sound like their own. "Valerie. My darling girl. I'm so sorry."

Rhia's heart forgot to beat. Her hand automatically reached for Valerie's, but Valerie flinched away. Her lips silently formed the word *no*, over and over again, but no sound escaped.

"I can't—th-they're watching," Quinn babbled. "She's not letting me up, and I can't breathe, and they're watching! *They're watching they're watching they're—*"

Philline Harms

With each word, their voice grew louder, quiet whimpers turning into hoarse screams that made Rhia's hair stand on end. She couldn't take it anymore—without thinking twice about it, she jerked forward and pried the necklace out of Quinn's cramping fingers.

Quinn froze the instant the pendant left their grasp. Their lips parted on an aborted scream; then, like a marionette with its strings cut, they crumbled inward, their chin dropping down to their chest in the sudden silence.

"Quinn?" Valerie asked, gently shaking their shoulders.

Quinn didn't react. Their skin was pale enough for their veins to show, their mouth going slack as all the tension drained out of them at once. When Valerie lowered them onto the bed, they went easily, body limp, eyes closed. Their chest was rising and falling evenly now, like they were fast asleep. Like they hadn't sounded like they were dying only a few seconds earlier.

Together, they moved Quinn's head onto the pillow and pulled a blanket up to their chin. Valerie's motions were mechanical as she tucked the blanket under their feet, throwing a glance over her shoulder to make sure that Quinn's binder was flung across the back of their chair and they didn't fall asleep wearing it.

"They used up too much magic," Rhia rasped while Valerie sank down on the edge of Quinn's bed and smoothed their tousled hair out of their face. "They're okay. They're just going to be asleep for a while."

"Magic?" Valerie echoed. Her voice sounded strange—cold, detached.

"I always had a feeling they had abilities, with them working at Obscura and everything, and then when you sleepwalked to the river, they were the one who knew where to find you."

Valerie stared down at Quinn's face as if she'd never seen it before. Huddled under the blanket, they looked so small. "Why didn't you say anything?"

"I . . . I thought that they should be the one to tell you."

Valerie's gaze found the pentagram necklace Rhia had dropped next to the bed. "So you got them to do divination with my mother's necklace?"

Guilt was a knife plunged right through Rhia's rib cage. "Yes."

"And you didn't think for one second to ask me first?" Valerie quietly asked.

"I did," Rhia managed. "I did think about it."

"But?"

"But I knew that you wouldn't agree to do this. I knew they had some kind of connection to the river. I didn't know they were also a Messenger, but if I'm correct—"

"A Messenger?" Valerie asked impatiently.

"A rare type of witch that can tap directly into the spirit world, no further rituals needed," Rhia rushed to clarify. "I think that's what they did. Somehow, they channeled your mom through her necklace."

Valerie tore her gaze away from Quinn and got to her feet. Her movements were slow; her eyes, when they met Rhia's, held a fire she'd never seen in them before. It wasn't the quiet kind that had warmed her when they'd shared a bed at the cabin or the steady flame she usually found leveled at her—it was the raging kind that itched to destroy, and it was visibly hard for Valerie to contain.

"Let me get this straight," Valerie said. "You knew that I would be against this, but you did it anyway. You came to *my* dorm room when you knew I'd be in class, got *my* best friend—whose abilities you decided to hide from me—to help you, and tried to contact *my* mother?"

"Valerie, I didn't think—"

"That I'd find out?"

"That it would be this bad." Rhia gestured at Quinn's still form. Tears were stinging in her eyes, but she blinked them away. "I just wanted to help."

"I didn't *ask* for your help!" For the first time, Valerie's voice rose in volume.

"I know, I—"

"Rhia." Valerie cut her off. Her hands were trembling at her sides, clenching and unclenching. The air between them was suddenly charged, prickling with all the static of an incoming thunderstorm. "I think you should go. I can't be around you when you're doing this."

"Doing what?" Rhia whispered.

"This." Valerie waved her hand around in a vague gesture. "Trying to control . . . *everything*."

Rhia's throat constricted. By now, the tears were coming too fast to hold back. On instinct, she wanted to defend herself, wanted to affirm that she wasn't in the wrong—but with Quinn unconscious next to them and the terrible look on Valerie's face, she knew that that wasn't the truth. She did the only thing she could do: she gave a jerky nod and turned.

The last thing she saw before she pulled the door shut behind her was Valerie sinking to her knees in front of Quinn's bed, one hand clutching the necklace to her chest while the other brushed absentmindedly over the spot where river water soaked the sheets.

21

THE HERMIT

solitude — introspection — searching for truth

Typically, Valerie didn't hold grudges. Her anger was a fickle thing; it could flare up in the blink of an eye and be snuffed out just as quickly.

However, *typically* her temper wasn't ignited by walking in on her girlfriend trying to contact her missing mom using a magical necklace. *Typically*, she didn't find her best friend coughing up river water on their bed. And *typically*, that wasn't how Valerie found out that her mother—the fairy-tale creature she'd spun stories about when she was little, the witch she'd tried to channel when she'd first discovered her abilities, the woman she'd moved towns and waded into rivers for—was most likely dead. It was too much, all of it.

The anger was so simple. It didn't ask any questions, and as long as it raged on, Valerie didn't have to face what lingered beyond the smoke. And so, this time, she didn't try to extinguish it—she let it smolder in her chest and stoked it when it threatened to dwindle.

~

Ten days passed, and Valerie didn't respond to Rhia's texts. Didn't go to the café. Didn't walk past her house. Definitely did *not* spend most of her time thinking about her. Instead, she spent the hours in her dorm room or in one of the school's art studios. Before magic, art had been the only way she'd known to express herself—a strange child with few friends, she'd spent her afternoons lying on her bedroom floor, her hands never free of paint stains. She'd quickly discovered that she had a knack for portraits, and so she'd started there: hyperrealistic drawings of classmates and people she saw on TV, the stranger the face the better. Next, she moved on to working without a reference. Most of those sketches were of women. Usually, they had red hair and looked a little like her, except older, wiser, more sure of themselves. She drew them sitting on the porches of houses in a town she knew only from late-night searches on Google Maps. Sometimes, when she felt self-indulgent, she would draw a girl her age next to them.

Enter her fire magic. As she discovered her abilities, her colors grew bolder. Realistic portraits turned into something more abstract, feverish strokes with layered texture. Her motifs turned from domestic scenes to something wilder: houses ablaze, hands cradling flames, women who looked like wildfires.

Now she stared at her empty canvas and didn't know what to paint. When she thought of her mother, she thought not of fire but of lungs filled with river water. Her paintings were in shades of blue and gray. None of her ideas sparked.

Quinn joined her sometimes, but only so long as Valerie didn't try to address their abilities. They were still shaken, and even more elusive than usual. Trying to get them to open up was like trying to hold on to water: one wrong word, and they slipped through Valerie's fingers again, disappearing somewhere and only returning to their room long after midnight. Even though they'd played just as big a part in going behind Valerie's back as Rhia had, she found it a lot harder to be mad at Quinn—*they* were the one who'd had their body hijacked by a dead woman, after all. Valerie wanted to talk to them about it—to ask if they were okay or, hell, just give them a hug—but no such luck.

Today was another day spent mostly alone. After class, Quinn had taken off to Obscura, leaving Valerie to wander the campus alone. Fitting her mood, it was a gloomy afternoon with a dark-gray sky. She kept her head down and her hands in her pockets as she picked her way through the groups of students standing outside the main building. Halloween was only two days away, and from the bits of conversations floating around, she'd gathered that there would be a big festival in the town center. All around her, people were making plans, talking about costumes and dinner arrangements, their topics of conversation perfectly mundane. Watching her peers chattering and laughing, Valerie regretted not having tried harder to make friends at the beginning of the semester.

She walked quickly down the path that led back to her dorm, leaving the Arts and Fashion Building behind—only to come to a halt when she glimpsed something pink flashing in her periphery.

Her fight-or-flight instinct kicked in immediately, but it was too late: Holly Greenbrook was already gliding straight towards her. "Valerie!" she exclaimed, drawing her bright-fuchsia coat tighter around herself. "So chilly today, isn't it?"

Valerie's smile felt more like a grimace. "Yeah. What are you doing here?"

"I just had coffee with my dad at Sugar & Spice, and I thought I'd swing by Tristan's dorm on the way back," Holly said. She sounded innocent enough, but Valerie knew her well enough by now to recognize that there was a weight behind her airy tone.

"How did you find me?"

"Air magic, remember?" Holly leaned in like she was telling her a secret. "The wind's a gossip."

Valerie could do nothing but blink at her.

"Anyways," Holly continued, undisturbed by her disbelieving stare, "now that I've found you, why don't you walk with me?"

She strolled down the narrow path before Valerie got the chance to respond. Valerie watched her go, rooted in place. This did not fit into her plan—the plan being to avoid all things Rhia until she could tell whether the confusing mix of emotions in her gut was harmless or a goddamn Molotov cocktail that would blow up as soon as Valerie saw her again. Then again, this wasn't Rhia. Just her cousin. Her cousin who'd hunted Valerie down to talk to her. Curiosity won over spite. Hurrying to catch up with her, Valerie panted, "Did Rhia send you?"

"Oh, no. In fact, she'll probably kill me when she finds out I talked to you," Holly said cheerily.

Behind the main building, there were a few empty wooden benches where students sat on the rare sunny days to do their coursework together or have a smoke between classes. Holly gracefully climbed onto one of them and perched on the back-rest with her pink rain boots planted on the seat. With her hands in the pockets of her jacket, Valerie sank down next to her.

"How are you, Valerie?" Holly asked.

Valerie froze. She'd expected a scolding for not reaching out to Rhia, some version of a fiercely protective lecture. She wasn't prepared for such a simple question, spoken in a way that was so sincere it momentarily put out the fire inside her rib cage. Staring down at the cigarette butts that littered the damp grass in front of the bench, she lifted one shoulder in a shrug. "Dunno." Holly didn't say anything, her imploring gaze flitting over Valerie's features. "How . . ." Valerie cleared her throat. "How's Rhia?"

"Sad," answered Holly, her lips curling into an unhappy frown. "Anxious. She feels terrible about the whole thing."

Valerie dug her nails into her palms. "I just don't understand why she did it."

Holly hummed, her eyes fixed on the edge of the woods in the distance. "You know, I've known Rhia her entire life. Before her dad died, and after. She told you about how she was unable to practice divination after he was gone, didn't she?"

Valerie gave a tense nod. She had no idea where this conversation was heading and wasn't sure she wanted to be a part of it.

But Holly was already continuing. "To lose a loved one like that . . . I don't need to explain to you how it changes everything." She paused, carefully choosing her next words. "Once you learn what that kind of loss feels like, you build a wall. In the beginning, it helps—you feel like it protects you. If you don't let anyone in, you can't lose anyone, right?"

Rain began to fall, an irregular pitter-patter on the treetops sheltering them that mirrored the erratic beating of Valerie's heart.

"The thing is, that wall? It doesn't go away. You spend so much time building it—arranging every brick, filling every

Philline Harms

crevice—that taking it down begins to feel impossible. So the wall stays, even after it's done serving you. And it doesn't make exceptions, either; no one gets in, and no one leaves. That's how you survive for years." Holly waited until Valerie met her eyes. "Until, one day, a person manages to get through."

Valerie stayed silent, her eyes burning. The anger was gone. In its place spread something else: a tangled mix of mourning, both for her and for Rhia. Their grief was the same entity, just with different faces: while Valerie's had driven her forward, into witchcraft and into Oakriver, Rhia's had paralyzed her.

"You know, for the longest time, I didn't think this would happen," Holly said. "And I saw how much she battled with it at first—letting you in."

Suddenly, Valerie understood. "Because love, next to death, is the ultimate loss of control."

"Exactly. Opening up *terrified* her. But not as much as the thought of losing you," Holly finished.

"But that still doesn't make what she did okay," Valerie whispered. "Right?"

"Of course not. None of this is an excuse. But maybe it can be an explanation." Holly offered her a small smile. "I know it must be difficult for you to understand, your Sagittarius energy is totally clashing with her Capricorn moon here—"

"How do you know I'm a—"

"But this is Rhia's way of loving people. Reluctantly, at first, and then irrevocably and with everything she has."

Tilting her head back, Valerie tried to blink back her tears. Above her, the wind was toying with the golden leaves of the trees that spanned over them, and all she saw was *her*. Rhia was everywhere she went. She was the swaying of the branches, the rustling of the leaves, the scent of wet soil and rain. She was autumn and all its colors. How was Valerie ever supposed to spend another October without thinking of her?

Irrevocably, indeed.

"I know it's not easy, but you need to understand that from her perspective, she really was trying to protect you," Holly said softly. "The things she does, they're born out of fear, not malice. She would jump into that goddamn river a dozen times if it meant keeping you safe."

Valerie didn't respond—couldn't, with how tight her throat was.

Holly got to her feet. "I'll leave you be now. You know where to find me if you need anything." She turned around once more to tell Valerie, "Whatever you decide to do—I'm grateful you came along. At least now we know that the wall can still crumble."

A moment later, she was gone, as if whisked away by the wind. Valerie was left sitting alone on the bench, rain clinging to her eyelashes and trailing down her collar. Its pattering was only getting faster; meanwhile, Valerie's heart was getting slower with every beat, falling back into a steady rhythm that spoke of a decision already made.

Her fingers wandered to her neck, closing around the persistent weight of the protection charm Rhia had given her.

Irrevocably.

~

It was eleven at night by the time Valerie found herself nearing the towering brick house in the center of Oakriver. The rain had stopped, but there was still a heavy mist in the air that rendered her walk hazy and dreamlike. As she neared the Greenbrooks' property, she could feel the familiar presence of witchcraft growing; what had started as a faint humming at the end of the street had turned into an acute awareness, the night air practically singing with magic by the time Valerie stepped through the creaking garden gate. Ahead of her, all the windows were dark—all, except for Rhia's.

Last time she'd been here, she'd jumped from that very ledge. Then, the leap had terrified her; now, staring up at the window, she realized climbing up was going to be far more difficult.

She honed in on the tree in front of the house that looked like it was older than the town itself. "Okay," she said to herself, resolutely tucking two strands of hair behind her ears, "you've got this. Climb the tree, get through the window, and make up." Even as she said it, she could feel her resolve begin to falter. She didn't know what part she was more intimidated by—the climb or the confrontation with Rhia. Still, she shoved her fear aside. Of the series of terrifying experiences she'd had since coming to Oakriver, this wasn't going to be the one that stopped her.

She climbed.

It was a slippery, shaky affair, but somehow she managed it, breathing a relieved sigh once her boots found purchase on the roof. Rhia's curtains were open, like always—she liked to fall asleep with the moon for company and wake up with the sun in her face. Presently, she was sitting on her bed, huddled under several blankets with a movie running on her laptop and a cat nestled in her lap. With her curls twisted into two thick braids and a knee hugged to her chest, she looked like a perfectly normal nineteen-year-old, but Valerie could sense it from a distance: even in a room full of candles and crystals, Rhia was the most magical thing there was. For a few seconds, Valerie felt just like she had the first time she'd seen her through this very window—Rhia, watering the herbs in the windowsill in her canary-yellow sweater, and Valerie, walking down unfamiliar streets without a plan or direction until she'd seen a face that felt like coming home.

She lifted her hand to the window.

At the first knock, Rhia gave a violent start, enough to make the cat dart through the open door in a heartbeat.

Blood rushed to Valerie's cheeks as she became aware of how she probably looked. In her mind, this whole undertaking had had a very *Romeo and Juliet*-esque vibe. In reality, she probably looked like some kind of nightmarish gargoyle crouching on the roof with her hair sticking to her forehead and a scratch on her cheek where the wind had whipped a branch into her face.

After a shivering eternity, Rhia ripped herself out of her disbelief and darted over to the window.

"Hey." Valerie shifted on her feet. "Can . . . can I come in?"

Rhia wordlessly stepped aside. While Valerie heaved herself through the window, landing on the wooden floorboards with a heavy thud, she walked over and shut the door to her room.

"What are you doing here?" Rhia asked when she turned around again, her arms wrapped around her own shaking frame.

Valerie realized then that Rhia wasn't looking at her like she saw a dripping wet gargoyle. Instead, her eyes were trained on the protection charm that had slipped out from underneath Valerie's sweater during her breakneck climb. At the sight of it, Rhia's tense shoulders relaxed almost imperceptibly.

"We need to talk," Valerie said. "I'm sorry I didn't come to speak to you sooner; I was going through some stuff. But I'm here now."

"No, I'm sorry. About everything. I didn't have the right to try and find out more about your mom." Tears glinted in Rhia's eyes in the soft light of her bedside lamp. "I was just so scared. There's so much happening that I can't explain. Every time I closed my eyes, I saw you wading into the river with that terrible look on your face, and I—I needed to do *something* to make me feel like I still had a grip on the situation. Like I could protect you from whatever it is that's doing this."

"I know," Valerie said. "I understand that now."

Rhia shook her head, her hands trembling at her sides. "I can't *lose* you, Valerie. Not like that. Not after the vision I had." The rest hung unspoken in the air: *Not like I lost my dad.*

Her voice had cracked halfway through the last sentence, and with it Valerie's self-restraint. She stepped forward before she could think better of it and pulled Rhia in. Rhia went easily, her face buried against Valerie's shoulder, even though her sweater was wet, even though they hadn't spoken in over a week.

"I'm really sorry, Val," Rhia said, words muffled in the fabric of Valerie's sweater. "It was selfish to go behind your back to find out if she was dead. That should've been your decision to make."

"Yeah," Valerie murmured, tightening her embrace around Rhia. "It should've been. But I think I understand now. I guess I was being a bit stupid."

"You weren't, though. Reckless, yes, but nothing you're feeling is ever stupid. If there was even the slightest chance that my dad was still alive, I would have done everything to hold on to him too."

"Yeah, well. It doesn't matter now anyway," Valerie said

tonelessly. "She's dead. *She's* the woman who drowned in the river. I have the answers I needed."

"How . . . how are you feeling now?"

Valerie gave a shrug, but it held none of the nonchalance she'd tried for. "It's fine. I mean, I didn't know her."

Rhia's eyebrows furrowed. "Well, no, but—"

"And besides," Valerie went on, "dead doesn't mean totally gone, right? We're witches. Surely there are rituals and spells to contact her. I mean, Quinn already did, kind of."

"What Quinn did wasn't really contacting her," Rhia said hesitantly. "It was more like a freeze-frame. They relived her death, or at least parts of it. I'm sure they *could* communicate with her if they learned how, but interacting with the spirit world requires knowledge and experience and, most of all, protection."

"But I could do it. Right?"

"I don't know, Valerie," Rhia said gently. "You'd need an object that belonged to the person—"

"I have her necklace."

"But even then, it's not a guarantee that you'll get through. And honestly . . ." Rhia halted for a second. "Maybe you shouldn't. Sometimes the best thing you can do is let go."

Valerie frowned. "Did you never try to contact your dad?"

"Of course I do. I talk to him all the time. I sit in front of my altar and offer him his favorite snacks, and I tell him about what's going on in my life. But that's different, Val. It's a way for me to feel closer to him and honor his memory. I don't expect him to pop up in my room. What you are talking about—*summoning* your mom—is necromancy, and that is nothing to be taken lightly. Once you open that door, you may never be fully able to close it." Her lips curved into a sad smile. "Having one foot in each world doesn't do you any favors, I promise. A wound can't heal if you keep poking at it."

Valerie gave only a noncommittal hum in response, her thoughts already racing. *Necromancy.* The word sent a tingle down her spine, but before she could decide whether it was pleasant or unsettling, Rhia commanded her attention again.

"Speaking of honoring the dead," she said, "my family has this celebration on the thirty-first. I was thinking, maybe we could . . . Would you like to celebrate with us?"

"You guys celebrate Halloween?" Valerie questioned.

Rhia chuckled. "Not exactly. Every witch around here has a different name for it. My family calls it the Unveiling, because it's the night that the veil between our world and the spirit world lifts. It's not a huge thing; mostly, we just eat a lot of food and dance and chat with our ancestors if they feel like hanging out."

"And you really think it'd be okay if I . . . I mean, you'd really want me to be there?"

"I do," Rhia said with a nervous smile. "That way, I could finally introduce you to my family. You could actually enter through the front door for once."

Valerie's heart fluttered in her chest at the thought. "I've never properly celebrated on the thirty-first," she admitted. "It was always just me sitting on my bedroom floor with my tarot cards and a candle from Target, getting interrupted by trick-or-treaters every five seconds."

Rhia's relief was almost tangible. "We usually start a little after sundown, so you could come by around six? And you could bring Quinn—I'd hate for them to be alone during the Unveiling after everything that's happened."

Valerie grimaced. "I don't think they'll want to come, but I'll pass it on. They'll probably prefer the Halloween festival."

"Oh, we can totally go to the festival after dinner!" With her eyes lighting up the longer she spoke, the sadness that had lingered at the corners of Rhia's mouth finally disappeared. "Tristan's family organizes it, so he'll be there all evening. He always gets us free snacks. This year there will even be a corn maze!"

"Mmm, I love a good corn maze."

"Yeah?"

"Yeah." Valerie laughed, and kissed her. Rhia melted into her arms the moment their lips brushed, her hands sliding into Valerie's hair when Valerie tugged her closer by the hips. After being deprived for ten days, kissing Rhia was enough to make her go weak in the knees and breathless within seconds. Everything about her was so *familiar*: the little gasp that got lost in Valerie's mouth when she nipped at Rhia's bottom lip; the softness of her body under Valerie's hands; the feeling of warmth enveloping both of them that had nothing to do with Valerie's magic. Valerie only leaned back once her lungs were screaming for air and her lips were tingling. When she opened her eyes again, she looked at Rhia—really *looked* at her for the first time that night—and grinned. "Is that my sweater?" she asked, giving a tug to one of the paint-spattered sleeves. "The one that I left here after the Fall Festival?"

Rhia's expression turned flustered as she looked down at herself. "Uh . . . no?"

"Strange." Valerie hooked one finger through the collar to pull Rhia closer. "I could've sworn I had one just like this."

"Hmm. Must've disappeared somehow," Rhia said, her voice

Philline Harms

a little distracted as her eyes strayed to Valerie's lips. "Maybe you can do a tracking spell or ask your tarot cards if—Mhh."

She was abruptly cut off when Valerie kissed her again, both of them smiling into it. "Stay the night?" Rhia asked. And hell, what was Valerie supposed to do other than nod?

A few minutes later, she found herself nestled behind Rhia in bed. Rhia seemed to drift off the instant they settled in under the blanket, but Valerie fought sleep for a little while. She didn't want to sleep. She wanted to stay like that, with her arms around Rhia and their legs tangled together, and not miss a single one of her steady breaths.

Here was Rhia, a girl who had built a wall around herself years ago; Rhia, who hadn't let anyone in since; Rhia, who protected herself with everything she had, but not as fiercely as she protected her loved ones. And here was Valerie, somehow lucky enough to be the one exception, the first person in forever to step through the gates. Lying there with Rhia in her arms, she felt the weight of her trust like a tangible thing.

Lips brushing the nape of Rhia's neck, she whispered, "Thank you." She'd been sure that Rhia was asleep; instead, she suddenly shifted, a soft, sleepy noise sounding from the back of her throat, and slipped her hand into Valerie's. The last thing Valerie felt before she drifted off was Rhia's lips brushing her knuckles and the weight of ten days of silence melting off her shoulders at once.

22

THE LOVERS

harmony — balance — complementary opposites

After the last few days, waking up to the sight of Valerie's face inches away felt like Rhia had stumbled into yet another dream. Their hands were loosely entangled on the pillow between them. Valerie was breathing evenly, eyelashes fluttering against her cheeks as the sunlight caught in the wisps of red hair that were fanned out against the pillows. Rhia could have watched her forever had it not been for the racket starting up downstairs.

It was October 30, the last day before the Unveiling. Rhia could *feel* the shift in energy, a pleasant prickle that started at the top of her spine and gradually spread into the rest of her body. It was one of the most important holidays her family celebrated, and Rhia's favorite next to the autumn equinox. The veil between the realm of the living and the spirit world had gradually lifted over the last few weeks—in the night between October 31 and November 1, it would vanish completely.

It was the best time of the year for divination and contacting the dead—and, as with any holiday, an occasion for an elaborate feast. Already, the kitchen looked like it had been swept up in a hurricane. The preparations were something not a single family member could escape, so Rhia knew that it was only a matter of time until someone would knock at her door to get her to come downstairs.

She allowed herself another full minute to study Valerie's features—so *soft* in her sleep—before she reached out a hand to gently tap her nose. "Val," she whispered. "Wake up."

There was a displeased groan, half-muffled into the pillow. "Why?"

"The Unveiling," said Rhia. "I need to get up and help."

Valerie gave another moan that eloquently articulated her discontent before she pried open her eyes and sat up. Rhia couldn't quite bite back a chuckle: unlike her own hair, which she'd put into a protective hairstyle before bed, Valerie's hair bore a significant resemblance to a bird's nest. After what had to have been an impressive climb up the tree outside, there were still a few twigs and leaves stuck in her lion's mane that neither of them had noticed yesterday.

"What are you laughing at?" Valerie asked around a yawn.

Smiling, Rhia reached out to smooth down a few strands. "Nothing." While Valerie closed her eyes again, looking like she might drift back to sleep despite sitting up, Rhia carefully plucked the bits of greenery out one by one, making a mental note to issue a formal apology to the oak outside her window later. "Look at you," she murmured. "You took the whole tree with you."

Valerie rubbed a hand over her eyes. Mellow in the hazy

morning light, features sleepy and movements languid, she wasn't that different from the cats Rhia usually woke up to.

"Mmm, yeah. Couldn't grab any flowers on the way, so I thought this would have to do."

"I love it, thank you." With a peculiar feeling of fondness, Rhia set the leaves down on her nightstand.

Valerie's eyes had drifted shut again. Rhia caught her drooping chin in one hand and pressed a kiss to her lips. The noise that left Valerie this time sounded much more pleased, one of her hands finding its way to the side of Rhia's face, fingers gently tracing the shell of her earlobe. One kiss turned into two, turned into three, turned into Rhia losing count in the pleasant fog that took over her brain.

Finally, she managed to lean back long enough to utter an unconvincing, "I *really* need to go downstairs."

"Do you?" Valerie asked. "Do you really?"

It took all her strength to nod, making Valerie's hands fall away. "Yeah," she said, "I *really* do."

Heaving a long-suffering sigh, Valerie reluctantly blinked her eyes open. Rhia held her gaze for a few seconds before she abruptly leapt to her feet.

"I almost forgot! I have something for you."

At that, Valerie visibly perked up. "Oh?"

"Remember how Holly found a bunch of old books in the attic of the café?"

"Yeah?"

"Well, I finally looked through them, and I found this." Rhia bent down to the cardboard box standing at the foot of her bed and procured what looked like a leather-wrapped journal.

Valerie gingerly accepted it, blowing away some of the dust

that coated the cover. There was no title or name on it. The only thing adorning the front was a pentagram carved into the leather.

"I think it's a spell book," Rhia said, sinking down next to her on the edge of her bed. She hadn't looked inside—these books were extremely personal, only to be read by family and future descendants—and even now, as Valerie flipped it open, Rhia kept her eyes trained on her face.

There was a furrow between her brows as she lifted it to her nose, followed by a look of recognition. "It smells like . . ."

"Fire magic," Rhia finished.

"Do you think it might be my mom's?" Valerie quietly asked. Her fingers traced the edge of a page, her touch so light it seemed like she was afraid the paper would disintegrate beneath her fingertips.

"I don't know. I asked my boss if she knew who owned the building before she turned it into the café, but she wouldn't tell me. Either way, whoever it belonged to had fire magic, so I felt like you should have it. For guidance."

"Thank you, Rhia," Valerie said earnestly. "This means everything."

Rhia tried to push down the sadness that washed over her as she watched her hug the book to her chest. "Of course. I hope there's something useful for you in there."

"I'm sure there is." Valerie leaned over for one last kiss. Then she got to her feet and gestured at the window. "I'm gonna have to jump from the roof again, huh?"

"One last time," Rhia promised. "At least you're not the one who has to face my grandma's wrath when she finds out I've been seeing you for the last month."

Valerie paused, one hand already on the window frame. "What? She hasn't even met me yet. I'm a goddamn delight."

"She had a vision about you during the autumn equinox." Rhia chuckled. "Something about you bringing doom and destruction to us all, I think?"

Valerie didn't look as offended as she maybe ought to—on the contrary, there was a smirk curling around her lips that told Rhia she didn't mind being perceived as a harbinger of chaos all that much. "Sick."

"Not sick! She'll murder me when I tell her we're together after she told me *very explicitly* to stay away from you. They'll be honoring *me* during dinner tomorrow!"

Valerie breathed an unconcerned laugh and leaned down to press a kiss to Rhia's forehead. "Tell me how it goes. Or give me a sign from the afterlife if you want me to avenge you. Either one."

"Will do."

Valerie opened the window and swung her legs outside, the spell book still clutched in one hand. With the other, she blew Rhia a kiss. "Farewell, my star-crossed lover."

"Get out of here," Rhia said, laughing.

Valerie gave another exaggerated bow before she swung herself onto the roof. Rhia watched her from the window, a stupid grin on her face that wouldn't vanish even after Valerie was long out of sight.

If she lived to see it, this year's Unveiling might turn out to be the best one yet.

~

Rhia spent the next few hours swept up in the familiar chaos that was the kitchen before the Unveiling. Already, the entire house was decorated: black, gold, and orange candles flickered on tables and mantelpieces, jack-o'-lanterns grinned from the windowsills, and garlands of dried autumn leaves spanned the walls. The air was filled with a mix of earth magic and fragrant food—the scent of *home*.

Like every year, they were making a mix of traditional Unveiling dishes—roasted vegetables, pumpkin pie, and corn bread—and her dad's favorite soul food. Her grandmother sat at the kitchen table chopping herbs while opposite her, Tristan was halfway through peeling an ungodly amount of sweet potatoes. He beamed at Rhia when she glanced over at him, his cheeks ruddy from the heat inside the kitchen, perfectly content in the whirlwind that was her family. Rhia smiled back at him before she turned back to the pots and pans on the stove in front of her, whistling to herself.

"Someone's in a good mood," her mother remarked, sidling up beside her. She was wearing an oversized checkered flannel with a denim patch on the left elbow that Rhia recognized as one of her dad's. The sight made her chest well with a familiar mix of acute longing and bittersweet fondness.

"Of course. It's almost Halloween!"

"Mmm. That the only reason?" Her mother leveled her with an unimpressed stare. "You were wallowing all week, and suddenly you're all better because it's almost October thirty-first?"

Rhia bit her lip. She'd been trying to find a way to sneakily steer the conversation towards Valerie all day but had chickened out every time. Now the night was pressing against the windows and she still hadn't mustered the courage. It was a challenge when her grandmother sat within earshot, hacking the rosemary on her cutting board as if it had personally wronged her. Maybe it was best to wait until she'd put down the cleaver?

"It's just, uh . . ." Rhia was cut off when the back door flew open and Holly bounced inside, followed by Sage and a chilly gust of autumn air.

"We're all set!" she announced, flopping onto the chair next to Tristan. "The circle's in place. No malevolent spirits entering the house anytime soon."

Their grandmother looked up, a grim expression on her face. "Are you absolutely sure?"

"Yes," confirmed Sage as she too sat down. "We double-checked. It's big enough to include most of the garden—we stopped somewhere near the greenhouse. Unless you're scared the eggplants are going to be haunted?"

Grandma Deloris offered a dry "Very funny" and went back to her task, a sure sign that she would have a walk around the perimeter in approximately fifteen minutes just to make sure. None of them were surprised—their grandmother's superstitious streak only increased with the lifting of the veil. The Unveiling was a celebration, but one that—like all things witchcraft—harbored its own dangers, which she was all too glad to remind them of every year.

Rhia's mother gave a fond shake of her head and turned back to Rhia. "You were saying?"

Rhia froze. She'd thought that Holly and Sage's entrance would be enough to distract her mother from the topic at hand, but judging by the inquisitive look she found when she turned to face her again, she'd let her guard down too soon.

With a sigh, she carefully set the spoon down on the counter-top. At least Holly and Sage were here now and could jump in to help—or, alternatively, send word to Valerie of her being chased out of town by her own grandmother.

"I need to tell you something," she announced, turning to face the entire room. "But you have to promise not to be mad."

The clamor that had filled the kitchen instantly reduced to nothing but the bubbling of the pots on the stove and the purring of the cat nestled on Sage's lap. Tristan sat up a little; Holly shot her a painfully obvious thumbs-up.

"Go on," her mother said warily.

"Right. So. I kind of . . . I've been seeing this girl."

A collective sigh of relief sounded through the room. "Oh, sweetheart," Aunt Tanisha cooed, patting her cheek. "Why would we be mad? That's wonderful! When will we—"

"I'm not finished," Rhia said quickly. "This girl may or may not be a witch?"

Silence fell, and silence lasted. Ten, twenty, thirty seconds ticked by, and no one said a word. Finally, Rhia dared to look at her grandmother.

"Rhiannon Greenbrook," she said, her voice deadly quiet. The furrow between her brows was even deeper than usual as she slowly pushed herself to her feet. "You mean to tell me that all this time you've been wooing the one person I told you to stay away from?"

"She did more of the wooing than me, I think," Rhia murmured.

"Do you not remember the cards I pulled? Death, the Tower—"

"You also pulled the Lovers," Rhia told the kitchen floor. "So, really, you could have seen it coming."

There were a few more seconds of tense quiet—then a snicker, the breathless kind that escapes unbidden. Rhia glanced up in surprise to find her *mother*, of all people, wiping tears of laughter from underneath her eyes.

"Oh, dear," she wheezed, trying hard to get herself under control but cracking every time her eyes fell on the sour look that had taken up residence on Grandma Deloris's face. "Ma, your scary stories really did a number on her. The poor thing had a whole clandestine affair because of you!"

While Rhia relaxed a fraction, her grandmother turned her head to glower at her daughter. "This is not a laughing matter, Zora! This girl is dangerous—"

"No, she's not," Holly interjected. "We took her to the cabin with us the other weekend. She's really lovely!"

"You took her to the *cabin*? Have you lost your minds?"

"Ma, seriously," Aunt Tanisha chided in her soft voice. "This is wonderful! Rhia has a girlfriend!" From the corner of the room, Tristan gave a loud whoop—the sound took the last of the tension out of Rhia's shoulders and made the room around her break into chuckles.

"So," she started, "is it okay if I invite her over for the Unveiling tomorrow? She's never had anyone else to celebrate with, and I thought it might be a nice opportunity for you to get to know her."

"Of course she can come over!" her mother said before her grandmother could open her mouth to protest. "Tell her she's more than welcome."

Rhia was about to thank her when the phone in the pocket of her dress vibrated. "Oh, that's her," she said with a glance at the display. "I'll just take this. Be right back!" Under the curious eyes of her family, she darted out into the hallway, pressing the phone to her ear as soon as she was out of earshot. "Hey."

"Oh, good, you're still alive!" Valerie observed on the other end of the line.

"Barely." Rhia leaned against the door frame to the living room. "Grandma might still disown me. But, for now, it looks like you'll be able to come tomorrow."

"Nice." There was some rustling in the background, a faint crackle. "Um, I'm calling because I have two questions."

"Yes?"

"Number one: What should I wear tomorrow night? Number two: Does the shape of a candle matter when you're doing a ritual?"

"Anything black should be fine." Rhia laughed. "And I don't think it does? We always use regular candles. Why are you asking?"

"Just curious," Valerie said, a smile in her voice. "I'll let you get back to your super important kitchen magic now."

"Okay. I'm looking forward to tomorrow."

"Me too. Good night, pumpkin."

"Night," Rhia softly said.

Exhaling, she pressed the phone to her chest. A disbelieving grin spread on her face as it finally sank in: she had a girlfriend who would meet her family tomorrow, whom she would get to celebrate her favorite holiday with.

When she looked up again, her grandmother stood at the kitchen door, her face shrouded in shadows. "I have a bad feeling about this, Rhiannon."

"You have a bad feeling about everything, Grandma," Rhia said. "It'll be fine, I promise. You'll *love* her."

Grandma Deloris studied Rhia. Whatever she saw on her face made her heave a small sigh. "You really care for this girl, don't you?"

"I do," Rhia said earnestly.

"All right."

"All right?"

"There's no sense in trying to reason when it comes to matters of the heart," Grandma Deloris said. Her hand came up to gently tuck a curl behind Rhia's ear. "And I know you well enough to know that you have already done more than enough of that inside your own head. Haven't you?"

"Yeah," Rhia confirmed with a teary laugh, and let her grandmother fold her into her arms. Closing her eyes, she breathed in her familiar scent: fresh laundry and coconut oil and the faint trace of Florida water that always seemed to cling to her skin.

"I *am* glad that you found someone who makes you act like a fool," Grandma Deloris murmured fondly into her hair. "You're too young to have so many worry lines."

"I get those from you," Rhia sniffed.

"Probably," her grandmother agreed.

Rhia pulled back enough to press a kiss to her grandmother's cheek. She knew she wasn't overly cautious just for the sake of it, nor was she a pessimist by nature. It was her father's death that had deepened Grandma Deloris's frowns and made her anxious to let any of them out of her sight. Rhia could only imagine what it had felt like for her to watch her daughter lose the love of her life and to pick up the pieces of her granddaughters' childhoods in the months that followed. Deloris had been the one who organized the funeral, who got them ready for school and made sure they did their homework, who imbued the doorways with spells for protection and burned orange and cinnamon in the hallways until Rhia's mother could get out of bed to take the task up herself.

Even though she no longer spoke healing spells over them every morning and night, traces of the old patterns had stuck. It was easy to forget sometimes where they came from, and easier still to laugh her grandmother's worries off as quirks, but in that moment, with her grandmother's warm hands on her shoulders and her serious gaze on her face, Rhia felt her chest grow tight with all the love she had for her.

She decided to tell her as much. "I love you, Grandma."

Her grandmother responded the same way she had when she'd tucked Rhia in every night, a familiar call and response. "And I you, little bug."

Together, they returned to the kitchen. Before, Rhia hadn't noticed how heavily the secret had weighed on her. Now, as she was once again enveloped in the glow and the noise and the comfort of the kitchen, she felt so light she could have floated up to the ceiling.

She watched the familiar scene unfold: her mother stirring one of the pots as she whispered a spell, Sage making a shopping list for her next trip to Obscura, her aunt laughing gleefully as she commanded a bag of flour to fly across the kitchen, making one of the cats sneeze in the white cloud that trailed behind it. She glanced at Holly sprawled across two chairs, her head resting in Tristan's lap while he told her about that afternoon's lacrosse practice, and then she looked at her grandmother, taking her seat at the table again with an expression that almost came close to acceptance. Drenched in the flickering light of candles and jack-o'-lanterns, they were a peculiar mix of magic and mundane that Rhia loved so dearly it hurt.

The ache was even sweeter now that she knew that, twenty-four hours from now, the two people she was missing—her dad and Valerie—would be a part of their strange patchwork as well; some parts knitted together by blood, others entirely by choice, and all of them rooted firmly in Rhia's heart.

23

THE DEVIL

destructive behavior — chaos — powerlessness

Valerie knew from the moment Rhia handed it to her that the spell book was something special. Pure, unadulterated witchcraft clung to every yellowed page, hid in every fold, sang in every drop of faded ink. It was magic that felt familiar—the kind that smelled like smoke and spices and made her fingertips tingle with potential.

Valerie also knew that this spell book was different from everything that Rhia had taught her. The Greenbrooks drew their magic from the air and the earth and used it in small doses, under strict conditions, and in ways that rarely affected others. The things that Valerie read in this book were a different brand of witchcraft altogether. She could tell by the alternating styles of handwriting and the dates scrawled in the corners of some pages—going all the way back to the nineteenth century—that several women over several decades had poured their knowledge into these pages. There were hexes to ruin an enemy's entire harvest for the season; spells to make someone fall madly in love or, if spoken backward, stir up blazing hatred for their betrothed; rituals that could burn an entire building down with nothing but a whisper. And then there was a chapter titled "Necromancy."

Valerie stayed up reading until her eyes were burning. The spell she chose was straightforward, its creator's words filled with glee as they led Valerie through the ritual.

And so, in the early afternoon of October 31, Valerie slipped the book into her tote bag along with a knife she'd swiped from the kitchen and set off towards the town center. She was already dressed for dinner at Rhia's; choosing an outfit to meet Rhia's family had somehow been more difficult than the decision to call on the dead. In the end, she'd settled on a long-sleeved black dress, black tights, and her trusty Doc Martens.

Her plan was to head to Obscura to buy the candles she needed, go into the woods to perform the ritual (Quinn would kill her if they found out she'd summoned spirits in their room, and she was scared she might accidentally trip the fire alarm), and be finished in time for dinner at Rhia's.

With the sky a spotless blue and the October sun warm on Valerie's face, it was one of the rare bright days Oakriver saw. Already, the air was buzzing with anticipation; everywhere she looked, Valerie saw jack-o'-lanterns grimacing from doorsteps and windowsills, little kids running around in their costumes, and adults chattering about the Halloween festival. It was currently being set up in the town square, but Valerie quickly brushed past the scene and instead headed into the more secluded alleyway where Obscura was tucked away.

The excited flurry in the streets became muffled as she stepped through the door, the scents of cinnamon and apple cider replaced by lavender and candle wax. Like the first time Valerie had stumbled into the shop, Quinn sat slouched behind the register. Unlike last time, they weren't alone. Deloris Greenbrook—Valerie recognized her from the photos in Rhia's house—stood at the counter, only her side profile visible in the low light. Not wanting to disturb them, Valerie softly pulled the door shut behind her and busied herself looking through a display of ritual knives.

". . . know we've only spoken a handful of times, but I did a tarot reading earlier, and I had to think of you." Deloris's voice carried across the shop. "Rhiannon told me you were having a bit of a magical crisis?"

"I guess you could call it that," Quinn murmured. Valerie's heart sank. They sounded so *tired*.

"It's your family, isn't it." From the old woman's mouth, the question sounded like a statement.

"Yeah." There was a beat of hesitation. Then, it was as if a dam broke. "All these years, I've been wondering why we didn't have anything to do with the Chinese side of the family. Why my mom wouldn't take us there more often. Why she didn't encourage me to learn Mandarin so I could talk to the rest of the family or teach me about the culture. Why she kept that part of my identity to herself, even though it's *my* family too."

"I understand," Deloris said. Through the gap in the shelves, Valerie could just barely make out the way her palm had settled on Quinn's hand. "It must be hard, feeling like you know yourself when you don't even seem to know your roots. Even more so when the beliefs you hold about yourself are challenged by a discovery as big as this one."

In the silence that followed, Valerie could hear her blood

rushing in her ears. Her throat felt tight all of a sudden. Although the words weren't meant for her, they rang true somewhere deep inside her chest. Of course, Quinn's pain ran deeper—Valerie couldn't imagine the confusion that came with being isolated from one parent's entire culture—but there was still a parallel here that she'd been too caught up in her own anger to see.

"What do you want to do about it?" Deloris finally inquired.

"About what?"

"Your magic. Will you use it? Or will you go on as if nothing happened?"

Quinn laughed. Without any real humor in it, the noise sounded wrong. "Do I have a choice?"

"Of course you do. We always have choices." There was silence, interrupted only by a quiet rustling. Valerie peered through the shelves to see Deloris pulling a thick book—not unlike the spell book her granddaughter had handed Valerie the day before—out of her shopping bag. "Would it help you to know more about your family?"

". . . Yes. I think it might."

Deloris opened the book, pointing at a page. If Valerie craned her neck, she thought she could catch a glimpse of an old photograph. "I met your grandmother when we were both younger—she was a regular at my pharmacy back when she lived in Oakriver, and we often ended up talking for hours on end over cups of herbal tea. Even then, Ying Yue was an impressive woman, overflowing with water magic the likes of which I haven't witnessed since. Oh, and the conversations we had! Before I met her, I never knew how limited my knowledge was. All my life, I never questioned that there are only four elements to draw from. Imagine my surprise when she told me about the five-element system in Nanjing!"

"Five elements?" Quinn echoed, voicing Valerie's question. "What's the fifth?"

"It's not just the number that's different, it's the classification as well," Deloris explained, her voice filled with the same breathless excitement that Rhia spoke with when she got the chance to launch into a monologue on magic. "In China, the elements that practitioners ascribe themselves to are water, fire, earth, and—get this—*wood* and *metal*. It made us wonder: Is wood magic included in what we call earth magic, and we just lumped it all together? Is air magic so unobtrusive it goes unnoticed unless you are actively looking for the signs? What other belief systems are there? What other knowledge slips through the cracks between cultures?"

Quinn cleared their throat. "You mentioned that she also has water magic. Did . . . did she ever speak about being able to communicate with spirits?"

"You're asking if she's also a Messenger?" Deloris chuckled. "It's a rather inelegant word, isn't it? Messenger. In Nanjing, many call it *qiáo*—bridge. You're not just an antenna for the spirit world to communicate through, some kind of paranormal one-way street. You form a *connection*. It's an incredibly precious talent, Quinn." She tilted her head. "But to answer your question: no, Ying Yue cannot communicate with spirits. I believe one of her sisters could, though. And so do a few witches around Oakriver."

While Quinn seemed to process this information, Deloris traced the edge of the book with a wistful expression. "Magic was everything to your grandmother. With her family—all witches, if memory serves—far away, in a country on the other side of the Pacific, it was the one thing that gave her comfort. And it was what pulled her back to Nanjing, eventually. There are a lot of water witches there; between the Yangtze and the Qinhuai rivers, there's so much power surging through the region, the Murmuring River probably felt like barely a dribble to Ying Yue."

Quinn made a thoughtful noise. Valerie, who had felt the strength of the Murmuring River herself, felt a shiver run down her spine as she tried to imagine its force multiplied.

Meanwhile, Deloris continued. "She asked your mother to go with her, but, as you know, she refused. She and Ying Yue had never been very close, and your mother felt no connection to a country she had never been to. So Ying Yue left, and your mother stayed to finish her college degree."

"It really was magic, then, that drove a wedge between them," Quinn said.

Deloris shook her head. "It's not magic that tears families apart, Quinn. It's people."

Quinn didn't respond, their expression hidden behind the curls that fell into their eyes as they studied the page in Deloris's book. "I don't know what to do with it. There's always been a part of me that felt different from everyone around me. I thought it was just part of growing up queer, trans, and mixed, but now it turns out it's also been *this*." They laughed helplessly. "It's absurd. I came to Oakriver to study art, and now I lie awake at night because I can hear the water moving through the pipes. *Calling* me."

"The two aren't mutually exclusive," Deloris said gently. "You can have magic and get a degree. You can be angry at your family and still find comfort in the things you have in common. You can have all the answers and still feel confused." The half of her face that Valerie could see softened into a smile. "At the end of the day, the only one who gets to decide what to make of all the pieces of your identity is *you*, Quinn. It takes time, but one day you will settle into a sense of self that feels comfortable—even if still malleable. Maybe *because* of it. Wouldn't it be terrible, staying the same forever, never questioning the beliefs we hold about who we are?" She waited for Quinn's timid nod before she added, "Discovering new things about ourselves can be frightening, but in the end it's these moments that bring us closer to who we truly are. Once you embrace the process and accept the uncertainty, it's really quite lovely."

Quinn ran a finger along the edge of the book, their gaze still glued to the yellowed pages. "Thank you for coming here," they said. "Truly."

"Oh, you've got nothing to thank me for." Deloris checked her watch. "Goodness, time flies! I really have to go back now. Will you come by for dinner tonight?"

"Um. Maybe." Quinn rubbed at their neck. "I think I need some time to think."

"Of course. If you change your mind, our door is always open. Always." With that, Deloris made her way towards the exit, leaving the spell book with Quinn. In her wake, the shop was left eerily quiet, the silence interrupted only by the ticking of the clock on the wall and the distant bustle from the street that filtered in before the door fell shut.

Then: "You can come out now."

Valerie jumped so hard she almost rammed her shoulder into the shelf next to her. Sheepishly, she stepped out from behind it and strolled up to the counter. "I'm sorry, I didn't mean to eavesdrop. I came in, and then I didn't know how to leave without interrupting."

"It's fine." Quinn gave a tired wave of their hand. "What are you doing here? I thought you'd be getting ready to charm your girlfriend's family by now."

"I think you already beat me to it." Valerie laughed. "I'm mainly here to get these."

She grabbed a few black candles from the basket on the counter.

"What do you need those for?" Quinn asked.

"Art project," Valerie lied easily. "I want to do something with wax."

The only answer she got was a vague hum as Quinn punched in the total. Valerie slid them a few dollar bills and put the change into the tip jar next to the register. She paused once more to lean over the counter and press a kiss into Quinn's hair. "Make sure you eat today, okay? And get some sleep. You look like you need it."

"I will." Valerie was nearly by the door when Quinn called, "Valerie? Please be careful tonight. I—I have a bad feeling."

"I'm always careful." Valerie shot them one last grin and slipped outside.

Back in the main street, she held her tote protectively to her chest and weaseled her way through the throngs of people heading towards the festival. The sun was starting to set by now, bleeding pink and orange across the deep-blue sky. Valerie had no time to waste; she still needed to find a spot in the woods and set everything up, and fast, if she wanted to make it to Rhia's in time.

As she hurried back to the campus, she was so immersed in going through the spell in her head that she almost didn't notice the sound of her phone going off. It was only after a few rings that she startled and dug it out of the depths of her bag, frowning when she saw the caller ID.

"Dad?" she asked in lieu of a greeting, sidestepping a group of students that came her way on the narrow sidewalk.

"Valerie," he responded.

His tone was smooth, giving her nothing to go off in terms of where they stood after their last phone call. It was strange how much had changed since then—and how, despite everything, Valerie's feelings towards him had remained stagnant. There was still the same anger she'd felt last time. Maybe even more. Overhearing the conversation between Quinn and Deloris Greenbrook had left her feeling strangely raw, a barely healed bruise that had been unwittingly pressed on too many times.

"How are you?"

"I'm good," she said warily. "How are you?"

"Good, good. Has everything been okay with—"

Down the road, the college campus came into view. "Dad, I don't really have time right now," Valerie said, cutting him off. "I'm kind of busy. Is there a reason you're calling?"

From the other end of the line came a sigh. "No. I guess I just wanted to ask what you're up to. Have any plans for tonight?"

"I'm having dinner at my girlfriend's house. Meeting the family."

"Girlfriend? When did that happen?"

"A few weeks ago," was all she said in response. With anyone else, she would've immediately launched into a ramble about Rhia. Not with him.

"Okay . . . well, that sounds nice. I'm glad, Valerie." He cleared his throat. "You know I hate Halloween. Just stay safe tonight, yeah? None of that weird stuff."

Valerie could feel her expression darkening. She knew exactly what he meant by that. She had heard that very same tone every time he'd caught her with her tarot deck or a pendulum or anything else that went beyond what Matthew Morgan, responsible stepfather of his quaint new family and levelheaded accountant, deemed appropriate for his teenage daughter.

Normally, Valerie would have stood her ground and argued about autonomy and self-reliance and her not being a child anymore. But as it was, the woods were already coming into view, and Valerie had a more important parent to contact. "Sure."

There was a silence so long she almost hung up. Finally, he asked, "What's her name? Your girlfriend."

Valerie blinked, surprised to find that he sounded genuinely interested. Her next words came out slightly less frosty. "Rhiannon Greenbrook. I can send you a picture of her later if you—"

"Repeat that." Her father suddenly sounded much more alert. "What's her name?"

"Rhiannon. Unusual name, I know."

"What? Valerie, *listen*—"

"I really have to go now," Valerie interrupted, and then, just to spite him, she added, "Happy Halloween, Dad." She hung up before he could utter another word. The display told her that it was four thirty by now. Valerie told herself that was chill. Everything was chill. She still had one and a half hours to do this.

During the call, she'd made her way into the woods behind

the dorms. It was much darker here than in the street; the setting sun's light barely made it through the treetops, and mist licked at her boots. Shaking her head, Valerie tried to focus not on the eerie silence but on the things she knew—the things that reminded her of Rhia. The leaves whispering in the wind. The heady scent of wet soil and dying leaves. The softness of the moss under her boots.

Ahead of her, the tree line opened into the same small clearing that she and Rhia had passed through on their first date. Unconsciously, she'd sought out a place far away from the river, its rumbling only audible in the distance if she strained her ears. Here, the trees at least stood far enough apart that she could see the darkening sky, the mist thinner than it had been in the underbrush.

Valerie sank to her knees in the damp grass. The spell book was a steadying weight in her hands as she pulled it out of her bag and placed it in her lap, flipping to the page she needed. In the dim light, she had to squint to make out the instructions, written in loopy strokes and accompanied by some comments written in the margins in darker ink by another woman years later. Last night, Valerie had lain awake tracing the words with her finger, comparing them to her own, trying to conjure up an image in her mind of whose pen they might have poured from. Were the bold, blue letters her grandmother's? Was the hasty writing that looked like it was trying to flee the page her mom's? Whose words would Valerie be speaking in a moment? She read the entire page once more, memorizing the spell. There was no mention of a protection circle like the one that Rhia had taught her, but there was a fire ring that seemed to serve the same purpose.

Setting the book aside, Valerie got to work.

First: Arrange twelve candles in a circle. Light them with a match or—if you're a Firebearer—with your magic, going counterclockwise.

Firebearer. The word gave her a small thrill.

One after another, she lit the black candles she'd bought at Obscura and placed them in a circle around where she was sitting. Her hands got steadier with each candlewick that crackled to life. By the time she was done, she found herself in a circle of light, the gentle flickering of the candles holding the darkness at bay as the sun disappeared behind the trees.

Second: Take the thirteenth candle and position it in front of you. Light it in the same manner.

Valerie placed the last candle in front of her crossed legs. *"Look,"* she whispered into the evening air, *"here comes a walking fire."* A flame sparked immediately, close enough to warm her hands where they were resting in her lap.

Third: Use a knife to draw blood. Feed it to the fire while chanting the spell.

Valerie drew in a shaky breath. This was the part where things got serious. She wasn't usually a squeamish person, but her hands still trembled when she reached for the knife she'd brought. The blade glinted menacingly in the firelight. Squeezing her eyes shut, she focused on the warmth of the candles surrounding her, the magic thrumming steadily in her veins. She was so close. If she did this right, she would be talking to her mother in a few minutes. She would finally meet the ghost she'd chased across town, the one person who could give her answers to what had happened to her all those years ago, where the rest of her family could be found, *who Valerie was.* Isabelle Morgan was the puzzle piece that, for years, had been missing in the grand picture that made up Valerie. If she got this right, it would at last be filled— she would know for the first time what it was like to be whole. And so, without another second of hesitation, she took the knife in one hand and sliced it across her open palm.

"Motherf—" she hissed, gritting her teeth at the sting of it, before she remembered that she was supposed to recite the spell. *"I call on you, spirits of the other side,"* she murmured shakily, turning her pulsing hand over so that the blood could drip onto the candle in front of her. With the other hand, she tightly gripped the pentagram necklace around her throat. *"Hear my voice and follow my light; for you I open the door tonight."*

A chill ran down her spine as the wind around her picked up.

"With my words I call you, so my word is law." Fire was licking at her palm from how close she was holding it to the flame, heat and pain blending into one, but Valerie didn't pull her hand away. *"Speak the truth and harm me not. Return to your realm when I've found what I've sought."*

There was a faint snapping sound from somewhere in the trees that made her jump. Valerie squinted into the dark, trying to determine if something was there, but she could barely see beyond the fire ring. She looked down at the blood dripping into the flame again.

"With fire, I summon you; with blood, I bind you; with my spell, I shall release you." She inhaled one last trembling breath. *"As I have spoken, so shall it be."*

Slowly, Valerie drew her hand away from the fire and raised her gaze. She wasn't sure what she had expected—an apparition to be standing right in front of her, probably, some kind of *The Woman in Black* situation. Instead, there was nothing except flickering candles and dark woods inching in on her from all sides.

Valerie's shoulders sagged. Of course there was nothing. It would've been too easy to just use a spell she'd gotten her hands on through coincidence and have it actually work. With a huff, she got to her feet, giving a frustrated little kick to the spell book lying in the grass. She couldn't believe she'd trekked all the way out here and given herself a flesh wound for nothing, like a goddamn—

"Valerie?"

She spun around so fast she almost stumbled over her own feet. "Mom?" Scanning the surrounding woods, she couldn't see anything besides her own breath forming frantic clouds. "Mom, is that you?"

There was a silence so long Valerie started to think the voice had only been in her imagination. But then it sounded again, so soft she had to strain her ears to understand the words it was saying.

"Valerie." The woman sounded far away, muffled as if through cotton. *"I've been waiting so long for you to call me."*

Valerie's hands shook as she stared into the unwavering darkness. "I can't see you," she said. Her teeth were chattering. "Can you see me? Mom?"

"No. I'm at the border, but I can't get through. Something is barring it."

"Did I do something wrong?"

"I don't think so . . ." Heavy silence fell, disturbed only by the rustling of leaves and the violent pounding of Valerie's heart. "Did you cast an additional circle? Or are you wearing something enchanted?"

Valerie's hand flew to the crystal around her neck. "Just smoky quartz."

This time, the wind carried a twinkle of laughter. "Silly girl. How am I supposed to get through to you? Go on, take it off. I want to see your beautiful face!"

Her thumb running over the coarse surface of the crystal in a practiced motion, Valerie hesitated. She could still feel the phantom touch of Rhia's fingers brushing her hair aside. *For protection.*

"Valerie?" her mother asked. "Don't you want to see me?"

"Of course I do," Valerie rushed to say. She wanted—no, *needed*—to see her, to compare the colors of their eyes and find similar constellations in their freckles, to know if it was true what her father said about them looking identical.

In one swift motion, she opened the clasp at the back of the necklace and tossed it behind the line of the fire circle.

Three things happened at once.

One: the candles that had been nothing but docile all evening suddenly flickered uncontrollably.

Two: a second voice, this one much brighter than the other, cried out a gut-wrenching "No!"

Three: a woman appeared.

There was no red hair. There were no freckles. There was no

warmth, nothing in her sunken, charcoal-gray eyes that spoke of affection. Her face was pale and narrow, all sharp edges and severe lines. "Hello, Valerie," she said. "How nice of you to open the door."

Wrong, whispered Valerie's instinct. *This is all wrong.*

Out loud, she managed: "Who are you?"

"Oh, sweetheart." The woman gave her a grin that was all teeth. "I'm your grandmother!"

Valerie took an unsteady step back, narrowly avoiding stepping on the knife at her feet. For a second, she was overcome by the impulse to bend down and grab it, but she knew that would have done her no good against someone who was very clearly not human. While the wind whipped Valerie's hair around her face, the woman in front of her was eerily still. The dim light filtered through her in spots, and her edges seemed frayed, blurring into the night around her. *Wrong wrong wrong.*

"Okay . . . well, sorry, Granny, but you're not the person I was hoping to reach, so . . ." She squinted down at the spell book still lying open in the grass. *"Spirits of the other side, I thank you for your help tonight—"*

"Now, why would you do that?" Her grandmother cut her off. In the split second that Valerie had taken her eyes off her, she'd floated several inches closer to her. "The fun has only just begun. We didn't wait all these years for nothing!"

We?

With a renewed sense of panic, Valerie spun around. Six other women were pressing closer to her from all sides, black dresses fading into the night. They circled her like vultures, all sharp features and hungry eyes, like Valerie was a feast and they'd been starving for decades.

Instincts took over. Valerie ran without thinking twice about it, towards the border of the circle and the protection charm lying in the grass just beyond it. No one tried to stop her; in fact, one of them even stepped out of the way. Valerie understood why when she reached the border of the circle and was stopped by an invisible barrier that was as firm as it was impossible. She tried to push against it with all her strength, her heart throwing itself against her ribs like a caged bird—still, it didn't budge. She tried to blow out one of the candles, but it immediately flickered back to life.

At last, she understood how truly fucked she was. The circle she'd cast wasn't meant to keep anything out; it was meant to keep things *inside*.

The blood-chilling realization was accompanied by a chorus of cackling laughter from all around her. In a fit of desperation, Valerie conjured a flame in her hands and aimed it at them. It was no use: where the fireball should have hit one of the women straight in the chest, it simply disappeared inside her, absorbed by her translucent form.

"You know," her grandmother mused, "I would've been content if I'd gotten you to join her in the river. All it would've taken were a few nights of forgetting to burn those pesky herbs, or maybe another little getaway without anyone interfering, but this is even better. This means we get to *use* you."

With her back against the barrier, Valerie dug her nails into her palms to stop herself from crying. She thought of her mother, whom she'd done all of this for and whom she still didn't know. She thought about her father's strained voice when he'd warned her not to do anything stupid tonight, and his identical tone when he'd begged her not to go to Oakriver all those weeks ago.

She thought of Rhia, her magical person, waiting on the other side of town for Valerie to come over, to meet her family, to become a part of her sacred little world for good. And then, she only thought that she'd never been more scared in her entire life.

"Silly thing." Her grandmother slowly stalked towards her. As she moved, something glittered on her hand: a silver signet ring engraved with an *H*. "You truly had no idea what you were getting yourself into, hmm? But don't worry—we'll take over for you now."

"Go to hell," Valerie spat.

The woman leaned closer to her, her eyes a bottomless black as she took in Valerie's trembling frame. "You really are just like her," she mused. "So much fight in you. Too bad it didn't do either of you much good."

Valerie bit down on her tongue hard enough to taste blood. Made another futile attempt at pushing through the wall. Breathed in the suffocating scent that wafted off the spirit in front of her: embers and ashes, things that were still fighting to exist and things that had already lost the battle, life and death and the narrow path in between that Valerie was balancing on. Finally, searing fingers clasped her chin, and the world slipped away.

24

THE TOWER

pain — confusion — destruction

"You've reached Valerie! If you're hearing this, I'm probably busy committing arson right now. Just kidding. Or am I? Either way, leave a message after the beep!"

Rhia slumped back against the kitchen counter with a groan.

"Still nothing?" Holly asked. Slouching at the kitchen table, dressed in black for once, she looked equal parts sympathetic and irritated, though the latter might have just been hunger. It was almost 7:00 p.m. now, a full hour after Valerie was supposed to be there, and none of them had eaten much over the day. Rhia had stopped her grandmother twice from opening the feast, reassuring her that everything was fine, Valerie was going to come, just a few more minutes.

"No," Rhia murmured. By now, her conviction was starting to fade.

"Maybe she overslept?" suggested Sage. She was leaning in the doorway wearing a sharp black suit, her braids falling over one shoulder as she glanced at the watch on her wrist. "Is she the type for afternoon naps?"

"I don't think so." Rhia lifted a hand to rub at her temple before she added, "And if that *were* the reason, I would kill her on the spot, threefold law be damned."

"Rhia," her mother chided.

Rhia pressed her lips together and stared down at her phone screen again. None of the messages she'd sent had gone through.

Standing there with her entire family watching her, dressed in their best Unveiling attire, the food already on the table, she felt so stupid she could have cried. "What if something bad happened to her?" she asked no one in particular.

"I don't think so, baby." Her mother gave her a pitying look. "Maybe she flaked. You're young. It happens."

No, it doesn't, Rhia wanted to say. *Not with her. Not after so many weeks of magic.* Instead, she let Holly take a hold of her wrist, tugging her down onto the seat next to her at the table. The rest of the family settled down around her, dresses rustling. Rhia willed herself not to look at their faces, staring instead at the candles in front of her, the overflowing pots and pans.

She barely listened to the short speech her grandmother gave, the usual spiel about thanking the earth for their meal and inviting their deceased loved ones to join them tonight. Like every Unveiling, the seat opposite Rhia was empty; it was tradition to keep one chair unoccupied so that her father, if he so chose, could sit with them. The sight of it only caused a dull pain, merely an echo of what it had been like in those first years. It was the empty chair next to Rhia that really stung this time.

"Chin up, little bug," her aunt said softly, a gentle hand

Philline Harms

brushing a stray curl behind Rhia's ear. "Your father would hate to see you so sad tonight." Rhia knew she was right. Even though she barely had an appetite, she forced herself to eat, trying to conjure up images of her dad instead of thinking about Valerie.

"Are you going to the festival later?" her mother asked, trying to distract her.

"Yeah." Rhia poked at her roasted potatoes. "Tristan is meeting us there."

Her mother nodded. Rhia didn't ask what she was going to do because she already knew: every Unveiling, after dinner, her mother would go to the cemetery to lay flowers at her dad's grave and sit there on a blanket with a warm drink in her hands, telling him all about the year that had passed. She always offered for Rhia and Sage to join her, but Rhia never went—it felt too intimate a moment for her to disturb, and she knew she'd likely just spend the entire time bawling.

"Well, I'm going to have another go at the cards, if anyone wants to—" her grandmother began, but she was abruptly cut off by a loud meowing.

At the other side of the kitchen, Medea and Hecate, two of the household cats, were scratching at the back door. Rhia cast a short glance over her shoulder before she went back to her food. Cats were more sensitive to the presence of spirits than humans, so it wasn't rare for them to respond to things the family couldn't see, especially on the night of the Unveiling.

"I don't really want to hear any other bad news tonight, so I'll pass," she quietly said.

Her grandmother's features softened at that, a weathered hand reaching across the table to give a warm squeeze to Rhia's fingers. Rhia was already bracing herself for the *I told you I had a bad feeling*. Instead, she only muttered, "Oh, sweetheart. The first one is always the worst."

Rhia knew what she meant, and she hated it. This wasn't her first heartbreak. This wasn't her first anything. This was simply a misunderstanding or an accident, and she was *fine*. She was about to open her mouth and tell her grandmother as much, but Sage beat her to it.

"Guys," she said. "Look outside."

There was something about her voice that made Rhia look up instantly. The cats had grown even louder, their mewling loud enough to nearly drown out Holly's strangled gasp. Rhia turned slowly, a hand flying to cover her mouth when she saw what had laced her sister's voice with terror.

The greenhouse stood on fire.

Rhia was the first one to move, throwing the back door wide open as she stumbled outside. Her knees threatened to buckle. The greenhouse's metal skeleton groaned as flames devoured its insides, ravaging the herbs and seeds, destroying the growth and potential and *life* that had been sprouting inside its glass walls.

Distantly, Rhia heard the rest of her family pouring into the garden behind her, panicked voices and frantic instructions overlapping, and the only nonsensical thought she had was *Valerie's fern is in there.*

While her aunt ran inside to search for the fire extinguisher, Rhia stood frozen, watching as the flames rose higher and higher under the glass roof. Dark smoke piled up, pressing against the windows with nowhere to go—until the door flew open, and it spilled into the garden, along with a dark silhouette.

"Valerie." Rhia staggered forward, snapping out of her daze in an instant. "Valerie!"

The other girl didn't give a single sign that she'd heard her. With the thick vapor billowing around her feet and her hair spilling over her shoulders in waves of flaming red, she looked barely human, more avenging angel than the girl who had smiled sleepily into Rhia's pillow the day before. Her spell echoed in Rhia's ears again: *Look, here comes a walking fire.*

"Valerie!" Rhia called again. The closer she got to Valerie, the more the smoke made her eyes water. "What happened? Are you okay?"

Valerie didn't respond. There was a strange look on her face, or what little of it Rhia could make out in the flickering firelight. Her hands were balled into fists. It was only when Rhia was right in front of her that Valerie met her eyes and whispered a single word, so quiet it almost got lost in the shouting and the hungry crackling of fire. "Run."

"What? Valerie, I—"

Behind her, Holly's voice cried out, "Rhia, watch out!"

She understood why when her eyes darted down to Valerie's left hand. Finger by finger, the fist was uncurling, as if each joint had to be commanded individually. When it opened, there was fire lapping at her palm.

"Valerie," Rhia said. Her hands came up in a soothing gesture. "Hey, Val, calm down. It's just me, I—"

Fire rushed towards her before she got to finish her sentence. She ducked on instinct, squeezing her eyes shut as it passed over her head with an audible *whoosh*. The smell of burnt hair stung her nostrils. When she raised her head, she was met with Valerie's green eyes, wide and vacant as the next fireball formed in her hand.

Rhia staggered back, unable to tear her gaze away from

Valerie for fear of what would happen if she turned her back on her. The glimmer of heat around her silhouette rendered it hazy and alien as Rhia watched everything play out in slow motion. The next fireball forming in Valerie's skilled hands. Her arm lifting. Her fingers releasing it. The fire rushing towards Rhia's face with deadly accuracy, a flurry of red-hot magic that came at her with such rapid speed that she didn't have time to—

A hand closed around her wrist and pulled her back, stumbling into the circle she hadn't even realized she'd left. The fire fizzled out inches away from her face, close enough for her to feel its heat on her skin before it was absorbed by her family's protective magic.

"You're okay." Sage hauled Rhia against her, one hand cradling the back of her head while Rhia clung to her for dear life. "I've got you, you're okay."

"What just happened?" Holly breathed.

Rhia couldn't answer. She twisted in her sister's arms to meet Valerie's gaze. From the other side of the wall that shielded her, she stared Rhia down, fire still licking up her forearms, her face terribly blank in the dancing shadows. Then, as suddenly as she'd appeared, she spun around and vanished into the woods, leaving the fire burning and Rhia trembling in her wake.

25

EIGHT OF SWORDS

helplessness — feeling trapped — inability to see a way out

Valerie was trapped.

She was in her head, and she was trapped.

She was—

She couldn't—

She remembered her grandparents' house.

It was old and stuffy and dank. At night, the wind howled around it, and the roof creaked like it was going to fly right off. Her grandmother creaked too. She was very old, and her husband was dead. That was why Valerie and her father were there.

I don't want to be here, Daddy. My room is scary, and Grandma doesn't like me.

Of course she likes you, honey. She's just very sad. I have to help her get some of my dad's things in order around here, okay? Just three days, and then we'll go home. Maybe you can spend some time with her, cheer her up.

Valerie didn't want to spend time with her. She had long

nails and yellow eyes, and she'd yelled at Valerie on the first day because she'd knocked over a glass of water.

She stayed close to her father instead.

Valerie remembered the cellar. Down there were all types of terrible things: spiders and towering mountains of boxes and monsters. Lots and lots of monsters. They were waiting in the shadows for when her father turned his back. As soon as he was gone, they would pounce and drag Valerie into the dark corners where he would never find her. She just knew it.

They couldn't touch her when she was with him, though, and so she sat on the creaky stairs and watched as he sorted old things into piles and stuffed the piles into garbage bags. He told her to wait there while he brought them upstairs. She didn't want to, but he said he would be *really quick, and I'll leave the door open, see?*

At first, that was okay. Maybe he'd told the monsters to stay in the dark, Valerie thought. He could do that. He was very good at telling people what to do, like when it was bedtime or when she had to shower. But then the one light bulb that swayed from the ceiling went out, and suddenly, the dark was everywhere. Valerie sat there, alone on the bottom step of the stairs, too scared to breathe or make a noise. She knew that if she moved even an inch, the monsters would hear her, so she stayed where she was, trembling with her knees pulled to her chest, staring up at the open door. It seemed ten thousand miles away. The staircase was big, and she was so small. The door was a tiny rectangle, and the light didn't reach her at all.

On the night of the Unveiling, Valerie felt the same way. If she strained, she could sense the world, make out bits and pieces of it. Trees scratching at her arms. A house in the distance. Fire in her palms and smoke in her lungs. But it was all so far away. No matter how hard she tried, she couldn't hold on to any of it.

She had always told herself that she was different now; there were no monsters to be scared of, no darkness that her fire couldn't banish. She'd lied to herself. She was still the little girl at the bottom of the staircase, only this time no one was coming to bring her back to the light. She was alone. Just her and the dark and the suffocating presence of seven other women in her head, holding her down.

"Valerie!"

The voice was like a blade, dispelling the darkness enough that, for just a few seconds, Valerie's eyes cleared. Rhia was running towards her, her face lit by orange flames. Fire. She'd caused that fire.

"What happened?" Rhia asked. "Are you okay?"

Valerie wanted so desperately to collapse. She wanted to throw herself at Rhia's feet and beg for forgiveness. She wanted to tell her everything that had happened and cry until she'd flushed the darkness out of her system.

Instead, she felt her palms growing hot. *No.* She desperately tried to resist the force that uncurled her fingers. *No, please, not her, don't—*

"Run," was all she managed to rasp before the darkness crashed over her and she went tumbling towards the bottom of the staircase once again, down and down and down.

White-hot anger surged through her as she went, but it wasn't hers. None of it was. Not the fire. Not her magic. Not her body as it began to move again, carrying her away from Rhia. The world blurred again, until suddenly—

Valerie.

It was the same voice that had cried out earlier, right after she'd taken off the protection charm. It came from nowhere and everywhere all at once. It felt like her father returning to the cellar and scooping her up in his arms; like Rhia holding her after she'd pulled her from the river; like a hot cup of tea and warm blankets and being curled up next to a fireplace.

Mom?

I'm here, baby. I'm here.

If Valerie could have cried, she would have. In her imagination, meeting her mother had always been victorious, running into her arms and studying her face, a feeling of coming home. It hadn't been this: stumbling through the night in a torn dress, seven pairs of hands tugging her along by the strings she'd tied to herself.

I'm so sorry, she thought. *I did everything wrong. I didn't know—*

You couldn't have known. The warmth spread, seeping into every corner of Valerie's mind. Her voice was so familiar: the velvety tone of it, the soothing cadence. *Your spell worked—without it, I wouldn't be able to talk to you right now. It's just that the necklace wasn't only mine. It was everyone's. A family heirloom.*

So she wanted *me to find that necklace.* The revelation did nothing to make Valerie feel any less numb. *That's the reason for the sleepwalking. She tried to lead me to the river from the moment I first set foot in Oakriver.*

It was between finding the pentagram or drowning you, her mother confirmed. Her voice was so soft. She sounded so young, a girl not much older than Valerie was now. *I was so scared she would manage it during those first nights. You must be so tired. You've spent so long resisting her.*

Valerie didn't know why the understanding in her mother's voice made her want to weep even more. She *was* tired. She'd never been this tired in her life. Still, she pressed on. *Quinn told me they heard a voice warning them during the Hunter's Moon. That was you, wasn't it? You reached out to them when the veil was thinning.*

I did. I didn't mean to frighten them—I just couldn't see another way.

There was silence as Valerie tried to sort her thoughts. Then: *I still don't understand why she did it. Why did she want to drown me?*

It's her version of revenge.

On whom?

Me. And your father, of course. Secondhand sadness washed through Valerie, strong enough to momentarily drown out every other sensation. *She knew I was watching you—or trying to, anyway. Apparently, the first punishment didn't satisfy her.*

The first *punishment? Why did she want to punish you at all? And what does Dad have to do with any of this?*

It doesn't matter now. What matters is that you regain control.

Valerie tried once again to will her body to stop its movements, to call on her fire. It didn't work. Her magic felt just like it had all those years ago, when she'd struggled to even light a candle; it was there inside of her, she knew it was, but she couldn't grasp any of it. Sometimes her fingertips would brush it, but then it was gone again in an instant, snatched away by someone else.

I can't. Mom, I can't.

The silence stretched so long Valerie was afraid her mother's presence had vanished again, or worse, that she'd imagined her being there in the first place. Finally, her mother's gentle voice inquired, *Do you remember your spell, Valerie?*

I—I think so.

Good. Hold on to it, okay?

But how am I supposed to say it? I barely managed one word. They have so much more magic than I do.

You're not alone, Isabelle told her, a firmness in her voice that, for just a second, calmed Valerie. *When the time is right, I will give you what's left of mine. It isn't much—guiding Quinn to the river used up most of it—and I won't be able to reach out to you again afterward, but . . . maybe* she *can help us too.*

Rhia?

You've shared magic before, haven't you?

Yes, but not a lot. And I don't think she'll know to give me any of hers. Valerie thought back to the reluctance on Rhia's face as she'd peered into the scrying bowl, the way that her control had to be coaxed out of her bit by bit. A few weeks ago, Valerie had thought of it like a game, getting Rhia to lay down her armor piece by cautious piece. Now all she could think about was how much of it was still left. *She doesn't let go of her power like that.*

Let's hope she surprises us, her mother said quietly.

Valerie didn't respond. Dimly, she was aware that she was still walking, her legs mechanically setting one foot in front of the other. She only understood where they were taking her when the town center came into view and the world turned into a kaleidoscope of flashing colors.

Oh, Valerie, her mother whispered. *You should've never come back to this town.*

26

FIVE OF CUPS

old wounds — regret — dwelling on past mistakes

Rhia wanted to run after Valerie the moment she was out of sight, but Sage had an iron grip on her and kept her firmly at her side. In the end, she sank into the grass, watching in a daze as the rest of her family put out the fire inside the greenhouse. Unlike Rhia, who had to wrap her arms around herself to stop from shaking, they were moving with purpose and surprising calm, using buckets of water and a fire extinguisher while Holly and Aunt Tanisha tried to limit the oxygen supply inside the structure.

When the fire died down, they returned to where Rhia was sitting, sweat glittering on their browbones in the moonlight. Guilt churned in Rhia's stomach as she trailed back inside after them, the kitchen still festively decorated and their food cold on the table. With their black dresses and solemn expressions, they suddenly had the air of funeral guests rather than a family of witches celebrating their most anticipated holiday of the year.

Rhia's mother was the first one to break the tense silence. "Was *that* your girlfriend?"

Rhia gave a small nod.

"Charming," her grandmother remarked.

"It wasn't *her*," Rhia said firmly. "Valerie wouldn't do this."

"Valerie?" Her mother fixed her with a stare Rhia couldn't read. "That's her name?"

Rhia frowned. "Yeah. Valerie Morgan. Why?"

She didn't get a response. The silence in the kitchen felt like it was getting heavier with every second that passed as her mother exchanged weighted looks with her aunt and grandmother. Rhia couldn't read the expressions on their faces, caught between disbelief, anger, and something that looked far too close to fear for Rhia's liking.

Finally, Rhia said, "Okay, I don't know what's going on here, but we really don't have time for this. We need to find her before she sets something else on fire or gets herself hurt."

"No," her grandmother said. "We won't go after her. It's far too dangerous."

"You're *scared* of her?" Rhia had to fight down a hysterical laugh. "That's ridiculous. I know what happened out there looks bad, but I promise this isn't like h—"

"You don't know what you're dealing with." Grandma Deloris's voice was alarmingly quiet.

"What? Of course I do, she's my *girlfriend*—"

"She's a Hawthorne!" Her grandmother all but spat the word. It sounded venomous from her mouth, like a rare poison she was driving out of her system.

Rhia gave an exasperated shake of her head. "What on earth does that mean?"

As always, it was her aunt's voice that was the gentlest. "Rhiannon, sweetheart." There was a strained smile on her face as she rested a featherlight hand on Rhia's shoulder and steered her towards the nearest chair. "Why don't you sit down?" To Rhia's mother, she said, "I think it's time we tell them, Zora."

"Tell us what?" asked Sage. She was leaning against the kitchen counter, a deep furrow between her brows as she observed the rapid derailing of her meticulously planned evening. Smoke was rising from the singed sleeves of her suit. Seeing her older sister look so frazzled only added to the uneasy feeling in Rhia's stomach.

"It's a long story, and a dark one," Rhia's mother reluctantly said. Sitting at the end of the table, with the candle in front of her hollowing out her features, she appeared wearier than Rhia had seen her in a long time. "We agreed not to tell you—we didn't want to frighten you when you were so young, and we thought it wasn't necessary anymore, after everything that happened. But apparently, that has changed."

"Oakriver wasn't always home to only three families of witches," Grandma Deloris said, the steel in her eyes belying her matter-of-fact tone. "There was another family, made up of seven cruel women . . . and one who didn't want anything to do with them."

"Isabelle Morgan," Rhia murmured.

"Isabelle Hawthorne," her grandmother corrected her. "They never got married."

Rhia turned the name over in her head. Hawthorne. "They're the fourth family who was in the Council," she realized. "The Council of the Four. Right?"

"Ah. I thought you might've stumbled upon something in

those spell books you were looking through." Her mother let out a long breath. "You're right. The Hawthornes used to be part of the Council."

"What happened to them?" Rhia asked, rubbing at the goose bumps on her arms.

"We'll get there," her grandmother said. "First, you must know who the Hawthornes *were*. Because trust me when I say they were nothing like you think. Witches, yes, but an entirely different kind. Their practices went beyond anything you can imagine. They had no rules, no moral compass. The threefold law meant nothing to them. The only thing they were ruled by was their greed."

"What did they do?" Holly asked. She was sitting at the table with the look of a child hearing a scary story at the campfire, her eyes wide and openly frightened.

"Anything that would give them more power. Hexes, curses, ghastly potions. Necromancy, communicating with the dead to gain information on the people of Oakriver. Nothing was holy to them."

"There were all these terrible rumors." Aunt Tanisha's eyes went unfocused as she stared into the candle in front of her. "It was said that Elvira, the oldest and the leader of their coven, had poisoned her husband after he'd given her three daughters and she decided she was done with childbearing and playing the doting wife." Her aunt shivered. "They despised anyone without abilities. Humans without magic were inferior to them, a stain on their family tree."

"But why have we never heard about them until now?" Sage questioned. "Did they leave Oakriver?"

Their grandmother gave a snort. "Oh, no. They never

would have abandoned the town, not when their claws were buried in its marrow. You see, over the decades they lived here, they gained more and more influence and wealth. Eventually, Elvira decided to run for mayor." Her lips curled in a snarl. "Unfortunately for her—and luckily for the entire town—all the dark magic in the world couldn't secure her win. I'm sure the people could sense that there was something wrong with her whole lot. They were afraid of her, and while fear *is* a motivator, it most definitely does not make you any friends. So she lost. And, boy, did she take that loss to heart."

"That's the biggest euphemism I've ever heard," Rhia's mother said bitterly. "They killed the elected mayor, his wife, and his two children. Set fire to their house in the middle of the night."

Rhia inhaled sharply. The floor beneath her seemed to tilt, as if this terrible new knowledge had knocked the world right off its axis. Never in her entire life had she witnessed another witch intentionally use their magic to hurt another being. It was the biggest crime one of them could commit, an atrocity so unimaginable it made her sick to her stomach.

In the eyes of Holly and Sage, she saw the same unspoken horror. "Did they get away with it?" Sage rasped.

"No," their grandmother said. "This is where Isabelle Hawthorne comes in."

Rhia sat up straighter.

Her mother met her eyes, the shadow of a sorrowful smile flitting over her face. "She was different from them. She was *good*. But she was also reckless. When she was twenty-one, she started seeing Matthew Morgan behind her family's back. He didn't know about them, and they didn't know about him. It was a dangerous game she played—even more so when she got pregnant."

Under the table, Rhia's nails were digging little crescent moons into her palms. Here was Valerie's story, the answers she'd been searching for all this time—a family portrait painted in the darkest of colors. With every ugly detail in stark relief, it was more terrible than anything she could've imagined.

"They were furious that she'd kept their affair hidden, but Isabelle had leverage: the baby. As much as the Hawthornes despised her relationship with a human, they loved the idea of new magical blood entering their family more. They struck a deal: Matthew would be left alone if in turn Isabelle kept the baby and raised it beneath their roof."

"But what if it'd been a child born without magic?" Rhia asked. The stifling silence that followed was answer enough. "Okay, so Isabelle gives birth to Valerie," she said, trying her best to keep her voice steady. "What happened then?"

"For two years, she continued living with them," her grandmother answered. "Magical abilities usually start to show at four years, as you know, so she had a cushion, a period of time before they could try to make use of Valerie in any way, and she could still be with Matthew. But that didn't mean Isabelle didn't hate every second that her child grew up in a household of dark magic and deceit. The murder of the mayor's family two years after Valerie was born was the final straw— and Isabelle's chance at freedom. She couldn't stop them, but what she *could* do was send anonymous letters to influential people around town, exposing the role the Hawthornes had played in their deaths."

While a shiver ran down Rhia's spine, Holly gasped softly.

"But wasn't that signing her own death sentence? She was the only one who could have known they'd done it, right?"

Rhia's mother tilted her head. "She had everything planned. On the day she sent out the letters, she made sure that Matthew was out of town. And Valerie . . . Valerie, she brought to us."

"What?" Rhia whispered.

Her grandmother's eyes looked glassy as she studied her hands. "Up until that point, we'd tried to keep our heads down as much as possible. We included them in the Council in hopes of being able to supervise their doings, maybe even guide them back onto the lighter path. It was no use. They still performed their darker brand of magic—they just got better at hiding it. We knew about some of their doings, but we never imagined the lengths they would go to. And we were frightened of what would happen if we called them out—with Sage barely six years old and you and Holly still toddlers, our family felt more vulnerable than ever."

Grandma Deloris rubbed a trembling hand over her eyes. The only other time Rhia had seen her as troubled had been the night her father had died; there was a similar mix of regret and frustration on her face now, still potent after more than a decade. "And so our family never took a stance. It was only that night, when Isabelle showed up on our doorstep with her crying two-year-old, that the invisible lines we'd drawn were blurred for the very first time."

"We knew what the consequences might be if they found out we'd stolen their magical offspring—because stealing was how they would have viewed it—and that it was dangerous," Rhia's mom added. "But I'd known Isabelle since high school. We were years apart, but we would grab lunch together sometimes or run into each other at Obscura. I knew what she dreamed of: a normal life with her partner and her baby. Who was I to deny her that? How could I, when you were laughing in the living room with your father, just as innocent as the little green-eyed girl in front of me?" She shook her head, a muscle leaping in her cheek. "So I took Valerie in. *Just for four or five days*, that was what Isabelle said. *Just until the worst has blown over*. Except it didn't."

"The town failed her," Rhia's aunt whispered. "They took too long to act. A week passed, and all they did was talk, talk, talk. Until word got to the Hawthornes."

In the dim light, the shine in Rhia's mother's eyes looked almost like tears. "Isabelle had taken protective measures for everyone but herself. She didn't want all hell to break loose before her actual plan could unfold, so she let her family believe that Matthew had taken their daughter with him on his trip while she stayed. When they found out that it was Isabelle who had sent the letters, there was nowhere left for her to run. Not to her partner, who was staying with his family at the other end of the state. Not to us because she would've led them straight to her daughter. The Lightbourns and the Fairloves had left town right after the fire for fear that they, as the two other most influential families, would be targeted next, so she couldn't turn to them either. In the end, she ran into the woods. And that's where she died."

"Because they drowned her."

All at once, all eyes were directed at Rhia. "Yes," her mother said. "How do you know that?"

Rhia hesitated for a moment, unsure of how much she should say. In the end, she settled on, "Valerie found her mother's necklace in the Murmuring River. What . . . what happened after she was dead?"

"Murdering Isabelle couldn't undo the damage, of course," Deloris answered. "The town knew what they'd done. Two days after Isabelle's death, they finally acted. In the middle of the night, someone burned down the barn in which they were performing their rituals, with all of them locked inside."

"The threefold law," Rhia murmured. *What harm you do shall return to you times three.* There was a cruel irony in the fact that most of them had probably been fire witches—untouchable by their own fire, but helpless to the flames set by others.

"Yes," Deloris agreed. "A week later, the Lightbourns and the Fairloves returned. In our first meeting as the Council of the Three, we swore an oath, formally agreeing to keep the existence of magic hidden from the townspeople like we had before the Hawthornes had interfered. It was the only way to quench the rumors that circulated—the only way to give you three the carefree childhood you deserved."

Silence fell once again. Holly sat chewing nervously at her nails. Sage looked pensive, still leaning against the kitchen counter with her arms crossed in front of her chest. And Rhia . . . Rhia didn't know how to feel. It was all too much and too terrible for her to comprehend right away. The only thing that remained a constant was the worry coiling tight in her stomach.

"None of this changes anything," she said. "I still need to go after her."

"But—"

"I know it's dangerous, but I also know that this . . ." Rhia shook her head. "This isn't her. I *know* it's not. When I tried to talk to her, I could see she was trying to hold herself back. She was trying to put out the fire in her hands, and when she couldn't, she told me to run."

"She's still a Hawthorne," her grandmother insisted. "Knowing their lot, that little trick with the greenhouse was only a taste of what she's capable of."

Rhia was about to object, but her mother beat her to it. "She might be a Hawthorne," she said, meeting Deloris's gaze head-on, "but she's also Isabelle's daughter. I made a promise to her all those years ago to keep that little girl safe. I don't intend to break it now."

"Thank you, Mom," Rhia said earnestly. "Valerie is—"

Frantic knocking at the front door cut her off before she got to finish.

Holly's hand shot across the table to grab onto Rhia's sleeve, but she leapt to her feet before anyone could stop her. It was irrational, but maybe whatever was going on with Valerie had stopped—maybe she could pass through the circle again and was coming to explain what had happened. Rhia threw open the door.

Outside stood the one person she'd least expected. "Quinn?" she asked, blinking at them. "What are you doing here?"

Quinn shook their head. "It's Valerie," they panted, doubling over. "Something's wrong with her. I think she—"

"I know," Rhia said quickly. "Where did you see her?"

"I ran into her when I was heading back to the dorm from work a few minutes ago. She didn't even look like she recognized me." Quinn gulped. "She was on the main road. I think she's heading towards the festival."

For the second time that evening, the ground seemed to tilt. The Halloween festival. The place where the entire town was gathered that night. The place where she'd agreed to later meet . . .

"Tristan." Holly suddenly stood right behind Rhia, the look

on her face like she'd seen a ghost. Behind her, the rest of the family was gathered, their expressions pulled taut with grim determination.

Quinn's words had made the decision for them.

"Let's go," said Deloris, clapping her hands. "Get a move on, everybody."

Quinn met her eyes over Rhia's shoulder with an expression she couldn't read. "Did you know this was going to happen?"

"I had a feeling," was all Deloris said.

"A good or a bad one?"

"A good one about you." She pulled on her knitted hat. "A bad one about everything else."

Quinn gave a nod, as if that made sense.

Without another word, coats were grabbed, crystals pocketed, candles snuffed. A moment later, the moon watched as six witches poured into the garden and marched towards whatever awaited them in the heart of the town, a seventh one trailing reluctantly after them.

27

NINE OF WANDS

perseverance — courage — standing one's ground

The Halloween festival was to the town what the Fall Festival was to the witches in the area. Organized by Tristan's mom, it took place every year, a brightly lit array of food stalls and small-town attractions that began in the town square and stretched all the way to Oakriver's outskirts.

Rhia could already hear the sounds from two blocks away, a flurry of excited voices layered over loud music and the metallic shrieking of a carousel. The narrow alleyways were bustling with bright-eyed families and tipsy college students, all grins and animated chatter as they made their way either to the festival or away from it. Meanwhile, Rhia's heart pounded in her chest as she strained her ears, dreading the moment when the delighted squeals would turn into screams and the twinkling lights be consumed by smoke.

She startled violently when a hand brushed hers. "Hey," Sage murmured, squeezing her fingers. "Everything will be okay. We'll find her and figure out what's wrong with her. You'll see."

"I wouldn't worry too much about her," their grandmother huffed. She was breathing heavily but stubbornly kept up with their unforgiving pace. "*She* will be just fine. It's the not-fireproof parts of the population I'm more concerned about."

"Grandma," Holly whispered. "Not the *time*."

Rhia once again quickened her stride. From the corner of her eye, she could see Quinn hurrying along half a step behind her, their gaze glued to the cracked cobblestones as they whispered, "I hate everything about this" to no one in particular.

They turned another corner, and the town square came into view. Bustling with festivalgoers in gaudy costumes and lit by black and orange lanterns, it was like stepping into another world. For a second, Rhia was disoriented, blinded by the lights and dizzy from the cloying scent of sugar and alcohol.

She was ripped out of her daze when her mother caught her eye. "Let's split up," she said. "If you find Valerie or Tristan, call. If you don't, we'll meet here again in fifteen minutes. Got it?"

Rhia barely managed to nod before Sage tugged her deeper into the overwhelming sea of light and noise. Together, they pushed their way through the crowds gathered in front of stalls that sold mulled wine and candy apples, pumpkin pie and neon-colored cocktails that were supposed to look like potions. "Spellbound" by Siouxsie and the Banshees was blasting through the speakers, loud enough to make Rhia's ears ring. From her right, a white woman wearing a deep-purple robe and a headscarf shouted at her to come closer to her booth, *Five dollars for a glimpse at your future, little girl!* Rhia tore her gaze away from her cheap deck of tarot cards just in time to catch a glimpse of red hair disappearing behind the stall that hosted a pumpkin-carving contest.

"That's her!" Rhia shouted over the racket. She didn't wait to see if the others had heard her before she took off. Valerie was only a few feet ahead of her, her long black dress gathered in both hands as she picked her way through the festival crowd. Rhia pushed even harder, barely dodging a group of vampires as she raced after her. "Wait!" she shouted. With one hand, she grabbed onto Valerie's arm to spin her around—

Except it wasn't Valerie. The girl in front of Rhia was at least five years older, confused blue eyes peering at Rhia from above a gigantic prosthetic nose, warts and all. Her red hair was a few shades too dark and, judging by the brunet strands that curled around her ears, clearly a wig.

"Sorry," Rhia said, quickly dropping her hand. "I thought you were someone else."

"Oh, it's okay!" With a giggle, the girl gestured at another woman passing by in a similar costume. "Lots of witches around here. Happy Halloween!"

She was carried away by the teeming stream of people before Rhia could respond. Her head spun. The entire festival felt like a fever dream, a parallel world too fast, too bright, too loud for her to find her footing.

"Where is she?" Holly appeared behind Rhia, Sage and Quinn in tow.

"Wasn't her." Rhia tried to push down the panic that bubbled up in her chest, but some of it still seeped into her voice when she said, "How are we supposed to find her? There are way too many people here, there's no way we'll—"

"Um," Quinn interrupted. "I . . . I think I found her."

Rhia spun around. In the very center of the town square, there was a black tent. It was set up there every year, serving as the space where Tristan's mom gave her annual speech and where people could dance once enough alcohol had been poured and the children had been brought home. Rhia could hear Sharon Moore's voice crackling through a microphone, but the words were drowned out by the blood rushing in her ears.

At the back of the tent crouched Valerie. Her hands were balled into fists, her red hair a curtain hiding her face from view. Even from afar, Rhia could see her entire frame trembling as she desperately clung to what little control she had left.

It wasn't much. In the next heartbeat, a flame flickered in her palm—small, but enough to set the tent that dozens of people were currently under alight. The tent in which Sharon Moore was speaking. And if she was in there, then so was Tristan.

Holly started running before any of them moved, the crowd parting in front of her when she gave no signs of slowing for anyone. Rhia sprinted after her, her eyes glued to Valerie as the flame flickered on and off. Slowly, inch by inch, her hand neared the tent, fingers almost brushing against it before a gust of wind came out of nowhere, strong enough to knock her off her feet. Her back hit the cobblestones with enough force to audibly punch the air out of her lungs, her face momentarily going slack. Aside from a little wince, Holly didn't look very apologetic as she slowly lowered her hands.

"Valerie." Rhia ground to a halt in front of her. "Get away from the tent."

Valerie stared up at her as if she'd never seen her before. The green in her eyes had been swallowed completely; all that remained was a bottomless black that Rhia saw nothing but her own reflection in. She was caught in that vacant gaze, her feet firmly rooted to the ground even as Valerie shot to her feet, faster than should have been possible after her fall. "Val, no—" Rhia began, but it was too late: she had already taken off. Frantic, Rhia threw a glance over her shoulder. Holly had vanished inside the tent, and Sage and Quinn hadn't caught up with her yet. She could wait here until they fought their way through the crowd, losing sight of Valerie once again—or she could chase after her, alone.

Rhia ran. To her surprise, Valerie moved *away* from the town center and into the dark alleyways where the stands were more scattered, the streets less packed. As the noise faded behind her, Rhia could hear the sound of her boots hitting the ground again, her own heavy breaths as she pumped oxygen into her lungs. More than once, she tripped on the hem of her dress—if she had known she was going to be doing so much running, she would've dressed more practically. Then again, if she'd known what was going to happen, she wouldn't have let Valerie out of her sight in the first place. What on earth had she *done*? And what did Rhia have to do to reverse it?

By now they had reached the outskirts of town. There was nothing out here aside from a few more houses and . . . a cornfield. With a start, Rhia remembered the conversation they'd had just two days earlier: *This year, there will even be a corn maze.* Sure enough, it came into view right as she rounded the next corner.

Valerie vanished into the field before Rhia had the chance to stop her. In the dark, the entrance looked like a gaping mouth. Rhia's legs tried to slow as she got closer to it, but she forced them to pump harder, ignoring the burning ache in her calves, and let it swallow her whole.

Inside, it was darker than she'd expected, her eyes slow to adjust after the bright lights of the festival. The walls of the maze towered above her, almost blocking out the tar-black night sky. The passage was barely wide enough for her to stretch her arms out on both sides. She lasted for maybe three more minutes before she had to pause, doubled over with her hands on her knees. Surrounded by corn on all sides, with every sound muffled and the town a million light-years away, she suddenly felt terribly claustrophobic. She could've asked the plants for guidance, but there was something artificial about them, planted in straight rows and drowned in pesticides. They weren't at all like the trees outside her house, who had watched her grow up and spoke to her like friends, or even like the woods around the cabin, to whom she was a loose acquaintance. Getting into contact with plants she didn't know was like switching through a dozen different radio frequencies until she found a channel that worked: it required time and calm, two things she decidedly did not have.

She swore quietly. Valerie was nowhere to be seen, her family didn't know where she was, and in her hurry she hadn't thought to bring a phone. Maybe it was better to turn around while she still could.

The sounds of steps coming her way made her straighten just in time to see a pair of pint-sized ghosts rounding the corner. "Happy Halloween!" said one of them, giddy voice muffled by the bedsheet thrown over his head.

"Happy Halloween," Rhia numbly repeated. "You two didn't happen to see a girl with red hair just now, did you?"

"We did! She's, like, almost in the middle of the maze." The other one eagerly waved an arm in the direction he'd seen her.

"Thank you," Rhia said, quickly pushing past them. She only glanced over her shoulder once more to see the two little ghosts waddling around the next corner. Her grandmother's words echoed in her head again: *It's the not-fireproof parts of the population I'm more concerned about.* Who knew who else was wandering around inside this labyrinth? She couldn't let anyone get hurt, least of all *children*.

With her resolve renewed, Rhia sped up her steps. Once, she'd heard that you could always find the exit of any maze if you kept your right hand on the wall at all times. She didn't know if it was true, but she felt slightly better as she grazed the wall with her fingertips, praying she wasn't just running in circles as she wandered farther and farther away from the entrance.

Time passed strangely inside the maze, so Rhia didn't know how long she'd been walking when she heard another pair of feet in front of her. She rounded another corner to find Valerie only a few steps ahead.

This time, Rhia didn't try to call out to her. Instead, she crouched, took a deep breath to momentarily calm herself, and dug her fingers into the soil at her feet. She didn't bother trying with the corn but addressed what she knew well—what was woven through the earth everywhere she went, and stirred like it had just been waiting to be called on. *"Stop her."*

Roots broke through the ground the instant the words were spoken, reaching for Valerie. She slowed, then stumbled, until finally she landed flat on her stomach. She barely managed to turn onto her back before they wound around her ankles and wrists, tethering her to the ground.

Releasing the breath she'd been holding, Rhia tentatively neared her. In Valerie's eyes flickered an expression Rhia had

Philline Harms

never seen on her. It was a white-hot fury even angrier than she'd looked when she'd found Rhia and Quinn in her dorm room.

"I'm sorry," Rhia said when she came to a halt in front of her. "Did I hurt you?"

Valerie didn't respond, her teeth gritted as she yanked at her restraints.

Rhia hesitated for a second before she sank to her knees beside her. Studying Valerie, her face a mask of hatred, it was hard to find any trace of the girl she knew. Still, she kept her voice gentle as she said, "Valerie, I know you're in there. It's me. I'm here to help you if you can tell me how."

A few inches away from her, Valerie's legs kicked out. The roots didn't loosen their grip.

Gulping, Rhia reached out a hand and rested it lightly on Valerie's knee. "Please, Val. You're stronger than them. You can do this."

Valerie struggled against her restraints one more time—then she went limp, her head hitting the ground with a soft thud. A whimper tore free from her throat, terrible and raw in the quiet. The anger melted away and gave way to just her, wide-eyed and frightened.

"*Spirits of the other side,*" she whispered, her voice cracking on the last word, "*I thank you for your help tonight.*"

A spell. "Go on," Rhia urged.

"*With my words, I called you, so my word is law.*" She inhaled sharply, her hands flexing at her sides. "*Return to where you came from, for I am . . . for I am . . .*"

"You can do it," Rhia pressed. "Valerie, you're almost there."

Valerie shook her head. With her tears glittering in the moonlight and her hair sticking to her sweaty forehead, she looked achingly helpless. The worst thing was that Rhia knew there was nothing she could do. Valerie had spoken whatever spell had caused this; she was the only one who could make it undone.

Rhia hated everything about this. She hated being so goddamn *useless* when inches away from her, Valerie was shaking with silent sobs, looking more afraid than Rhia had ever seen her. "Valerie." Rhia's voice sounded pathetically pleading as she looked down at her, watching the way her hands twitched, fire sparking at her fingertips again. "Please."

Valerie's eyes finally met hers. A jolt went through Rhia. Even though they weren't touching, she suddenly felt the bond between them drawing taut, followed by a familiar tug at her very core.

Valerie was trying to draw on her magic.

On instinct, Rhia scrambled back, pushing away the insistent presence of Valerie's abilities—or whoever else it was who had made themselves at home inside her.

Valerie held her gaze for a few more stuttering heartbeats, her eyes brimming with tears. When she blinked again, they were gone, and her face turned blank, like a blackboard wiped clean of chalk. The sparks at her fingertips grew as golden flames spilled from her hands and consumed the roots around her wrists and ankles. By the time Rhia got her own legs to cooperate and run after her, the only thing she found was a smoking hole burned into the wall of the maze, and behind it the infinite night.

28

THE HIGH PRIESTESS

inner knowledge — psychic insight — stepping into one's power

Rhia wanted nothing more than to crumble to the ground and let the earth claim her. Her head was pounding. Her legs were trembling from the exertion of running. Worst of all, her heart *ached* as the image of Valerie replayed over and over: her shaking hands, her lips parting on a helpless whimper, the raw fear in her eyes.

It was the latter detail that got Rhia to move. She couldn't afford to fall apart now. But she also couldn't keep playing cat and mouse with Valerie now that she'd run off into the dark again. She needed her family and a plan.

And so, as much as she hated the feeling of turning her back on the smoldering hole that Valerie had disappeared through, she rushed in the opposite direction, back the way she'd come. No one paid her any mind as she stumbled through the exit of the corn maze and headed down the dark alleyway towards the noise of the festival. From above the roofs, the moon looked down at her. Rhia wished she could ask her what she was seeing, if things made sense from her vantage point in the sky.

The festival was even more overwhelming as Rhia entered it this time, all shouts and swirling colors and a frenetic hum in the air that made her skin prickle as she shoved through the crowd. By the time she made it back to their agreed meeting spot, she was so exhausted her knees almost buckled.

Her mother was the first to spot her. "Rhiannon!" she exclaimed, immediately pulling her into a hug. Her arms were tight enough around Rhia to knock the air out of her lungs; tight enough that, for just a few seconds, Rhia allowed herself to lean into her and share a fraction of her weight. "You scared me," her mother whispered into her hair. "What on earth happened?"

It took all the strength she had in her to step out of her mother's embrace and face the rest of her family, already gathered around her with a million questions hanging unspoken in the air. "I chased after her to the corn maze," she said. "I managed to stall her for a few seconds. She was trying to say a spell to banish them, but she couldn't finish it. She was so close, but then *someone* took over, and she ran."

"So it's true what I thought," her grandmother said. "The family took control of her."

"They aren't in control," Rhia said. "She's fighting. She almost got there, but they dragged her under again somehow."

"Of course they did," her aunt murmured. "Poor thing. If it's true and all *seven* of them have a hold of her, I can't imagine how much strength it took to utter even a few words of the spell."

"Wait." Quinn took a staggering step forward. Rhia only noticed them now that they were peeling out of the shadows, their arms crossed in front of their chest. It looked less like a defensive gesture and more like they were desperately trying to hold themself together. "I don't get it. Is she *possessed*?"

Rhia gave a tired nod. "Something like that, yeah." Quinn looked like they were seconds away from throwing up. Sage gave their shoulder a sympathetic squeeze.

Around the corner, the festival raged on, but the cheers and music barely reached them; it was as if their little pocket of darkness was an entire world away from the unknowing townspeople. Rhia suddenly wished nothing more than to be one of them, just a normal girl drinking and dancing in a cheap costume. Anything but a witch having to save her girlfriend who had somehow gotten herself possessed by her dark-magic-performing, mayor-killing, revenge-seeking family on the most magically charged night of the year.

"What are we supposed to do now?" she asked, looking at her family again. "I have no idea where she went."

"No, you don't," her mother agreed. "But maybe you can find out where she *will* go."

"What do you mean?"

"You should try divination."

"No," Rhia objected. "That's a waste of time. I've only managed it once, and that was with Valerie. One of you has to do it."

"You know that's not possible, sweetheart," Grandma Deloris said. "We can only tell the future for ourselves or a person who's physically with us. Anything else requires a strong emotional connection between you and the one you seek answers about." She took a step forward, gently taking Rhia's face in both hands. "You're the only one who can do it, Rhiannon."

"No. Grandma, I *can't*. You told me yourself that I'm too bad at letting go to ever manage it—"

"That's not what I said." The familiar impatience gave her voice an edge. "I said that if you learn to let your magic flow freely, you will be as fantastic at divination as you are at everything else."

Rhia shook her head. There had to be another way that didn't depend on *her* and her messed-up brain getting in the way. She couldn't bear the thought of failing—not when Valerie was on the line. Turning around, she caught Quinn's gaze. "What about you?" she all but pleaded. "You guys are close. Have you ever done divination?"

Quinn grimaced. "The one time I consciously used my magic was when I held the necklace, and that wasn't exactly controlled."

While Rhia tried to stop herself from panicking, Sage gently touched her shoulder. "You've already managed it once. I think you should try again."

"But what if I fail? I don't think I can do it alone."

"Who says you have to do it alone?" It was the first time that Holly had spoken. When Rhia glanced over at her, her cousin looked more serious than Rhia had ever seen her. "All of us will be with you. We'll shield you."

Around her, the others nodded—even Quinn, despite the sickly color of their face.

Rhia swallowed hard. Holly was right. Of course she was right. Rhia had never been alone: not when she'd first discovered her abilities, not when she'd performed her first rituals, not when she'd started building her altar or writing in her spell book or all the many small firsts after that. Her entire life, her family had been the light guiding her, the roots keeping her grounded, the protective circle ensuring she was safe. Rhia trusted them blindly. If they believed she could do this—if *Valerie* believed she could do this—then she had to at least try.

"Okay." She lifted her gaze to meet theirs. "But I can't do it here."

~

The walk into the woods was a silent affair disturbed only by the snapping of twigs under their boots and the rustling of their dresses. Rhia and Quinn walked at the front, Holly and Sage right behind them. The older women were at the rear.

They were following the same path behind the college dorms that Valerie and Rhia had walked that golden afternoon when Rhia had finally given up on trying to run from her feelings. Then, she'd been so sure. Now her feet were sore and unsteady, the path ahead of her dark and winding. Craning her head back, she looked up at the trees swaying high above her.

Have you seen her? she asked them.

The answer was a confusing tangle of overlapping voices, so overwhelming that Rhia couldn't get a hold of a single one. The trees had witnessed something they hadn't seen in years, something that felt so unnatural it made even the tallest of them shiver with dread. Rhia could feel their panic seeping into her, but then a hand slipped into hers, and the connection broke, agitated whispers fading into rustling leaves and groaning branches once again.

"Steady," Holly said, her palm warm against Rhia's.

Rhia wondered if Holly could hear a similar clamor in the whispering of the wind. She didn't think she wanted to know.

Instead, she asked, "Is Tristan okay?"

"Yes. I brought him home, and he promised to stay there until tomorrow morning."

The anxious knot in Rhia's stomach loosened the tiniest bit. At least one of her loved ones was safe.

Ahead of them, the narrow path opened into a clearing. Rhia had chosen this spot because it reminded her of the afternoon with Valerie, and because here, surrounded by trees, she felt more grounded than in the streets of the town. Apparently, she hadn't been the only one to have that idea.

The second she set foot into the clearing, an uneasy chill ran down her spine. Magic lingered in the air, so thick she feared she would choke on it. There was the unmistakable scent of Valerie's witchcraft, smoke and spices, but it was overpowered by something else. Rhia had never encountered a corpse in real life, but she was sure that the sickly sweet fragrance that hung over the meadow like a cloying perfume was what death smelled like. Its stench grew stronger as she neared the remains of a ritual spread out in front of her. Twelve candles were arranged in a circle, a thirteenth knocked over in its middle. The tote bag that had been slung over Valerie's shoulder every time she'd visited the café had been dropped into the grass. Right next to it lay the spell book Rhia had handed Valerie only yesterday. Her stomach twisted at the sight of the word *Necromancy* scrawled at the top of the open page in jagged handwriting.

"Where did she get that?" her grandmother asked. She looked like she was itching to step inside the circle and pick it up, but none of them dared to move any closer to it.

"I gave it to her," Rhia said tonelessly. "It was in the box of old books that Holly found in the attic of the café."

Holly's eyes widened. "What? How did it get there?"

"That building was one of the many the Hawthornes owned," Rhia's mother explained. Her long skirt brushed against the tall grass as she slowly neared the circle. "Everyone thought it was madness when Anne bought it and turned it into Sugar & Spice, but somehow she managed to rid it of its bad name." Her lips curled in disgust as her eyes fell on the book. "Just not all its ghosts, I suppose."

"I always did get a weird vibe in the attic," Holly murmured. "I thought it was just haunted."

"Oh, it probably is," said Aunt Tanisha. "I don't even want to know what they used it for. Why do you think I tried to talk you out of moving your workshop there?"

Holly quipped something in response, but Rhia wasn't listening anymore. From the corner of her eye, she'd caught a glimpse of something sparkling in the grass. Sinking to her knees, she picked up the protection charm she'd given Valerie. Somehow, it was this sight that came the closest to undoing her. Rhia could still remember the way Valerie had looked at her in the café all those weeks ago when Rhia had asked her why she hadn't cast a circle. Even then, Rhia had wanted to shake her, to make that amused glimmer in her eyes go away, to make her understand that this was *serious*. And now Valerie, a girl to whom magic had always been a game without rules, was the playing piece being toyed with by a force that was so much bigger than anything even Rhia had feared. The thought made her feel sick.

"Did you find something?" Sage's voice asked from right above her.

Rhia uncurled her fingers so the moonlight hit the crystal in her hand. "Her protection charm," she quietly said. "She must've taken it off."

"That's good," Sage said. "I mean, it's not good that she took it off, obviously, but now you at least have something of hers that you can use to channel her energy."

Rhia nodded. When she looked up again, she found her entire family, plus Quinn, standing around her.

"Ready?" her grandmother asked.

"Ready as I'll ever be." Rhia clutched the necklace a little tighter in her hand. "I can't promise it'll work."

"Just try." Her mother offered her a smile that was as encouraging as it was worried. "The worst thing that can happen is that you won't see anything."

Rhia wanted to tell her that that was a pretty big *worst thing* considering the circumstances, but she swallowed the words. Around her, the others got into formation, hands lacing together. Quinn was the last one to reach theirs out.

As soon as their fingers slipped into Holly's, the energy around Rhia shifted. Gone was the stench of dark magic; in its place spread a steady warmth that draped over her like a heavy blanket. The air hummed with witchcraft, but it was a different kind: one that smelled like a gentle summer breeze and fallen leaves and a clear blue river, three different elements combined to protect her. This was magic that felt like being *held*, like love in its purest form. Rhia understood then. She didn't need to cast a circle; her family already formed one.

All that she had to do was let herself fall into the magic that surrounded her. It should have been so easy, but, as she let her eyelids flutter shut, she was seized by the same anxiety that had overcome her every other time she'd tried this. All she saw were the backs of her eyelids. All she heard was her own ragged breathing. She'd spent so many years burying this part of her that the idea of digging it out again felt impossible.

Then again, maybe she didn't have to dig it out. Maybe it would come to her if she just *let it*.

Seeds can sprout and grow, Valerie's words echoed in her mind.

Clutching the protection charm close to her chest, Rhia tried to focus on the memory of Valerie: her steady presence at her side, the smile in her voice, the warmth of her hand when it had rested against the back of her neck.

Clear your mind, Valerie murmured in her ear. *Don't force it. The visions will come to you when you're ready.*

Rhia drew in a shaky breath. The darkness behind her eyes was bottomless. She wanted nothing more than to escape it; instead, she dragged her mind to its edge and let herself drown in its depths.

Time dissolved. Behind her closed eyes, the world splintered into a thousand tiny pieces and put itself back together, slowly at first and then all at once.

A door came into view. Rhia recognized it for what it was: her subconscious giving her a last out. She could remain in the present, open her eyes, and tell her family that she couldn't do it. Or she could walk through the door that led her to Valerie—the door to the future.

It wasn't really a choice.

Rhia put a hand to the doorknob and tumbled forward into a moonlit sky. Floating several feet above the trees, she spotted her: Valerie, her hair setting the dark ablaze as she staggered down a winding path. From afar, she simply looked like a girl who was exhausted, moving like there was an iron ball fastened to her leg, some invisible weight that she had to drag along with every step she took. In reality, Rhia knew that she was more dark magic than girl at this point, and that the only thing slowing her body down was spite and her own cast-iron will.

But even Valerie, stubborn as she was, wasn't inexhaustible. Her strides gained momentum the longer she walked, the flame in her hand growing steadier. It lit what lay ahead of her: the narrow path that led to the Murmuring River.

Rhia's heartbeat stuttered. Around her, the vision trembled, fraying at the edges—or maybe it was she who was trembling. Rhia drew in a shallow breath, the rough surface of the crystal digging into her palm as she gripped it harder.

Steady, the magic around her seemed to say. *You're not alone in this.*

Focus, Valerie whispered.

From her vantage point, Rhia could see the river slicing through the woods like a jagged wound. It wouldn't take much longer for Valerie to reach it if she continued at this speed.

Nausea took a hold of Rhia as the puzzle pieces slotted into place. The Hawthornes had wanted Valerie to exact revenge on the Greenbrooks for sheltering Valerie all those years ago. When they hadn't succeeded, they'd led her to the festival to do the same thing that had been done to them: revenge through fire, with as many victims as possible. But Valerie had resisted, and Holly and Rhia had stopped her. In failing all her tasks, Valerie had become dispensable. Even worse: in resisting her family, Valerie had shown her alliance with the Greenbrooks. *We knew what the consequences might be if they found out we'd stolen their magical offspring—because stealing was how they would have viewed it.* If they couldn't have her, then neither could anyone else. History would be repeating itself—unless Rhia stopped it.

Philline Harms

She ripped her eyes open at once, a gasp tearing from her throat as the vision shattered. Her hands pressed into the grass, fingertips digging into the soil to ground herself as she frantically gulped air into her lungs. She'd done it. For the first time in years, she had seen the future without any help, but she didn't have time to celebrate. Instead, she looked up into the anxious faces surrounding her and rasped, "They're taking her to the river. We need to hurry before it's too late."

Dropping her hands, her grandmother gave a stern nod. As the magical connection broke, so did the circle; the chill took a hold of Rhia once again, the cold hands of autumn creeping under her dress and raising goose bumps on her skin.

The solemn silence that had fallen over the clearing vanished. Rhia was the first to rush back to the path they'd come from, Quinn at her heels. Over her shoulder, she asked them, "Last time, you could sense that she was heading towards the river, right? Do you hear it now? The water?"

"Yes," Quinn said, their head tilted as they listened. "I think the current will tell me once she's close to the riverside. At least it did last time." They paused. "I don't hear the other voice, though. I can't sense her at all."

Rhia nodded. She didn't know how much time they had left. There was no time stamp to visions, no clear indicator of when they would take place. All she could do was hope that they would get to the river before Valerie did. Her dress snagged on branches and roots as they raced through the thicket, following the familiar path to the Murmuring River. *"Move,"* she told the trees, her voice taking on a commanding tone in her panic, and they pulled back to clear a wider passage for them.

Behind her sounded the footsteps of her family; ahead of

her, she could faintly hear the rumbling of water. It sounded even more vicious tonight, hungry and ruthless. Did it know what was coming? Was it yearning for another body to pull under, another soul to claim?

Rhia startled when right next to her, Quinn's breath audibly caught in their throat. "She's almost there."

"So are we," Rhia ground out. The river was growing louder with every second, nearly drowning out their steps. It only took another minute until they broke through the tree line.

The sight in front of Rhia was a prelude to the scene she'd seen in the scrying bowl, and again in Quinn's drawing. There was the moon, pale and apathetic as it drenched the riverside in silver. The Murmuring River, dark and untamable. And Valerie—helpless, shaking Valerie—wearing the same black dress she'd worn in every vision. She wasn't facedown in the river, but seeing her wading into the water was enough to freeze the blood in Rhia's veins.

"Valerie!" she shouted, her voice loud enough to echo from the trees. "Valerie, *look at me*." Valerie's hands twitched at her sides, but she didn't turn around.

Rhia forced her tired legs to run one last time, fighting against the helplessness that threatened to slow her steps. Even after all they'd learned and done, it hadn't prevented what Rhia had foreseen; every time she'd thought they'd evaded the hands of fate, they'd pulled Valerie back in.

Fate. All of a sudden, a clear, burning rage coursed through Rhia. When had she started to see the future as set in stone? There was no fate. There was no destiny. There was only the present and what she made of it—a million minute choices, each moment malleable as clay. She could still shape it. *She* was in control.

She forced her feet to speed up.

Valerie was still close to the riverside, in a shallow spot where the water only reached up to her knees, but she was advancing. Rhia knew where she was heading: a few feet ahead of her, there was a spot where the river was so deep it would reach up to her chin. With how ruthless the current was tonight, it would be a miracle if it didn't pull her under.

Gathering her dress in both hands, Rhia lowered herself into the water, inhaling sharply as it swallowed her legs up to the knees. She'd forgotten just how biting its cold was. The current tore at her with a force that almost knocked her over, roaring with an ancient hunger. Here, there wasn't the stability of earth—only the elemental power of the water, wild and capricious and a servant only to itself. A sob ripped from Rhia's throat. After all the running, her legs felt like lead. She was barely four steps into the river, and already she felt like she couldn't go on.

She took a deep breath. Forced her legs forward. Tried not to let the current knock her off her feet.

And then, it stopped.

Perplexed, Rhia glanced over her shoulder. Quinn knelt at the riverside, both hands plunged into the water. The air around them hummed with something unfamiliar. When their eyes met Rhia's through the strands of blue hair falling into them, they were brighter than she had ever seen them.

Without the roaring of the current, an eerie silence settled over the woods. In a matter of seconds, the water had turned from a murderess into something docile and calm, like a child abruptly ceasing its tantrum once held by its parent. "How long can you keep it like this?" Rhia called out.

Quinn swayed slightly where they were kneeling. "Not long."

It had to be long enough. Praying that the rest of her family would make it there soon, Rhia turned around. The water had reached Valerie's chest by now, soaking the tips of her hair. Rhia's heart pounded as she gathered all her strength to wade towards her. Her dress was weighing her down, and even unmoving, the river was working against her as she painstakingly set one foot in front of the other.

"Valerie!" she called out again. "Remember your spell!"

Valerie slowed in her mechanical movements, every inch of her trembling. Her breathing turned into choking gasps—in them, Rhia could hear all the exertion, all the desperation, all the fear that simmered just below the surface. How easy it would have been for her to simply stop fighting, to give in and let the water drag her under.

Her slowing down bought Rhia enough time to catch up to her. With numb fingers, she reached out and grasped Valerie's shoulders to turn her around. Seeing her face only made her heart hurt more: tears glittered against Valerie's cheeks, her lips moving silently without a single noise escaping.

"Rhia," Quinn ground out, their voice strained. The current was starting to pick up, lapping at Rhia's back as it grumbled its displeasure at being tamed. Glancing behind her, she saw that Holly and Sage had arrived, each one holding Quinn up by their shoulders with a mix of worry and awe on their faces.

Rhia had to get Valerie out of there, and soon. But when she tugged at her arm to get her to move, her body was stiff as wood and cold as marble. She was still firmly in the grasp of her family; unless she managed to free herself, there was no moving her towards the riverside.

"Val." She tried to catch Valerie's gaze, but her eyes were so glazed Rhia wasn't sure if Valerie even *saw* her. "Valerie," she said again. "Look at me."

For a split second, Valerie's eyes became sharp, startlingly intense as they burned into Rhia's. There it was again: the tug of her magic trying to draw on Rhia's, an unspoken plea.

Rhia's heartbeat stuttered. It was madness. Every single cell in her body rebelled against the mere *idea* of it. But maybe . . .

"Rhia!" Holly called out. "You need to get out of there, the river—"

Rhia tuned her out. She knew that the current was getting stronger, could feel it in the way it was tugging at her dress. It didn't matter. She wasn't letting go of Valerie. The magical tether between them wound tight as she locked eyes with her again. Suddenly, she understood what she had to do with perfect clarity.

"Okay." She caught Valerie's face in her hands, took a deep breath, and whispered, "It's yours."

And then, with the river roaring around them and her forehead leaning against Valerie's, Rhia did the one thing she'd spent the last fifteen years of her life fearing: she let go.

Her magic stirred as soon as she called upon it, warm and familiar as it traveled through her limbs before, in one terrifying rush, it surged out of her. She didn't try to hold on to any of it, didn't attempt to slow it—instead, she let her eyes flutter shut as she leaned into the feeling of complete surrender.

It was sweeter than she'd thought it would be, especially when, through the fog, she heard Valerie's voice.

"Spirits of the other side, I thank you for your help tonight. With my words, I called you, so my word is law; return to where you came from, for I am closing the door. With fire, I summoned

you—the fire is out. With blood, I bound you—the blood has run dry. With this spell, I release you—farewell and goodbye." The last of Rhia's magic poured through her fingertips, sputtering as it ran out. There was a trembling gasp; whose it was, she didn't know. *"As I have spoken, so shall it be."*

Heavy silence fell as soon as the last word rang out. The air smelled like magic, fire and earth. Mostly earth.

"Rhia?" Valerie's voice was right next to her ear, soft and familiar.

With a hum, Rhia leaned forward to rest her forehead against the shoulder that was so conveniently in front of her. Standing was suddenly very difficult.

"Stay with me," Valerie murmured.

"I'm here," Rhia assured her. It was possible that her speech came out slurred. She knew that she had to move, that the river was picking up speed, but her body was so heavy. Maybe it was easier to just lie down here. The water didn't even feel that cold anymore.

As if she knew what Rhia was thinking, Valerie's grip on her tightened. There were a few seconds of silence, a quiet "Oh no."

A moment later, the world tilted very slowly backward until a new set of arms wound around Rhia's middle. She blinked her eyes open just long enough to catch a glimpse of her mother's concerned frown and a sliver of velvety night sky. The stars were brighter than she'd ever seen. She wanted to reach up and pluck one of them out, give it to Valerie and put it in her hair—wouldn't that have looked nice? She was sure the sky wouldn't mind; it had so many of them. But before she could lift her arm, the stars already came tumbling down, and with them the darkness.

29

THE STAR

peace — healing — purification

The world was an elusive thing. Valerie could only grasp it for a few seconds at a time before it slipped through her fingers again. Here, a blanket being pulled up to her chin. There, a tickle of dark curls against her cheek. Hushed murmurs and a sliver of light through a crack in the door. Gentle hands smoothing her hair out of her face.

When the world finally settled down, Valerie regarded it with as much confusion as if she'd never seen it before. She was in a bed that wasn't hers; the mattress was much softer than those in the dorms, and a silk pillowcase lay cool against her cheek. It smelled like sugar and lavender, cinnamon and magic. It smelled . . . like the girl curled up in the armchair next to her.

"Hey," said Rhia. In the golden light streaming through the window—was it the sunset or the sunrise?—she looked sleepy and warm.

"Hey," Valerie rasped, at once wide awake as she pushed

herself up on her elbows. "Are you okay? You passed out, and then we carried you home, and I didn't—"

Rhia cut her off with a small laugh. "Valerie, breathe. I just slept for twenty-nine hours. I feel more rested than probably ever."

"Twenty-nine hours?" Valerie echoed disbelievingly. "What time—what *day* is it?"

"November second. Just past four p.m." Rhia stretched a little, much to the displeasure of the cat curled up in her lap. "*You* slept for almost forty hours. How are you feeling?"

"Like I got hit by a bus," Valerie mumbled. "But, like, psychically."

Rhia reached over to her bedside table and poured something from a Thermos bottle into a mug. Valerie obediently accepted it, cradling it in both hands as she breathed in the steam curling from its rippling surface. It smelled sweet, like honey and a blend of herbs too complex for her to recognize in her daze. "What's this?"

"An herbal tea that Sage made. It's for healing and anxiety relief, I think."

Valerie's throat suddenly felt tight. She managed two tiny sips before she had to set the mug down, her grip on it white-knuckled. "I'm so sorry," she said. "If I had known what would happen—"

"You couldn't have known, Val. Not without knowing about your family first."

Her family. The memories crashed over Valerie like an avalanche. Her grandmother's cruel grin. Her aunts' and cousins' gleeful cackles. Their overwhelming presence inside her head, pushing her down time and time again as she struggled to stay above the surface of her consciousness and keep her magic contained.

But also: her mother. A flicker of light in the darkness that poisoned her mind, a feeling of warmth, a soft voice reminding her to keep fighting, to remember her spell, to remember who she *was*.

"What are they?" Valerie managed to ask.

"Are you sure you want to hear everything now?"

"Yes."

Rhia told her. By the time she was done, Valerie's tea had gone cold, and her head was throbbing. So many things clicked into place: the ghastly spells in the spell book she'd read, the charred rubble she'd stumbled upon in the woods on her way to the river, the way the witches at the Fall Festival had blanched upon seeing her face, so similar to that of her mother. As the fragments arranged themselves into the horrifying bigger picture, Rhia watched her with barely concealed concern. "How are you feeling?" she asked again.

"I don't know," Valerie slowly said. "I think I need some time."

"Of course." Gently setting the cat down, Rhia lowered herself to her knees next to the bed. "I just need you to know that you're not like them. You're *good*, Valerie."

"Am I, though?" Warmth began to pool behind her eyes, but through sheer force of will, she managed to keep the tears at bay. "I almost burned down the tent with everyone inside. I threw *fire* at you. I—God, I burned down the greenhouse, I'm so sorry—"

Rhia's fingers tightened around Valerie's. Her voice was so much firmer than Valerie's when she said, "None of that was you. *You* spent the entire night resisting them. I don't think there are many people who would've been strong enough to do that."

Valerie lifted one shoulder in a weak shrug. She didn't *feel* particularly strong. But Rhia was still watching her, looking up at her with an expression that made every objection get stuck in her throat. "How did you know where to find me?" she asked instead.

"I saw what was going to happen," said Rhia.

Valerie's head snapped up. "You mean, you performed divination? And it worked?"

"Yeah," Rhia chuckled breathlessly.

"That's . . ." Valerie began before some kind of too-large-for-words emotion choked her off. "Rhia, that's amazing. I knew you could do it. I'm so proud of you."

"Me too," Rhia said. She held Valerie's gaze with a smile. Then she suddenly asked, "Do you think you can get up?"

Valerie flinched. "Oh. Y-yeah, I can go. I'm sorry—" After a brief fight with the blankets, she managed to get to her feet, only swaying a tiny bit. "I didn't mean to stay so long."

"Val." There was a frown on Rhia's face as she reached out to steady her. "I don't want you to *go*. Ever."

"You don't?"

"No." She reached up, brushing a strand of hair behind Valerie's ear. The gesture was so unexpectedly tender that it made Valerie's heart do something strange. "I was going to ask if you'd like to have a bath."

Valerie blinked. "Oh." For the first time, she looked down at herself. She was still wearing the dress she'd put on for Samhain along with her tights, though the latter were little more than scraps of fabric by now. "I'd like that. But only if it isn't too much trouble. I don't want to—"

Rhia shook her head, an exasperated sigh leaving her as she tugged at Valerie's hand, leading her towards the door. "It's okay," she said, more to herself than to Valerie. "We'll work on that."

"Work on what?" Valerie asked, stumbling after her through the hallway.

"All that stupid *guilt* you're carrying with you for no reason. Sit."

In a daze, Valerie let herself be guided onto the closed toilet lid. Somehow, she was out of breath even after the very short walk from Rhia's room to the bathroom. Her entire body was aching, especially her feet. She supposed that was to be expected after running through the woods for hours.

From her position, she watched as Rhia closed the door behind them and walked over to the bathtub that took up most of the room. It was an old one, the kind with claw feet, but that wasn't what Valerie paid attention to. It was the several rows of herbs, neatly labeled in mason jars, on the small shelf next to the tub that Rhia now rifled through. Over the sound of running water, Valerie tentatively asked, "What are you doing?"

"Searching for anything with cleansing or healing proper-ties." Looking up, Rhia offered Valerie a smile. "You can start undressing if you want. Or you can keep your clothes on. Whatever you like."

Valerie couldn't help the way her heartbeat stumbled at that, her cheeks involuntarily flushing. She had to remind herself that Rhia had already seen her naked—and that her current postpossession look wasn't exactly swoon-worthy—before she began the painstaking process of getting out of her dress. It was oddly stiff and reeked of river water and smoke. Valerie wanted to burn the goddamn thing along with every other memory of that night.

By the time she was done, a light mist filled the bathroom and scented the air with a pleasant mix of herbs. The bathwater had taken on a pinkish tint, delicate leaves and pastel-colored blossoms floating on the surface as Rhia turned off the faucet. Valerie had never been more desperate to take a bath in her life.

As if reading her mind, Rhia turned around, eyes only trained on Valerie's face. "You can get in."

On unsteady legs, Valerie crossed the short distance and accepted Rhia's hand as she helped her lower herself into the water. Her eyes fluttered shut the moment she was fully submerged.

"Is the temperature okay?" Rhia asked.

Nodding, Valerie let her head tip back. Through half-lidded eyes, she watched as Rhia procured several small crystals from one of the jars.

"Amethyst for healing," Rhia explained as she knelt in front of the bathtub and placed the first crystal into Valerie's open palm, "obsidian for protection. And rose quartz." She paused as she curled Valerie's fingers around the three crystals, pressing a lingering kiss to her knuckles. "For love and forgiveness."

"Thank you," Valerie whispered. She wasn't even sure what she was thanking her for—the crystals, or the bath, or the way she looked at her, without a trace of disdain despite everything that had happened.

Rhia's hands, still so gentle, smoothed Valerie's hair out of her face. "I want to do a healing ritual with you. Is that okay?"

"You gave me so much of your magic, shouldn't you—"

"It's already coming back," Rhia said. "And besides, this doesn't require much energy at all. At least, not from me."

"Okay."

"Okay," Rhia echoed. "Can you lie back for me?"

Valerie did as she was told, allowing herself to relax against the rim of the bathtub. Clutching the crystals a little tighter, she asked, "Do I need to close my eyes?"

"No." Rhia's lips curved into a small smile. "You can keep looking at me if you want."

Valerie wanted to. At that moment, there was nothing in the world that she would have rather looked at than Rhia, with her features unguarded and her eyes warm, wearing one of her too-large knit sweaters.

"It's simple," Rhia said. "I'm going to say a sentence, and I want you to repeat whatever I say until you mean it."

Valerie nodded, the fingers of her free hand twitching against the rim of the bathtub.

"We'll start off easy: I am safe."

That *was* easy. Even without the scent of jasmine and lavender filling the air, Valerie would have felt perfectly secure. She always did when she was with Rhia.

Her voice was firm when she repeated, "I am safe."

"Good." Although they weren't touching, their magical tether hummed between them. "I am loved."

For a second, Valerie had to fight the urge to close her eyes. Instead, she kept them trained on Rhia's face and spoke the simple truth she found there. "I am loved."

Rhia's smile softened. "Yeah, you are," she agreed, her fingertips carefully tracing the inside of Valerie's wrist. "Now say: I am *worthy* of love."

Valerie wanted to tell her that those two were basically the same thing, but she knew that wasn't true. Knowing you were loved didn't automatically mean that you felt deserving of it. Especially when you'd almost gone on a killing spree forty-eight hours earlier.

Her voice wavered. "I am worthy of love."

"Try that again," Rhia gently said.

Valerie drew in a shaky breath, her fingers tightening around the crystals. She tried to focus on Rhia's face, but all she could see were images from the night of the Unveiling: the fire burning in her hands; the smoke pouring from the greenhouse; a flame flickering inches away from the wall of a tent. Rhia passing out after spending all her magic, her body limp as she collapsed in her mother's arms. Quinn kneeling at the riverside, their hands red and raw from the cold of the water. Her fault her fault her fault.

"I am worthy of love," she whispered. It didn't sound convincing in the slightest.

"Oh, Valerie," Rhia murmured, cupping her face in both hands. "*You* didn't do those things."

The lump in her throat was so big she could barely breathe around it, much less speak.

"You couldn't have known it would turn out like this," Rhia continued. "All you wanted was to talk to your mom. That's not really something to beat yourself up about, is it?"

Valerie helplessly shook her head. "I don't know."

"Would you be angry with me if I'd done it? If I'd accidentally summoned some evil spirits I had no idea would be there because I wanted to talk to my dad? After not knowing anything about him or my family for my entire life?"

"No," Valerie said tonelessly. "I guess not."

"Exactly." With her hands still cradling Valerie's face, Rhia tipped Valerie's head back to make her meet her gaze. "They might be of the same blood, but that doesn't necessarily mean you have anything in common with them. We get to choose who we call our family. And we also get to choose what kind of people we want to be, every single day."

She didn't know what it was, but looking at Rhia, with her sure hands and steady gaze, Valerie couldn't help but believe her. She took a deep breath, focused on the touch of Rhia's fingers against her skin, the magical tether drawn taut between them, and said, "I am worthy of love."

"That's it." Rhia's gaze was soft and encouraging and deeply, unwaveringly kind. "You're doing so well. Just one more. Say: I am good."

After the previous one, the words rolled off her tongue with ease. It was a logical conclusion: Rhia was the best person Valerie knew, so if Valerie was deserving of her love, she couldn't be as terrible as the voice in her head suggested. "I am good."

"Well done." Rhia leaned forward to press a kiss to Valerie's forehead.

Instinctively, Valerie closed her eyes, letting herself sink into the touch of Rhia's hands still holding her face. She was safe. She was loved. She was *worthy* of love. She was good. The crystals in her hand clinked quietly in agreement.

Comfortable silence fell, disturbed only by the quiet running of water as Rhia added more to keep the bath from cooling. Under different circumstances, Valerie would have laughed and told her that she could keep it warm herself. As it was, she wasn't confident she would have been able to heat up even a single cup of tea if she'd tried.

Eventually, Rhia carefully asked, "Did you get to talk to your mom at all?"

Valerie trained her eyes on the water lapping at her skin. "Kind of. While I was . . . possessed, I could hear her. She was telling me to remember my spell." She paused for a moment, thinking back to the sound of her voice. It had been lovely, bright and melodic, like wind chimes in a summer breeze. Valerie never wanted to forget it. "And I could *feel* her. Her warmth. How much she loves me. How much it hurt her to leave me."

One of Rhia's hands came up to caress her cheek; Valerie only realized she was crying when Rhia wiped the tears away with her thumb.

Valerie didn't try to hold them back. For the first time since she could remember, she let herself break down—and for the first time since she could remember, someone held her. "It's just . . ." She hiccupped, her face pressed into Rhia's neck. "Even though she was gone the entire time, I feel like I lost her again."

Rhia hummed quietly. Valerie braced for the inevitable *I'm sorry*, but it never came. Rhia knew better than anyone else that that wasn't what Valerie needed to hear. *I'm sorry* required the response of something like *It's fine* when they both knew it wasn't. Instead, she softly said, "You're allowed to grieve, Valerie. Not just for her—for yourself too."

And so Valerie did. She cried for her mother, who had died before she'd ever truly lived. She cried for her father, who had lost his first love to something he would never understand. She cried for the little girl who'd believed with all her heart that her mother was still out there. She cried for the girl she'd been when she'd first arrived in Oakriver, full of wonder as she'd wandered the streets and imagined her mother just around the corner, or around the

Philline Harms

next one, or the next. She cried for the girl she'd been only two days ago when she'd gone into the woods with a book and a few candles and the certainty that this was it, the moment she'd been waiting for, only for it all to come crashing down. Between two rib-cracking sobs, she managed, "Does it ever go away?"

There was a pause as Rhia laid out her words, her fingers running soothingly up and down Valerie's spine. "No. It's like a weight you take everywhere with you. It doesn't really get lighter, but with time, *you* get stronger, I think. You learn how to carry it, and it becomes less noticeable."

"I don't know if I can do it," Valerie hiccupped.

"Of course you can. You *are*. And whenever it gets too heavy, I'll be there to hold you up." Rhia's arms tightened almost imperceptibly around her. "You're not alone, Val. Not anymore."

At that, Valerie leaned back. She looked at Rhia and said with every ounce of sincerity she had in her, "I love you so terribly much."

For a few heart-stopping seconds, Rhia didn't respond. Her hand was still cradling the back of Valerie's head; her expression suddenly looked very close to crying as well. "Me too," she finally whispered. "God, me too."

Before Valerie could reply, she was already being pulled into a kiss that tasted like tea and salt and magic. The crystals hit the bottom of the bathtub with a quiet clink as they tumbled from her fingers, but she didn't care—she was already sliding her hand to the back of Rhia's neck, feeling her pulse fluttering under her fingertips, quick and alive and *real*.

"I never told you," she said when she pulled back, "but the afternoon at the café wasn't the first time I saw you. It was the first day I moved here. I saw you watering your herbs in the windowsill, and I just looked at you and thought, *There she is.*"

Love and Other Wicked Things

Rhia's smile, though small, was a dizzying, disarming thing. "I always wondered how our magic could connect so quickly when I barely knew you." Her thumb carefully traced the side of Valerie's jaw, the touch so light it made her shiver. "*I* didn't recognize you, but my magic did. Even after all these years."

"What the fuck," Valerie sobbed. This entire thing wasn't her most dignified moment, but it didn't matter. Her heart felt so full at the improbability of it all; the fact that she was here right now, crying in a bathtub in front of the most beautiful girl she'd ever known, felt like the least likely outcome that her move to Oakriver ever could have had. And yet, here they were, and it felt more right than anything she could've ever imagined. "That's the most romantic shit I've ever heard."

"Oh, good." Chuckling wetly, Rhia rested her forehead against Valerie's. "You're swearing again. You had me worried there."

Despite herself—despite everything that had happened—Valerie couldn't help but laugh.

"Come on." Rhia leaned back. "Let's get you out of there. You're already getting all pruney."

By the time Valerie stepped out of the bath with a fluffy towel wrapped around her, she felt tender in more ways than one. Under Rhia's careful gaze, she got into the clothes she'd laid out for her, a pair of sweats and a warm sweater that smelled like Rhia.

"One last thing," Rhia said once Valerie was dressed, brushing her damp hair out of the way. "Promise me you won't take it off again?"

Valerie felt the last of the tension leaving her as the weight of the protection charm returned to her neck. "Promise."

~

Philline Harms

It was dark outside by the time they made their way downstairs. Nerves fluttered in Valerie's stomach as the chatter from the kitchen grew louder. Sensing her anxiety, Rhia slipped a hand into hers, her grip gentle but decisive as she tugged Valerie along.

The room fell silent the moment they stepped inside. Rhia's entire family was gathered: Holly and Sage, Tristan, Rhia's grandmother, and two other women Valerie hadn't yet met. And there, wedged between Tristan and Sage at the table, was Quinn. The last time Valerie had seen them had been on the way back to the Greenbrooks' house from the river. Valerie thought they would've gone home by now—instead, they'd waited.

Quinn wasn't much of a hugger, so Valerie was surprised when a few seconds later, they were crashing into her, blue hair tickling Valerie's face as their fingers curled into Valerie's sweater. "Fuck you, Valerie," they said into Valerie's shoulder. "Great art project you made there. Ten out of ten."

"What can I say. Performance art, baby." Eyes burning, Valerie pressed a kiss into Quinn's hair. "I love you. Thank you."

"Thank me by never getting yourself possessed again." Quinn sniffled. They drew back. "Top ten sentences I didn't think I'd have to say in my first semester of college."

Before Valerie could do much more than snort, one of the women—Rhia's mother, Valerie guessed—touched her shoulder.

"Valerie," she said, "it's so good to see you. How are you feeling, honey?"

Valerie shifted on her feet as she became aware of every single person in the room studying her. "Um. I'm okay, I think. Feeling very . . . cleansed. Healed, almost."

"That's wonderful to hear." Zora Greenbrook's eyes grew more serious as they studied Valerie's face, one hand coming up to gently brush her knuckles over her cheek. "You really do look just like her."

An unfamiliar feeling of pride welled up in Valerie. "Thank you," she murmured. She wanted to say more: *Thank you for letting me stay here. Thank you for helping my mother and taking me in all those years ago. Thank you for looking at me and seeing her, not the others.*

Judging by the look on her face, Zora Greenbrook knew what she was thinking all the same. "Of course," she said, a warm smile so similar to Rhia's lighting up her eyes. "She would be so proud of you."

She was. Valerie knew she was.

After a heartbeat of silence, Valerie quietly asked, "My father . . . does he know?"

"I'm not sure. I told him everything when he came back to Oakriver to get you, but I don't know how much of it he believed. At least enough to leave town with you like I told him to."

Enough to flinch every time Valerie so much as mentioned anything remotely related to magic, she thought. Enough to hate Halloween. Enough to be terrified when she'd told him about her plan to study in Oakriver.

"I still think of her often, you know," Rhia's mom said. "If you stay here a little longer, maybe I can find our old yearbook."

Valerie's throat felt tight from the sheer kindness contained in that simple offer. "I would like that." Before she could stop herself, she admitted, voice catching, "I'm just scared that I'll forget. Her voice. The way her magic felt."

"Maybe you will," said Rhia's mother. When she smoothed a hand over Valerie's hair, it was with so much maternal affection that it made something deep inside of her ache. "But that's nothing to be afraid of, Valerie. We might forget their voices or the exact shade of their eyes, but never the important things. Never the love."

Valerie's eyes burned as the words slotted into place inside her. For so long, there had been a hole behind her ribs, some kind of starving absence, aching and raw and growing hungrier with each year that passed. Rhia had been right: poking at a wound did nothing to heal it. But the acknowledgment of its existence and the acceptance that there was still pain there, no matter how much she had conditioned herself to ignore it . . . that, at least, felt like a start.

"Oh, and I have something else." Rhia's mother abruptly whirled around to fetch something from the kitchen counter.

Valerie sucked in a breath when she saw that it was an old photograph. Sitting in the living room of the Greenbrooks' house were two little girls: one with flaming-red hair in tiny pigtails, a look of pure mischief on her face as she pulled the tail of a much younger, less chubby Salem, the other sitting with her arms crossed as she watched the scene from a safe distance.

"Oh my God." Hands trembling with giddiness, Valerie turned to Rhia. "You were frowning even as a toddler."

"That's because you were a menace even then!" Rhia accused her, her shoulder flush against Valerie's as she pressed closer to see the photo. "Look at poor Salem. He's probably traumatized."

Laughing, Valerie turned her head a little so she could compare Rhia to the girl in the picture. No wonder she'd felt so familiar that first day Valerie had spotted her in Oakriver. No wonder that falling for her had been as easy as breathing.

Valerie didn't care much for fate, but at that moment, she decided that maybe she believed in luck.

"Well, don't just stand there," a voice cut in. Valerie's head snapped up to find Rhia's grandmother gesturing at the table. "The food's getting cold."

They obligingly sat, Valerie taking the free seat between Rhia and Tristan. The latter offered her a dimpled smile. "Hey, you. Good to see you're alive. I really missed out on something, huh?"

Valerie felt her lips pulling into something that almost felt like her usual grin. "Next time I feel like getting possessed, I'll be sure to notify you beforehand," she assured him.

"Or maybe we'll hold off on the whole dark magic thing for now," Rhia threw in. "How's that sound?"

Valerie shifted her gaze to Quinn as they settled down at the other side of the table. "Have you been staying here the entire time?"

"Yeah. I was dead asleep until a few hours ago. I didn't know using magic was so draining."

Sage chuckled. "Most people start by controlling individual drops of water, not commanding an entire *river*. Maybe after this, you can go back and start with the basics?"

At that, Valerie saw Quinn genuinely laugh for the first time in days, their eyes crinkling at the corners as their shoulders finally lost their remaining tension. Below the table, Valerie softly nudged their foot with her own. Then she looked at the dozens of bowls and plates in front of her, her stomach giving a loud rumble as it remembered how long it'd been since she'd last eaten.

"What is all this?" she quietly asked Rhia.

"Leftovers from the Unveiling dinner," she replied. "We didn't get to eat much that night."

"Oh. Right." Valerie looked up to meet the gazes of the women on the other side of the table. "I'm really sorry about ruining the festivities," she said, hoping they could tell she was being sincere. "And about the greenhouse. If there's anything I can do to make it up—"

"Oh, sweetheart," a woman with big golden hoops said. She looked like Holly, if Holly had been twentysomething years older and less pink. In front of her, a bottle was levitating a few inches above the table to pour wine into her glass, but her eyes were fixed only on Valerie. "The Unveiling is every year. And the greenhouse was old and rickety anyways. Isn't that right?"

Rhia's mom nodded in agreement. "We've been meaning to build a new one for years. I've already ordered some parts. Tristan, you'll help us set it up, won't you?"

"Sure," Tristan said around a spoonful of mashed potatoes. "I'll be the big, strong man helping you. Makes my ego feel really good."

Laughing, Holly leaned over to peck his cheek before pushing the bowl of mashed potatoes towards Valerie. "Come on, Valerie, eat something! You must be starving."

As she obediently helped herself to food, Valerie noticed that Rhia's grandmother was watching her.

Valerie smiled nervously at her. "Rhia told me that you saw me coming. I guess you were right to warn her."

The old woman hummed, cocking her head to the side as she scrutinized Valerie. "No, I don't think I was. You did bring chaos. But you also brought a lightness I've never seen on her." She paused. "It takes more than a little strength to defy the kind of darkness you've encountered. You should give yourself some credit for that."

"Hear, hear!" Holly said in a stage whisper.

Valerie cleared her throat. "I couldn't have done it alone. I don't know what would've happened if it hadn't been for Rhia, or Quinn, or all of you." She paused. "Well, all of you except Tristan."

"Excuse you," he said, a hand to his heart in faux offense. "I think my performance as the oblivious damsel in distress was *spectacular*."

As the entire table broke into laughter, Valerie finally allowed herself to relax into the cheerful warmth of the kitchen. From her seat, she took in the comforting chaos: Quinn smiling at her with sauce smudged on their chin; Tristan pressed way too close to her in the tiny space, groaning when their elbows kept knocking together because she was a lefty; Holly and Sage squabbling about who got to eat the last slice of pumpkin pie; Rhia's socked foot nudging against hers under the table; the older women watching everything play out with fond exasperation. With every passing minute, the unfamiliar feeling inside Valerie's chest solidified until it turned into dizzying certainty: the family she'd been so desperate to find was right here, and she clicked into place as if it had always been meant to be this way.

It was the best dinner Valerie had ever had.

~

Later that night, Valerie and Quinn made their way back to the dorm. The Greenbrooks had offered for them to stay, but Valerie knew that if she spent one more night in Rhia's bed, chances were slim she would ever muster the strength to return to her own. Besides, as distant as they felt, there were still other duties for her to fulfill.

"I can't believe we have classes tomorrow," she said, piercing the delicate quiet that had draped itself over the sleepy alleyways. In the glow of the streetlights, her breaths came out as clouds. "Sitting in a studio and painting my silly little assignments feels so stupid after everything that happened."

Quinn gave a quiet laugh. "I don't know. I think I'm looking forward to a bit of normalcy."

Balancing on the curb, Valerie studied them. Their cheeks were flushed from the cold, their shoulders pulled up to their ears to brace against the crisp night air. They looked like they always did, and yet there was something subtly different about the way they held themself. Taller. Looser, somehow. "I've been meaning to ask . . ." Valerie began, coming to a halt. There were so many questions she felt she hadn't asked yet. In the end, she settled on the most important one. "Are you okay?"

"I think so. It still hasn't quite sunk in, the whole magic thing. But it's . . ." Quinn pushed a curl out of their eyes, thinking. "These last few years, I always had this odd feeling. Like I was missing something, but I couldn't say what. You know how it feels when you have art block?"

Valerie nodded.

"That's what it was like. There's so much potential inside you, but you just can't get it out, and it drives you *insane*. That feeling's finally gone. The moment I plunged my hands into the river, it all came rushing out, and it felt so *good*. Now it's as if, for the first time in my life, there's an equilibrium." They exhaled. "Does that make sense?"

"It does." With something like awe, Valerie remembered the sight of Quinn kneeling at the riverside. "I can't believe you've been keeping all of this in for so long. I mean, you have enough power to command an entire *river*. I'm surprised it didn't burst out of you sooner."

At that, Quinn ducked their head, scratching sheepishly at their neck. "I, uh. I feel like it might've."

"What? No way. When?"

"Remember the flooding at the dorm?"

Valerie clapped a hand to her mouth. Of course—the burst pipe that had damaged the better part of the dorm that Quinn had been staying in at the time. *It was my first night here*, they had told her. "Quinn," she breathed, and this time the feeling was definitely awe. "And people say that *I* am unpredictable."

"It wasn't on purpose, I swear!" They covered their face with their hands. "It's something about this town. I guess the water was just . . . excited to have me."

"Oh, I bet it was," Valerie snorted. She tilted her head. "What about the other stuff? The whole *messenger of the spirit world* thing?"

"God, I don't even know where to start with that one. I don't ever want to relive what it felt like when your mom was inside me." Valerie opened her mouth, but Quinn pointed a threatening finger at her. "Do not even say it," they told her, lips twitching as they suppressed their own laugh. "It was genuinely terrifying. Next time I communicate with a spirit, I want it to be on my terms."

"That's understandable." Valerie shivered as she recalled the distant look in Quinn's eyes as they'd held the necklace.

"That being said," Quinn added, "if you want me to reach

out to your mom again, I can try. You know, if it would help you get closure or anything."

"That's okay. I think I'll let her rest for now. I've found what I needed to know."

"Yeah?" Quinn asked curiously.

Valerie thought so. In hindsight, she wasn't sure what she had expected to learn from meeting her mother. When she'd been little, it had felt imperative to find her—like she would be able to answer every question Valerie had about herself, her powers, her identity. Now Valerie was nineteen, and she realized that she wasn't her mother any more than she was her father. She was a messy, reckless, firebearing art student who fell in love too fast and secretly loved every moment of it. She had spent almost two decades getting to know herself. For the first time, she didn't need anyone else to hold up a mirror for her to see who she was.

She was too exhausted to explain all of this aloud, so all she said was: "Yeah."

Quinn's eyes searched her face, questioning. "You seem different."

"So do you," Valerie said with a grin.

"Touché," said Quinn, bumping their shoulder against Valerie's as they began walking again.

Returning to their room felt strange. Everything looked exactly as it had the day Valerie left for her ritual: a cluttered, cozy freeze-frame of the life she had built for herself here. Her paintings had dried. Her coursework for the next day still lay unfinished on her desk.

Stepping back into the routine she'd briefly broken away from, she realized she had no idea how to proceed. What did one do after completing the goal one had been chasing ever since one could think? "So . . . what's next?" she asked Quinn.

Quinn plopped down on their bed so hard the springs complained. "We make art," they said, glancing around the room. "We study. We try to survive college. We go for walks and call our parents and have coffee with our friends. We do a little magic, and try not to cause the school thousands of dollars in property damage." They met Valerie's eyes, cheeks dimpling. "Too boring?"

"No." Valerie draped her coat over her chair and set her bag down in its familiar spot by the door. She exhaled. "Just boring enough, I think."

Epilogue

THE WORLD

wholeness — abundance — the completion of a journey

As an earth witch, Rhia had been taught to appreciate the beauty in every season, but if asked, she would have readily admitted that November was one of her least favorite months. September and October were where the real beauty of fall lay: the long walks through orange-and-red woods, the joyful novelty of seeing her breath in the air after closing the café, the autumn equinox and the Unveiling and the bustling period in between. In November, the weather was too bad for her walks and the ground so frozen she sometimes could not sense the life beneath it at all. To Rhia, the month was just the dreary, miserably cold stretch before December started and the winter solstice marked the slow return of the brighter days.

However, this November felt different—after all, it was impossible to be cold when there was a girl made of fire in your life. Valerie laughed every time Rhia inched closer to her in the evenings, slipping freezing hands under her shirt and tucking her face into the warmth of her neck. Being held by Valerie was like being held by the sun. Rhia didn't think she'd ever be cold again.

Even the blue skies didn't seem so rare this year. As she leaned against the wall next to the cemetery gate, Rhia turned her face towards the light of the low-hanging sun. The air was crisp and smelled like smoke and new beginnings. During her last try at divination, she'd seen that it was going to snow soon, though she didn't have enough practice yet to be able to pinpoint exactly when. Valerie had told her she would get there. Her clairvoyance was like a muscle that she had to train for it to grow stronger, so now she practiced every day, trying to forecast whatever she could: the weather for the next week, the date of the next book delivery, the outfit Valerie would be wearing the next time they saw each other. These kinds of predictions were child's play, but they still felt like small victories every time they turned out to be correct. To Valerie's delight, Rhia had also discovered her love for tarot—almost every day, she drew cards to help her decide as she scrolled through college websites and drafted essays. Next semester, Oakriver College would be offering courses in environmental science. Rhia and the latest cards she'd pulled seemed to be in agreement about how they felt about it.

She opened her eyes just as Valerie stepped through the gates with her hands buried in the pockets of her jacket. From her neck dangled both the protection charm and her mother's pentagram necklace.

"What are you smiling about?" Valerie asked.

"Nothing," Rhia said, getting onto her tiptoes to press a kiss to the corner of her mouth. Landing on the balls of her feet again, she reconsidered. "Everything."

Philline Harms

Valerie laughed, the sound a bright, bewitching thing, and caught Rhia's face in one hand to pull her in for a real kiss. The rings on her fingers were cold against Rhia's cheek; her lips tasted like the cinnamon buns they'd had for (a very late) breakfast in bed.

There was something heady about this new familiarity between them, a foreign sense of comfort that grew with every little thing they learned about each other now that they had nothing else to worry about. Like the fact that Valerie preferred almond milk over oat milk and that she picked at her nail polish when she was anxious and that her guilty pleasure was terrible splatter movies from the '80s that had Rhia covering her eyes the entire way through.

Like a dragon hoarding its gold, Rhia took each new piece of knowledge about Valerie and pocketed it for safekeeping, watching her treasures pile higher and higher while Valerie did the same. Rhia didn't think she'd ever get enough, but luckily Valerie was just as greedy—it was their thirst for knowledge that had brought them together, after all, and as it turned out, they were each other's favorite subject.

"Are you ready to go?" Rhia asked once they separated. Her hands had found their way into the pockets of Valerie's jacket, always seeking more of her warmth and always receiving it.

"Yeah. There wasn't much to do." Valerie's fingers playfully flicked one of Rhia's earrings (today, they were tiny frogs wearing witch's hats). "Did you do something to those flowers, or is it normal for them to still look that good?"

"Maybe," Rhia teased. "A witch has to keep some of her secrets." She had, in fact, performed a little spell on the flowers. A few days after the Unveiling—once her magic had fully returned and Valerie's cheeks had color again—they'd visited the cemetery together. While Rhia hadn't found Isabelle Morgan's headstone when she'd come looking for it all those weeks ago, the one for Isabelle *Hawthorne* was hard to miss. It sat right next to the chapel, overgrown but still standing proudly. In addition to regular phone calls with her father, it was part of Valerie's new routine to come by once a week and take care of the grave. Rhia had helped by banishing the weeds and ivy that had covered it and making a little wreath of flowers that were enchanted to last at least until the next full moon. Headstones for the rest of the family, they had noted with grim satisfaction, were nowhere to be found. Now that Valerie had burned their spell book, there was truly nothing left of them but whispered ghost stories, and even those were sure to fade as the years went by.

Hand in hand, Valerie and Rhia walked through the winding alleyways, making their way past Obscura, the town square, and the college campus, until finally Sugar & Spice came into view. It greeted them with its usual hustle and bustle, but this time they walked straight past the tables and up the stairs. In one of the more secluded corners of the second floor, hidden behind the "Light & Fluffy" book section, was a second staircase that led to the attic.

"Have you seen it yet?" Valerie inquired as they neared it.

"No." Rhia scratched at the back of her neck. "I haven't been up there since that day I hid from you."

"Memories," Valerie said fondly.

Rhia gave her arm a light swat and climbed the stairs, hearing Valerie following close behind. The last time she'd been in the attic, it had been dusty, dominated by towering heaps of old books and furniture, musty clothes and boxes of scratched

Philline Harms

records. Now the chaos was gone, and in its place had appeared something that truly did look like the workshop Holly had always described. Tall shelves lined the walls, stocked with boxes that held envelopes for mailing, utensils for crafting jewelry, and instruments for performing magic. The crystals that filled the neatly labeled jars scattered tiny specks of light onto the wooden floorboards and the workstation that sat right beneath the window.

"Rhia! Valerie!" Holly exclaimed when she spotted them, her voice as delighted as if they hadn't all been together just two hours ago. "You came!"

"Of course we came." Rhia laughed, stumbling slightly when Holly launched herself at her. "This is amazing! I can't believe you did this all by yourself."

"I mean, I didn't do it *all* alone. Tristan helped a lot, and so did my dad." Holly stepped back, beaming with pride. "I've already gotten so many orders!"

"They'd be stupid *not* to order." Valerie tugged at her own protection charm. "Ten out of ten, really works for warding off evil family members as long as you're not stupid enough to take it off."

"I'll include that in the customer reviews," Holly giggled. She turned to where Quinn was lingering near the shelf with the crystals, curiously studying its contents. "Pick any crystal you like! I'll make you a charm for free."

The surprise that passed over Quinn's face was nearly palpable. "Really?"

"Of course! You're family."

Quinn blinked once before a soft smile lit up their face and they turned back to the crystals.

After an hour or so, Rhia and Tristan had to make their way back downstairs for the beginning of their shift. Quinn and Valerie came with them. "Are you going to stay here for a bit?" Valerie asked Quinn.

"Can't." Quinn's lips quirked. "I have a phone call with my mom and my grandmother in a few minutes."

Valerie and Rhia gasped in unison. "No way," said Valerie. "How long as it been since they've talked?"

"Three years, I think." Quinn shifted their weight from one foot onto the other. "I figured it was time to finally talk about everything. Clearly, this whole *keeping family secrets until they blow up in everyone's faces* strategy hasn't been working out too great for any of us."

Rhia gave a small snort. With her family not telling her about the Hawthornes, Valerie's dad not speaking about her mother, and Quinn being left to figure out their magic on their own, there was a definite pattern. "Good luck. Tell us how everything goes!"

Nodding, Quinn let Valerie press an exaggeratedly loud kiss to their cheek before they pulled on their beanie and headed outside.

Meanwhile, Valerie stayed and hunted down a table in the café.

Rhia wasn't sure if she was imagining it or if they really had more customers than ever. A glance into the cake display confirmed her suspicions. She grinned. A week ago, she'd asked Anne if she would consider letting Rhia put out a few of her own treats. Next to regular brownies and warm slices of apple pie now sat Rhia's cleansing lemon cake and the magical banana bread Tristan so loved. They weren't labeled as such, of course, but Rhia had overheard several patrons gushing about the effects they'd felt. It was subtle enough to fly under the Council's radar while still having a positive impact on the people she cared about. The perfect compromise.

Past Rhia would have been appalled, but if Valerie had taught her anything, it was that nothing was ever black-and-white. She wasn't taking the world off its hinges—just cracking the door open wide enough to allow the tiniest sliver of magic to seep through.

Dancing through the whirlwind that was the café, Rhia felt Valerie's gaze following her. She couldn't help but smile every time their eyes locked from across the room, the tether of their magic giving a little tug even as Valerie pretended to focus hard on her art history book.

Once all other patrons were cared for, Rhia allowed herself to sink down on the chair opposite Valerie. Whether by luck or by coincidence, it was the same table where she had sat the first time Rhia had seen her. Back then, Valerie had seemed like the personification of danger, slouching in the armchair with a smirk on her face and the scent of magic clinging to her as naturally as if it were perfume. Now, as Rhia studied the familiar curve of her lips, the amused tilt of her head, the way the she wore the sweater she'd stolen from Rhia, all she felt was a giddy kind of happiness.

She didn't realize she was staring until a faint blush rose to Valerie's cheeks—something Rhia hadn't thought possible the first time they'd met—and she leaned slightly forward. "Well, pumpkin?" Valerie asked, offering her hand.

Rhia placed her hand in Valerie's without hesitation, palm facing up. She remembered the first time Valerie had run her fingertips along the lines there, and the way she'd shivered, drawn in by her strange charm even as her heart had raced with fear. This time, Rhia leaned closer, brushing her knuckles across the familiar constellation of freckles on Valerie's cheek, and said, "Tell me, then. How does the future look?"

"Mmm. Let's see." Valerie's eyes met Rhia's again, bright and mischievous as ever; her finger traced Rhia's heart line without having to look. "Looks pretty magical to me."

Rhia could only agree.

ACKNOWLEDGMENTS

As I sit here writing these acknowledgments, I still can't fully comprehend that I am, in fact, writing acknowledgments. A second time, no less! And for one of my favorite stories I have ever written!

Every time I got to open this book, I was struck by how many versions of myself it contains. There's the Philline that spent recess talking to the trees like they were friends and brewing potions on the elementary school playground (I was a very strange child). The Philline who held a deck of tarot cards for the first time at thirteen years old and felt like maybe magic did exist, and it lived in the half-lit corners of her grandparents' house. The Philline who daydreamed about two teenage witches falling in love on foggy mornings while walking to school in twelfth grade, and during train rides soundtracked to Hozier and Florence + The Machine. I like to think that all the little Phillines over the last two decades would be pretty proud of the book that's now on shelves, even if she would be incredibly confused about how we got here.

Anyways. Acknowledgments! Time to acknowledge.

First and foremost, I would like to thank my wonderful

editor, Rebecca Sands, for her enthusiasm and gentleness during the editing process. I felt from the very beginning that this story would be in safe hands with you, and I was right! Thank you for caring about my girls and for turning my rough-around-the-edges baby into something much shinier than I ever could've managed on my own. You made working on this book extra magical.

To Irina Pintea, for putting up with all the emails and for the emotional support. Meeting you in LA was the loveliest thing, and our calls always make me feel so warm inside. I couldn't have asked for a better person to navigate this journey with.

Thank you also to the entire rest of the team at Wattpad Books, especially Deanna McFadden, Delaney Anderson, Rachel Wu, and Tammy Kung. Working with you is always a joy.

A big thanks also to Tom McGee, who coached me through writing the very first draft! I feel like without your pointers, the structural edits would've taken twice as long.

To Andrea Waters, who read this story with more attention to detail than anyone else could and caught the typos that would've haunted me forever.

To Spiros Halaris and Lesley Worrell, for crafting the whimsical cover of my dreams. I want this entire thing tattooed on me.

To the wonderful sensitivity readers who lent me their time and invaluable insight: Brittany Campbell, Idris Grey, R.E. Levy, Heather Sanderson, and Zhui Ning Chang. A special thanks also to Tora Shae Pruden for sharing their knowledge on the practices of Black witches in the US with me. Thanks to all of you, this book has grown into something so much deeper and more layered than I ever could have written on my own.

Of course, I also need to thank some of the people who have not touched this book but who have made an impact on it all the same. To my family: thank you for always believing in me, for taking photos of my books in bookstores, for gushing about my writing to your friends, and for being there every step of the way. You *are* the light, the roots, the circle. Thank you also to my grandpa, Alfred Harms. *Lieber Opa: danke für die Geschichten und das Tarot. Ohne dich wäre meine Kindheit nur halb so magisch gewesen.*

To Sarah: in this book, I've written a lot about how there's no such thing as fate, but you and I both know there's little other explanation for the two of us meeting. Thank you for the bookstore trips, the therapy sessions, and for enduring my rambling about this story and all the others. You are the Valerie to my Quinn, the Tristan to my Rhia. I am forever grateful our paths crossed and can't wait to marry you for the tax benefits in ten years.

Vera, Lorena, Elise, Merle, Linda, Louisa: you were there when I got the email that this story would become a book, and you were there while I was writing the first chapters and scribbling notes during school breaks. I adore each of you with my entire heart and am so grateful to have known you for twelve (!!!) years.

Thank you also to my internet friends, who cheer me on every step of the way, from the little orange app into the bookstore. To Stell, Olivia, Tess, Gray, Kay, Sol, and Wren: I love you, little people in my phone. To Akriti: you know that every book I write, I write exclusively for you. A thousand forehead kisses for you, mwah.

To the incredible writers who inspire me every day and

who I'm so grateful to call my friends: Loridee De Villa, Brianna Joy Crump, Jessica Cunsolo, Auburn Morrow, Matthew Dawkins, Romi Moondi, Rebecca Sullivan, Nicole Nwosu, Warona Jolomba, and so many more. Insert big orange heart here!

To my Wattpad readers, who have read this book when it was but a fledgling: thank you for returning week after week to read my words and for the infinite kindness you continue to gift me with despite being handed the most atrocious first drafts. You are the reason I get to do this.

Lastly, thank you to the booksellers, the librarians, the reviewers, the bookstagrammers, and of course you, dear person reading this! Whether you've been with me on Wattpad since 2016 or just randomly picked this up in a library or bookstore: thank you for spending some time in Oakriver. I hope this story could bring a tiny bit of magic to your life as well.

ABOUT THE AUTHOR

Philline Harms is a writer of queer contemporary YA romances, including *Never Kiss Your Roommate*. When she's not working on a novel, she can be found analyzing her friends' birth charts, drinking her body weight in tea, or crafting obscurely specific Spotify playlists—sometimes simultaneously. Living in Germany, she is currently pursuing a bachelor's degree in psychology.

Love and Other Wicked Things

BONUS CONTENT

LOVE AND OTHER WICKED THINGS
THE SOUNDTRACK

🟢 ·|||·|·|··|||··|·||·

Season Of The Witch - Lana Del Rey
Autumn Equinox

People Are Strange - The Doors
Exploring Oakriver

Leather and Lace - Stevie Nicks & Don Henley
The Girl in the Window

Heavy Weather - Billie Marten
Sugar & Spice

Devil Woman - Cliff Richard
The New Witch

Mr. Fox in the Fields - Alexandre Desplat
Kitchen Magic

Hurricane Drunk - Florence + The Machine
The Party

Rhiannon - Fleetwood Mac
Garden Serenade

I Put A Spell On You - Nina Simone
A Slow Saturday Morning

Ophelia - The Lumineers
The Trouble Begins

Witches - Alice Phoebe Lou
Tutoring

The Secret Garden - AURORA
The Greenhouse

bad idea! - girl in red
What the Hell Just Happened?

It Will Come Back - Hozier
Rhia's Not Here

Sisters of the Moon - Fleetwood Mac
Moon Tea

Curses - The Crane Wives
Far from Sleepy

Deep Green - Marika Hackman
The Fall Festival

Pumpkin - The Regrettes
Morning, Pumpkin

Every Other Freckle - alt-J
The Storage Closet (Short-Circuit)

ivy - Taylor Swift
An Intervention

Moderation - Florence + The Machine
Never Done Anything Casual

we fell in love in october - girl in red
This Is a Date?

Woodland - The Paper Kites
Driving to the Cabin

Turn To Dust - Wolf Alice
Scrying Lessons

Would That I - Hozier
Here Comes a Walking Fire

Bedroom Hymns - Florence + The Machine
Let Me Take Care of You

Blood Moon - Saint Sister
Cold Sheets

I Follow Rivers - Marika Hackman
Down to the River

Meet Me in the Woods - Lord Huron
An Inexplicable Pull

Riverside - Agnes Obel
Down to the River (II)

Secrets (Cellar Door) - Radical Face
The Family Archive

Drown - Marika Hackman
Water Magic

Bottom of the River - Delta Rae
My Darling Girl

Something in the Orange - Zach Bryan
Autumn and All Its Colors

Shrike - Hozier
Romeo-and-Juliet-esque

Spooky - Classics IV
Unveiling Preparations

Open Wide - Marika Hackman
Spirits of the Other Side

Seven Devils - Florence + The Machine
All Wrong

Arsonist's Lullabye - Hozier
Fire in the Garden

Run Baby Run - The Rigs
Run

The Yawning Grave - Lord Huron
Trapped

Family Portrait - Radical Face
She's a Hawthorne

Spellbound - Siouxsie and the Banshees
The Halloween Festival

Demon Host - Timber Timbre
In the Corn Maze

Fuel to Fire (David Lynch Remix) - Agnes Obel
Divination

Which Witch - Florence + The Machine
Down to the River (III)

As It Was - Hozier
I Don't Want You to Go

Work Song - Hozier
The Healing Ritual

Let The River In - Dotan
Back to the Dorm (An Equilibrium)

Dog Days Are Over - Florence + The Machine
November

LOVE AND OTHER WICKED THINGS
THE TAROT CHAPTERS

Chapter 1: The Hierophant
family – shared beliefs – established conventions

Chapter 2: Knight of Wands
passion – boldness – pursuing ideas

Chapter 3: Wheel of Fortune
fated encounters – unexpected events – a turning point

Chapter 4: Queen of Pentacles
stability – earthly comforts – self-sufficiency

Chapter 5: The Sun
fruitful encounters – childlike enthusiasm – authentic self-expression

Chapter 6: Four of Swords
recovery – reflection – self-protection

Chapter 7: Page of Swords
intellectual debates – thirst for knowledge – new ways of thinking

Chapter 8: Two of Cups
finding common ground – mutual attraction – a deep connection

Chapter 9: Four of Cups
melancholy – frustration – feeling disconnected

Chapter 10: The Moon
facing one's fears – uncertainty –the subconscious

Chapter 11: Temperance
moderation – perspective – blending of opposites

Chapter 12: Three of Cups
celebration – joy – community

Chapter 13: Eight of Cups
withdrawing – disappointment – walking away

Turn the page for a preview of
Philline Harms's debut novel!

Available now, wherever books are sold.

1

Evelyn

Long train rides, to me, had always felt a little bit like slipping out of reality.

There was something about the smooth glide of the wheels on the rails and the monotonous hum of the engine, the way there was nothing interesting to focus on except the landscape outside and the bored faces of other passengers, that made it so easy to get lost in my fantasy.

All I had to do was close my eyes and I was in another time, another place, another one of those lives I had lived vicariously through the pages of some tattered paperback. I could be a young farm girl on her way into the city for the first time. Or maybe a detective on his way to a small town where he would investigate a mysterious murder. Or maybe some aristocrat's daughter sent off to marry an unknown spouse—a noble*woman*, of course, because although I had a vivid imagination, it wasn't *that* creative—the ambient noise of the train morphing into the rattling of a carriage across cobblestones in my mind.

It was all there, a whole world inside my head in which to immerse myself, and once I got bored of it, I could simply dive into the next one.

That was, unless the train came to a stop.

Right now, it stood in a train station somewhere in the middle of nowhere, the doors open to spit out people whose travel ended here. I blinked open my eyes and stifled a yawn behind my hand as I looked out at the platform, watching as people kissed their loved ones good-bye or hello while others strolled off alone.

Not many passengers were left around me and the announcement about the train's departure that crackled through the speakers led me to the conclusion that no one else would be getting on—until a boy suddenly skidded inside, his large suitcase almost getting stuck between the closing doors.

He turned around, swearing under his breath when the duffel bag he had slung across his shoulder got caught on one of the seats. After heaving his suitcase into the overhead carrier, he slumped down on a seat on the left-hand side, level with where I was sitting. His third piece of luggage, a large backpack that looked like it was stuffed full to the very top, he placed on the seat next to him. Only then did he release a relieved exhale, one hand coming up to brush aside the strands of unruly brown hair that had fallen into his eyes. After what I assumed had to be an impressive sprint to the train platform, there was a bright flush that spread from his pale cheeks all the way to the tips of his ears.

The train left the station with a steadily increasing rumbling sound, the landscape outside turning into a blur of browns and greens once again, the sky a steely gray that promised rain. I hoped that it would wait until I reached my destination.

My destination. So far, I had managed to distract myself from the looming unknown, but now, with nightfall fast approaching and only a few stations left until the train would reach it, an anticipatory shiver ran down my spine.

Luckily, a loud rustling sound ripped me out of my thoughts before panic truly set in. In the reflection of the window, I could see the boy digging around in his backpack until he finally pulled out a paperback book. A quiet gasp tore free from my throat when I recognized the cover: a train driving down snowy train tracks, headlights cutting through the night.

In the deserted carriage, the noise was loud enough to make the boy look up, shooting me a confused glance. His bewilderment seemed to ease when his eyes drifted down to the book I was balancing in my lap, my train ticket serving as a bookmark after I had put it down an hour ago—a similarly tattered copy of Agatha Christie's *Murder on the Orient Express.*

His lips quirked into the hint of a smile. "Good book, huh?"

"It's one of my favorites," I said. I was silent for a moment but then, because I hadn't had anyone to talk to in over five hours, much less anyone my age who also happened to read, I asked, "What chapter are you on?"

"Chapter five. But I've already read it a hundred times, so . . ."

"Me too."

His smile widened. "Nice." He hesitated for a moment before he lifted his backpack, previously acting as a barricade between us, and slid over to the seat closer to the aisle. "So . . . is this your first year at Seven Hills?"

My heart skipped a beat at the name I had previously tried to block out. "How do you know I'm going there?"

"You look about seventeen, meaning you're the right age to be a student. You're carrying a lot of luggage, indicating you might have packed for a pretty long stay." He pointed up at the two suitcases occupying the overhead carriers. "And finally, there are only two more stops. The next one is in some small village, so it's unlikely that you'll get off there. That leaves only the last stop, which happens to be within walking distance of the school."

"All right, Sherlock," I laughed. "You're right, it's my first year. What about you?"

"Me too."

I was more relieved than I cared to show. The prospect of having to enter the school all alone had been terrifying, to say the least, so this was a lovely turn of events.

Leaning into the aisle, I stretched out a hand. "I'm Evelyn."

He shook my hand with a grin, blowing a strand of hair out of his eyes. "Seth. Seth Williams."

"You're not from around here, are you?"

It took no deduction skill to be able to tell that; his thick Northern accent was hard to mistake.

"No," he laughed. "I'm from Manchester. You?"

"Leicester."

Outside a light drizzle had begun, raindrops trailing down the windows and blurring the landscape behind them. The carriage's overhead lights flickered a little.

Seth was still studying me, his head cocked slightly to the side. "Why did your parents want to get rid of you?"

"They didn't want to *get rid of me*." In fact, that had been exactly what my mom had said: *Sweetheart, it's not like we want*

to get rid of you. We just think that a change of scenery would be nice, don't you think? "I didn't exactly like my last school."

"I see," he said slowly. "No heart-wrenching sob story there? You just wanted to go?"

"Yes." I changed the subject. "Why do you ask? Are your parents forcing you?"

"They got divorced over the summer and didn't know what to do with me. Said that I could come back around Christmas if everything is *sorted out* by then." The dark expression clouding his face mirrored the gloomy weather outside. "It's a bloody shit show, the whole thing."

"I'm sorry."

Seth shrugged, but there was a tension in his shoulders that contradicted the casual gesture. "It's not your fault. Just sucks that I'm away from my sister."

"Is she too young to go to Seven Hills?"

"No, we're twins. But I got held back in primary school, so she's going to uni already." He was silent for a moment, chewing on his thumb. Finally, he looked at me again and asked, "Did you visit Seven Hills beforehand?"

I nodded. "They had an open house earlier this summer that my parents and I went to. Why, have you not been there before?"

"No. Everything was pretty . . . spontaneous," he murmured.

In hopes of calming him, I said, "I was only there for an hour, but it looked nice. The castle is lovely, and the teachers seemed really friendly."

Seth didn't seem convinced, his expression only darkening when a female voice announced the train's final destination, Gloomswick, just then. With a groan, he shoved his copy of *Murder on the Orient Express* into his backpack.

While carefully storing mine away, I said, "Maybe it won't be so bad. Who knows, Seven Hills might even be fun?"

Seth's snort gave away his opinion on that statement. "Right. I'm sure everyone at this posh private boarding school is going to be dead funny. I'm buzzing for it."

The train rocked to a stop before I could reply. After Seth helped me get my luggage from the overhead carrier (this boy was *tall*), we stepped out onto the platform. He swore quietly when a cold gust of wind took a hold of us, tearing at our clothes and whipping rain into our faces.

Gripping tighter onto my suitcases, I glanced around the train station. It consisted of nothing but the platform we were standing on and a small brick building where you could purchase tickets during the day, with a map of Gloomswick mounted on the wall next to the door. The small town slumbered at the feet of the hills that gave the school its name, but covered in a blanket of woods and with night falling, it was hard to see all seven.

Together, we left the train station and took off on a road that led right into the woods. Streetlamps stood every few yards or so, illuminating the road but not the forest, which seemed to edge closer to us from both sides. I kept throwing wary glances into the woods every time I heard a creak or a snap, but there was nothing to be seen except shadows and even darker shadows.

"You would think this rich-ass school would have some sort of shuttle to get us there," Seth grumbled.

"Probably part of the *discipline* thing they're all about," I chuckled. We were walking uphill, and I was out of breath already. "This is just the first endurance test."

Seth's only response was a stream of colorful swear words as he pulled his hood farther over his face. Keeping my head down,

I dragged my two suitcases along with me. My left shoulder was hurting from the heavy bag slung over it, the strap digging into it, and the rain was soaking through my clothes to the point where they clung to my body like a second skin.

Lightning flickered across the sky, followed by deafening thunder that made us both jump. The rain fell even heavier now and I dimly worried about the books in my backpack, when Seth suddenly let out an incredulous laugh.

"Are these the gates of heaven?"

Blinking against the rain clinging to my eyelashes, I raised my head enough to see what he was talking about. Seven Hills was an old castle with protruding alcoves and sprawling turrets that reached into the night sky, the windows in them a hundred unblinking eyes watching us warily as we neared the entrance. On the mild summer day I had come here with my parents, the building had looked enchanted with its arched doorway and the ivy climbing its stone facade; however, with the thunder roaring in the distance and lightning tearing through the sky behind it, right now it just looked haunted.

"*Lovely*, you said?" Seth grimaced. "This looks a little less Hogwarts and a lot more *Dracula* than I expected."

"Let's just go inside," I said, my teeth chattering.

"Do you want to go first, or . . . ?"

"Oh, I'm good."

With a sigh, Seth reluctantly walked up the steps leading up to the front door and pushed down on the handle. He made a surprised noise when it swung open just like that, luckily without the scary creaking sound I had already braced myself for.

Instead of the gloomy vault the outside of the castle suggested, the hall in front of us was drenched in the warm glow of a chandelier hanging overhead. The stone walls were covered in certificates from several sports tournaments Seven Hills had won and photos hung in golden frames, each one showing widely grinning teenagers from all different decades. There were large doors on each end of the hall that led to the different wings of the building, and then there were two flights of stairs leading to the first floor.

I nudged Seth when I spotted the figure descending the stairs on the left, but he had already seen her. With ginger hair that shone like copper in the chandelier's light, the girl was hard not to notice.

"There you finally are!" she said as she reached the end of the stairs. "Mrs. Whitworth was already worried you'd gotten lost on the way."

The way she carried herself, with an air of confidence and authority that was almost tangible, contradicted the look of her face, which, with soft features and a splatter of freckles, seemed no older than seventeen. Her gray eyes studied us appraisingly when she came to a stop in front of us.

"Sorry to keep you waiting," I said apologetically. "Are you supposed to give us the tour?"

"Yes, I am," she said. "My name is Amelia Campbell, head of the student council, and captain of our cheerleading team. First of all: Welcome to *Seven Hills International School for Boys and Girls*. We are happy to welcome you to our community."

She paused for a second as if waiting for an answer but continued before either of us could open our mouths. "Community is the most valued thing at this school, as you probably gathered from our website. You two are welcome, and even encouraged, to join one of our clubs or sports teams. It is important to get

8

involved and contribute to our school's success and reputation."

Seth shot me a pained look that echoed his earlier statement about the *dead funny* private school students.

"With that said, let's get into the rules." Amelia flipped through the papers on her clipboard. "You are not allowed to leave school grounds without notifying a teacher. You must wear your school uniform and stick to the dress code. This is just another factor in establishing a community. Boys are not allowed to be in the girls' wing and vice versa. Intimate relationships are not encouraged."

"Bit heteronormative, isn't it?" Seth said, quiet enough that only I could hear him.

Amelia continued without taking notice. "You need to attend every meal in the cafeteria. If you are ill, you must see the nurse and either go to classes or remain in bed according to her judgment. Bedtime is at ten o'clock to ensure peak performance."

There was a meaningful pause. "Any breaches of these rules will be punished with community service at our school or, in the worst case, expulsion. Are there any questions?"

"What are we actually allowed to do?" Seth asked.

"You are allowed to study and serve the school's community, as I previously stated. That is the sole purpose of Seven Hills, and hopefully the reason you are here."

"Um . . . sure."

"Fantastic," Amelia replied and handed us a few papers. "Here is some information regarding the dress code and possible clubs or teams you might consider joining. Now, I will take you, Evelyn, to your room in the girls' wing. Seth, you will wait here— your roommate, Gabe, should be here at any moment to bring you to your room and help you settle in."

Seth didn't look happy at the prospect of being left alone here, but nodded.

I reached out and lightly squeezed his arm. "See you at breakfast tomorrow?"

His expression brightened a little bit at that. "It's a date."

"Hurry, Evelyn!" Amelia called, already climbing the stairs. "Bedtime is less than twenty minutes away, and we still need to get you settled in. You do not want to break the rules your first night here, do you?"

"Of course not," I murmured. Seth chuckled quietly behind me.

Amelia either didn't hear me or didn't pick up on the sarcasm. Instead, she wordlessly led me up the stairs and down a narrow corridor with tall windows that looked out onto the front yard, the thick red carpet swallowing the sound of our footsteps. Glancing over my shoulder, I could see the wet footprints I was leaving behind and hoped that Amelia didn't notice them. She seemed like the kind of person who would notice if anything was out of step, maybe fine me for an infraction I didn't even know existed.

At the end of that corridor, we climbed another flight of stairs where I struggled with all my luggage.

When Amelia suddenly spoke, it wasn't to offer help, but to say, "Evelyn, I do have to warn you about something."

"What is it?" I asked, almost tripping over my suitcases as I tried to keep up with her.

"Your roommate . . . let me phrase it like this: she is not easy."

"What do you mean?"

"She is impossibly rude and does not care about anyone else other than herself and that boy, Jasper, that she's always with.

Never Kiss your Roommate

Fact is, all of the girls she's shared a room with moved out within a few weeks. But I am sure you will last longer than that," she said. "Let us hope so, at least. There is no other girl at this school that would volunteer to move in with Noelle Daniels. Everyone is rather . . . intimidated by her."

"*Intimidated*?" I laughed. "I'm sure she can't be that bad."

Amelia spared me another, almost pitying look before she said, "See for yourself. This is your room."

With that, she pushed a key into my palm and pointed at the door at the end of the corridor. I hesitantly closed my fingers around the cool metal and walked past her, raising a hand to knock. When a few seconds had passed and no answer came, I inserted the key and turned it slowly, surprised when the lock only opened with a *click* after a second turn.

The room behind the door was almost exactly like I had imagined. The walls were bare stone, the floor a dark wood marred with scratches and dents left there by decades of girls. Two beds, two drawers, and two desks with one chair each occupied the two halves of the room. The left side was obviously taken by the other girl, books and magazines scattered all over her desk and clothes lying on the unmade bed.

Only after I had taken all of this in did my eyes fall on her. Noelle Daniels was sitting in the window, one foot standing on the sill, the other dangling outside like she had a death wish.

Her skin was a rich brown that, illuminated by the lamp on her desk, glowed golden, but that was all I could tell about her: the springy dark curls falling into her face made it impossible for me to see her features as she lifted the cigarette between her fingers to her lips, and she didn't react to the door opening. Sitting by the open window with lightning flashing and rain pouring behind her, unimpressed and unblinking, she looked like an avenging angel.

Only when Amelia cleared her throat behind me did Noelle turn her head. In a voice that was deeper than I had expected, she said, "What is it, Amanda?"

"Amelia. My name is Amelia. You know that," Amelia hissed and pushed past me. "Oh my God, is that a *cigarette*?"

"No, Amanda. Why would you think that?" Noelle flicked ashes onto the windowsill.

"Put that out right this second, Daniels. Your new roommate is here. Can't you at least *pretend* to be interested?"

"I suppose I could, couldn't I?" she mused, glancing my way. Suddenly overly conscious of my soaked state, I crossed my arms in front of my chest, aware that my hair was matted across my forehead and I was dripping onto the hardwood floor. In anyone else's face, Noelle's chocolate brown eyes, framed by long lashes, would have looked warm and comforting; however, as they slowly raked me up and down, a shiver that had nothing to do with the gust of cold air blowing through the open window ran down my spine.

Surprisingly, Noelle was the first one to look away, but the expression on her face made it clear the reason wasn't that I had beat her in the staring contest—she had simply lost interest. Lazily waving a hand in my direction, she said, "You know, there *is* a question I have. What the fuck is *she* doing here?"

"She lives here with you now. Didn't you hear me?"

"Not what I meant, Amanda. I remember clearly telling Whitworth not to bring another girl in here. So: What. Is. She. Doing. Here?"

"Evelyn will be living here," Amelia repeated. "Your hissy fits won't change that."

Never Kiss your Roommate

Noelle took another long drag from her cigarette before stubbing it out on the windowsill and tossing it outside. "We'll see about that."

"A map of the school grounds and additional information are on your bed, Evelyn," Amelia curtly said, fed up with the pointless discussion. "Breakfast begins at seven. Good luck with her."

I gave an uncertain nod, fighting the childish urge to cling onto her sleeve and beg her not to leave. When the door had fallen shut behind her and I turned back around, Noelle was sliding off the windowsill, not even looking at me anymore.

"I'm Evelyn," I said after a few tense seconds of silence. "Do you know where I can get a towel? I'd like to dry off."

Noelle lit another cigarette. I tried not to wrinkle my nose as the smell spread through the room.

"Noelle? I know you don't want me to be here, but maybe we can get along? I'll try not to be too annoying—"

At that, she finally turned around and walked up to me, not stopping until we were almost touching, and I could smell not only the cigarette smoke but also her perfume. "Try harder."

Breathing suddenly felt like a Herculean task. Noelle waited a few seconds, slowly exhaling the smoke from her nose. When I didn't say anything, she laughed—a short, raspy sound that made the blood in my veins freeze—and disappeared through the door that Amelia had left open. Looking after her, I realized that Noelle *was* as intimidating as Amelia had said. Almost as intimidating as she was beautiful.

And right now I wasn't sure which was worse.